Praise for *The Blackhouse*

'Impressive writing and a clammy, claustrophobic atmosphere'
The Times

'A novel of subtlety and horror . . . A story that gets into the heart
of human darkness . . . An intriguing novel you won't be able to
put down' *City A.M.*

'A beautifully written, haunting and powerful examination of
the darkness of men's souls . . . An outstanding page-turning
murder mystery' *Irish Independent*

'Pitch-perfect dialogue and creepy, spine-tingling storytelling . . .
[A] bleak, wild, atmospheric novel' *Scotsman*

'An intriguing foundation for an outstanding thriller that is as
dark and chilling as the stormy Scottish seas on a winter's night'
Daily Record

'A tense, edgy and evocative read' *Glasgow Evening Times*

'May handles the plot, pace and characterisation with a fresh-
ness and fluidity that make it a delight to read' *Big Issue*

'A magnificent and gripping story of murder and long held
resentment that grabs the attention from the very first word . . .
Much, much more than a murder mystery, revealing the depths
to which human beings are driven by passion and jealousy'
CrimeSquad

'What a truly fantastic book this is! The nature of the story gets
into your mind and won't leave you alone. It haunts you, taunting you to put down what you're doing and carry on with the
story' *Euro Crime*

Also by Peter May

FICTION

The Lewis Trilogy
The Blackhouse
The Lewis Man
The Chessmen

The China Thrillers
The Firemaker
The Fourth Sacrifice
The Killing Room
Snakehead
The Runner
Chinese Whispers

The Enzo Files
Extraordinary People
The Critic
Blacklight Blue
Freeze Frame
Blowback

Standalone Novels
Virtually Dead
Entry Island
Runaway

NON-FICTION

Hebrides (with David Wilson)

PETER MAY
THE BLACK HOUSE

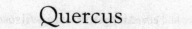

Quercus

First published in Great Britain in 2011 by Quercus Publishing Limited
This paperback edition first published in 2011 by

Quercus Publishing Limited
Carmelite House
50 Victoria Embankment
London
EC4Y 0DZ

An Hachette UK company

A CIP catalogue reference for this book is available
from the British Library

ISBN 978 1 84916 386 6
EBOOK ISBN 978 0 85738 216 0

16

Typeset by Ellipsis Digital Limited, Glasgow

Printed and bound in Great Britain by Clays Ltd, Elcograf S.p.A.

PRONUNCIATION

Here is a simple guide to the English pronunciation of some of the Gaelic names and words in the book. *ch* is pronounced as in the Scottish word *loch*, and the emphasis is placed on the underlined syllable:

An Sgeir	Eilidh	Niseach
An Skerr	Aylay	Neeshuch
Beag	Fionnlagh	Ruadh
Beg	Feeonlach	Rooagh
Ceit	Gaelic	Seonaidh
Kate	Gahlick	Shawnay
Coinneach	Iain	Seoras
Coinyach	Yan	Shawrass
Dubh	Mairead	Sine
Doo	Myrad	Sheenuh
Eachan	Mamaidh	Slàinthe mhath
Yachan	Mammy	Slange e vah
Eilean	Marsaili	Uilleam
Yaylan	Marshally	Willyam

Machair, pronounced *macher*, is the Gaelic word for the fertile sandy soil around the coastal areas of the Western

Isles of Scotland. It has passed into the English language as a result of international concern over the problem of 'machair erosion'. Much of the machair is gradually being reclaimed by the sea.

That is the land of lost content,
I see it shining plain,
The happy highways where I went
And cannot come again.

– A. E. Housman,
'Blue Remembered Hills'

*Tri rudan a thig gun iarraidh: an t-eagal, an t-eudach 's
an gaol.*
(Three things that come without asking: fear, love and
jealousy.)

– Gaelic proverb

For Stephen, with whom I travelled those happy highways.

PROLOGUE

They are just kids. Sixteen years old. Emboldened by alcohol, and hastened by the approaching Sabbath, they embrace the dark in search of love, and find only death.

Unusually, there is just a light wind. And for once it is warm, like breath on the skin, caressing and seductive. A slight haze in the August sky hides the stars, but a three-quarters moon casts its pale, bloodless light across the compacted sand left by the outgoing tide. The sea breathes gently upon the shore, phosphorescent foam bursting silver bubbles over gold. The young couple hurry down the tarmac from the village above, blood pulsing in their heads like the beat of the waves.

Off to their left, the rise and fall of the water in the tiny harbour breaks the moonlight on its surface, and they hear the creaking of small boats straining at ropes, the soft clunk of wood on wood as they jostle for space, nudging each other playfully in the darkness.

Uilleam holds her hand in his, sensing her reluctance. He has tasted the sweetness of the alcohol on her breath and felt the urgency in her kiss, and knows that tonight she will finally succumb. But there is so little time. The Sabbath is close. Too close. Just half an hour, revealed in a stolen glance at his watch before leaving the street lights behind.

Ceit is breathing rapidly now. Afraid, not of the sex, but of the father she knows will be sitting by the fire, watching the embers of the peat fade towards midnight, timed with a practised perfection to die before the coming day of rest. She can almost feel his impatience slow-burning to anger as the clock ticks towards tomorrow and she has not yet returned. How is it possible that things can have changed so little on this God-fearing island?

Thoughts crowd her mind, fighting for space with the desire which has lodged there, and the alcohol which has blunted her youthful resistance to it. Their Saturday night at the Social Club had seemed, just a few short hours ago, to stretch ahead to eternity. But time never passes so quickly as when it is in short supply. And now it is all but gone.

Panic and passion rise together in her chest as they slip past the shadow of an old fishing boat canted at an angle on the pebbles above the watermark. Through the open half of the concrete boatshed, they can see the beach beyond, framed by unglazed windows. The sea seems lit from within, almost luminous. Uilleam lets go of her hand and slides open the wooden door, just enough to allow them past. And he pushes her inside. It is dark here. A rank smell of diesel and salt water and seaweed fill the air, like the sad perfume of hurried, pubescent sex. The dark shadow of a boat on its trailer looms above them, two small rectangular windows opening like peepholes on to the shore.

He pushes her up against the wall, and at once she feels his mouth on hers, his tongue forcing its way past her lips, his hands squeezing the softness of her breasts. It hurts, and she pushes him away. 'Not so rough.' Her breath seems to thunder in the darkness.

'No time.' She hears the tension in his voice. A male tension, filled at the same time with desire and anxiety. And she begins to have second thoughts. Is this really how she wants her first time to be? A few sordid moments snatched in the dark of a filthy boatshed?

'No.' She pushes him aside and steps away, turning towards the window and a breath of air. If they hurry there is still time to get back before twelve.

She sees the dark shape drift out of the shadows almost at the same moment she feels it. Soft and cold and heavy. She lets out an involuntary cry.

'For God's sake, Ceit!' Uilleam comes after her, frustration added now to desire and anxiety, and his feet slide away from under him, for all the world as if he has stepped on ice. He lands heavily on his elbow and a pain shoots through his arm. 'Shit!' The floor is wet with diesel. He feels it soaking through the seat of his trousers. It is on his hands. Without thinking, he fumbles for the cigarette lighter in his pocket. There just isn't enough damned light in here. Only as he spins the wheel with his thumb, sparking the flame, does it occur to him that he is in imminent danger of turning himself into a human torch. But by then it is too late. The light is sudden and startling in the dark. He braces himself. But there is no ignition of diesel fumes, no sudden

3

flash of searing flame. Just an image so profoundly shocking it is impossible at first to comprehend.

The man is hanging by his neck from the rafters overhead, frayed orange plastic rope tilting his head at an impossible angle. He is a big man, buck naked, blue-white flesh hanging in folds from his breasts and his buttocks, like a loose-fitting suit two sizes too big. Loops of something smooth and shiny hang down between his legs from a gaping smile that splits his belly from side to side. The flame sends the dead man's shadow dancing around the scarred and graffitied walls like so many ghosts welcoming a new arrival. Beyond him Uilleam sees Ceit's face. Pale, dark-eyed, frozen in horror. For a moment he thinks, absurdly, that the pool of diesel around him is agricultural, dyed red by the Excise to identify its tax-free status – before realizing it is blood, sticky and thick and already drying brown on his hands.

ONE

I

It was late, sultry warm in a way that it only ever gets at festival time. Fin found concentration difficult. The darkness of his small study pressed in around him, like big, black, soft hands holding him in his seat. The circle of light from the lamp on his desk burned his eyes, drawing him there like a moth, blinding now, so that he found it hard to keep his notes in focus. The computer hummed softly in the stillness, and its screen flickered in his peripheral vision. He should have gone to bed hours ago, but it was imperative that he finish his essay. The Open University offered his only means of escape, and he had been procrastinating. Foolishly.

He heard a movement at the door behind him and swivelled angrily in his seat, expecting to see Mona. But his words of rebuke never came. Instead, he found himself looking up in astonishment at a man so tall that he could not stand upright. His head was tipped to one side to avoid the ceiling. These were not big rooms, but this man must have been eight feet tall. He had very long legs, dark trousers gathering in folds around black boots. A checked cotton shirt was tucked in at a belted waist, and over it he wore an anorak, hanging open, the hood falling away from an upturned collar. His arms dangled at his sides, big hands protruding from sleeves that were too short. To Fin he looked about sixty, a lined, lugubrious face with dark, expressionless eyes. His silver-grey hair was long and greasy and hung down below his ears. He said nothing. He just stood staring at Fin, deep shadows cut in stony features by the light on Fin's desk. What in the name of God was he doing there? All the hair on Fin's neck and arms stood on end, and he felt fear slip over him like a glove, holding him in its grasp.

And then somewhere in the distance he heard his own voice wailing, childlike, in the dark. 'Funny ma-an . . .' The man remained staring at him. 'There's a funny ma-an . . .'

'What is it, Fin?' It was Mona's voice. She was alarmed, shaking him by the shoulder.

And even as he opened his eyes and saw her frightened face, perplexed and still puffy from sleep, he heard himself wail, 'Funny ma-an . . .'

'For God's sake, what's wrong?'

He turned away from her on to his back, breathing deeply, trying to catch his breath. His heart was racing. 'Just a dream. A bad dream.' But the memory of the man

6

in his study was still vivid, like a childhood nightmare. He glanced at the clock on the bedside table. The digital display told him it was seven minutes past four. He tried to swallow, but his mouth was dry, and he knew that he would not get back to sleep.

'You just about scared the life out of me.'

'I'm sorry.' He pulled back the covers and swung his legs down to the floor. He closed his eyes and rubbed his face, but the man was still there, burned on his retinas. He stood up.

'Where are you going?'

'For a pee.' He padded softly across the carpet and opened the door into the hall. Moonlight fell across it, divided geometrically by ersatz Georgian windows. Halfway down the hall he passed the open door of his study. Inside, it was pitch-black, and he shuddered at the thought of the tall man who had invaded it in his dream. How clear and strong the image remained in his mind. How powerful the presence had been. At the bathroom door he paused, as he had every night for nearly four weeks, his eyes drawn to the room at the end of the hall. The door stood ajar, moonlight washing the space beyond it. Curtains that should have been drawn but weren't. It contained only a terrible emptiness. Fin turned away, heart sick, a cold sweat breaking out across his forehead.

The splash of urine hitting water filled the bathroom with the comforting sound of normality. It was always with silence that his depression came. But tonight the usual void was occupied. The image of the man in the anorak had displaced all other thoughts, like a cuckoo in the nest. Fin wondered now if he knew him, if there was something familiar in the long face and straggling hair. And suddenly he remembered the description Mona had given the police of the man in the car. He had been wearing an anorak, she thought. Had been about sixty, with long, greasy, grey hair.

II

He took a bus into town, watching the rows of grey stone tenements drift past his window like the flickering images of a dull monochrome movie. He could have driven, but Edinburgh was not a town where you would choose to drive. By the time he reached Princes Street the cloud had broken, and sunlight swept in waves across the green expanse of the gardens below the castle. A festival crowd was gathered around a group of street entertainers who were swallowing fire and juggling clubs. A jazz band played on the steps of the art galleries. Fin got off at Waverley Station and walked over the Bridges to the old town, heading south past the university, before turning east into the shadow of Salisbury Crags. Sunshine slanted across the sheer green slope rising to the cliffs that dominated the skyline above the city's 'A' division police headquarters.

In an upstairs corridor familiar faces nodded acknow-ledgement. Someone put a hand on his arm and said, 'Sorry for your loss, Fin.' He just nodded.

DCI Black barely looked up from his paperwork, waving a hand towards a chair on the other side of his desk. He had a thin face with a pasty complexion, and was shuffling papers between nicotine-stained fingers. There was something hawklike in his gaze when, at last, he turned it on Fin. 'How's the Open University going?'

Fin shrugged. 'Okay.'

'I never asked why you dropped out of university in the first place. Glasgow, wasn't it?'

Fin nodded. 'Because I was young, sir. And stupid.'

'Why'd you join the police?'

'It was what you did in those days, when you came down from the islands and you had no work, and no qualifications.'

'You knew someone in the force, then?'

'I knew a few people.'

Black regarded him thoughtfully. 'You're a good cop, Fin. But it's not what you want, is it?'

'It's what I am.'

'No, it's what you were. Until a month ago. And what happened, well that was a tragedy. But life moves on, and us with it. Everyone understood you needed time to mourn. God knows we see enough death in this business to understand that.'

Fin looked at him with resentment. 'You've no idea what it is to lose a child.'

'No, I don't.' There was no trace of sympathy in Black's voice. 'But I've lost people close to me, and I know that you just have to deal with it.' He placed his hands together in front of him like a man in prayer. 'But to dwell on it, well, that's unhealthy, Fin. Morbid.' He pursed his lips. 'So it's time you took a decision. About what you're going to do with the rest of your life. And until you've done that, unless there's some compelling medical reason preventing it, I want you back at work.'

The pressure on him to return to his job had been mounting. From Mona, in calls from colleagues, advice from friends. And he had been resisting it, because he had no idea how to go back to being who he was before the accident.

'When?'

'Right now. Today.'

Fin was shocked. He shook his head. 'I need some time.'

'You've had time, Fin. Either come back, or quit.' Black didn't wait for a response. He stretched across his desk, lifted a manilla file from a ragged pile of them and slid it towards Fin. 'You'll remember the Leith Walk murder in May?'

'Yes.' But Fin didn't open the folder. He didn't need to. He remembered only too well the naked body hanging from the tree between the rain-streaked Pentecostal church and the bank. A poster on the wall had read: *Jesus saves*. And Fin remembered thinking it looked like a promotion for the bank and should have read: *Jesus saves at the Bank of Scotland*.

'There's been another one,' Black said. 'Identical MO.'

'Where?'

'Up north. Northern Constabulary. It came up on the HOLMES computer. In fact it was HOLMES that had the bright idea of attaching you to the inquiry.' He blinked long eyelashes and fixed Fin with a gaze that reflected his scepticism. 'You still speak the lingo, don't you?'

Fin was surprised. 'Gaelic? I haven't spoken Gaelic since I left the Isle of Lewis.'

'Then you'd better start brushing up on it. The victim's from your home village.'

'Crobost?' Fin was stunned.

'A couple of years older than you. Name of . . .' He consulted a sheet in front of him. '. . . Macritchie. Angus Macritchie. Know him?' Fin nodded.

III

The sunshine sloping through the living-room window seemed to reproach them for their unhappiness. Motes of dust hung in the still air, trapped by the light. Outside they could hear the sounds of children kicking a ball in the street. Just a few short weeks ago it might have been Robbie. The tick-tock of the clock on the

11

mantel punctuated the silence between them. Mona's eyes were red, but the tears had dried up, to be replaced by anger.

'I don't *want* you to go.' It had become her refrain in their argument.

'This morning you *wanted* me to go to work.'

'But I wanted you to come home again. I don't want to be left here on my own for weeks on end.' She drew a long, tremulous breath. 'With my memories. With . . . with . . .'

Perhaps she would never have found the words to finish her sentence. But Fin stepped in to do it for her. 'Your guilt?' He had never said that he blamed her. But he did. Although in his heart he tried not to. She shot him a look filled with such pain that he immediately regretted it. He said, 'Anyway, it'll only be for a few days.' He ran his hands back through tightly curled blond hair. 'Do you really think I want to go? I've spent eighteen years avoiding it.'

'And now you're just jumping at the chance. A chance to escape. To get away from me.'

'Oh, don't be ridiculous.' But he knew she was right. Knew, too, that it wasn't just Mona he wanted to run away from. It was everything. Back to a place where life had once seemed simple. A return to childhood, back to the womb. How easy it was now to ignore the fact that he had spent most of his adult life avoiding just that. Easy to forget that as a teenager nothing had seemed more important to him than leaving.

And he remembered how easy it had been to marry Mona. For all the wrong reasons. For company. For an excuse not to go back. But in fourteen years all they had achieved was a kind of accommodation, a space that each of them had made for the other in their lives. A space which they had occupied together, but never quite shared. They had been friends. There had been genuine warmth. But he doubted if there had ever been love. Real love. Like so many people in life, they seemed to have settled for second best. Robbie had been the bridge between them. But Robbie was gone.

Mona said, 'Have you any idea what it's been like for me these last few weeks?'

'I think I might.'

She shook her head. 'No. You haven't had to spend every waking minute with someone whose very silence screams reproach. I know you blame me, Fin.'

'I never said that.'

'You never had to. But you know what? However much you blame me, I blame myself ten times more. And it's my loss, too, Fin. He was my son, too.' Now the tears returned, burning her eyes. He could not bring himself to speak. 'I don't *want* you to go.' Back to the refrain.

'I don't have a choice.'

'Of course you have a choice. There's always a choice. For weeks you've been *choosing* not to go to work. You can *choose* not to go to the island. Just tell them, no.'

'I can't.'

'Fin, if you get on that plane tomorrow . . .' He waited for the ultimatum while she screwed up the courage to make it. But it didn't come.

'What, Mona? What'll happen if I get on that plane tomorrow?' He was goading her into saying it. Then it would be her fault and not his.

She looked away, sucking in her lower lip and biting on it until she tasted blood. 'Just don't expect me to be here when you get back, that's all.'

He looked at her for a long time. 'Maybe that would be best.'

The two-engined, thirty-seven-seater aircraft shuddered in the wind as it tilted to circle Loch a Tuath in preparation for landing on the short, windswept runway at Stornoway airport. As they emerged from thick, low cloud, Fin looked down at a slate-grey sea breaking white over the fingers of black rock that reached out from the Eye Peninsula, the ragged scrap of land they called Point. He saw the familiar patterns carved into the landscape, like the trenches which had so characterized the Great War, though men had dug these ditches not for war but for warmth. Centuries of peat-cutting had left their distinctive scarring on the endless acres of otherwise featureless bogland. The water in the bay below looked cold, ridged by the wind that blew uninterrupted across it. Fin had forgotten about the wind, that tireless assault blowing in across three thousand miles of Atlantic. Beyond the shelter of Stornoway harbour there was barely a tree on the island.

On the hour-long flight, he had tried not to think. Neither to anticipate his return to the island of his birth, nor to replay the dreadful silence which had accompanied his departure from home. Mona had spent the night in Robbie's room. He had heard her crying from the other end of the hall as he packed. In the morning he had left without a word, and as he pulled the front door shut behind him knew that he had closed it not only on Mona, but on a chapter of his life he wished had never been written.

Now, seeing the familiar Nissen huts on the airfield below, and the unfamiliar new ferry terminal shining in the distance, Fin felt a rush of emotion. It had been so very long, and he was unprepared for the sudden flood of memories that almost overwhelmed him.

TWO

I have heard people who were born in the fifties describe their childhood in shades of brown. A sepia world. I grew up in the sixties and seventies, and my childhood was purple.

We lived in what was known as a whitehouse, about half a mile outside the village of Crobost. It was part of the community they called Ness, on the extreme northern tip of the Isle of Lewis, the most northerly island in the archipelago of the Outer Hebrides of Scotland. The whitehouses were built in the twenties of stone and lime, or concrete block, and roofed with slate, or corrugated iron, or tarred felt. They were built to replace the old blackhouses. The blackhouses had dry-stone walls with thatched roofs and gave shelter to both man and beast. A peat fire burned day and night in the centre of the stone floor of the main room. It was called the fire room. There were no chimneys, and smoke was supposed to escape through a hole in the roof. Of course, it wasn't very efficient, and the houses were always full of the stuff. It was little wonder that life-expectancy was short.

The remains of the blackhouse where my paternal grandparents lived stood in our garden, a stone's throw from the house. It had no roof, and its walls had mostly fallen down, but it was a great place to play hide and seek.

My father was a practical man, with a shock of thick black hair and sharp blue eyes. He had skin like leather that went the colour of tar in the summer, when he spent most of his waking hours outdoors. When I was still very young, before I went to school, he used to take me beach-combing. I didn't understand it then, but I learned later that he was unemployed at that time. There had been a contraction in the fishing industry, and the boat he skip-pered was sold for scrap. So he had time on his hands, and we were up at first light scouring the beaches for whatever might have washed up in the night. Timber. Lots of timber. He once told me he knew a man who had built his whole house from timber washed up on the shore. He himself had got most of the timber for build-ing our attic rooms from the sea. The sea gave us plenty. It also took plenty. There was barely a month went by when we didn't hear of some poor soul drowning. A fish-ing accident. Someone in bathing and dragged out by the undertow. Someone falling from the cliffs.

We dragged all manner of stuff home from those trips to the beach. Rope, fishing net, aluminium buoys that my father sold to the tinkers. Pickings were even better after a storm. And it was after one that we found the big forty-five-gallon drum. Although the storm itself had subsided, the wind was still blowing a gale, the sea still high and angry, and thrashing at the coast. Great ragged clumps of broken cloud blew overhead at sixty miles an hour or more. And in between them, the sun coloured the land in bright, shifting patches of green and purple and brown.

Although the drum was unmarked, it was full and heavy, and my father was excited by our find. But it was too heavy for us to move on our own, leaning at an angle and half buried in the sand. So he organized a tractor and a trailer and some men to help, and by the afternoon we had it safely standing in an outbuilding on the croft. It didn't take him long to open it and discover that it was full of paint. Bright purple gloss paint. Which is how it came to be that in our house every door and cupboard and shelf, every window and floorboard was painted purple. For all the years that I lived there.

My mother was a lovely woman with tight blond curls that she dragged back in a ponytail. She had pale, freckled skin, and liquid brown eyes, and I can't ever remember seeing her wear make-up. She was a gentle person with a sunny disposition, but a fiery temper if you got on the wrong side of her. She worked the croft. It was only about six acres, and it ran in a long, narrow strip from the house down to the shore. Fertile machair land that was good grazing for the sheep that brought in most of the croft's income from government subsidies. She also grew potatoes and turnips and some cereals, and grass for hay and silage. My lasting image of her is seated on our tractor in her blue overalls and black wellies, smiling self-consciously for a photographer from the local paper because she had won some prize at the Ness show.

By the time I came to start school, my father had got a job in the new oil-fabrication yard at Arnish Point in Stornoway, and he and a bunch of men from the village left early every morning in a white van on the long drive to town. So it was my mother who was to run me to school in our rusted old Ford Anglia on my first day. I was excited. My best friend was Artair Macinnes, and he was as eager to start school as I was. We were born only a month apart, and his folks' bungalow was the nearest house to our croft. So we spent a lot of time together in those days before we started school. His parents and mine were never the best of friends, though. There was, I suppose, something of a class difference. Artair's father was a teacher at Crobost School, where they not only took the seven years of primary, but also the first two years of secondary. He was a secondary teacher and taught maths and English.

I remember it was a blustery September day, low cloud bumping and bruising the land. You could smell the rain coming on the edge of the wind. I had a brown anorak with a hood, and wore short trousers that I knew would chafe if they got wet. My black wellies clopped against my calves, and I swung my stiff new canvas schoolbag over

19

my shoulder, sandshoes and a packed lunch inside. I was keen to be off.

My mother was backing the Anglia out of the wooden shed that served as a garage, when a horn sounded over the noise of the wind. I turned to see Artair and his dad pulling up in their bright orange Hillman Avenger. It was second-hand, but it looked almost new, and put our old Anglia to shame. Mr Macinnes left the engine running and got out of the car and crossed to speak to my mother. After a moment, he came and put a hand on my shoulder and said I was to get a lift to the school with him and Artair. It wasn't until the car was drawing away, and I turned to see my mother standing waving, that I realized I hadn't said goodbye.

I know now how it feels on the day your child goes to school for the first time. There is an odd sense of loss, of irrevocable change. And, looking back, I know that's what my mother felt. It was there in her face, along with the regret that she had somehow missed the moment.

Crobost School sat in a hollow below the village, facing north towards the Port of Ness, in the shadow of the church that dominated the village skyline on the hill above. The school was surrounded by open grazing, and in the distance you could just see the tower of the light-house at the Butt. On some days you could see all the way across the Minch to the mainland, the faintest outline of the mountains visible on the distant horizon. They always said if you could see the mainland the weather was going to turn bad. And they were always right.

There were a hundred and three kids in Crobost primary, and eighty-eight in the secondary. Another eleven fresh-faced kids started school with me that day, and we sat in class at two rows of six desks, one behind the other.

Our teacher was Mrs Mackay, a thin, grey-haired lady who was probably a lot younger than she seemed. I thought she was ancient. She was a gentle lady really, Mrs Mackay, but strict, and she had a caustic tongue on her at times. The first thing she asked the class was if anyone couldn't speak English. Of course, I had heard English spoken, but at home we had only ever used the Gaelic, and my father wouldn't have a television in the house, so I had no idea what she'd said. Artair put his hand up, a knowing smirk on his face. I heard my name, and all eyes in the class turned towards me. It didn't take a genius to work out what Artair had told her. I felt my face going red.

'Well, Fionnlagh,' Mrs Mackay said in Gaelic, 'it seems your parents didn't have the good sense to teach you English before you came to school.' My immediate reaction was anger at my mother and father. Why couldn't I speak English? Didn't they know how humiliating this was? 'You should know that we only speak English in this class. Not that there's anything wrong with the Gaelic, but that's just how it is. And we'll find out soon enough how quick a learner you are.' I couldn't raise my eyes

21

from the desk. 'We'll start by giving you your English name. Do you know what that is?'

With something like defiance, I raised my head. 'Finlay.' I knew that because it's what Artair's parents called me.

'Good. And since the first thing I'm going to do today is take the register, you can tell me what your second name is.'

'*Macleoid*.' I used the Gaelic pronunciation which, to an English ear, sounds something like *Maclodge*.

'Macleod,' she corrected me. 'Finlay Macleod.' And then she switched to English and ran through the other names. Macdonald, Macinnes, Maclean, Macritchie, Murray, Pickford . . . All eyes turned towards the boy called Pickford, and Mrs Mackay said something to him that made the class giggle. The boy blushed and muttered some incoherent response.

'He's English,' a voice whispered to me in Gaelic from the next desk. I turned, surprised, to find myself looking at a pretty little girl with fair hair tied back in pleated pigtails, a blue bow at the end of each. 'He's the only one whose name doesn't begin with *m*, you see. So he must be English. Mrs Mackay guessed that he's the son of the lighthouse keeper, because they're always English.'

'What are you two whispering about?' Mrs Mackay's voice was sharp, and her Gaelic words made her even more intimidating to me because I could understand them.

'Please, Mrs Mackay,' pigtails said. 'I'm just translating for Finlay.'

'Oh, *translating* is it?' There was mock wonder in Mrs Mackay's voice. 'That's a big word for a little girl.' She paused to consult the register. 'I was going to reseat you alphabetically, but perhaps since you are such a linguist, Marjorie, you'd better continue sitting next to Finlay and . . . *translate* for him.'

Marjorie smiled, pleased with herself, missing the teacher's tone. For my part, I was quite happy to be sitting next to a pretty girl with pigtails. I glanced across the class and saw Artair glaring at me. I thought then it was because he had wanted us to sit together. I know now it was because he was jealous.

I took him to task in the playground at breaktime. 'Why did you clype on me about not being able to speak the English?'

But he was blasé. 'They were going to find out anyway, weren't they?' He slipped a small blue-and-silver inhaler from his pocket, shoved the nozzle in his mouth and sucked in a breath as he pressed down on the refill tube. I didn't think anything of it. He'd had a puffer ever since I'd known him. He was asthmatic, my folks had said, which didn't mean much to me then. I just knew that sometimes he found it difficult to breathe, and if he sucked on his puffer he would be okay.

A big, red-haired boy snatched it from him. 'What's this?' He held it up to the light as if he might be able to see through to its inner secrets. It was my first encounter with Murdo Macritchie. He was taller and heavier built than the other boys, and had a shock of distinctive, carrot-red hair. I found out later that they called him Murdo Ruadh. *Ruadh* is the Gaelic word for *red*. Literally, Red Murdo. It was to distinguish him from his father, who was also Murdo Macritchie. He had black hair, and was called Murdo Dubh. Everyone ended up with a nickname, because so many of the given and surnames were the same. Murdo Ruadh had a brother, Angus, a couple of years older than us. They called him *Angel* because he was the bully in his year, and Murdo Ruadh seemed set to follow in his footsteps.

'Gimme it!' Artair tried to snatch back his puffer, but Murdo Ruadh held it out of reach. Sturdy though Artair was, he was no match for big Murdo, who tossed it to another boy who threw it to another, who tossed it back to Murdo. Already Murdo Ruadh, like all bullies, had drawn followers, like flies to shit. Feeble-minded boys, but smart enough to avoid being victims.

'Come and get it then, wheezy.' Murdo Ruadh was taunting him. And as Artair grabbed for it, he threw it on to one of the flies.

I could hear that distinctive rasping sound in Artair's chest as he chased after his puffer, panic and humiliation rising together to block his airways. And I grabbed one of the acolytes and pulled the puffer from his hand. 'Here.'

I handed it back to my friend. Artair sucked on it several times. I felt a hand on my collar, and an irresistible force propelled me up against the wall. Sharp roughcast drew blood from the back of my head. 'What the hell do you think you're playing at, Gaelic boy?' Murdo Ruadh's face was two inches from mine, and I could smell his rotten breath. 'Can't speak English. Can't speak nothing.' The irony, although it didn't strike me at the time, was that his jibes were in Gaelic. It was the language of the playground. We only ever spoke English in class.

'Leave him alone!' It was just a small boy's voice, but it carried such authority that it quieted the barracking of the boys who had gathered to see me get a doing from Murdo. A frown of incomprehension clouded Murdo Ruadh's big, ugly face. Challenged twice in the space of a minute. He was going to have to put a stop to this. He let go of my collar and turned around. The boy was no bigger than me, but something in the way he held himself stopped Murdo Ruadh in his tracks. The only thing you could hear was the sound of the wind, and the laughter of the girls skipping on the other side of the playground. Everyone was watching Murdo. He knew his reputation was on the line.

'Any trouble from you . . . and I'll get my big brother.'

I wanted to laugh.

The other boy held Murdo Ruadh in his gaze, and you could see that Murdo was unnerved by it. 'If you want to go running to your big brother . . .' the boy spat out the words *big* and *brother* with something like contempt, '. . . then I'll just have to tell my father.'

Murdo paled beneath that shock of wiry, red hair. 'Well, just . . . just stay out my way.' It was a feeble comeback, and everyone knew it. He pushed away through the group and across the playground, his followers trotting after him, wondering if maybe they'd backed the wrong horse.

'Thanks,' I said to the boy as the group dispersed.

But he just shrugged, like it was nothing. 'Can't stand fucking bullies.' It was the first time I had ever heard anyone swear. He pushed his hands in his pockets and walked off towards the annexe.

'Who is he?' I asked Artair.

'Don't you know?' Artair was amazed. I shook my head. 'That's Donald Murray.' His tone was hushed and filled with awe. 'He's the minister's son.'

The bell rang then, and we all headed back to class. It was just chance, really, that I was passing the headmaster's door when he opened it and scanned the flood of pupils in the corridor for a likely candidate. 'You, boy.' He pointed a finger at me. I stopped in my tracks and he thrust an envelope into my hand. I had no idea what he said next, and just stood there with growing panic.

'He doesn't speak English, and Mrs Mackay said I had to do the translating for him.' Marjorie was hovering on my shoulder like a guardian angel. She gave me a winning smile as I turned to look at her.

'Oh, did she now? Translating, eh?' The headmaster surveyed us with interest, raising one eyebrow in mock severity. He was a tall, bald man with half-moon glasses, and always wore grey tweed suits a size too big for him. 'Then you'd better go with him, young lady.'

'Yes, Mr Macaulay.' It was amazing how she seemed to know everybody's name. 'Come on, Finlay.' She slipped her arm through mine and steered us back out to the playground.

'Where are we going?'

'That note you're holding is an order for the Crobost Stores, to restock the tuck shop.'

'The tuck shop?' I had no idea what she was talking about.

'Don't you know anything, stupid? The tuck shop's where we buy sweets and crisps and lemonade and stuff in school. So we won't go traipsing up and down the road to the store and risk getting knocked down.'

'Oh.' I nodded and wondered how she knew all this. It wasn't until some time later that I discovered she had a sister in primary six. 'So it's only us that's to get knocked down?'

She giggled. 'Old Macaulay must have thought you looked like a sensible type.'

'He got that wrong, then.' I remembered my confrontation with Murdo Ruadh. She giggled again.

The Crobost Stores was in an old stone barn about half a mile away at the road end. It stood on the corner by the main road. It had two small windows, which never seemed to have anything in them, and a narrow doorway between them that opened into the shop. We could see it in the distance, next to a stone shed with a rust-red corrugated roof. The single-track road was long and straight, without pavements, and delineated by rotting wooden fenceposts leaning at angles. The fence made a poor job of keeping the sheep off the road. The tall grasses along the ditch were burned brown and bowed by the wind, and the heather was all but dead. On the slope beyond, houses were strung along the main road like square beads on a string, no trees or bushes to soften their hard edges. Just a jumble of fences and the rotting carcasses of dead cars and broken tractors.

'So whereabouts in Crobost do you live?' I said to Marjorie.

'I don't. I live on Mealanais Farm. It's about two miles from Crobost.' And she lowered her voice so that I could hardly hear it above the wind. 'My mother's English.' It was like a secret she was telling me. 'That's why I can speak English without a Gaelic accent.'

I shrugged, wondering why she was telling me this. 'I wouldn't know.'

She laughed. 'Of course not.'

It was cold and starting to rain, and I pulled up my hood, stealing a glance at the girl with the pigtails. They were blowing out behind her in the wind, and she seemed to be enjoying the sting of it in her face. Her cheeks had turned bright red. 'Marjorie.' I raised my voice above the wind. 'That's a nice name.'

'I hate it.' She glowered at me. 'It's my English name. But nobody calls me that. My real name's Marsaili.' Like *Marjorie*, she put the emphasis on the first syllable, with the *s* becoming a soft *sh*, as it always does in the Gaelic after an *r*, a Nordic inheritance from the two hundred years that the islands were ruled by the Vikings.

'Marsaili.' I tried it out to see if it fitted my mouth, and I liked the sound of it fine. 'That's even nicer.'

She flicked me a coy look, soft blue eyes meeting mine for a moment then dancing away again. 'So how do you like *your* English name?'

'Finlay?' She nodded. 'I don't.'

'I'll call you Fin, then. How's that?'

'Fin.' Again, I tried it out for size. It was short, and to the point. 'It's okay.'

'Good.' Marsaili smiled. 'Then that's what you'll be.'

And that's how it happened that Marsaili Macdonald gave me the name that stuck with me for the rest of my life.

In those days, for the first week, the new intake at the school only stayed until lunchtime. We had our lunch and then left. And although Artair and I had been given a lift to school that first morning, we were expected to walk home. It was only about a mile. Artair was waiting for me at the gate. I had been held up because Mrs Mackay

29

had called me back to give me a note for my parents. I could see Marsaili up ahead on the road, walking on her own. We had got soaked on the walk back from the stores and had spent the rest of the morning sitting on a radiator together drying off. The rain had stopped for the moment.

'Hurry up, I've been waiting for you.' Artair was impatient to get home. He wanted us to go searching for crabs in the rock pools below his house.

'I'm going back by Mealanais Farm,' I told him. 'It's a shortcut.'

'What?' He looked at me as if I were mad. 'That'll take hours!'

'No, it won't. I can cut back by the Cross–Skigersta road.' I had no idea where that was, but Marsaili had told me that was the quick way from Mealanais to Crobost.

I didn't even wait for him to object, but took off at a sprint up the road after Marsaili. By the time I caught up with her I was out of puff. She gave me a knowing smile. 'I thought you would be walking home with Artair.'

'I thought I'd walk with you up by Mealanais.' I was dead casual. 'It's a shortcut.'

She looked less than convinced. 'It's a long way for a shortcut.' And she gave a little shrug. 'But I can't stop you walking with me, if that's what you want.'

I smiled to myself, and restrained an urge to punch the air. I looked back and saw Artair glaring after us.

The road to the farm branched off the other side of the

main road before the turnoff to Crobost. Punctuated by the occasional passing place, it wound its way south-east across acres of peatbog that stretched off to the far horizon. But the land was more elevated here, and if you looked back you could see the line of the road as far as Swainbost and Cross. Beyond that, the sea broke white along the west coast below a forest of gravestones standing bleak against the sky at Crobost cemetery. The northern part of Lewis was flat and unbroken by hills or mountains and the weather swept across it from the Atlantic to the Minch, always in a hurry. And so it was always changing. Light and dark in ever-shifting patterns, one set against the other, rain, sunshine, black sky, blue sky. And rainbows. My childhood seemed filled by them. Usually doublers. We watched one that day, forming fast over the peatbog, vivid against the blackest of blue-black skies. It took away the need for words.

The road tipped down a gentle slope then, to a cluster of farm buildings in a slight hollow. The fences were in better repair here, and there were cattle and sheep grazing in pasture. There was a tall, red-roofed barn, and a big white farmhouse surrounded by a clutch of stone outbuildings. We stopped at a white-painted gate at the opening to a dirt track that ran down to the house.

'Do you want to come in for some lemonade?' Marsaili asked.

But I was sick with worry by this time. I had no real idea where I was or how to get home. And I knew I was going to be very late. I could feel my mother's anger already. 'Better not.' I looked at my watch trying not to seem concerned. 'I'm going to be a bit late.'

Marsaili nodded. 'That's what happens with shortcuts. They always make you late.' She smiled brightly. 'You can come and play on Saturday morning if you want.'

I pushed at a clump of turf with the toe of my welly and shrugged, playing it cool. 'I'll think about it.'

'Please yourself, then.' And she turned and skipped off down the track towards the big white farmhouse.

I've never really been sure how I managed to find my way home that first day, because after Mealanais the road petered out to a stony track. I had been walking along it for some time with a growing sense of despair when I saw the top of a car flashing past along the near horizon. I ran up the slope and found myself on what must have been the Cross–Skigersta road that Marsaili had talked about. Looking both ways along it, the road seemed to disappear into the peatbog. I didn't know which way to turn. I was scared and close to tears. Some guiding hand must have prompted me to go left, because if I had turned right I would never have got home.

Even so, it was more than twenty minutes before I came to a turnoff where a crooked black-and-white signpost pointed uncertainly towards Crobost. I was running now, the tears burning my cheeks, the rims of my wellies rubbing my calves raw. I smelled the sea, and heard it before I saw it. And then as I came over the rise, there was the familiar silhouette of the Crobost Free Church looming over the disparate collection of houses and crofts that huddled around it on the cliff road.

As I reached our house my mother was pulling up outside it in the Ford Anglia. Artair was in the back seat. She jumped out of the car and grabbed me as if I might blow away in the wind. But her relief turned quickly to anger.

'For God's sake, Fionnlagh, where have you been? I've been up and down that road to the school twice looking for you. I'm just about demented.' She brushed away tears from my face as I tried to stop more of them leaking from my eyes. Artair had got out of the car and was standing watching with interest. My mother glanced at him. 'Artair came looking for you after school and didn't know where you were.'

I gave him a look, and made a mental note that where girls were concerned he was not to be trusted.

I said, 'I walked the girl from Mealanais Farm home. I didn't know it would take so long.'

My mother was aghast. 'Mealanais? Fionnlagh, what were you thinking? Don't you ever do that again!'

'But Marsaili wants me to go and play there on Saturday morning.'

'Well, I forbid it!' My mother had turned steely. 'It's far too far, and neither your father or me have the time to run you there and back. Do you understand?'

I nodded, trying not to cry, and she suddenly took pity

on me, giving me the warmest of hugs, soft lips brushing my burning cheeks. That was when I remembered the note that Mrs Mackay had given me. I fumbled for it in my pocket and held it out.

'What's this?'

'A note from the teacher.'

My mother frowned and took it and ripped it open. I watched her face flush, and she folded it quickly and stuffed it in the pocket of her overalls. I never knew what the note said, but from that day on we only ever spoke English in the house.

Artair and I walked to school the next morning. Artair's dad had to go to Stornoway for some education meeting, and my mother was having a problem with one of her ewes. We walked most of the way in silence, battered by the wind, and in turn warmed by brief scraps of sunshine. The sea was throwing whitetops over the sand on the beach below. We were nearly at the bottom of the hill when I said, 'Why did you pretend to my mother you didn't know I'd gone to Mealanais?'

Artair puffed his indignation. 'I'm older than you. I'd have got the blame for letting you go.'

'Older? Four weeks!'

Artair cocked his head and shook it with great solemnity, like the old men who stood around the Crobost Stores on a Saturday morning. 'That's a lot.'

I was less than convinced. 'Well, I told my mother I was going to your house to play after school. So you'd better back me up.'

He looked at me, surprised. 'You mean, you're not?' I shook my head. 'Where are you going, then?'

'I'm going to walk Marsaili home.' And I gave him a look that defied him to object.

We walked in more silence until we reached the main road. 'I don't know what you want to go walking girls home for.' Artair was not pleased. 'It's sissy.' I said nothing, and we crossed the main road and on to the single track that ran down to the school. There were other kids now, converging from all directions, and walking in groups of two and three towards the little clutch of school buildings in the distance. And suddenly Artair said, 'Okay, then.'

'Okay what?'

'If she asks, I'll tell your mum you were playing at ours.'

I stole a glance at him, but he was avoiding my eye. 'Thanks.'

'On one condition.'

'What's that?'

'That I get to walk Marsaili home with you.'

I frowned my consternation, and gave him a long, hard look. But he was still avoiding my eye. Why, I wondered, would he want to walk Marsaili home if it was so *sissy*?

Of course, all these years later I know why. But I had no idea then that our conversation that morning marked the beginning of a competition between us for Marsaili's affections that would last through all our schooldays, and beyond.

THREE

I

Fin had barely lifted his bag from the luggage carousel when a large hand grabbed the handle and took it from him. He turned, surprised, to find a big friendly face grinning at him. It was a round face, unlined, beneath thickly oiled black hair that grew into a widow's peak. It belonged to a man in his early forties, broad built, but a little shorter than Fin's six feet. He wore a dark suit with a white shirt and blue tie, beneath a heavy, quilted, black anorak. He thrust another large hand into Fin's. 'DS George Gunn.' He had an unmistakable Lewis accent. 'Welcome to Stornoway, Mr Macleod.'

'It's Fin, George. How the hell did you know who I was?'

'I can spot a cop at a hundred paces, Mr Macleod.' He grinned, and as they stepped out to the car park said, 'You'll probably see a few changes.' He leaned into the strong westerly and grinned again. 'One thing that never changes, though. The wind. Never gets tired of blowing.'

But today it was a benign wind with a soft edge to it, warmed by an August sun that burst periodically through broken cloud. Gunn turned his Volkswagen on to the roundabout at the gate to the airfield, and they drove up over the hill that took them down again to Oliver's Brae. They took a right towards the town, and the conversation turned towards the murder.

'First of the new millennium,' Gunn said. 'And we only had one in the whole of the twentieth century.'

'Well, let's hope this is the last of the twenty-first. Where are post-mortems usually held?'

'Aberdeen. We have three police surgeons here on the island. All doctors from the group practice in town. Two of them are locum pathologists. They'll examine the bodies of any sudden death, even carry out a post-mortem. But anything contentious goes straight off to Aberdeen. Forester Hills.'

'Wouldn't Inverness be nearer?'

'Aye, but the pathologist there doesn't approve of our locums. He won't do *any* post-mortems unless he does them all.' Gunn flicked Fin a mischievous look. 'But you didn't hear that from me.'

'Hear what?'

Gunn's face split into a smile that told Fin they had connected.

As they headed down the long straight road towards Stornoway, Fin saw the town laid out before them, built around the shelter of the harbour and the tree-covered hill behind it. The glass-and-steel ferry terminal at the head of the new breakwater which had been built in the nineties looked to Fin like a flying saucer. Beyond it, the old pier seemed neglected. It gave him an odd jolt seeing the place again. From a distance it appeared almost exactly as he remembered it. Only the flying saucer was new. And no doubt it had brought a few aliens with it.

They passed the yellow-painted former mills of Kenneth Mackenzie Limited, where millions of metres of homespun Harris tweed had once been stored on thousands of shelves awaiting export. An unfamiliar terrace of new houses led down to a big metal shed where government money financed the production of television programmes in Gaelic. Although it had been unfashionable in Fin's day, the Gaelic language was now a multi-million-pound business. The schools even taught maths and history and other subjects through the medium of Gaelic. And these days it was hip to speak it.

'They rebuilt Engebret's a year or two ago,' Gunn said as they passed a filling station and minimarket at a roundabout that Fin did not remember. 'It's even open on a Sunday. And you can get a drink or a meal most anywhere in town now on the Sabbath.'

Fin shook his head in amazement.

'And two flights from Edinburgh every Sunday. You can even get the ferry from Ullapool.'

In Fin's day the whole island shut down on a Sunday. It was impossible to eat out, or go for a drink, or buy cigarettes or petrol. He could remember tourists wandering the streets on the Sabbath, thirsty and hungry and unable to leave until the first ferry on Monday. Of course, it was well known that after the churches of Stornoway had emptied, the pubs and hotels filled up with secret Sunday revellers who slipped in by the back door. It was not illegal, after all, to drink on the Sabbath, just unthinkable. At least, to be seen doing it.

'Do they still chain up the swings?' Fin remembered the sad sight of children's swings chained and padlocked on the Sabbath.

'No, they stopped that a few years ago.' Gunn chuckled 'The Sabbatarians said it was the thin end of the wedge. And maybe they were right.'

Fundamentalist Protestant churches had dominated island life for centuries. It was said that a publican or a restaurateur who defied the Church would be quietly put out of business. Bank loans called in, licences withdrawn. The power of the Church had seemed medieval to those looking on from the mainland. But it was real enough on the island, where some sects condemned any kind of entertainment as sinful, and any attempt to undermine their authority as the work of the devil.

Gunn said, 'Mind you, even though they don't chain the swings up any more, you'll never see a kid using one on a Sunday. Just like you'll still not see anyone hanging out their washing. Not outside of the town, anyway.'

A new sports centre hid Fin's old school from view.

They passed the Comhairle nan Eilean island council offices, and the former Seaforth Hotel opposite a terrace of traditional step-gabled sandstone houses. A mix of new ugly and old ugly. Stornoway had never been the prettiest of towns, and it hadn't improved. Gunn turned right into Lewis Street, traditional harbour homes cheek by jowl with pubs and dark little shops, then left into Church Street and the police station halfway down. Fin noticed that all the street names were in Gaelic.

'Who's running the investigation?'

'A crew from Inverness,' Gunn said. 'They were helicoptered in in the early hours of Sunday morning. A DCI, a DS and seven DCs. Plus a forensics team. They didn't hang around once the balloon went up.'

The police station was a collection of pink, harled buildings on the corner of Church Street and Kenneth Street, next door to the Kingdom Hall of Jehovah's Witnesses and the Peking Cuisine Chinese Takeaway. Gunn drove through a gate and parked beside a large white police van.

'How long have you been based at Stornoway, George?'

'Three years. I was born and brought up in Stornoway. But I've spent most of my time in the force at other stations around the islands. And then at Inverness.' Gunn slipped out of the car with a quilted nylon swish.

Fin got out of the passenger side. 'So how do you feel about all these incomers taking over the investigation?'

Gunn's smile was rueful. 'It's no more than I'd expect. We don't have the experience here.'

41

'What's the CIO like?'

'Oh, you'll like him.' A smile crinkled Gunn's eyes. 'He's a real bastard.'

The real bastard was a short, stocky man with thick, sandy hair Brylcreemed back from a low brow. He had an old-fashioned face and an old-fashioned smell (was it Brut?), and Fin could have guessed he was a Glaswegian even before he opened his mouth. 'Detective Chief Inspector Tom Smith.' The chief investigating officer rose from behind his desk and held out a hand. 'I'm sorry for your loss, Macleod.' Fin wondered if they all knew, and thought that they had probably been warned. Smith's handshake was firm and brief. He sat down again, the sleeves of his pressed white shirt neatly folded up to the elbows, his fawn suit jacket carefully arranged over the back of the seat behind him. His desk was covered in paperwork, but there was a sense of order about it. Fin noticed that his thick-fingered hands were scrubbed clean, and that his nails were immaculately manicured.

'Thank you.' Fin's response was mechanical.

'Sit down.' Smith spent more time looking at his papers than at Fin as he spoke. 'I've got thirteen CID, including the local boys, and twenty-seven uniforms working on this. There's more than forty officers on the island I can count on.' He looked up. 'I'm not sure why I need you.'

'I didn't exactly volunteer, sir.'

'No, you were volunteered by HOLMES. It certainly wasn't my idea.' He paused. 'This murder in Edinburgh. Do you have *any* suspects?'

'No, sir.'

'After three months?'

'I've been on leave for the last four weeks.'

'Aye. Right.' He appeared to lose interest, and returned again to his paperwork. 'So what grand illumination is it you think you'll be able to cast on our little investigation here?'

'I've no idea, sir, until I've been briefed.'

'It's all in the computer.'

'I have a suggestion, though.'

'Oh, do you?' Smith looked up sceptically. 'And what might that be?'

'If the post-mortem hasn't been carried out yet, it might be an idea to bring in the pathologist who did the PM on the Edinburgh murder. So we'll have a first-hand comparison.'

'Great idea, Macleod. Which is probably why I already had it.' Smith leaned back in his chair, his self-satisfaction almost as overpowering as his aftershave. 'Professor Wilson arrived on the last flight yesterday.' He checked his watch. 'PM should be starting in about half an hour.'

'You're not flying the body to Aberdeen, then?'

'The facilities are good enough here. So we brought the mountain to Mohammed.'

'What would you like me to do?'

'Frankly, DI Macleod, nothing. I've got a perfectly good team here that's quite capable of running this inquiry without your help.' He sighed in deep frustration. 'But HOLMES seems to think you might be able to say whether or not there's a connection with the Leith Walk murder. And God forbid we shouldn't do what HOLMES tells us. So why don't you sit in on the post-mortem, take a look at the parallel evidence, and if you come up with anything we'll give it a gander. Okay?'

'I wouldn't mind casting an eye over the crime scene.'

'Feel free. Detective Sergeant Gunn can give you the tour. The local boys aren't really equipped to be of much use to us anyway. Except as dogsbodies.' His contempt for everyone outside of his own team, including Fin, was clear.

'And I'll want to take a look at the files.' Fin was pushing his luck. 'Maybe talk to some of the witnesses. Suspects, if there are any.'

Smith pursed his lips and gave Fin a long, hard look. 'I can't stop you doing that, Macleod. But you might as well know that I expect to have this whole thing wrapped up in a matter of days. And just so you're not under any illusion, I don't believe there is an Edinburgh connection.'

'Why's that?'

'Call it instinct. People here aren't very sophisticated.' He smirked. 'Well, you'd know that.' He was tapping his pencil on his desk now, irritated by having to explain himself to a junior officer from another force. 'I think this is a crude copycat killing. There were plenty of details published in the papers at the time. I think the killer's a local man with a grudge trying to cover his tracks, trying to make us look somewhere else. So I'm going to shortcut the whole process.' Fin resisted the temptation to smile. He knew all about shortcuts. He'd learned very early in life that they could lead you off at tangents. But DCI Smith was not privy to such wisdom. He said, 'Unless the PM throws up something unexpected, I'm going to take DNA samples from every adult male in Crobost, as well as any additional suspects we might come up with. I figure a couple of hundred at the most. Economy of scale. A whole hell of a lot cheaper than a long-running investigation tying up officers in the field for weeks on end.' Smith was one of the new breed of senior cops whose primary concern was the bottom line.

Still, Fin was surprised. 'You have a DNA sample of the killer?'

Smith beamed. 'We think so. Despite local sensibilities, we put out teams of uniforms to search the locus on Sunday. We found the victim's clothes in a plastic binbag dropped in a ditch about half a mile away. The clothes are covered in vomit. And since the police surgeon is pretty sure the victim wasn't sick, we have to assume the murderer was. If the forensic pathologist can confirm that, we should have a perfect sample of the killer's DNA.'

II

In Church Street, and all the way down to the inner harbour, little hanging baskets of flowers swung in the wind, a brave effort to bring colour into grey lives. Pink- and white- and green-painted shops lined the street, and at the bottom of it Fin could see a cluster of fishing boats tied up at the quay, moving with the rise and fall of the ocean. A blink of sunlight caught the white boatshed on the opposite shore, and swept across the tops of trees in the Lews Castle grounds.

'What did you make of the CIO, then?' Gunn said.

'I'd pretty much concur with your assessment.' Fin and Gunn shared a grin.

Gunn unlocked the car and they got in. 'Thinks he's a superstar, that one. My old boss in Inverness used to say of the brass, they're no different from you and me. They still have to get their legs out of their breeks one at a time.'

Fin laughed. He liked the image of DCI Smith struggling to get his stocky little legs out of his trousers.

'Listen,' Gunn said, 'I'm sorry I couldn't give you the inside line on the pathologist. I didn't even know he was on the island. Shows you how much they're keeping *me* in the loop.'

'That's okay.' Fin brushed the apology aside. 'Actually, I know Angus pretty well. He's a good guy. And at least he'll be on our side.' They backed out into the street.

'Why do you think Smith's not attending the PM himself?'

'Maybe he's squeamish.'

'I don't know. A man who uses that much aftershave can't be too sensitive.'

'Aye, right enough. Most corpses smell better than he does.'

They slipped out of Kenneth Street on to Bayhead, heading north out of town. Fin looked from the passenger window at the children's playpark, the tennis courts, the bowling green, the sports ground beyond and the golf course on the hill behind it. On the other side of the street, tiny shops were crammed together beneath the dormer windows of flats above. It almost felt as if he had never been away. He said, 'Friday, Saturday nights in the eighties, the kids used to cruise up and down here in their old bangers.'

'They still do. Regular as clockwork, every weekend. Whole processions of them.'

Fin reflected on what a sad existence it was for these kids. Little or nothing to do, strangled by a society still in the grips of a joyless religion. An economy on the slide, unemployment high. Alcoholism rife, a suicide rate well above the national average. The motivation to leave was as compelling now as it had been eighteen years ago.

The Western Isles Hospital was new since Fin's day, replacing the old cottage hospital on the hill below the war memorial. It was a fully equipped, modern facility, better than many of those serving urban populations on the mainland. They turned in off Macaulay Road, and Fin saw the low, two-storey structure built in shallow angles around a sprawling car park. Gunn drove to the foot of the hill and turned right into a small, private parking area.

Professor Angus Wilson was waiting in the mortuary room. His goggles were pushed up over his shower cap, his mask pulled down below his chin, pushing out a thick beard of fusewire copper shot through with silver. He wore a plastic apron over green surgical pyjamas covered by a long-sleeved cotton gown. On the stainless steel table in front of him he had laid out plastic sleeve covers to protect his forearms, a pair of cotton gloves, a pair of latex gloves, and the characteristic steel-mesh glove he wore on his non-cutting hand to guard against an accidental slip of the blade. He was impatient to begin.

'About bloody time!' A twinkle in his green eyes betrayed the outward appearance he liked to give of bad-tempered eccentricity. It was an image he cultivated as an excuse for the rudeness that was almost expected of him now. 'How the hell are you?' He held out a hand to shake Fin's. 'Same killer, is it?'

'That's what you're here to tell us.'

'Godforsaken bloody place! You'd think if there was anywhere in the world you could get fresh fish this would be it. I ordered plaice in the hotel last night. Aye, and it was fresh alright. Fresh out the fucking freezer and into the deep-fat fryer. Christ, I can get that in my own house!' He looked at Gunn and leaned over the table to pull the folder from under his arm. 'Is that the report and the photographs?'

'Aye.' Gunn held out his hand. 'DS George Gunn.' But the professor had already turned away to look at the report and lay out the photographs. Gunn withdrew his hand self-consciously.

'You'll find head covers, shoe covers, goggles, masks and gowns in the pathologist's room across the hall.'

'You want us to put them on?' Gunn said. Perhaps, Fin thought, he hadn't been at a post-mortem in a while.

'No.' Professor Wilson wheeled around. 'I want you to gather them into a little pile and set them on fire.' He glared. 'Of course I want you to put the fucking things on. Unless you want to catch AIDS or whatever viral particles might be lurking in the bone dust that'll fill the air when we take the oscillating saw around the victim's skull. Alternatively, you can stand out there.' He waved a hand towards the large window that opened on to the corridor beyond. 'But you'll not be able to hear a fucking thing I say.'

'Jesus,' Gunn said, as they pulled on their protective clothing in the pathologist's room. 'And I thought the CIO was bad.'

Fin laughed, and almost stopped dead at the sound of it. It was the second time he had laughed today, and he hadn't laughed in such a long time. Becoming aware of it, whatever he had thought amusing was quickly choked off by a tidal wave of returning emotion. He took a moment to recover himself. 'Angus is okay. His bark's worse than his bite.'

'I'd be frightened I caught rabies if he bit me.' Gunn was still reeling from the sharp edge of the pathologist's tongue.

When they went back into the mortuary room, the professor had spread photographs across almost every available space. He was examining the victim's clothes on the table. The stainless steel was covered by a large sheet of white butcher's paper to collect any stray fibres or dried particles of vomit that detached themselves from the material. The victim had been wearing a zip-up fleece over a white cotton shirt and blue denim jeans. Big, dirty-white misshapen running shoes sat on the end of the table. The pathologist had slipped on his protective gloves and was holding a square magnifying glass in his left hand and picking delicately at the dried vomit on the dark-blue fleece with a pair of tweezers. 'You didn't tell me the victim was my namesake.'

'They never called him Angus,' Fin said. 'Everyone knew him as Angel. You could send him a letter addressed to Angel, Ness, Isle of Lewis, from anywhere in the world and it would get to him.'

DS Gunn was shocked. 'I didn't know you knew him, Mr Macleod.'

'I was at school with him. His younger brother was in my class.'

'Angel . . .' Professor Wilson was still focusing on his tweezers. 'Does he have wings?'

'The nickname was ironic.'

'Ah. Maybe that explains why someone wanted to kill him.'

'Maybe it does.'

'Gotcha, you little bugger!' The professor straightened up and held his tweezers up to the light, with what looked like a small white bead pinched delicately between its prongs.

'What is it?' Gunn said.

'It's a ghost.' He looked at them, grinning. 'Of a pill. One of these extended-release pills. The shell is full of micropores that let the medicine leak out slowly. This one's empty. But these pill casings can sometimes survive in the stomach for hours after they've served their purpose. We see them all the time.'

'Is there any significance in it for us?' Fin said.

'Maybe. Maybe not. But if this really is the killer's vomit, then it could tell us something about him that we wouldn't otherwise have known. Whatever medicine this contained may or may not show up on a tox screen, but we'll still know what it was he was taking.'

'How?'

The professor held up his magnifying glass to the tiny

shell. 'You can't really see it with this, but stick it under a dissecting scope and we'll almost certainly find numbers or letters etched on the surface, even a drug company symbol. We can check the markings against those listed in drug books to identify the medication. It might take a little time, but we'll get there.' He dropped the ghost pill carefully into a plastic evidence bag and sealed it. 'You see, we're clever bastards these days.'

'What about DNA?' Fin looked at the dried lumps of undigested food stuck to the fabric of the fleece, and could not begin to guess what they were. It seemed that no matter what you ate, it nearly always came back up looking like diced carrots in porridge. 'Will you be able to get any out of that lot?'

'Oh, I imagine so. We're sure to find mouth mucosa cells in the saliva. We'll get DNA from the nuclei of any of the cells lining the mouth, or the oesophagus, or the stomach itself. They slough off all the time, and will certainly be part of the vomitus.'

'Will it take long?' Gunn said.

'If we get the specimen to the DNA lab some time this afternoon. Extraction, amplification . . . we should have a result by late tomorrow morning.' The professor put a finger to his lips. 'But don't tell anyone, otherwise everyone'll want their results that fast.'

Fin said, 'The CIO says he's going to take anything up to two hundred DNA samples to run past whatever you extract from this lot.'

'Ah.' Professor Wilson smiled, and his beard bristled. 'That'll take a little longer. And, besides, we have not yet established that this isn't the victim's own vomitus.'

Two white-coated assistants wearing large yellow rubber gloves wheeled the body in from the six-shelved refrigerator across the hall and transferred it to the autopsy table. Angel Macritchie was a big man. Bigger than Fin remembered him, and probably fifty pounds heavier than when he had last seen him. He would not have disgraced the front row of a rugby scrum. The thick black hair he had inherited from his father was a good deal thinner now, more silver than black. His skin was a pale putty grey in death. The lips that taunted, and the fists that damaged, were slack and powerless now to inflict the emotional and physical pain that they had dispensed with such ease through all those childhood years.

Fin looked at him, trying to remain dispassionate, but even Angel's dead presence made him tense, and knotted his stomach so that he felt physically sick. He let his eyes wander to the dreadful opening across his abdomen. Inflated loops of shiny small intestine, pink tan in colour, had burst through the opening in the abdominal wall, held by a sheet of fat that Fin knew, from the Edinburgh post-mortem, was called the mesentery. There also seemed to be a balloon of large bowel pushing through. Dried blood and body fluid streaked his thighs. His tiny, flaccid penis looked like a dried fig. Fin turned to see DS Gunn standing towards the back of the room, almost pressed against the window. He was very pale.

Professor Wilson drew blood from the femoral veins at the top of the legs, and vitreous fluid from the eyes. Fin always found it hard to watch a needle entering an eyeball. There was something peculiarly vulnerable about the eyes.

Muttering almost inaudibly into a hand-held recorder, the professor examined first the feet and then the legs, noting reddish-purple bruising on the knees, before coming to the opening in the abdomen. 'Hmmm. The wound starts higher up on the left side of the abdomen, with the terminus lower on the right, tapering away almost to a skin scratch at the very tip.'

'Is that significant?' Fin said.

The professor straightened up. 'Well, it means that the blade used to inflict the wound was slashed across the abdomen right to left, from the killer's perspective.'

Fin suddenly saw his point. 'It was left to right in Edinburgh. Does that mean one was right-handed, the other left?'

'We can't tell handedness, Fin. You should bloody well know that by now! You can slash either way with the same hand. All it means is, they were different.' He ran a latexed finger along the upper edge of the wound, where the skin had darkened as it dried. 'The wound inflicted on the Edinburgh victim was deeper, too, more violent, severing the mesentery from the retroperitoneum. You'll remember, there were about three feet of small intestine hanging between the legs in loops that had been partially severed and drained.' Fin recalled the smell of it at the scene, streaks of pale green and yellow marbling the blood on the pavement. And at the post-mortem the small bowel, emptied of its juices, had been a dull, dark gold in appearance, quite unlike Angel's. 'There's just a wedge of omentum which has pushed out here, and a bulb of the transverse colon.' The professor worked his way around the wound and its protrusions. He measured it. 'Twenty-five and a half centimetres. Shorter, I think, than in Edinburgh, but I'll need to check that. And this man's much heavier. He would have presented a bigger target area.'

The external examination moved on to the hands and arms. The professor noted bruising around both elbows. There were old scars on hands ingrained with oil, and he scraped some of the black accumulation of it from beneath bitten fingernails. 'Interesting. These certainly do not look like the hands of a man who put up a desperate struggle to ward off his attacker. There is no sign of trauma, no skin beneath the fingernails.'

Careful scrutiny of the chest showed no trauma there either. But there was clear bruising on the neck, the same reddish-purple as the knees and the elbows. A row of four round bruises on the left side of the neck, two of them close to half an inch in diameter, one larger oval on the right side. 'Consistent with having been caused by fingertips. And you can see the little crescent-shaped abrasions associated with them. Made by the killer's fingernails. There are tiny flakes of skin heaped up at the concave side.' The professor glanced up at Fin. 'It's interesting, you know, how little pressure it takes to strangle someone. You don't have to stop them breathing, just prevent the blood draining from the head. The jugular veins that carry blood away from the head only require about four and a half pounds of pressure to cut them off. Whereas the carotid arteries carrying blood *to* the head require about eleven pounds to put them out of action. You'd have to apply about sixty-six pounds of pressure to cut off the vertebral arteries, and thirty-three pounds to choke off the trachea. In this case you can see the florid petechial haemorrhaging around the face.' He peeled back the eyelids, beneath a large purple bruise on the right temple. 'Yes, and also here around the conjunctivae. Which would suggest that death might have been caused by cutting off the venous drainage.'

He moved back to the neck. 'Interesting, though, that again there is no indication that our angel put up any kind of a fight. Someone defending themselves might be likely to scratch their own neck as they tried to prise away their attacker's hands. Which is another reason one would have expected to find skin beneath the fingernails. Interesting, too, that the trauma around the neck here, inflicted by the rope, the colour of the bruising, would indicate that he was almost certainly dead by the time he was strung up.'

He moved towards the bench where he had laid out the photographs. 'And if you look at the photography, the pooling of the blood on the ground, and compare it with the way the blood and fluid has streaked down the body, one could only be drawn to conclude that the disembowelling took place once our angel had been suspended from the roof, and after he was dead. The blood was not under pressure when the wound was inflicted, otherwise there would have been tell-tale spatter patterns on the floor. It simply drained from the body through the wound.'

Gunn said, 'So you're saying that the order of things was that he was strangled to death, then hung from the rafters and disembowelled?'

'No, I'm not saying anything of the sort.' The professor was short on patience. 'I'm thinking aloud. Jesus Christ, we've only just started the fucking examination.'

The assistants carefully turned the body over, and loose flesh fell away from folds of fat around the midriff and settled on cold steel. Great flabby white buttocks were dimpled and streaked with wiry black hair. The same pubic body hair that grew in tight curls around the neck and shoulders. There was no visible sign of trauma except, once more, at the neck.

'Ahhh . . .' The professor shook his head, disappointed. 'I had half hoped to find the roots of wings beneath his shoulder blades.' He moved on up to the scalp and started working carefully through the hair, parting and reparting it as if he were looking for fleas.

'Think you might find horns instead?' Fin said.

'Would you be surprised if I did?'

'No.'

'Ahhh . . .' This time the professor had found something that did not disappoint him. He crossed to his toolkit, removed a scalpel and then returned to the body to start paring away an area of hair high up on the back of the scalp, revealing a purple-red patch a little bigger than the size of a walnut, and an oval indentation that was soft beneath the fingers. The skin was broken, and there was evidence of dried blood. 'A nasty little crack on the skull.'

'Someone took him out from behind,' Fin said.

'It would appear that way. Bruising his knees and arms and forehead as he went down, pretty heavily by the looks of it. The shape of the indentation in the skull would indicate that he was hit with a metal tube, a baseball bat, something round like that. We'll get a better idea when we open up the skull.'

With the body turned face-up, and the head supported on a shaped metal block, Professor Wilson began peeling back the layers of Angel's hidden secrets. He made a 'Y' incision, cutting in from each shoulder to a point at the breastbone, and then drawing the blade down through the centre of the chest, stomach and abdomen to the pubes so that he could lay back the flesh on either side to reveal the ribcage. He used a pair of heavy shears to cut through the ribs before dislocating them at the clavicle, removing the breastbone and both halves of the shield that the human body has evolved to protect the delicate internal organs. One by one those organs were removed – heart, lungs, liver, kidneys – and taken to the workbench at the far end of the room to be weighed. Each measurement was chalked up on a blackboard, before the organs were sectioned into wedges, like slices of bread, for examination.

Angel had been in average condition for a man of his age and weight, lungs darkened from years of smoking, arteries hardened, but not in imminent danger of shutting down completely. His liver showed the ravages of too much alcohol consumed over too many years, the pale grey-brown colour of mild cirrhosis, nodular and scarred. The professor had to dig through thick layers of retroperitoneal fat to retrieve the kidneys.

The slimy, fluid-filled purse of the stomach was drained into a stainless steel bowl. Fin recoiled from the smell, but Professor Wilson seemed to savour it. He sniffed several times, like a dog, his eyes closed. 'Curry,' he said. 'Could be lamb bhuna.' His eyes twinkled as he caught Fin's revulsion.

DS Gunn said in a small voice, 'He had a curry at the Balti House in Stornoway about eight o'clock on Saturday night.'

'Hmmm,' said the professor. 'I wish I'd tried it last night.'

Fin exhaled deeply with distaste. 'Smells like alcohol, too.'

'According to witnesses he had a fair few pints at the Crobost Social after he got back from town,' Gunn told them.

'Well,' the professor said, 'I'd say the contents of his stomach are pretty much intact. Partially digested. No medication residue grossly identified. Ethanol odour is noted. Whatever cretinous cocktail of curry and alcohol he threw down there, he didn't throw it up again. So I think we might begin to lean towards the thought that the vomitus found on his clothing was, indeed, that of his killer.'

The pathologist began, then, to cut the guts free of their layers of fat, unlooping them and slicing them open along their length with a pair of scissors. The smell of excrement was almost unbearable. It was all Fin could do to stop himself from gagging. He heard Gunn gasping, and turned to see him with a hand placed firmly across his mouth and nose. But he clearly intended to stick it out.

Finally, the discarded intestine was dropped into a lined bucket and removed. 'Grossly unremarkable,' Professor Wilson said, apparently unaffected. He turned to the neck, pulling the flap of skin from the 'Y'-shaped incision up over the face to reveal the damage caused to the bony and cartilaginous structures by the act of strangulation, and the subsequent hanging, although he quickly established that the neck itself was not broken.

An incision was made to the back of the head, running

from one ear to the other, and the pathologist peeled the scalp down over the face to reveal the skull. He moved Fin back from the table as one of the assistants took an oscillating saw around the skull cap before removing it and allowing the brain to plop out into another stainless-steel bowl. The professor examined the skull and nodded his satisfaction. 'As I thought. There's an area of subgaleal haemorrhage over the left parietal bone, two and a half to three and a half centimetres, roughly the same dimensions as the scalp contusion. And a small amount of deep subdural haemorrhage. The parietal bone shows a matching fracture, pretty much consistent with what I suspected. A metal tube, a baseball bat, something of that nature, used to club him down from behind. If he wasn't completely unconscious, he'd have been in no condition to resist.'

Fin wandered over to the bench where the pathologist had laid out the photographs taken at the crime scene. It looked as if the boatshed had been lit by an overzealous theatrical lighting director. The colours were lurid and startling, blood already dried to a rust brown. Angel's dead weight seemed impossibly large, layered folds of blue-white flesh. The intestine looping from his grinning abdomen appeared unreal. It all had the cheap and nasty veneer of a bad sixties B-movie. But Fin was beginning to get a picture of Angel's last hours.

He had gone into Stornoway for a curry, returning afterwards to Ness, where he had consumed several pints at the Crobost Social Club. He had either accompanied his killer to the boatshed at Port of Ness or met him there. For what reason, it was unclear. But in any event, he must either have known his killer, or been sufficiently unsuspecting to turn his back on him, allowing the opportunity to attack him from behind. Knocked unconscious by a blow to the back of the head, he had been turned over and strangled. The murderer must have been in a state of high nervous tension, excitable, adrenalin pumping. He had vomited all over his victim.

Undaunted, apparently, he had proceeded to strip Angel of his clothes. That would have taken some time, and been a far from simple task, given the dead weight of a man of around two hundred and fifty pounds. Even more incredibly, he had proceeded to tie a rope around his neck, thread it through a beam in the roof and hoist him upright so that he was eventually hanging with his feet more than six inches clear of the ground. Which told them something about the murderer. This was a powerful man. And in spite of the act of murder making him physically sick, very determined. The longer it took, the greater the risk of being caught. He must have known that the boatshed was a Saturday night haunt for young lovers, and that he might be discovered at any moment. Murder interrupted instead of the more usual coitus interruptus. And yet not content simply with killing him, he had undressed him, hanged him and disembowelled him. Time-consuming and messy. Something in all these thoughts made Fin uneasy.

He turned back towards Professor Wilson. 'How do you think it compares with the Leith Walk murder? Are we talking about the same killer here?'

The professor pushed his goggles up on his forehead and pulled his mask down below his beard. 'You know how it is, Fin. Pathologists never give you a straight answer. And I'm not about to break with tradition.' He sighed. 'On the face of it, the MO is very similar. Both men attacked from behind, struck on the head, rendered unconscious and strangled. Both men stripped of their clothes and found hanging by the neck. Both men disembowelled. Yes, there are differences in the angle and depth of the wound. And our Angel's killer was agitated to the point of throwing up over his victim. We don't know if that happened in Edinburgh. There were no traces of vomitus on the body, and we never found the clothes. What we did find on that body, you'll recall, were carpet fibres, suggesting that perhaps the victim had been murdered elsewhere and brought to Leith to be strung up for exhibition. There was certainly less blood in Edinburgh, which probably meant that some time had elapsed between the victim's death and the disembowelling.'

The professor began the process of reassembling the carcass on the table in front of him. 'The thing is, Fin, the circumstances and the setting are so very different, the detail is bound to be different, too. So the truth is, that without definitive evidence pointing one way or the other, it is impossible to say whether these killings were carried out by the same individual or not. Perhaps the ritualistic nature of the murders might lead you to think that they were, but on the other hand salient features of the Leith Walk murder were carried in some detail by several of the tabloids. So if someone had wanted to replicate the murder they could do so fairly easily.'

'But why would somebody *want* to do that?' Gunn said. He looked a little less green around the gills now.

'I'm a pathologist, not a psychiatrist.' The professor cast Gunn a withering look, before turning back to Fin. 'I'll take skin swabs, and we'll see what, if anything, toxicology turns up. But don't expect much in the way of further illumination.'

III

The Barvas road wound up out of Stornoway, leaving behind spectacular views towards Coll and Loch a Tuath and Point, sunlight coruscating across the bay, torn clouds chasing their own shadows over the deep blue water. Ahead lay twelve miles of bleak moorland as the road straightened out and took them north-west towards the tiny settlement of Barvas on the west coast. It was a brooding landscape that in a moment of sunlight could be unexpectedly transformed. Fin knew the road well, in all seasons, and had never ceased to marvel at how the interminable acres of featureless peatbog could change by the month, the day, or even the minute. The dead straw colour of winter, the carpets of tiny white spring flowers, the dazzling purples of summer. To their right the sky had blackened, and rain was falling somewhere in the hinterland. To their left the sky was almost clear, summer sunlight falling across the land, and they could see in the distance the pale outline of the mountains of Harris. Fin had forgotten how big the sky was here.

Fin and Gunn drove in silence, thoughts filled by the images of clinical post-mortem carnage they had witnessed at the mortuary. There was no greater reminder of your own mortality than to witness another human being laid bare on a cold mortuary table.

At just about the halfway point, the road took a dip before rising again to a peak from which the Atlantic was distantly visible, venting its relentless anger on a crumbling coastline. In the hollow of the dip, about a hundred yards from the north side of the road, stood a small stone house with a brightly painted green tin roof. A shieling, once used by coastal crofters as a home during the summer, when they would move their beasts inland for better grazing. They were everywhere on the island. Most of them, like this one, had long since fallen into desuetude. Fin had seen the green-roofed shieling on the Barvas moor every Monday on his way to the school hostel in Stornoway. And again on the way back on the Friday. He had seen it in all weathers. And he had seen it often, as it was today, lit by the sun from the south, standing in vivid outline against the blackest of skies in the north. It was a landmark that almost every man, woman and child on the island would recognize. For Fin, however, it had a special significance, and the sight of it now filled him with a pain he had long since forgotten, or at least buried in a dark place he had no wish to revisit. But for as long as he was on the island, he knew that there were memories from his past he could not avoid. Memories which, like childish things, he had put away when he became a man nearly twenty years before.

The drive up the west coast was a trip that took him deeper into that past, and Fin sat silently in the passenger seat while Gunn drove. Long stretches of empty road linked bleak and exposed settlements huddled around churches of various denominations. The Church of Scotland. The United Free Church of Scotland. The Free Church of Scotland. The Free Church of Scotland Continuing – the *Wee Frees*, as the free churches were universally known. Each one was a division of the one before. Each one a testimony to the inability of man to agree with man. Each one a rallying point for hatred and distrust of the other. He watched the villages drift by, like moving images in an old family album, every building, every fencepost and blade of glass picked out in painfully sharp relief by the sun behind them. There was not a soul to be seen anywhere. Just an occasional car on the road, or at the odd village store, or filling station. The tiny village primary schools, too, were empty, still shut for the summer holidays. Fin wondered where all the children were. To their right, the peatbog drifted into a hazy infinity, punctuated only by stoic sheep standing firm against the Atlantic gales. To their left, the ocean itself swept in timeless cycles on to beaches and into rocky inlets, creamy white foam crashing over darkly obdurate gneiss, the oldest rock on earth. The outline of a tanker, like a distant mirage, was just discernible on the horizon.

At Cross, Fin saw that the tree which had once grown tall in the shelter of the Cross Inn had been cut down. A landmark gone. The only tree on the west coast. The village seemed naked without it. The Cross Free Church still dominated the skyline, dark granite towering over the harled and double-glazed homes of stubborn islanders determined to see off the elements. And occasionally their prayers were answered. For sometimes, on days like today, the wind took pity and the sky let the sun through to soften its razor edge. Hard lives rewarded with fleeting moments of pleasure.

Not far beyond the church the road peaked, and they had a view down towards the northernmost tip of the island. The gable ends of white-painted cottages caught the sunlight all along the eastern horizon, in between the ruins of old blackhouses, textured stone in random patterns pushing up out of the turf. And Fin saw the familiar curve of the land dipping away to the village of Crobost on the cliff road, and the distinctive silhouette of a church built to show the people of Cross that the people of Crobost were just as devout.

The road took them down through Swainbost and Lionel to the tiny village of Port of Ness, past the single-track roads that turned off towards Crobost and Mealanais. There the road ended, and the cliffs formed a natural harbour at the the north-west end of half a mile of empty golden beach. Man had enhanced nature by building a breakwater and harbour wall. At one time trawlers and fishing boats had plied their trade in and out of the harbour. But nature had struck back, smashing down the breakwater at one end, where great chunks of semi-submerged rock and concrete had fought and failed to stand firm against the irresistible assault of the sea. The harbour was all but deserted now, used as a haven only by small fishing boats, crabbers and dinghies.

Gunn parked outside Ocean Villa opposite the harbour road. A black-and-yellow crime-scene tape whipped and snapped in the wind, stretched across the road to prevent public access. A uniformed officer, leaning against the wall of the Harbour View Gallery, hastily ditched his cigarette as he recognized Gunn getting out of the driver's side. Some comedian had obliterated the *s* from the *To the Shore* sign pointing towards the harbour. Fin wondered if it was a comment on the succession of teenage girls who had lost their virginity over the years in the boatshed where, on Saturday, a fallen angel had died.

They stepped over the tape and followed the winding

road down to the shelter of the quay. The tide was in, green water over yellow sand. A crabber and a group of dinghies were tied together at the inner wall, creels piled on the quay above them beside a tangle of green netting, and pink and yellow marker buoys. A larger boat, dragged up out of the water, was tilting at a dangerous angle in the sand.

The boatshed was much as Fin remembered it. Green corrugated-iron roof, white-painted walls. The right-hand side of it was open and exposed to the elements. Two window slits in the back wall opening out to the beach beyond. There were two large wooden doors on the left-hand side. One was shut, the other half-open, revealing a boat on a trailer inside. There was more crime-scene tape here. They stepped into the semi-dark of the closed-off half of the building. Angel's blood still stained the floor, and the smell of death lingered with the diesel fumes and the salt water. The wooden cross-beam overhead revealed a deep groove cut by the rope where Angel's murderer had hauled him up to hang there. The sounds of the sea and the wind were muted in here, but still a presence. Through the narrow window openings, Fin could see that the tide was just turning, seawater starting to recede over smooth wet sand.

Apart from the staining, the concrete floor was unnaturally clean, every scrap of debris carefully collected by men in Tyvek suits for scrupulous forensic examination. The walls were scarred with the graffiti of a generation.

Murdo's a poof; *Anna loves Donald*; and that old classic, *Fuck the Pope*. Fin found it almost unbearably depressing. He stepped outside and into the open half of the shed and took a deep breath. A crudely fashioned swing hung from the rafters, two strips of wood bound together with plastic orange rope to create the seat. The same orange rope which had been used to suspend Angel from the rafters next door. Fin became aware of Gunn at his shoulder. He said, without turning, 'So have we any idea why someone might have wanted to kill him?'

'He wasn't short of enemies, Mr Macleod. You should know that. There's a whole generation of men from Crobost who suffered at one time or another at the hands of Angel Macritchie or his brother.'

'Oh, yes.' Fin spat on the floor as if the memory brought a bitter taste to his mouth. 'I was one of them.' He turned and smiled. 'Maybe you should be asking me where I was on Saturday night.'

Gunn cocked an eyebrow. 'Maybe I should, Mr Macleod.'

'Do you mind if we walk along the beach, George? It's been a long time.'

The beach was bordered on the landward side by low, crumbling cliffs no more than thirty feet high, and at the far end the sand gave way to rocky outcrops that reached tentatively into the water, as if testing it for temperature. Odd groups of rock, clustered together at points in the bay, were always just visible above the breaking waves. Fin had spent hours on this beach as a boy, beachcombing, catching crabs in the rock pools, climbing the cliffs. Now he and Gunn left virgin tracks in the sand. 'The thing is,' Fin said, 'being bullied at school twenty-five years ago is hardly a motive for murder.'

'There were more people it seems, Mr Macleod, who bore him a grudge, than just those he bullied.'

'What people, George?'

'Well, for a start, we had two outstanding complaints against him on the books at Stornoway. One of assault, one of sexual assault. Both, in theory, still subject to on-going inquiry.'

Fin was surprised only by the complaint of assault. 'Unless he'd changed since I knew him, Angel Macritchie was always fighting. But these things were aye settled one way or another, with fists in the car park, or a pint in the bar. No one ever went to the police.'

'Oh, this wasn't a local. Not even an islander. And there's no doubt that Angel gave him a doing. We just couldn't get anyone to admit they saw it.'

'What happened?'

'Och, it was some bloody animal rights campaigner from Edinburgh. Chris Adams is his name. Campaigns Director of a group called Allies for Animals.'

Fin snorted. 'What was he doing here? Protecting sheep from being molested after closing time on a Friday night?'

Gunn laughed. 'It would take more than an animal rights campaigner to put an end to that, Mr Macleod.' His smile faded. 'No, he was here – still is – trying to put a stop to this year's guga harvest.'

Fin whistled softly. 'Jesus.' It was something he hadn't thought about in years. *Guga* was the Gaelic word for a young gannet, a bird that the men of Crobost harvested during a two-week trip every August to a rock fifty miles north-north-east of the tip of Lewis. *An Sgeir*, they called it. Simply, *The Rock*. Three hundred feet of storm-lashed cliffs rising out of the northern ocean. Encrusted every year at this time by nesting gannets and their chicks. It was one of the most important gannet colonies in the world, and men from Ness had been making an annual pilgrimage to it for more than four hundred years, crossing mountainous seas in open boats to bring back their catch. These days they went by trawler. Twelve men from the village of Crobost, the only remaining village in Ness to carry on the tradition. They lived rough on the rock for fourteen days, clambering over the cliffs in all weathers, risking life and limb to snare and kill the young birds in their nests. Originally, the trip was made out of necessity, to feed the villagers back home. Nowadays the guga was a delicacy, in great demand all over the island. But the catch was limited by Act of Parliament to only two thousand, a special dispensation written into the Protection of Birds Act, passed in the House of Commons in London in 1954. And so it was only by good luck, or good connections, that a family would get a taste of the guga now.

Fin could still recall with mouth-watering clarity the oily flavour of the flesh on his tongue. Pickled in salt, and then boiled, it had the texture of duck and the taste of fish. Some said it was an acquired taste, but Fin had grown up with it. It had been a seasonal treat. Two months before the men left for the rock, he would begin to anticipate the taste of it, just as he relished each year the rich flavour of the wild salmon during the poaching season. His father always managed to acquire a bird or two, and the family would feast on them in the first week. There were those who would store them in kegs of salt water and ration them through the year. But stored like that, they became too gamey for Fin's taste, and the salt would burn his mouth. He liked them fresh from the rock, served with potatoes and washed down with milk.

'You ever tasted the guga?' he said to Gunn.

'Aye. My mother had Ness connections, and we usually managed to get a bird every year.'

'So these Allies for Animals are trying to stop the trip?'

'Aye, they are.'

'Angel was a regular on the rock, wasn't he?' Fin remembered that the only time he had been among the twelve men of Crobost, it was already Angel's second time there. The memory was like a shadow passing over him.

'Regular as clockwork. He was the cook.'

'So he wouldn't take too kindly to someone trying to sabotage it.'

'He didn't.' Gunn shook his head. 'And neither did

anyone else. Which is why we couldn't find anyone who saw what happened.'

'Did he do much damage?'

'A lot of bruising about the body and face. A couple of broken ribs. Nothing too serious. But the boy'll remember it for a while.'

'So why's he still here?'

'Because he's still hoping to stop the trawler from taking the men out to the rock. Mad bloody fool! There's a bunch of activists arriving on the ferry tomorrow.'

'When are they due to leave for An Sgeir?' Just forming the words in his mouth sent a slight shiver through Fin's body.

'Sometime in the next day or two. Depending on the weather.'

They had reached the far end of the beach, and Fin started climbing up over the rock.

'I'm not really wearing the right footwear for this, Mr Macleod.' Gunn slid dangerously on slick black rock.

'I know a way up to the top of the cliff from here,' Fin said. 'Come on, it's easy.'

Gunn scrambled after him, almost on his hands and knees as they struggled up a narrow scree path that cut back on itself before leading to a series of natural, if uneven, steps that took them finally to the top. From here they could see across the machair to where the houses of Crobost nestled in the dip of the cliff road, gathered around the grim, dominating presence of the Free

Church where Fin had spent so many cold and miserable childhood Sundays. The sky behind it was blackening for rain, and Fin could smell it on the wind, just as he had done as a child. He was exhilarated by the climb, and enjoyed the soft pummelling of the stiffening breeze, all thoughts of An Sgeir banished. Gunn was breathless, and concerned by the scuffs on his shiny black shoes. 'Haven't done that in a long time,' Fin said.

'I'm a townie, Mr Macleod.' Gunn was gasping. 'I've never done that.'

Fin smiled. 'It's good for you, George.' He was feeling better than he had done in quite a while. 'So, do you think your animal rights man murdered Angel Macritchie in revenge for his beating?'

'No, I don't. He's not the type. He's a bit ...' He searched for the right word. 'Fey. You know what I mean?' Fin nodded thoughtfully. 'But I've been around long enough, Mr Macleod, to know that the most unlikely people sometimes commit the most terrible crimes.'

'And he comes from Edinburgh.' Fin was thoughtful. 'Has anyone checked to see if he has an alibi for the Leith Walk murder?'

'No, sir.'

'Might be an idea. DNA evidence will rule him in or out of the Macritchie killing, but that'll take a day or two. Maybe I should have a word with him.'

'He's at the Park Guest House in town, Mr Macleod. I don't think Allies for Animals has the biggest of budgets.

And DCI Smith has told him not to leave the island.'

They started walking across the machair towards the road, sheep scattering before them as they went. Fin raised his voice over the wind. 'And sexual assault, you said. What was all that about?'

'A sixteen-year-old girl accused him of rape.'

'And *did* he rape her?'

Gunn shrugged his shoulders. 'It's very difficult to get the proof you need to bring a charge in a lot of these cases.'

'Well, it's probably not an issue. Not in this case, anyway. I'd have said it was virtually impossible for a sixteen-year-old girl to have done to Macritchie what his killer did.'

'Maybe so, Mr Macleod. But her father would have been more than capable.'

Fin stopped mid-stride. 'Who's her father?'

Gunn nodded towards the church in the distance. 'The Reverend Donald Murray.'

FOUR

Guy Fawkes night was just three days away. We had collected a huge stash of old rubber tyres and were looking forward to the biggest bonfire in Ness. Every village had one, and every village wanted theirs to be the best. It was a competition we took very seriously in those days. I was thirteen, and in my second year of secondary school at Crobost. The exams I would sit at the end of that year would pretty much determine my future. And the rest of your life is a lot of responsibility to carry when you're thirteen.

If I did well I would go to the Nicolson in Stornoway and sit my Highers, maybe Sixth Year Studies, even A levels. I would have a chance of going to university, the opportunity to escape.

If I did badly I would go to the Lews Castle School, still at that time in the castle itself. But there my education would be vocational. The school had a proud tradition of turning out first-rate mariners, but I didn't want to go to sea, and I didn't want to learn a trade and be stuck in some building yard like my father when the fishing no longer offered him a living.

The trouble was, I hadn't been doing too well. The life of a thirteen-year-old is full of distractions. Like bonfire night. I had also been living with my aunt for five years by then, and she kept me busy on the croft, cutting peats, dipping the sheep, tupping, lambing, bringing in the hay. She wasn't interested in how well or badly I was doing at school. And it is not easy at that age to motivate yourself to burn the midnight oil over some dry history book, or mathematical equation.

That was when Artair's dad first came to see my aunt and offered to tutor me. She told him he was daft. How could she afford a private tutor? He said she didn't have to. He was already tutoring Artair, and it would be no more bother to tutor me as well. Besides, he told her (and I know this because she relayed it to me later, word for word, and with no little amount of scepticism in her voice), he believed that I was a smart boy who was under-achieving. And that with a little push in the right direction he was sure I could pass my exams at the end of the year and graduate to the Nicolson. And, who knows, maybe even university.

Which is how I came to be sitting at a table that night in the little back room of Artair's bungalow that his dad liked to call his study. One whole wall was lined with shelves that sagged under the weight of books stacked along their length. Hundreds of books. I remembered wondering how it was possible for one person to read so many books in a lifetime. Mr Macinnes had a mahogany desk with a green leather-tooled top and a matching captain's chair. It was pushed against the wall opposite the bookshelves. There was a big, comfortable armchair where he sat to read, a coffee table beside it with an Anglepoise lamp. If he cared to look up, he would have a view out of the window to the sea. Artair and I were tutored at a fold-up card table that Mr Macinnes placed in the middle of the room. We sat in hard chairs facing away from the window, in case we would be distracted by the world outside. Sometimes he would take us together, usually for maths. But more often he took us separately. Boys together have a habit of encouraging each other to a failure in concentration.

I don't remember much, now, of those long tutoring sessions through dark winter nights and early spring light, except that I didn't enjoy them. Funny, though, the things I do remember. Like the chocolate-brown colour of the felt-topped card table, and the pale, sharply defined coffee stain that marred it and looked like a map of Cyprus. I remember an old brown water stain on the ceiling in the corner of the room that made me think of a gannet in flight, and the crack in the plaster which transected it, running at an angle through the cornice before disappearing behind cream-coloured anaglypta wallpaper. I remember, too, a crack in a windowpane, seen during stolen glances to that other world out there, and the smell of stale pipe smoke that always seemed to hang about Artair's dad. Although I don't ever remember seeing him smoking.

Mr Macinnes was a tall, thin man, a good ten years older than my father had been. I suppose the seventies was the decade when he probably finally admitted to himself that he was no longer a young man. But he clung on to a hairstyle well into the eighties that was longer than fashionable then. It's odd how people can get locked into a kind of timewarp. There's a time in their lives that defines them, and they hang on to it for all the subsequent decades: the same hair, the same style of clothes, the same music, even though the world around them has changed beyond recognition. My aunt was locked in the sixties. Teak furniture, purple carpets, orange paint, The Beatles. Mr Macinnes listened to The Eagles. I recall tequila sunrises and new kids in town, and life in the fast lane.

But he wasn't some soft academic. Mr Macinnes was a fit man. He liked to sail, and he was a regular on the annual trip to An Sgeir to harvest the guga. He was irritated with me that night, because my concentration was poor. Artair had been dying to tell me something when I arrived, but his dad had hustled me into the backroom and told Artair to keep his peace. Whatever it was could wait. But I could feel Artair's impatience from the other side of the door, and eventually Mr Macinnes realized he was fighting a losing battle and told me to go.

Artair couldn't wait to get me out of the house, and we hurried up the front path to the gate in the dark. It was a freezing cold night, the sky as black as you might ever see it, and inset with stars that seemed fixed like jewels. There was no wind, and a thick white frost was settling already, like dust, across the moor, slow sparkling as the moon lifted itself into its autumn elevation, casting its wonderful light on a rare, tranquil sea. There was a high-pressure zone sitting right over the Hebrides, and they said it was going to be there for a few days. Ideal weather for bonfire night. I could hear Artair's excitement wheezing in his breath. He had developed into a big, strong lad, taller than me, but cursed still with the asthma that threatened at times to shut down his airways. He took a long pull on his puffer. 'The Swainbost boys have got hold of an old tractor tyre. It's more than six foot in diameter!'

'Shit!' I said. A tyre like that would burn better than anything we had. We had collected more than a dozen, but they were just car tyres, and bike tyres, and inner tubes. And no doubt the Swainbost boys would already have stockpiled something not dissimilar themselves. 'Where did they get it?'

'Does it matter? The fact is they've got it, and they're going to have a much better bonfire than us.' He paused, watching for my disappointment, and then smiled. 'Maybe.'

I felt myself frowning. 'What d'you mean, *maybe*?'

Artair became conspiratorial. 'They don't know we

know they've got it. They have it stashed away some- where, and they're only going to wheel it out on bonfire night.'

Maybe it was the hour I'd spent cooped up in Mr Macinnes's study, but I seemed to be missing his point. 'So?'

'They think if we knew about it we'd be jealous and try to sabotage them.'

I was starting to get cold now. 'Well, we do know about it. But I don't see how the hell we could sabotage a tractor tyre.'

'That's just it, we're not going to sabotage it.' Artair's excitement was glistening in his eyes. 'We're going to steal it.'

Which took me completely by surprise. 'Says who?'

'Donald Murray,' Artair said. 'He's got a plan.'

The frost was still lying thick on the ground at playtime the next day. Everyone was out in the playground. There were half a dozen slides going. The best of them was at the end farthest from the gate, where the tarmac sloped away towards a drainage ditch. It was a good fifteen feet long. A short run-up, and gravity did the rest. But you had to jump off quick at the end or you would finish in the ditch.

I was itching to take my place in line and have a go, but Donald Murray had called a meeting of the Crobost boys and we were gathered in a huddle by the technical block, and I could only watch enviously from afar.

Donald was a tall, angular, good-looking boy, with a fine head of sandy hair that flopped down over his brow. All the girls fancied him, but he was dead casual about it. He was a boy's boy, a leader of men, and if you were with Donald you felt safe from the Macritchie brothers. Angel had left Crobost School by that time and gone to pursue vocational studies at the Lews Castle. But Murdo Ruadh was still an ever-present threat.

Initially Donald had drawn his power from the fact that everyone was afraid of his father. Everyone, that is, except Donald himself. The minister, then, was still a very powerful figure in the community, and Coinneach Murray was a fearsome man. Coinneach is the Gaelic for Kenneth, and although it was *Kenneth Murray* on the board outside the church, everyone knew him as Coinneach. Although not to his face. You would only ever refer to him in person as Mister or Reverend Murray. We always imagined that his wife called him Reverend, too. Even in bed.

Donald, however, always referred to his father as *the old bastard*. He defied him at every turn, refused to go to church on a Sunday and, as a result, was confined to the manse every Sabbath.

There was one Saturday night we were having a party at someone's house. The parents were at a wedding in Stornoway, and had decided to stay overnight rather than risk the drive back after drinking. It wasn't terribly late, ten thirty maybe, when the door burst open and

Coinneach Murray stood there like some avenging angel sent by the Lord to punish us for our sins. Of course, half the kids were smoking and drinking. And there were girls there, too. Coinneach roared his disapproval at us, and told us he would be sure to speak to every one of our parents. Did we not know it was the eve of the Lord's Day, and that children of our age should be home in bed? We were all terrified. Except for Donald. He stayed where he was, lounging on the sofa, a can of beer in his hand. And, of course, it was Donald he had come for really. He pointed a trembling finger of accusation at his son and told him to get out. But Donald just sat there, a sullen look of defiance on his face, and shocked us all by telling his father to fuck off. You could have heard a pin drop in Stornoway.

Red-faced with anger and humiliation, Coinneach Murray strode into the room and knocked the can from Donald's hand. The beer went everywhere. But nobody moved. And nobody spoke. Not even Coinneach. He had a powerful physical presence beyond anything that the dog collar gave him. He was just a big, strong man. He physically lifted Donald out of the settee by the scruff of his neck before frog-marching him out into the night. It was an awesome display of power in the face of defiance, and there was not one of us who would have wanted to be in Donald's shoes when his father got him home.

And true to his word, the Reverend Coinneach Murray visited the parents of every boy and girl who was in the house that night, and there was hell to pay. Although not in my house. My aunt was nothing if not eccentric, and in a God-fearing community it was somehow only natural that she would be a devout atheist. She told the minister in no uncertain terms, although not as colourfully as Donald, where he could stick his self-righteous indignation. He told her she was certain to go to Hell. 'I'll see you there, then,' she said as she slammed the door on his back. I suppose I learned my contempt for the Church from my aunt.

So Donald had gained a kind of legendary status in his own right. Not because of who his father was, but because of the way he defied him and went against everything he stood for. Donald was the first in our year to smoke. The first to drink. He was the first of my contemporaries whom I ever saw drunk. But there was a positive side to him, too. He was good at sports. He was second-top of our class. And although he was no match, physically, for Murdo Ruadh, intellectually he could run rings around him. And Murdo knew it. So by and large he gave him a wide berth.

There were six of us gathered there in the playground that day. Donald, me and Artair, a couple of boys from the bottom end of the village, Iain and Seonaidh, and Calum Macdonald. I always felt sorry for Calum. He was smaller than the rest of us, and there was something soft about him. He was good at art, he liked Celtic music and played the *clàrsach*, a small Celtic harp, in the school orchestra. He was also mercilessly bullied by Murdo Ruadh and his gang. He never told, and he never complained, but I always imagined him crying himself to sleep at nights. I dragged my eyes away from the slide at the far side of the playground to focus on the plan for tonight's raid on Swainbost.

'Okay,' Donald was saying, 'we'll meet up at the cemetery road end at Swainbost, one o'clock tomorrow morning.'

'How will we get out of the house without being caught?' Calum was wide-eyed and full of trepidation.

'That's your problem.' Donald was unsympathetic. 'Anyone doesn't want to come, that's up to them.' He paused to give anyone who wanted to a chance to back out. No one did. 'Okay, about a hundred yards down the road to the cemetery there's the remains of an old blackhouse with a tin roof on it. It's used mainly for storing agricultural equipment, and it's got a padlock on the door. That's where they've hidden the tyre.'

'How do you know all this?' Seonaidh said.

Donald smirked. 'I know a girl in Swainbost. She and her brother don't get on.' We all nodded, none of us surprised that Donald knew a girl in Swainbost, each of us thinking there was a good chance he knew her in the biblical sense as well.

'What the fuck's going on here, then?' Murdo Ruadh forced his way into the group, flanked by the same two boys who'd fallen in with him that first day at school all those years before. One of them had developed terrible acne, and you would find your eyes drawn to the clusters of suppurating, yellow-headed spots around his nose and mouth. Our circle quickly widened out away from him.

'Nothing to do with you,' Donald said.

'Aye, it is.' Murdo seemed unusually sure of himself in Donald's presence. 'You're going to steal the tyre the Swainbost boys have got stashed away up there.'

We were all shocked that he knew. Then beyond that initial shock came the realization that one of us must have told him. All eyes turned towards Calum. He squirmed uncomfortably.

'I didn't tell, honest.'

'Doesn't matter how I know,' Murdo Ruadh growled. 'I know. Alright? And we want in. Me and Angel and the boys. After all, we're all Crobost boys. That right?'

'No.' Donald was defiant. 'There's enough of us as it is.'

But Murdo was quite relaxed. 'It's a big tyre. It's gonna weigh a ton. Gonna take a lot to carry it.'

'We're not going to carry it,' Donald said.

Which knocked Murdo momentarily off-balance. 'How're you gonna get it back to Crobost then?'

'We're going to roll it, stupid.'

'Oh.' Murdo Ruadh clearly hadn't thought of that. 'Well, it's still gonna take a lot of hands to get it upright and keep it that way.'

'I told you.' Donald stood his ground. 'We don't need you.'

'Look!' Murdo jabbed a finger in his chest. 'I don't give a shit what you told me. Either we're in, or we blow the whistle on you.' He'd played his trump card and stood back triumphantly. 'What's it to be?'

I could tell by the slump of Donald's shoulders that for once he was beaten. None of us wanted the Macritchie brothers and their pals along. But, then, neither did we want the Swainbost boys to have the best bonfire on Guy Fawkes night. 'Okay,' Donald sighed. And Murdo Ruadh beamed his satisfaction.

I couldn't have slept that night, even if I'd wanted to. I sat up late doing my next week's homework for Mr Macinnes. There was a small two-bar electric heater with a concave reflector in my room, but it made no impact on the cold, unless you were six inches from it, and then it would burn you. I had two pairs of socks on, and my big crofter's leather boots. I wore a pair of jeans, a T-shirt, a shirt, a heavy woollen jumper and a donkey jacket. And still I was cold. It was a big, cheerless house this, built in the 1920s, and when the wind gusted in off the sea the windows and doors rattled and let it blow through at will. There was no wind tonight, but the temperature had dropped below twenty degrees, and the peat fire in the living room seemed a long way away. At least if my aunt looked in on me before she went to bed I would have an excuse for wearing all these clothes. But, of course, I knew she wouldn't. She never did.

I heard her coming upstairs about ten-thirty. Normally she was a late bird, but tonight it was too cold even for her. And bed, along with a hot water bottle, offered the only prospect of warmth. I worked on by the light of my bedside lamp for another hour and a half before finally closing my study books and listening at the door for any sign of life. I heard nothing, so I crept out into the darkness of the hall. To my horror I saw a line of light under my aunt's bedroom door. She must have been reading. I slipped quickly back into my bedroom. The wooden staircase was old and creaky, and I knew there was no way I could negotiate it without being heard. The only alternative was to climb out of the window on to the roof and slither down the rone pipe. I had done it before, but with the frost lying thick on the slates tonight it would be a treacherous undertaking.

I eased the rusted metal window frame off its latch and swung it open. The hinge screeched horribly, and I froze, waiting for the call of my aunt's voice. But all I could hear was the constant rhythm of the sea washing up on the shingle beach fifty feet below. The cold air pinched my face and penetrated my fingers as I held on to the window frame to lever myself out on to the roof. The tiles dropped away steeply from the dormer to the gutter below. I found it with my feet and inched my way along it to the gable, where I was able to hold on to the coping and lower myself until my boots found a grip on the rone. And it was with a huge sense of relief that I let myself slide down the cold metal pipe to the ground. I was out.

The air smelled of winter frost and peat smoke. My aunt's old car stood on the tarmac apron in front of the house. Beyond the shadow of the ruins of an older dwelling, the shingle shore below was lit as bright as day by the moon. I looked up and saw the light still burning in my aunt's window, and hurried to the concrete shed that abutted the east gable of the house. I retrieved my bicycle, and with a glance at my watch, pedalled hard off along the single-track road towards Crobost, the moor sparkling darkly on my left, the ocean shimmering on my right. It was just on half-past midnight.

My aunt's house was about a mile south of the village itself, standing on its own on the cliffs near the tiny Crobost harbour cut into a deep cleft in the rock. I covered the distance back to the village in a matter of minutes, passing my old home, dark and empty, closed up now and falling into sad disrepair. I always tried not to look at it. It was an almost unbearable reminder of how my life once was, and how it might still have been.

Artair's bungalow sat down below the level of the road, the shadowy mound of its peat stack silhouetted against the silver ocean, moonlight picking out the carefully constructed herringbone pattern of the peats. I pulled up at the gate and peered into the shadows that pooled around the house. Artair had long ago been nicknamed *Wheezy*, but I could never bring myself to call him that. 'Artair!'

My whispered call seemed awfully loud. But there was no sign of him. I waited more than five minutes, becoming increasingly agitated, glancing time and again at my watch, as if by doing so I could slow the progress of time. We were going to be late. I was on the point of giving up, when I heard a loud clatter from the side of the house next to the peat stack. Artair came wheezing out of the darkness, shaking off a plastic bucket whose handle had managed to attach itself around his ankle. He ran across the grass and almost somersaulted over the fence, propelled by the tension of the top wire which he had somehow failed to see. He landed on his backside at my feet, grinning up at me in the moonlight.

'That was subtle,' I said. 'What the hell kept you?'

'My old man only went to bed about half an hour ago. He's got ears like a bloody rabbit. I had to wait till I could hear him snoring before I was sure he was asleep.' He scrambled to his feet and cursed. 'Oh Jesus! I've got sheep shit all over me.'

My heart sank. I was giving him a backie, and he'd have his shitty breeks on my saddle and his shitty hands around my waist. 'Get on!' He swung a leg over the saddle, still grinning idiotically. And I could smell the shite off him. 'And don't get that stuff on me!'

'What are friends for, if not for sharing.' Artair grabbed hold of my donkey jacket. I gritted my teeth and pushed off down the single-track towards the main road, Artair's legs shoved out wide on either side of the bike for balance.

We hid the bicycle in a ditch a couple of hundred yards from the cemetery road at Swainbost and ran the rest of the way. The others were waiting impatiently at the road end, huddled in the shadow of the old Co-op building which had been taken over by Ness Builders. 'Where in God's name have you been?' Donald whispered.

Angel Macritchie ballooned out of the darkness and pushed me up against the wall. 'You stupid wee bastard! The longer we're hanging about here waiting for you, the more likely we are to get caught.'

'Jeeesus!' Murdo Ruadh's voice fizzed in the shadows. 'What the fuck is that smell?'

I glared at Artair, and Donald said, 'Come on, let's get on with it.'

Angel's big hand released me, and I followed the others as we slipped out of the cover of Ness Builders and into the moonlight that slanted across the road. It seemed very exposed out here. Higgledy-piggledy fence-posts marked out the line of the road all the way to the cemetery itself, sparkling headstones on the distant headland. Our footsteps crunched on the frost beneath us and seemed inordinately loud as we hurried past the gardens of the houses on our left. Our breath condensed in the freezing air and billowed around our heads like smoke.

Donald stopped outside an old blackhouse with a corrugated-iron roof. It had stout wooden doors with a large padlock threaded through a sturdy iron clasp. A triangle of roof had been built up above the door to allow bigger agricultural machinery in and out. 'This is it.'

Murdo Ruadh stepped forward and pulled a heavy-duty cutter from beneath his coat.

'What the hell's that for?' Donald whispered.

'You told us it was padlocked.'

'We're here to steal a tyre, Murdo, not go damaging people's property.'

'So how're we gonna get the padlock open?'

'Well, a key's the usual way.' Donald held up a big key on a leather tab.

'Where the fuck'd he get that?' This from Acne Boy, whose spots seemed to glow in the moonlight.

'He knows a girl,' Calum said, as if that explained everything.

Donald unlocked the padlock and pushed one half of the door open. It creaked into the dark interior. He pulled a torch from his pocket and we all crowded in behind him as he flashed its beam around an amazing accumulation of junk. There was the rusted shell of an old tractor, an ancient plough, a broken-down bailer, trowels, hoes, forks, spades, rope, fishing net suspended from the rafters, orange and yellow plastic buoys dangling just above our heads, the bench seat from the back of an old car. And there, leaning against the far wall, a huge old tractor tyre, bigger than any of us, and with a tread you could lose your fist in. It had a ten-inch gash on the side facing us, damage inflicted by a careless driver. Perhaps insurance had covered the cost of its replacement, but the tyre itself was no longer of any use to man nor beast. Just perfect fodder for a bonfire. We stared at it in hushed awe. 'She's a beauty,' Artair whispered.

'She'll burn for fucking days,' Angel said.

'Let's get her out of here.' There was a sense of triumph in Donald's voice.

She weighed a ton, that tyre, just as Murdo Ruadh had predicted. It took all of us just to keep her from falling over as we manoeuvred her out of the door and on to the road. Donald detached himself from the group, closed the door and refastened the padlock. He returned, grinning with anticipation. 'They'll not have a clue what happened. It'll be just like she disappeared into thin air.'

'Aye, until she goes up in smoke on our bonfire.' Murdo was gleeful.

It was heavy going, pushing that tyre up the slope to the main road. And it wasn't much of a slope either. It gave us a good idea of just how difficult it was going to be to get it up the hill to Crobost. A long night loomed ahead of us.

When we got to the road end, we leaned it up against the gable of the old Co-op building and took a break, panting and perspiring. We had generated enough of our own heat not to be bothered by the cold any more. Cigarettes got handed around, and we all puffed away in silent self-congratulation. We were pretty pleased with ourselves.

'It's going to get difficult from here,' Donald said, cupping his hand around the glowing ember of his cigarette.

'Whatdya mean?' Murdo glowered at him. 'It's downhill from here to the Crobost turnoff.'

'Exactly. Gravity's going to increase the weight of that thing and we're going to have a job keeping it from running away from us. We'll need the biggest, strongest boys at the front to keep it under control.'

And so the Macritchie brothers, Acne Boy and his pal were delegated to control the tyre from the front, walking backwards down the hill. Me and Artair were at one side, Iain and Seonaidh at the other. And Donald and Calum took a rim each at the rear.

We had just wheeled it out into the main road, when car headlights appeared suddenly over a blind bend at the top of the hill. None of us had even heard it coming. There was panic. There wasn't time to get the tyre back into the shadow of the building, and so Donald put his shoulder to it and pushed it over into the ditch. It took Murdo Ruadh with it. We heard the crack of thin ice breaking and, as we dived for cover, the muted cursing of the younger Macritchie. 'Ya fucking bastard!'

The car flew past and its lights receded towards the distant turnoff to Fivepenny and the Butt of Lewis. A dripping Murdo Ruadh, his face streaked with mud and God knew what else, staggered out of the ditch, spluttering in the cold and still cursing. Of course, the rest of us were in stitches, until Murdo strode angrily across the metalled road and smacked me on the side of the head, making my ears ring. He'd never liked me much, Murdo Ruadh. 'Think that's fucking funny, ya wee shite?' He glared around the other faces, their owners trying desperately to keep them straight. 'Anyone else think it's funny?' No one else was willing to admit that they did.

'Let's get on with it,' Donald Murray said.

It took us a full five minutes to get the tyre out of the ditch and upright again, my face stinging all the while. I was going to have a big bruise on my cheek tomorrow, I knew. We took up our positions again, and began slowly and carefully rolling the tyre down the hill towards the Crobost road end. At first it seemed easier than it had pushing it up the slope. Then, gradually, as the angle of descent increased, the tyre began to get heavier and gain a momentum of its own.

'For Christ's sake,' Donald hissed, 'slow it down!'

'What d'you think we're fucking trying to do?' You could hear the beginnings of panic in Angel's voice.

The tyre got heavier and faster, our hands burning on the rubber as we tried to hold it, trotting now alongside it as it gathered pace all the time. The Macritchie gang couldn't hold it back any longer. Acne Boy fell and the tyre bumped over his leg. Calum tripped over Acne Boy and went sprawling in the road.

'We can't hold it, we can't hold it!' Murdo Ruadh was almost shouting.

'For Christ's sake keep the volume down,' Donald

hissed. There were houses on either side of the road. But, in truth, volume was the least of our problems. The tyre was already out of our control. Angel and Murdo leapt out of the way, and it finally ripped itself free of Donald's last desperate attempts to stop it.

Off it went, with a life and direction of its own. We, all of us, went chasing after it, helter-skelter down the hill. But it just got faster and faster, and further and further away. 'Oh God . . .' I heard Donald groan, and I realized what he realized. The tyre was heading straight for the Crobost Stores, which stood face-on at the bend in the main road at the bottom of the hill. What with its weight and speed, it was going to do a lot of damage. And there was not a single thing we could do about it.

The sound of breaking glass sent shards of shockwaves through the night air. The tyre had gone straight into the window to the left of the door. I swear the whole building shook. And then nothing. The tyre remained standing upright, wedged solidly in the window opening like some bizarre modern sculpture. We arrived, gasping for air and shocked to silence, about thirty seconds after impact, and just stood there looking at it in abject horror. Lights went on in the nearest houses, about a hundred and fifty yards away.

Donald was shaking his head in disbelief. 'I don't be-lieve it,' he kept saying. 'I don't believe it.'

'Got to get the fuck out of here,' Murdo Ruadh gasped.

'Naw.' Angel put a hand on his brother's chest to stop

him going anywhere. 'We just run off, they're never going to give up till they find out who it was.'

'What're you talking about?' Murdo looked as if he thought his big brother had lost his mind.

'I'm talking about a scapegoat. Someone to take the fall and not rat on the rest of us. They'll be happy as long as they've got someone to blame.'

Donald shook his head. 'That's crazy. Let's just go.' We could hear voices now in the distance. Voices raised in query, wondering what on earth had happened.

But Angel stood his ground. 'Naw. I'm right on this. Trust me. We need a volunteer.' His gaze fell on each of us in turn. And then stopped on me. 'You, orphan boy. You've got least to lose.' I didn't even have time to object before a big fist hit me full in the face and my legs folded under me. I hit the ground with such force it knocked all the wind out of me. Then his boot in my stomach curled me up into a helpless foetal position and I vomited on the gravel.

I heard Donald shouting, 'Stop it! Fucking stop it!'

And then Angel's low, threatening tone. 'You gonna make me, God boy? Two's better than one. It could be you next.'

There was a moment's silence, and then Calum wailing, 'We gotta go!'

I heard footsteps running off into the distance, and then an odd peace settled on the night along with the frost. I couldn't move, did not even have the strength to roll over. I was vaguely aware of more lights coming on in nearby houses. I heard someone shouting, 'The store! There's a break-in at the store!' The beams of torches pricked the night air. Then hands pulled me roughly to my feet. I could barely stand. I felt a shoulder support me under each oxter, then Donald's voice.

'You got him, Artair?'

And Artair's familiar wheeze. 'Aye.'

And they dragged me, running, across the road and into the ditch.

I'm not sure how long we lay there in the ice and mud, hidden by the long grass, but it seemed like an eternity. We saw the locals arriving in their dressing gowns and wellies, beams of light flashing around the road and the shopfront. And we heard their consternation. A six-foot tractor tyre embedded in the shop window and not a soul around. They decided that no one had actually broken into the shop, but that they had better call the police, and as they headed back towards their houses, Donald and Artair got me to my feet and we staggered off across the frozen peatbog. At a gate in the shadow of the hill, Donald waited with me while Artair went off to retrieve my bike. I felt like hell, and worse. But I knew that Donald and Artair had risked being caught by coming back to get me.

'Why'd you come back?'

'Och, it was my stupid idea in the first place,' Donald sighed. 'I wasn't going to let you take the blame for it.'

And then he paused. I couldn't see his face, but I heard the anger and frustration in his voice. 'One day I'm going to rip that fucking Angel Macritchie's wings off.'

They never did find out who had run the Swainbost tyre through the window of Crobost Stores. But they weren't about to give it back to the Swainbost boys. The police impounded it, and Crobost had the best bonfire in Ness that year.

FIVE

I

Fin walked up the single-track road towards the village with the wind blowing soft in his face. He glanced down the hill and saw the distant figure of Gunn heading back to Port of Ness to retrieve the car. He felt the first spots of rain, but the black sky overhead was breaking up already, and he thought that perhaps it wouldn't come to anything.

It might have been August, but someone had a fire lit in their hearth. That rich, toasty, unmistakable smell of peat smoke carried to him on the breeze. It took him back twenty, thirty years. It was extraordinary, he thought, how much he had changed in that time, and how little things had changed in this place where he had grown up. He felt like a ghost haunting his own past, walking the streets of his childhood. He half expected to see himself and Artair coming around the bend in the road at the church, heading on their bikes for the store at the foot of the hill to spend their Saturday pennies. The cry of a child made him turn his head, and he saw two small boys playing on a makeshift swing next to a house on the rise above him. Clothes flapped on a drying line and, as he watched, a young woman came hurrying out of the house to gather them in before the rain came.

The church sat proud on the bend, looking out over the village below, and the land that fell away to the sea. The large metalled car park was new since Fin had last been here. *In* and *Out* gates were protected from sheep and their shit by cattle grids, and the tarmac was marked out with freshly painted white lines, worshippers guided to park their cars in orderly Christian rows. In Fin's day, people had walked to church. Some of them from miles around, black coats blowing about their legs, free hands holding on to hats, the others clutching bibles.

Steps led up from the car park to the manse, a large two-storey house built in the days when the Church had expected its ministers to require three public rooms and five bedrooms: three for family, one for any visiting minister and one for use as a study. The manse had stunning views over the north end of the island, all the way across to the distant skyward-pointing finger of the lighthouse. It was also exposed to the wrath of God in the form of whatever weather might descend on it from the Heavens. Even the minister was not spared the Lewis weather.

Beyond the curve of the hill, the road rose higher again with the land, along the clifftops, and the rest of Crobost was strung out along it for nearly half a mile. Although he couldn't see them from here, Fin knew that the bungalow where Artair used to live, and his parents' croft, were only a few hundred yards away. But he was not sure that he was ready yet for that. He pushed open the gate beside the cattle grid and crossed the car park to the steps leading to the manse.

He knocked on the door several times and rang the bell, but there was no reply. He tried the door and it opened into a gloomy hallway. 'Hello! Anyone home?' He was greeted by silence. He closed the door again and looked across towards the church. It was still massively impressive, built of great blocks of stone hewn out of local rock. Flanked by two small turrets, a bell tower rose high above the arched doorway. There was no bell in it. Fin had never known there to be. Bells were frivolous. Perhaps they smacked of Catholicism. All the windows were arched, two above the main door, one on either side of it, and four down each of the flanks. Tall, plain windows. No colourful stained glass in this austere Calvinistic culture. No imagery. No crosses. No joy.

One half of the double doors was lying open and Fin walked into the hallway where the minister would greet the congregation coming in, and shake their hands on the way out. A cheerless place, with worn floorboards and dark, varnished wood. It smelled of dust and damp clothes and time. A smell, it seemed, that had not changed in thirty years. Evocative of those long Sabbath days when

Fin's parents had made him sit through an hour and a half of Gaelic psalm-singing and a fiery midday sermon, followed by another dose at six o'clock. In the afternoon he'd had to endure two hours of Sunday school in the hall at the back of the church. When he wasn't at church, or at Sunday school, he would have to stay in the house while his father read from the Gaelic Bible.

Fin traced his childhood footsteps through the left-hand door and into the church itself, rows of unforgiving wooden pews flanking two aisles leading to the raised and railed area at the far end, from which sombre elders would lead the psalm-singing. The pulpit rose high above, an elaborately carved dais set into the wall and reached by curving staircases on either side. Its position of elevation placed the minister in his dominant position of authority over the mere mortals whom he berated each Sunday with threats of eternal damnation. Salvation was in their own hands, he would tell them week in and week out, if only they would put themselves in the hands of the Lord.

In his head, Fin could almost hear the singing of the Gaelic psalms. A strange, unaccompanied tribal chanting which could seem chaotic to the untrained ear. But there was something wonderfully affecting about it. Something of the land and the landscape, of the struggle for existence against overwhelming odds. Something of the people amongst whom he had grown up. Good people, most of them, finding something unique in themselves, in the way they sang their praise to the Lord, an expression of gratitude for hard lives in which they had found meaning. Just the memory of it brought him out in goose-pimples.

He heard a knocking sound that seemed to fill the church, rattling around the balconies that ringed three sides of it. Metal on metal. He looked about, puzzled, before realizing that it was coming from the radiators along each wall. The central heating was new. As was the double glazing in the tall windows. Perhaps the Sabbath was a little warmer today than it had been thirty years ago. Fin went back out to the entrance hall, and saw a door open at the far end. The banging was coming from somewhere beyond it.

The door gave on to what turned out to be the boiler room. A large oil-fired boiler stood with its door open, a protective cover removed to reveal its byzantine interior workings. Bits and pieces harvested from the interior were scattered around the concrete apron on which it stood. A toolbox lay open, and a man in blue overalls lay on his back trying to loosen the joint on an exiting pipe by banging on it with a large spanner.

'Excuse me,' Fin said. 'I'm looking for the Reverend Donald Murray.'

The man in the overalls sat up, startled, and banged his head on the boiler door. 'Shit!' And Fin saw the dog collar underneath the overalls where they were open at the neck. He recognized the angular face below a mop of untidy sandy hair. There was grey in that hair now, and it was a little thinner. As was the face, which had somehow shed its boyish good looks and become mean, pinched in lines around the mouth and the eyes. 'You've found him.' The man squinted up at Fin, unable to see his face because of the light behind it. 'Can I help?'

'You could shake my hand for a start,' Fin said. 'That's what old friends usually do, isn't it?'

The Reverend Murray frowned and got to his feet, peering into the face of the stranger who knew him. And then the light of recognition dawned in his eyes. 'Good God. Fin Macleod.' And he grabbed Fin's hand and shook it firmly, a smile splitting his face. And Fin saw in him again the boy he had known all those years before. 'Man, it's good to see you. Good to see you.' And he meant it, but only for as long as it took other thoughts to crowd his mind and cloud his smile. And as the smile faded, he said, 'It's been a long time.'

Fin had found it hard to believe, when Gunn told him, that Donald Murray had succeeded his father as minister of Crobost Free Church. But he could not deny the evidence of his own eyes. Although that still did not make it any easier to believe. 'About seventeen years. But even if it had been seventy I'd never have thought I'd see you in a dog collar, except maybe at a vicars and tarts party.'

Donald inclined his head a little. 'God showed me the error of my ways.'

Ways, Fin recalled, which had taken him on a long

diversion off the straight and narrow. Donald had gone to Glasgow at the same time as Fin. But while Fin had gone to university, Donald had got into the music promotion business, managing and promoting some of the most successful Glasgow bands of the eighties. But then things had started going wrong. Drink had become more important than work. The agency went to the wall. He got involved with drugs. Fin had met him at a party one night and Donald offered him cocaine. And a woman. Of course, he'd been smashed, and there was something dead in eyes that had once been so full of life. Fin heard later that after being arrested and fined for possession, Donald had left Scotland and headed south to London.

'Caught the *curàm* then?' Fin asked.

Donald wiped his oily hands on a rag, assiduously avoiding Fin's eyes. 'That's not a term I care for.'

It was a condition so prevalent on the island that the Gaelic language had subverted a word to describe it. *Curàm* literally meant *anxiety*. But in the context of those who had been born again, it was used in the sense of something you might catch. Like a virus. And in a way, it was. A virus of the mind. 'I've always thought it was very apposite,' Fin said. 'All that brainwashing as a kid, followed by violent rejection and a dissolute life. Drink. Drugs. Wild women.' He paused. 'Sound familiar? And then, I suppose, the fear and the guilt kick in, like belated indigestion, after all that early diet of hellfire and damnation.' Donald eyed him sullenly, refusing to be drawn.

'That's when they say that God talks to you, and you become very special to all those people who wish that God would talk to them, too. Is that how it was with you, Donald?'

'I used to like you, Fin.'

'I *always* liked you, Donald. From that first day you stopped Murdo Ruadh from punching my lights out.' He wanted to ask him why he was throwing his life away like this. And yet he knew that Donald had already been engaged in the act of flushing it down the toilet with drink and drugs. Maybe this really was some kind of redemption. After all, not everyone harboured the same bitterness towards God as Fin. He relented. 'I'm sorry.'

'Are you here for a reason?' Donald was clearly not as ready to forgive as Fin was to apologize.

Fin smiled ruefully. 'All those hours of study to get myself a place at university, and I threw it away.' He gave a small, bitter laugh. 'Ended up a cop. Now, that's a turn-up for the book, isn't it?'

'I'd heard.' Donald was guarded now. 'And you still haven't told me why you're here.'

'I'm investigating the murder of Angel Macritchie, Donald. They brought me in because he was killed in exactly the same way as a murder I'm investigating in Edinburgh.'

A smile flitted briefly across Donald's face. A glimpse of his old self. 'And you want to know if I did it.'

'Did you?'

Donald laughed. 'No.'

'You once told me you were going to rip the fucking wings off Angel Macritchie.'

Donald's smile vanished. 'We're in the house of God, Fin.'

'And that should bother me, why?'

Donald looked at him for a moment, then turned away and crouched to start putting tools back in his box. 'It was that atheist aunt of yours who turned you against the Lord, wasn't it?'

Fin shook his head. 'No. She'd have been pleased to have me be a happy heathen like her. But she got me too late. The damage was done. I was already infected. Once you've believed, it's very hard to stop believing. I just stopped believing God was good, that's all. And the only one responsible for that was God Himself.' Donald swivelled to look at Fin, incomprehension in his frown. 'The night he took my parents on the Barvas moor.' Fin forced a smile. 'Of course, I was just a kid then. These days, in my more rational moments, I know it's all just crap, and that such things happen in life.' And he added bitterly, 'More than once.' One more reason for resentment. 'It's only when I can't shake off the feeling that maybe there really is a God, that I start getting angry again.'

Donald turned back to his tools. 'You didn't *really* come here to ask me if I killed Angel Macritchie, did you?'

'You didn't like him much.'

'A lot of people didn't like him much. That doesn't

mean they would kill him.' He paused, balancing a hammer in his hand, feeling its weight. 'But if you want to know how I feel about it, I don't think he was any great loss to the world.'

'That's not very Christian of you,' Fin said, and Donald dropped the hammer into the box. 'Is it because of all the shit we took off him as kids, or because your daughter claimed that he raped her?'

Donald stood up. 'He raped her alright.' He was defensive, challenging Fin to contradict him.

'That wouldn't surprise me at all. Which is why I'd like to know what happened.'

Donald pushed past him and out into the hallway. 'I imagine you'll find everything you need to know in the police report.'

Fin turned after him. 'I'd rather hear it from the horse's mouth.'

Donald stopped in his tracks. He wheeled around and took a step back towards his old classmate. He was still a good three inches taller than Fin. Well over six feet, and well capable, Fin thought, of hoisting Macritchie's eighteen stone on a length of rope to hang him by the neck from the rafters of the boatshed in Port of Ness. 'I don't want you, or anyone else, talking to her about it again. That man raped her, and the police treated her like she was a liar. As if rape isn't humiliating enough.'

'Donald, I'm not going to humiliate her, or accuse her of lying. I just want to hear her story.'

'No.'

'Look, I don't want to force the issue, but this is a murder inquiry, and if I want to talk to her, I'll talk to her.'

Fin saw a father's anger in Donald's eyes. It flared briefly, then some inner control dulled its flame. 'She's not here just now. She's in town with her mother.'

'I'll come back, then. Maybe tomorrow.'

'It might have been better, Fin, if you hadn't come back at all.'

Fin felt the chill of a threat in Donald's words, and in his tone, and found it hard to remember that this was the same boy who had stood up for him against bullies, and risked his own hide to come back and rescue him the night that Angel Macritchie had felled him outside Crobost Stores. 'Why's that? Because I might find out the truth? What's anyone got to fear from the truth, Donald?' Donald just glared at him. 'You know, if Macritchie had raped *my* daughter, I'd probably have been tempted to take matters into my own hands myself.'

Donald shook his head. 'I can't believe you'd think me capable of something like that, Fin.'

'All the same, I'd be interested to know where you were on Saturday night.'

'Since your colleagues have already asked me that, I think you'll probably find it's a matter of record.'

'I can't tell when the record's lying. With people, usually I can.'

'I was where I always am on a Saturday night. At home

writing my sermon for the Sabbath. My wife will vouch for me if you care to ask her.' Donald walked to the door and held it open for Fin, signalling that their exchange was over. 'In any case, it is not for me to deliver retribution to sinners. The Lord will deal with Angel Macritchie in his own way.'

'Maybe he already has.' Fin stepped out into the blustery afternoon as the rain began falling in earnest. Horizontally.

By the time Fin reached Gunn's car idling in the car park, he was soaked. He dropped into the passenger seat with the rain clinging to his curls and running down his face and neck, and slammed the door shut. Gunn turned on the blower and glanced over at Fin. 'Well?'

'Tell me what happened the night the girl claimed Macritchie raped her.'

II

The cloud was shredded all across the sky as they drove back to Stornoway, ragged strips of blue and black and purple-grey. The road stretched straight ahead of them, rising to the horizon and a strip of light beneath the bruising where you could see the rain falling in sheets.

'It happened about two months ago,' Gunn said. 'Donna Murray and a bunch of her pals were drinking at the Crobost Social.'

'I thought you said she was only sixteen.'

Gunn sneaked him a look to see if he was joking. 'You have been away a long time, Mr Macleod.'

'It's illegal, George.'

'It was a Friday night, sir. The place would have been jumping. Some of the girls would have been over eighteen. And nobody's paying that much attention anyway.'

Sunlight unexpectedly split the gloom, wipers smearing light with rain across the windscreen, a rainbow springing up out of the moor away to their left.

'There was all the usual stuff going on between boys and girls. You know how it is when you mix alcohol with teenage hormones. Anyway, Macritchie was at his habitual place at the bar, sitting up on a stool, leaning in his elbow groove and casting a lascivious eye over all the young girls. Hard to believe he still had any hormones after the amount of beer he'd flushed through his system over the years.' Gunn chuckled. 'You saw the state of his liver.' Fin nodded. Angel had been a big drinker, even as a teenager. 'Anyway, for some reason young Donna seems to have caught his eye that night. And inexplicably, he seems to have thought she might find him attractive. So he offered to buy her a drink. I guess when she turned him down that might have been the end of it. But, then, apparently someone told him that she was Donald Murray's girl, and that seemed to encourage him.'

Fin could imagine how putting his hands all over Donald Murray's daughter might tickle Macritchie's sick sense of irony, particularly if her father got to hear about it.

'He spent the rest of the night badgering her, buying drinks that she wouldn't touch, trying to put his arm around her, making lewd suggestions. Her friends all thought it was a great laugh. Nobody saw Macritchie as a real threat. Just some drunken old fart in the bar. But Donna got really pissed off. He was ruining her night out, so she decided she was going home. Flounced out in a right tid, according to her pals. Most people didn't notice it, but about a minute later the barmaid saw Macritchie slipping off his stool and heading out after her. This is where different accounts start to conflict.'

Their car passed a bunch of teenage girls huddled in a concrete bus shelter at South Dell. They were peculiar to Lewis, these constructions, flat-roofed, with four open compartments that would provide shelter regardless of the direction of the wind. Fin remembered that they used to call them giants' picnic tables. The youngsters looked about Donna's age, waiting for a bus to take them into Stornoway for a night out. Alcohol and teenage hormones. Fin felt certain that these girls had no idea just how dangerous a cocktail that could be. Smiles on pale faces that flew past rain-streaked windows. Lives headed on a course that none of them could predict but which were, at the same time, utterly predictable.

'It was about thirty-five minutes from the time Donna left the Social till the time she got home,' Gunn said.

Fin exhaled through pursed lips. 'It would take about ten minutes at the most.'

'Seven. We got a policewoman to time it.'

'So what happened during the missing half-hour?'

'Well, according to Donna, Macritchie sexually assaulted her. Her words. She was dishevelled when she got back to the house. Which was the word her father used. Red-faced, make-up all smeared, blubbing like a baby. He called the police, and she was taken to Stornoway for questioning and examination by the police surgeon. That was when she used the word *rape* for the first time. So between Ness and Stornoway it had changed from sexual assault to rape. Of course, as we always do, we had to establish the exact nature of the assault. When we started getting into detail, the girl got hysterical. But, yes, she confirmed, Macritchie forced her to the ground and put his penis inside her vagina. No, she had not consented. Yes, she was a virgin. Or had been.' Gun glanced uneasily at Fin. 'But I have to be honest with you, Mr Macleod, there was no blood on her, or her clothes, and there was no outward indication that she had been forced to the ground on a wet night. There was no bruising visible on her arms, her clothes did not appear to be wet or dirty.'

Fin was puzzled. 'What did the medical examination show?'

'Well, that's just it, Mr Macleod, she wouldn't submit to a medical examination. Point-blank refused. Said it would be too humiliating. We told her that it was unlikely that charges could be brought against Macritchie unless we had physical, or witness, evidence. As it turned out, the only witness we could find outside the Social said that Macritchie had headed off in the opposite direction from Donna. And since she refused a medical examination . . .'

'What did her father say?'

'Oh, he backed her all the way. Said that if she didn't want to be examined by a doctor then that was her right. We explained the position to him, but there was no way he was going to try to persuade her to do it if she didn't want to.'

'What was his demeanour through all this?'

'I'd say he was angry, Mr Macleod. Kind of tight, balled-fist angry, you know, pent up inside. He seemed calm enough on the exterior. Too calm. Like water in a dam before they open the sluice gates.' Gunn sighed. 'In any event, the investigating officers questioned just about everybody who was at the Social Club that night, but there was no one who could corroborate Donna's story. In theory, the case remains open, but in fact the investigation was shelved.' He shook his head. 'Of course, shit sticks. There was rumour, and gossip, and a lot of people were convinced that Macritchie raped the girl.'

'Do you think he did?'

Scraps of water, tiny lochan lying in fragmented pools across the moor, glinted a cold blue in the sunlight. The rain had blown over, clearing the sky to the south. Siadar lay behind them, and the white cottages of Barvas as they approached it caught the western sun slanting across the land, lighting the gentle slopes of the southern mountains in the far distance.

'I'd like to say I did, Mr Macleod. From everything I know about the man he seems to have been a bad bastard. But, you know, there was no evidence.'

'I didn't ask you about the evidence, George. I asked you what you thought.'

Gunn held the wheel firmly in both hands. 'Well, I'll tell you what I think, Mr Macleod, as long as you don't quote me on it.' He hesitated just for a moment. 'I think that girl was lying through her teeth.'

III

The Park Guest House stood in a terrace of sandstone houses opposite what was now the Caladh Inn – dark, rain-streaked stone brooding behind black-painted wrought-iron fencing. It was home to one of the better restaurants in town, a conservatory built on to the dining room to make the most of the summer light. Around the solstice, it was possible to eat at midnight with the sun still streaking the sky pink.

Reluctantly, Chris Adams led Fin up to his small single-bedded room on the first floor, after Fin told him that the guest sitting room on the ground floor was not an appropriate place for them to talk. The floorboards creaked like wet snow underfoot. Fin noticed that Adams held himself

117

stiffly, and appeared to be in some discomfort as he climbed the stairs. He was English, which Fin had not expected, betrayed by a creamy Home Counties accent. He was around thirty years old, tall and thin, with very blond hair. And for someone who apparently spent much of his time outdoors in the pursuit of animal welfare, he had an unhealthily pale complexion. The ivory skin was marred, however, by yellowing bruising around the left eye and cheekbone. He wore baggy corduroy trousers and a sweatshirt with a slogan about not being able to eat money. His fingers were unusually long, almost feminine.

He held the door open for Fin to enter his room, and then cleared a fold-up chair of clothes and paperwork to allow him to sit. The bedroom appeared to have been at the centre of a paper explosion in which a thousand bits of paper and Blu-tack had stuck to the walls. Maps, memos, newspaper cuttings, Post-its. Fin was not certain how pleased the proprietor would be. The bed was strewn with books and ring-binder folders and notebooks. A laptop computer on the chest of drawers in the window shared its space with more paperwork, empty plastic cups, and the remains of a Chinese carry-out. Adams's outlook was across James Street to the grim glass and concrete edifice that used to be the Seaforth.

'I've already given you people more time than you deserve,' he complained. 'You do nothing to apprehend the man who beat me up, then accuse me of murdering him when he turns up dead.' His mobile phone rang.

'Excuse me.' He answered it and told his caller that he was busy right now and would call back. Then he looked expectantly at Fin. 'Well? What do you want to know now?'

'I want to know where you were on Friday, May the twenty-fifth this year.'

Which caught Adams completely off-balance. 'Why?'

'Just tell me where you were, Mr Adams, please.'

'Well, I have no idea. I'd need to check my diary.'

'Then do it.'

Adams looked at Fin with a clear mixture of consternation and irritation. He tutted audibly, and sat on the end of his bed, making his long fingers dance flamboyantly across the keyboard of his laptop. The screen flickered to life and flashed up a diary page. It jumped from a daily to a monthly layout, and Adams scrolled back from August to May. 'May twenty-fifth I was in Edinburgh. We had a meeting at the office that afternoon with the local representative of the SPCA.'

'Where were you that night?'

'I don't know. At home probably. I don't keep a social diary.'

'I'll need you to confirm that for me. Is there anyone who can corroborate?'

A deep sigh. 'I suppose Roger might know. He's my flatmate.'

'Then I suggest you ask him and get back to me.'

'What on earth is all this about, Mr Macleod?'

Fin ignored the question. 'Does the name John Sieve-wright mean anything to you?'

Adams did not even stop to think about it. 'No, it does not. Are you going to tell me what this is about?'

'In the early hours of May twenty-sixth this year, a thirty-three-year-old Edinburgh conveyancing lawyer called John Sievewright was found hanging from a tree in a street near the foot of Leith Walk. He had been strangled, stripped and disembowelled. As you know, just three days ago, one Angus John Macritchie suffered almost exactly the same fate right here on the Isle of Lewis.'

A tiny explosion of air escaped from the back of Adams's throat. 'And you want to know if I'm going around Scotland disembowelling people? Me? That's laughable, Mr Macleod. Laughable.'

'Do you see me laughing, Mr Adams?'

Adams gazed at Fin in studied disbelief. 'I'll ask Roger what we were doing that night. He'll know. He's better organized than I am. Is there anything else?'

'Yes, I want you to tell me why Angel Macritchie beat you up.'

'Angel? Is that what you call him? I imagine he'll have flown off to Hell by now rather than Heaven.' He frowned. 'I've already made an official statement.'

'Not to me you haven't.'

'Well, there's not much point in investigating the assault now, since the perpetrator is beyond even your reach.'

'Just tell me what happened.' Fin controlled his impatience, but something in his tone clearly communicated itself to Adams, who sighed again, this time even more theatrically.

'One of your local newspapers, *The Hebridean*, carried a story about how I was on the island to organize a demonstration to try to prevent the annual guga cull on An Sgeir. They kill two thousand birds a year, you know. Just slaughter them. Clambering about the cliffs strangling the poor little things while the adults are flying frantically overhead crying for their dead chicks. It's brutal. Inhumane. It may be a tradition, but it just isn't right in a civilized country in the twenty-first century.'

'If we could skip the lecture and just stick to the facts . . .'

'I suppose, like everyone else in this godforsaken place, you're in favour of it. You know, that's one thing I hadn't expected. Not a single person on the island has offered me one word of support. And I had hoped to rally local opposition to swell our numbers.'

'People enjoy their taste of the guga. And it may seem barbaric to you, but the method they use to kill the birds is almost instantaneous.'

'Sticks with nooses on the end, and clubs?' Adams curled his lips in distaste.

'They're very effective.'

'And you would know.'

'Actually, I would. I've done it.'

Adams looked at him as if there were a foul taste in his mouth. 'Then there's no point even discussing it with you.'

'Good. So could we get back to the assault, please?'

Adams's mobile rang again. He answered. 'Adams . . . Oh, it's you.' He lowered his voice to something like intimacy. 'You're in Ullapool? Good. What time does the ferry get in . . . ? Okay I'll meet you at the ferry terminal.' He glanced self-consciously at Fin. 'Look, I'll call you back a little later. I've got the police here . . . Yes, again.' He rolled his eyes. 'Alright. Ciao.' He dropped the phone on the bed. 'Sorry about that.' But he wasn't.

'Is that your protesters arriving?'

'Yes, if you must know. It's not a secret.'

'How many?'

'There'll be twelve of us. One for each member of the killing crew.'

'What are you going to do? Lie down in front of the trawler?'

'That's very amusing, Mr Macleod.' He curled his lips in mock amusement. 'I know we can't stop them. Not this year, anyway. But we can influence public opinion. There'll be press and television on hand. We'll get nation-wide coverage. And if we can persuade the Scottish Executive to withdraw their licence, then it'll become illegal. And people like you simply won't be allowed to go out there and kill those poor birds.'

'And you said all this in the piece in *The Hebridean*?'

'Yes, I did.'

'That'll have made you popular.'

'My mistake was in allowing them to carry a photograph of me. It meant I lost my anonymity.'

'So what happened?'

'I went out to Ness on a recce. Apparently the trawler leaves from Stornoway, but the Crobost men go out to meet her in a small boat from the Port of Ness. I wanted to get some photographs of the area, for reference as much as anything else. I suppose I might have been a little indiscreet. I had lunch at the Cross Inn and someone recognized me from the piece in the paper. I'm not used to language like that, Mr Macleod.'

Fin restrained the urge to smile. 'Did you talk to anyone up there?'

'Well, I got lost a couple of times and had to ask the way. The last person I spoke to before I was attacked was at a small pottery just outside Crobost. A strange, hairy sort of man. I'm not sure he was entirely sober. I asked him where I could find the road to the harbour. And he told me. I went back out to my car, which was only about twenty yards away down the road. That's when it happened.'

'What, exactly?'

Adams shifted slightly on the bed and winced. Whether from the memory or from the pain, Fin could not tell. 'A white van overtook me. A Transit van. Something like that. Funnily enough, I'd noticed it a couple of times earlier in the day. I suppose he must have been following me, awaiting his moment. Anyway, the van pulled over in front of me, and a large man whom I later identified as Angus Macritchie jumped out from the driver's side. The odd thing was, I had the impression there were others in the van. But I never saw anybody else.'

'Did he say anything?'

'Not a word. Not then, anyway. He just started punching me. I was so surprised I didn't even have time to try to get out of the way. I think it was after the second punch that my knees just sort of gave way under me, and I went down like a house of cards. And then he started kicking me in the ribs and the stomach. I curled up to try to protect myself, and he got me a couple of times on my forearms.' He pulled up his sleeves to show the bruising. 'Nice people your bird killers.'

Fin knew how it felt to be on the receiving end of a beating from Angel Macritchie. It wasn't something he would wish on anyone, even someone as naive as Chris Adams. 'Macritchie wasn't typical of the men of Crobost. And it might surprise you to know that he didn't go out to the rock to kill birds. He was the cook.'

'Oh, well, that's a comfort to me, I'm sure.' Adams's voice dripped with sarcasm.

Fin ignored it. 'What happened then?'

'He bent down and whispered in my ear that if I didn't pack up my bags and go he was going to stuff a whole guga down my throat. Then he got back into his van and drove off.'

'And you got the number?'

'Amazingly, I did. I don't know how I had the presence of mind, but yes, I made certain I committed that number to memory.'

'What about witnesses?'

'Well, there were several houses around. How people can claim they didn't see anything, I don't know. I *saw* curtains twitching in the windows. And then there was the chap from the pottery. He came down and got me to my feet and took me into his house to give me a drink of water. He said he didn't see a thing, but I don't believe him. I insisted he call the police, and he did. But very reluctantly, I have to tell you.'

'So if Macritchie threatened to stuff a guga down your throat, Mr Adams, why were you still here on Saturday night?'

'Because I couldn't get a booking on the ferry till Monday. Then, of course, someone with exquisitely good taste went and killed him, and now your people won't let me leave.'

'About which, I'm assuming, you have no complaints. Since you're able to go ahead with your protest after all.'

'With two broken ribs, Mr Macleod, I think I have plenty to complain about. And if the police had done their job a little better, your Mr Macritchie would probably have been alive today. Languishing in a police cell, rather than murdered in a boatshed.'

Which, Fin thought, was probably true. 'Where were you on Saturday night, Mr Adams?'

'Right here in my room, with a fish supper. And, no, unfortunately there isn't anyone who can confirm that, as your people have gleefully reminded me more than once.'

Fin nodded thoughtfully. Perhaps Adams might, physically, have been capable of doing the deed. In normal circumstances. Just. But with two broken ribs? Fin thought not. 'You like fish, Mr Adams?'

Adams seemed surprised by the question. 'I don't eat meat.'

Fin got to his feet. 'Have you any idea how long it takes a fish to die, starved of oxygen, literally suffocating, when a trawler hauls its nets on board?' But he wasn't waiting for an answer. 'A damned sight longer than a guga in a noose.'

IV

The incident room had been established in a large conference room at the far end of the first-floor corridor of Stornoway police station. Two windows looked out over Kenneth Street and the roofs of houses stepping steeply down to the inner harbour below. Beyond the masts of trawlers tied up for the night, the towers of Lews Castle were just visible above the trees on the far side of the water. Desks and tables were pushed up against walls, carefully trunked cabling feeding telephones and computer terminals and chattering printers. Graphic crime-scene photographs were pinned to one wall, copious notes scribbled on a whiteboard with blue felt pen. A projector sat humming quietly on a small table.

There had been nearly a dozen officers at work, taking phone calls, tapping computer keyboards, when Fin sat down at one of the four HOLMES terminals to bring himself up to date. Not only on the Macritchie murder, but also on the rape and assault claims made against him. In addition he had been able to access all the files on the murder of John Sievewright, refreshing his memory on the dozens of statements which had been taken, and on the forensic and pathology reports. But he was tired now, uncertain how clearly he was thinking. The number of officers in the incident room had dwindled to three. It had been a long day, following a sleepless night. He thought for the first time about Mona. Her threat. *Just don't expect me to be here when you get back.* And his response. *Maybe that would be best.* In those two brief exchanges, they had effectively brought their relationship to an end. Neither of them had planned it. And doubtless there would be regrets, most of them for the fourteen wasted years of their marriage. But there had also been an enormous sense of relief. A weight of silent unhappiness lifted from Fin's shoulders, even though it had been replaced almost immediately by the uncertainty of an unpredictable future. A future he did not want to contemplate right now.

'How's it going, sir?' Gunn wheeled up alongside him on a typist's chair.

Fin leaned back in his seat and rubbed his eyes. 'Downhill at a rapid rate of knots, George. I think I'm going to call it a day.'

'I'll walk you over to your hotel, then. Your bag's still in the boot of my car.'

They walked together past the armoury and the area admin office, pale-yellow walls, pastel-purple carpet. On the stairs they bumped into DCI Smith. 'Good of you to report back after the autopsy,' he said.

'Nothing to report.' Fin paused, and then added, 'Sir.' He had long ago discovered that dumb insolence was the only way to deal with sarcasm from senior officers.

'I had a verbal from the pathologist. Seems there are quite a few parallels with Edinburgh.' He had moved past them on the stairs so that he could make up for his lack of height by being on the step above.

'Inconclusive,' Fin said.

Smith looked at him thoughtfully for a moment. 'Well, you'd better have some conclusions for me by close of play tomorrow, Macleod. Because I don't want you here any longer than necessary. Understood?'

'Yes, sir.'

Fin turned away. But Smith wasn't finished. 'HOLMES has come up with another possible connection. I want you to go with DS Gunn first thing tomorrow to check it out. Gunn'll fill you in.' And he turned and took the stairs two at a time to the top landing without looking back. Fin and Gunn carried on down to the ground floor.

Fin said, 'So if he's sending us two, I guess that means he doesn't attach too much importance to it.'

Gunn smiled wryly. 'Your words, Mr Macleod, not mine.'

'Is there an Edinburgh link?'

'Not that I can see.'

'So what's the story?'

Gunn held the door open for Fin, and they headed up steps past the charge bar to the rear entrance. Early evening sunlight cast long shadows across the car park. 'Macritchie got done for poaching about six months ago. On a big estate down in the south-west of the island. Owned by an Englishman. They charge a bloody fortune down there for the salmon fishing, so the owner's keen to protect the river from poachers. Just over a year ago he brought in some heavyweight from London. Ex-army. You know the type. A thug, really. Knows bugger all about the fishing, but if he catches you at it, boy you'll know all about it.'

They retrieved Fin's bag from the boot. 'And he caught Macritchie at it?'

Gunn slammed the boot shut, and they headed down the road towards the harbour. 'He did that, Mr Macleod. And a few things besides. Macritchie was a bit the worse for wear by the time he ended up in our hands. But he wasn't going to complain about it. Loss of face, you know, to admit that somebody gave him a doing. Macritchie might have been a big lad, but this London boy was a pro. And it doesn't matter how big you are, you don't stand much chance against those fellas.'

'So what's the connection here?' Fin liked the idea of someone giving Macritchie a doing, but he couldn't see where Gunn's story was leading.

'About three weeks ago, the boy from London got jumped one night on the estate. There was a bunch of them, masks, the lot. He took a hell of a beating.'

They passed the charity shop on the corner of Kenneth Street and Church Street. A notice in the window read, *World Fair Trade – Trade not Aid*. 'So the computer, in its wisdom, thinks Macritchie might have been getting in a wee bit of revenge. And, what? That this ex-army boy finds out and goes and murders him?'

'I guess that's about the size of it, Mr Macleod.'

'So Smith saw that as a good excuse for getting you and me out of his hair for a while.'

'It's a nice run down to the south-west. Do you know Uig, Mr Macleod?'

'I know it well, George. We picnicked down there often in the summer. My father and I used to fly a kite on Uig beach.' He remembered the miles of dead flat sand that stretched away between tendrils of rock to the distant breakers. And the wind that took their home-made box kite soaring into the blue, whipping the hair back from their faces, tugging at their clothes. And the smile that creased his father's face, blue eyes shining in startling contrast to his deep summer tan. And he remembered, too, his disappointment if the tide was in, so that all those acres of sand lay under two feet of turquoise sea and they had to sit among the doons eating sandwiches.

High tide had pushed into the inner harbour, and the boats tied up along Cromwell Street Quay towered over them as Fin and Gunn headed south towards North Beach Quay, past a forest of masts and radar grilles and satellite pods. Stornoway extended along a spit of land that separated the inner harbour from the deep-water piers of the outer harbour where the ferry and the oil tankers docked. The Crown Hotel, where Fin had been booked a room, occupied a prime site on the spit, between Point Street and North Beach, overlooking the inner harbour and Lews Castle. Not much, to Fin's eye, appeared to have changed. A few commercial premises under new ownership, some freshly painted shop fronts. The hat shop was still there, its window full of bizarre creations that women pinned to their heads on the Sabbath. Hats, like the burka, were obligatory headwear on Lewis for churchgoing women. The clock tower on the town hall could be seen above the steeply pitched slate roofs and dormer windows. The two men skirted piles of lobster creels, and great heaps of tangled green fishing net. Skippers and crew were offloading supplies from vans and four-by-fours on to trawlers and small fishing boats, today not yet over before preparations were being made for tomorrow. And overhead the gulls wheeled endlessly, scraps of white against a clear blue sky, catching the last flashes of sunlight and calling plaintively to the gods.

On Point Street they stopped outside the entrance to the Crown. Fin looked along the length of this pedestrianized street with its ornamental flowerbeds and wrought-iron benches. Known to the locals as The Narrows, Point Street on a Friday and Saturday night would be thick with teenagers gathering in groups and cliques, drinking beer from cans, smoking dope, feasting on fish suppers and burgers from the fish and chip shop. In the absence of any other form of entertainment, this was where the kids made their own. Fin had spent many a night here, squeezed in shop doorways with his schoolfriends sheltering from the rain, waiting for some of the older boys to show up with a carryout. It had seemed exciting then, full of possibilities. Girls, drink, perhaps a puff on someone's joint. If you were still there at closing time, there was a good chance of seeing a fight. Or two. If you were lucky, you had heard about a party somewhere and were long gone. Each generation followed in the footsteps of the last, like the ghosts of their fathers. And mothers. Right now The Narrows were all but deserted.

Gunn handed Fin his bag. 'I'll see you in the morning, Mr Macleod.'

'Come on, I'll buy you a drink, George.'

Gunn looked at his watch. 'Just the one, then.'

Fin signed in and dropped his bag in his room. Gunn

had two pints waiting for them on the bar when he came back down. The lounge bar was almost deserted at this hour, but they could hear the thump of music from the public bar below and the loud thrum of voices as thirsty fishermen and construction workers from the reopened yard at Arnish took their reward for a hard day's work. There was a plaque here commemorating the scandal of an underage Prince of Wales ordering a cherry brandy on a stopover during a sailing tour of the Western Isles with his school. The fourteen-year-old Charles had subsequently been smuggled away by car, back to his school at Gordonstoun on the mainland. How times had changed.

'Did you manage to get through all the files?' Gunn said.

'Most of them.' The beer was cold and refreshing, and Fin took a long pull at his pint.

'Find anything interesting?'

'Actually, yes. The witness who said he'd seen Angel Macritchie heading off in the opposite direction from Donna Murray the night she claimed he raped her . . .'

Gunn frowned. 'Eachan Stewart. What about him?'

'You weren't directly involved in the Adams assault case, then?'

'No, I wasn't. That was DS Fraser.'

'Well, I guess we can't expect HOLMES to make all the connections. Do you know Eachan Stewart?'

'Aye, he's an eccentric old dopehead. Got a pottery just outside of Crobost. Been there for years. Selling his pots to the summer tourists ever since I can remember.'

'Since I was a kid,' Fin said. 'It was outside Eachan Stewart's pottery that Chris Adams got beaten up by Macritchie. Stewart was talking to him a minute before the attack, and picked him off the road a minute after it. Yet he claims to have seen nothing. Very convenient for Macritchie to have the same cast-iron witness in his favour at both events. Was there some connection between these two?'

Gunn thought about it. 'It's possible, I suppose, that Macritchie was supplying Stewart with dope. We'd suspected him of dealing for some time, but never caught him at it.'

'I think maybe I'll have a word with our Mr Stewart tomorrow.' Fin took another long draught of his beer. 'George, you said this afternoon that there were other people who bore Macritchie a grudge, other than those he'd bullied as a kid.'

'Aye, according to his brother. But it's just hearsay.'

'Murdo Ruadh?' Gunn nodded. 'What's he been hearsaying?'

'I don't know how much credence to give it, Mr Macleod, but Murdo seems to think there was some kind of feud between his brother and a boy he was at school with. A fella called Calum Macdonald. Apparently he was crippled in an accident years ago and works a loom in a shed behind his house. I've no idea what it was that happened between them.'

Fin laid his pint carefully on the bar. He felt sick just remembering. 'I do.' And Gunn waited for an explanation which never came. Eventually Fin seemed to snap out of his trance. 'Even if he wasn't crippled . . .' Fin remembered the look on the boy's face as he fell, '. . . I doubt if Calum Macdonald would have been capable of inflicting that kind of damage on anyone.'

'Murdo thinks this Calum Macdonald could have put someone else up to it.'

Fin flashed him a look, wondering if that were possible, if Calum would have been capable even of the thought. But why, after all this time? 'I don't think so,' he said, finally.

Again, Gunn waited for an explanation, but it quickly became clear to him that Fin did not intend to elucidate. He glanced at his watch. 'I'd better be going.' He drained his glass and pulled on his jacket. 'By the way, how did you get on with Adams?'

Fin paused for a moment, conjuring in his mind a vivid image of the tall, languid animal rights campaigner. 'It's interesting, I'd kind of figured a man with two broken ribs wouldn't have been up to dealing with Macritchie. But, then, it occurred to me there was a connection I was missing.'

'What's that?'

'Adams is gay.'

Gunn shrugged. 'Well, that hardly comes as a surprise,

Mr Macleod.' Then he was struck by a thought that drew a frown. 'You're not telling me Macritchie was gay?'

'No, but the Edinburgh victim, John Sievewright, was.'

SIX

Fin drifted through the bar in a trance. The music was pulsating here, competing with the babble of voices and drink-induced laughter. He was aware of the lights of a gaming machine flashing somewhere in his peripheral vision, the pips and beeps and whirrs of an electronic age. He ordered a pint and leaned on the bar waiting for the barmaid to pull it. He felt as if he were hermetically sealed inside an invisible bubble. As if he simply did not exist in this place. He had decided on a drink, a fish supper and an early night, but unable to face the solitude of the lounge bar he had come downstairs to the public bar in the hope of being distracted from his own thoughts. Now he was learning again how easy it was to be lonely in a crowd. Whoever these people were, he did not know them, and he was no longer one of them.

His pint arrived, thumped down in a beer puddle on the bar. He dropped his money in the same puddle and caught the look the barmaid threw him. She swept the money into her hand and returned a moment later with a beer towel to wipe the counter dry. Fin gave her a winning smile and she replied with a sullen scowl.

This was depressing. He raised the glass to his lips and stopped before he could take a drink. A group of workmen, some of them still in their overalls, was gathered around a table in the window, empty glasses accumulating in large numbers. The banter was in Gaelic, and there was loud, raucous laughter. It was the voice, really, which had drawn his attention, like a familiar tune caught in snatches that you can't quite place. Then he saw the face, and the shock of it was like a fist in the solar plexus.

Artair had changed. He looked ten years older than Fin. He had put on more weight than even his big frame could carry comfortably. Fine childhood features were lost in a round red face, and hair that once had been thick and black was now a fine grey stubble. Broken veins on his cheeks betrayed an over-fondness for the drink, but his eyes were clear and sharp and the same rich, warm brown.

Artair was throwing back the remains of a whisky when he caught Fin's eye. He lowered the glass slowly from his lips and looked across the bar with something like disbelief.

'Hey, Wheezy,' one of the men at the table said. 'What's wrong? You look like you've just seen a ghost.'

'I just have.' Artair stood up, and the two men looked at one another across the heads of the drinkers for a very long moment. The others at his table turned and looked at Fin. 'Jesus wept and shrank His waistcoat,' Artair muttered. 'Fin-fucking-Macleod.' He squeezed out from the table and pushed through the bodies between them, and to Fin's embarrassment threw his arms around him in a huge hug. Fin spilled half his beer on the floor. Then Artair stood back and gazed into his face. 'Hell, man. Where the fuck have you been all these years?'

'Here and there,' Fin said uncomfortably.

'There, maybe.' Artair's voice carried a tone. 'Certainly not here.' He looked at the remnants of Fin's pint. 'Let me fill that up for you.'

'No, I'm fine, honest.'

Artair caught the barmaid's eye. 'Gimme another dram, Mairead.' He turned back to Fin. 'So what have you been up to?'

Fin could never have imagined how awkward this would be. He shrugged. What do you say? How do you fill in eighteen years in a sentence? 'This and that,' he said.

Artair smiled, but it was forced friendly, and he still couldn't keep the tone out of his voice. 'That must have kept you fully occupied.' He snatched his whisky from the bar. 'I hear you joined the polis.' Fin nodded. 'Hell, you could have done that here, man. We could still have been rock'n'rollin' all these years, you and me. What happened to the big degree?'

'I flunked out of university in second year.'

'Shit. All that time my old man put in, getting you through your exams, and you blew it?'

139

Fin nodded. 'Big time.'

'Well, at least you've got the good grace to admit it.' Artair coughed and found himself short of breath. He took an inhaler from his pocket and sucked on it twice. Phlegm rattled in his throat as he drew oxygen deeply through widening airways. 'That's better. Nothing changes, eh?'

Fin grinned. 'Not much.'

Artair took Fin's elbow and steered him towards a table in the far corner. He stumbled slightly, and Fin realized that there had been a few whiskies before this one. 'We need to talk, you and me.'

'Do we?'

Artair seemed surprised. 'Of course we do. Eighteen fucking years to catch up on.' They sat down opposite each other and Artair looked carefully into his face. 'Jesus, it's not fair. You don't look any bloody older. Look at me. Big, fat, fucking porpoise. Must suit you, being a polisman.'

'Not a lot. I'm trying to get out. Doing a degree in the Open University.'

Artair shook his head. 'What a fucking waste. Me? Well, that was to be expected. But you, Fin. You were a cut above. Made for better things than the polis.'

'So what have *you* been doing all this time?' Fin felt obliged to ask, although in a strange way he didn't really want to know. The truth was, he didn't want to know anything about this man. He wanted to remember Artair the way he was, the way they had been together as boys. This was like making conversation with a stranger.

Air exploded from Artair's lips, an expression of self-contempt. 'Finished my apprenticeship at Lewis Offshore just in time for them to shut the fucking place down. I suppose I was lucky to get back in when it reopened in ninety-one. Then it closed again in May ninety-nine. Went into liquidation. Turfed us all on to the street again. Now it's reopened making wind turbines. Can you imagine? They're trying to persuade the government to plant big fucking windmills all over the island. It'll make us self-sufficient in energy, they say. But it'd kill the tourist industry. I mean, who's going to want to come to the fucking place to look at a lot of bloody windmills? Whole fucking forests of them.' His grin was sour as he upended his glass and poured its liquid gold down his throat. 'But Marsaili says I'm lucky they took me on. Again.' The mention of her name gave Fin a tiny jolt. Artair's smile was mirthless. 'And you know what? I feel lucky, Fin. I really do. You have no idea how fucking lucky I feel. You want another drink?'

Fin shook his head, and Artair pushed back his chair wordlessly and headed off to the bar to get his glass refilled. Fin sat staring fixedly at the table. It was sad beyond words seeing his old childhood friend bitter like this. Life went past you in a flash, like a bus on a rainy night in Ness. You had to be sure it saw you and stopped to let you on, otherwise it was gone without you, and you would be left with a miserable walk home in the wind and the wet. He supposed that, in his own way, he was just like Artair, dogged by a sense of what might have been, of somehow having missed that bus, embittered by his failures and daunted by the weary trudge into an uncertain future. All those childhood dreams lost for ever, like tears in rain. They were not so different, really, he and Artair. In a way, looking at him now was like seeing a reflection of himself, and he did not much like what he saw.

Artair dropped back into his seat and Fin saw that he had got himself a double. They served quarter gills here. 'You know, I was thinking, when I was up there at the bar. Just the mention of her. I saw that look in your face. That's why you never came back all these years, isn't it? Because of bloody Marsaili.'

Fin shook his head. 'No.' But he wasn't certain that was the truth.

Artair leaned across the table, staring discomfitingly into Fin's eyes. 'Not a phone call, not a letter, nothing. You know, at first I was just hurt. And then I was angry. But you can't keep stuff like that going. A flame always burns itself out in the end. That's when I started feeling guilty. That maybe you thought I'd taken her away from you.' He shrugged his shoulders helplessly, not knowing how else to express it. 'You know?'

'It wasn't like that, Artair. It was over between me and Marsaili.'

Artair held the eye contact, like a hand held too long in a handshake, and Fin became self-conscious. 'You know, I never believed that. Not really. I might have got her in the end, but you and Marsaili ... well, that's how it was supposed to be, wasn't it? That's what it should have been.' Finally the eye contact was broken and Artair took a mouthful of whisky. 'You married?'

His hesitation was imperceptible. 'Yeh.'

'Kids?'

A month ago the answer would have been, yes. But he could no longer lay claim to being a father, and it was not a story he was about to tell. Not here, not now. He shook his head.

'We just got the one. Finished school this year. Takes after his old man. Not too bright. I'm trying to get him a job at Arnish.' Artair tipped his head gently, smiling fondly now. 'Good kid, though. He's coming out to the rock with us this week to kill himself a few gugas. His first time.' He chuckled. 'Come to think of it, he's just the same age as you and me when we went out there the first time.' He emptied his glass and banged it on the table. Fin could see the effects of it dulling his eyes. He looked up at Fin, suddenly serious. 'Is that why you never came back? Is it?'

In a way Fin had dreaded the moment. But it was a confrontation with the past he had known he could not avoid from the moment he set foot on the island. 'What?' he said, disingenuously.

'What happened that year on An Sgeir.'

Fin couldn't meet Artair's eye. He shook his head. 'I don't know,' he said, and meant it. 'I really don't know.'

'Well, if it was, it was no fucking reason at all.'

'If I hadn't been so bloody careless . . .' Fin realized he was wringing his hands on the table in front of him, and he laid them palms down to stop himself.

'What happened, happened. It was an accident. Not anybody's fault. Nobody ever blamed you, Fin.'

Fin looked up quickly to catch Artair's eye, and wondered if he meant, nobody except Artair. But he saw no sign of hostility there, no indication that his old friend meant anything other than what he had said.

'Are you ready for that refill now?'

There was an inch of beer left in Fin's glass, but he shook his head. 'I've had enough.'

'Fin,' Artair leaned confidentially across the table, 'there's never enough.' And his face divided itself into a big infectious smile. 'I'm for one for the road.' And he headed off again to the bar.

Fin sat nursing his glass, memories crowding his thoughts. An Sgeir, Marsaili. The sound of voices calling across the bar made him look up. Artair's workmates were leaving, shouting their goodbyes, waving from the door. Artair raised a cursory hand of acknowledgement and made his way unsteadily back to the table. The seat creaked as he dropped himself into it. He banged another double down on the table. There was a smile fluttering around his lips like a butterfly trying to find a place to settle. 'I was thinking . . . You remember that history teacher we had in second year?'

'Shed? William Shed?'

'That's him. Remember he had that gap between his front teeth, and every *s* came out as a whistle?'

Fin remembered very clearly, although he hadn't thought about William Shed in more than twenty years. And the memory made him laugh. 'He used to make us read paragraphs from our history book out loud around the class . . .'

'And everybody made their *s*'s whistle, like his.'

'And he would say, "Stop that whistling!"' Fin said, making his *s*'s whistle just like Shed's had done. And the two of them laughed like schoolboys at the absurdity of it.

'And you remember that time,' Artair said, 'when he tried to separate us, and he grabbed my ear to drag me off to another desk?'

'Aye, and you kept reaching to get your bag, and he thought you were trying to get away from him, and the two of you ended up wrestling in front of the class.'

Artair was almost helpless with laughter remembering it. 'And you, you bastard, you just sat there laughing.'

'Only because he kept whistling, "Stop that, sonny!"'

Which sent Artair off into a fresh paroxysm of laughter, tears streaming down ruddy cheeks, until he couldn't breathe and had to resort to his puffer. The laughter somehow unlocked all the tension in Fin, releasing him from the stress of dealing with a friend who'd become a stranger. They were both just schoolboys again, laughing inanely at childish memories. No matter how much they had grown apart in the intervening years, their memories were something they would always have in common. A bond for life.

The laughter faded as they regained control, and they sat looking at each other, serious again. Adults once more. Until laughter exploded suddenly from Artair's trembling lips and they started all over again. Several heads in the bar turned towards them, wondering what the joke was. But they would never get it.

When, finally, Artair regained his composure he looked at his watch. 'Aw shit, gotta go.'

'To Ness?' Artair nodded. 'How are you getting back?'

'Car's parked at the quay.'

'You're not driving?'

'Well, the fucking thing doesn't drive itself.'

'You're in no state to drive. You'll kill yourself. Or somebody else.'

'Oh,' Artair wagged a finger at him. 'Forgot. You're a polis now. What're you gonna do? Arrest me?'

'Give me your keys and I'll drive you.'

Artair's smile faded. 'Serious?'

'Serious.'

Artair shrugged and fished the car keys from his

pocket and dropped them on the table. 'My lucky day, eh? Get a police escort all the way home.'

The sky was a dusky blue, the sun disappearing behind pewtery clouds bubbling up on the western horizon. From mid-August the nights start shortening very quickly, and yet it was still lighter than it would ever get in London, even at the height of summer. The tide had begun to recede, and the boats at the quayside stood lower in the water now. In an hour or two you would need ladders to get down to them.

Artair's car was a badly resprayed Vauxhall Astra that smelled inside like old trainers which had been left out in the rain. An ancient air freshener in the shape of a pine tree swung ineffectively from the rearview mirror, having long since given up the unequal struggle of trying to sweeten rank air. The upholstery was tashed and torn, and the speedometer was about to reset itself for a second go round. It struck Fin as ironic how their fortunes had reversed themselves. Artair's father had been the teacher, middle-class, good income, driving the shiny new Hillman Avenger, while Fin's folks had struggled between un-employment and the croft and driven a battered old Ford Anglia. Now Artair worked in a Stornoway construction yard and drove a car that would probably fail its next MOT, and Fin was a ranking CID officer who drove a Mitsubishi Shogun. He made a mental note never to tell Artair what kind of vehicle he owned.

He slipped into the driver's seat, snapped on the seatbelt and turned the key in the ignition. The engine coughed, spluttered and died.

'Christ,' Artair said. 'It could do with my puffer. There's a wee trick. Clutch and accelerator to the floor. Soon as she kicks in, feet off the pedals. She'll run sweet as a nut. What are you driving these days, Fin?'

Fin concentrated on the *wee trick*, and as the engine exploded into life, he said casually, 'Ford Escort. Not much call for a motor in the city.' And telling the lie left a bad taste in his mouth.

He pulled out on to Cromwell Street, and there was virtually no traffic as he headed north on to Bayhead. The headlights made little impact in the twilight, and he almost failed to notice the hump in the road at the crossing to the children's playpark. They bumped over it too quickly, and the car juddered.

'Hey, take it easy,' Artair said. 'I've got to get a few more miles out of this old lady yet.' Fin could smell the whisky on his breath as Artair exhaled deeply. 'So, you still haven't told me why you're here.'

'You never asked.'

Artair turned his head and delivered a look that Fin assiduously avoided. 'Well, I'm asking now.'

'I've been attached to the inquiry into the death of Angel Macritchie.' He felt Artair's sudden interest, aware of him turning physically in the passenger seat to look at him.

'No shit! I thought you were based in Glasgow.'

'Edinburgh.'

'So why'd they bring you in? Because you knew him?'

Fin shook his head. 'I've been involved in a case in Edinburgh which was . . . well, very similar. Same MO. That's *modus*—'

'—*operandi*. Yeh, I know. I read fucking detective stories, too, you know.' Artair chortled. 'That's funny, that. You ending up back here to investigate the murder of the guy who beat us all up when we were kids.' He was struck by a sudden thought. 'Did you see him? I mean, were you at the autopsy, or whatever they call it?'

'Post-mortem. Yes.'

'Well . . . ?'

'You don't want to know.'

'Maybe I do. There was never any love lost between me and Angel Macritchie.' He thought about it for a moment before issuing his considered opinion. 'Bastard! Whoever did it deserves a fucking medal.'

As they crossed the moor road towards Barvas, the sky was still light in the west, streaks of dark purple-grey and fading pink. Clouds, like billowing black smoke, were gathering out at sea, The sky in the east was dark. By the time they passed the green-roofed shieling, it was barely visible, and Fin became aware of Artair snoring gently in the seat beside him. The streetlights were on in Barvas, Fin swung the car north and they headed towards Ness.

He had nearly twenty minutes to think, undisturbed

by Artair's drunken ramblings. Nearly twenty minutes to anticipate the moment when he would find himself face to face with Marsaili for the first time since his aunt's funeral. Close to eighteen years. He had no idea what to expect. After all, Artair had changed so much. Would he even recognize the girl with the pigtails and the blue ribbons after all this time?

They drifted through deserted villages, yellow lights in cottage windows the only sign of habitation. A dog came barking out of nowhere and Fin had to swerve to avoid it. The smell of peat smoke seeped in through the car's ventilation system, and Fin remembered those long weekly bus journeys he and Artair had shared to their respective school hostels in Stornoway. He glanced across and saw, in the flash of the streetlights, Artair's jaw slack, hanging open, a tiny dribble of saliva running from one corner of his mouth. Dead to the world. A drink-induced escape. Fin's escape from the island had been physical. Artair had found other means.

By the time they reached Cross, Fin realized that he had no idea where Artair lived. He reached over and shook him by the shoulder. Artair grunted and opened an eye and then wiped his mouth with the back of his hand. He was disorientated for several moments, staring unseeing through the windscreen, before pulling himself upright in the seat. 'That was quick.'

'I don't know where you live.'

Artair turned to look at him, face distorted by disbelief.

'You what? You can't have forgotten where I live! I've lived there all my fucking life!'

'Oh.' It had never occurred to Fin that Artair and Marsaili would have made their home in the Macinnes bungalow.

'Yeh, I know, sad isn't it? Still living in the same house I was fucking born in.' The bitterness was back in his voice. 'Unlike you, I had responsibilities.'

'Your mother?'

'Aye, my mother.'

'She's still alive?'

'Naw, I took her to the taxidermist and had her stuffed so she could sit in the chair by the fire and keep us company at night. Of course she's still alive! Do you think I'd have stayed here all these years if she wasn't?' He gasped his frustration, and the smell of stale alcohol filled the car. 'Jesus. Eighteen years of spoon-feeding the old bitch morning, noon and night. Lifting her to the toilet, changing her fucking nappies – sorry, *incontinence* pads. And d'you know what really fucks me off? She maybe can't do much else, but she can talk nearly as good as you and me, and there's a big part of her brain as sharp as ever it was. I think she just revels in making my life a misery.'

Fin didn't know what to say. He wondered who fed her and changed her when Artair was working. And almost as though he'd read his mind, Artair said, 'Of course, Marsaili's good with her. She likes Marsaili.' And Fin had a sudden picture of what their lives must have been like for all these years, trapped in the same house, chained by family responsibility to the needs of an old woman robbed of most of her physical and mental faculties by a stroke she'd suffered when Artair was still in his teens. Again, as if he were inside Fin's head, Artair said, 'You'd think after all this time she'd at least have had the good fucking grace to die and give us our lives back.'

Fin turned off on the single-track that took them up the hill to the streetlights of Crobost strung out for half a mile along the cliff road. They passed beneath the shadow of the church, and Fin saw lights on at the manse. Around the curve of the hill, the road rose steeply towards the Macinnes bungalow built into the slope of the land as it fell away towards the clifftops. Light spilled out from its windows, falling on to the peat stack, illuminating its carefully constructed herringbone pattern, built just as if Artair's father had done it himself. A couple of hundred yards further on, Fin saw the dark silhouette of his parents' crofthouse smudged against the night sky. No lights, no life there.

He slowed and turned down on to the Macinnes drive and stopped the car in front of the garage doors. A blink of moonlight splashed a pool of broken silver on the ocean beyond. There was a light on in the kitchen, and through the window Fin could see a figure at the sink. He realized, with a start, that it was Marsaili: long fair hair, darker now, drawn back severely from her face and tied in a ponytail at the nape of her neck. She wore no make-up and looked weary somehow, pale, with shadows beneath blue eyes that had lost their lustre. She looked up as she heard the car, and Fin killed the headlights so that all she could see would be a reflection of herself in the window. She looked away quickly, as if disappointed by what she'd seen, and in that moment he glimpsed again the little girl who had so bewitched him from the first moment he set eyes on her.

SEVEN

It was a whole year before I plucked up the courage to defy my parents and go to Marsaili's farm on a Saturday.

Telling lies was something I didn't do very often. But when I did, I made sure they were plausible. I'd heard other kids spinning yarns to their parents, or their teachers, things that even I could tell weren't true. And you could see immediately in the faces of the grown-ups that they knew it, too. It was important that you made the lie believable. And if you didn't get found out, then you had a useful tool to keep in your locker for when the right, or wrong, moment arose. Which was why my parents had no reason to doubt me when I told them I was going down the road to play at Artair's that Saturday morning. After all, what possible reason could a six-year-old have for lying about something like that?

Of course, I told them in English, since we never spoke Gaelic in the house any more. I had found it much easier to learn than I could have imagined. My father had bought a television. Reluctantly. And I spent hours glued to it. At that age, I was like a sponge, soaking up everything around me. It was simple enough, there were just two words now for everything, where before there had only been one.

My father was disappointed that I was going to Artair's. He had spent all summer restoring an old wooden dinghy which had washed up on the beach. There was no name on her. All the paintwork had been bleached off by the salt water. All the same, he had put a notice in the *Stornoway Gazette*, describing her, and offering to restore her to her rightful owner should that person come forward to claim her. He was scrupulously honest, my father. But I think he was quite glad when no one did, and he was able to begin the rebuilding with a clear conscience.

I spent long hours with him that summer rubbing the wooden hull down to the bone, holding the worktable steady while he sawed new lengths of cross-planking from yet more timber which had been washed up on the shore. He got rowlocks very cheaply at an auction in Stornoway and fashioned new oars for her himself. He said he wanted to put a mast in her and make a sail out of some canvas we had found on one of our beachcombing adventures. And he had an old outboard motor in the shed that he wanted to try to make serviceable. Then we could propel her by oars, wind or petrol. But all that could wait. Right now he just wanted to get her into the water on the first good day, and row her around the bay from Port of Ness to Crobost harbour.

He had painted her inside and out to protect her from the salt. Purple, of course, like everything else in our lives. And on either side of the bow, in flamboyant white lettering, he had painted her name, *Eilidh*, which to the non-Gaelic ear sounds like *Ay-lay*. It was the Gaelic for Helen. My mother's name.

It was a perfect day for it, really. A fine September Saturday before the equinoctial gales kicked in. The sun was bright and strong, and still warm, and there was just a light breeze ruffling a tranquil sea. Today, my father said, was the day, and I was sorely torn. But I said I had told Artair I'd be there and didn't want to disappoint him. My father said we couldn't wait until next Saturday, because it was probable that the weather would have broken by then, and that the *Eilidh* would have to stay under her tarpaulin in our garden until the spring. If I didn't want to go with him, he was just going to have to take her out on his own. I think he was hoping that would make me change my mind, and that the two of us would take the *Eilidh* on her maiden voyage together. He couldn't understand why I would pass up the chance just so that I could go and play with Artair. I could play with Artair any time. But I had promised Marsaili, in spite of being strictly forbidden by my mother, that I would come to the farm that Saturday. And though it broke my heart, and probably my father's, I wasn't about to break my promise.

So it was with mixed feelings that I said goodbye and headed off down the road towards Artair's bungalow, the lie weighing heavily on my conscience. I had told Artair I was busy that Saturday, and not to expect me. And as soon as I was out of view of my house, I took off across country on a peat track, running until I was certain I could no longer be seen from the Crobost road. It took me about ten minutes from there, cutting back across the moor, to get on to the Cross–Skigersta road and turn west towards Mealanais. It was a route I knew well by now, having spent the last year walking Marsaili home after school with Artair. But this was the first time I had dared to go on a Saturday. A rendezvous arranged in secret during a snatched conversation in the playground. Artair was to know nothing about it. My stipulation. I wanted Marsaili to myself for once. But as I scrambled down the slope to the track that led to Mealanais farm, I felt the guilt of my deception like the sick feeling you get when you have eaten more than you should.

At the white gate I hesitated with my hand on the latch. There was still time to change my mind. If I ran all the way, I could probably get back before my father had got the boat on to its trailer, and no one would be any the wiser. But a voice came to me on the breeze, bright and cheerful.

'Fi-in . . . Hiya, Fin.'

And I looked up to see Marsaili running up the path from the farmhouse. She must have been watching for me. And now there was no going back. She arrived, breathless, at the gate, her cheeks rosy red, blue eyes shining like flowers in a cornfield. Her hair was plaited in pigtails as it had been that first day at school, blue ribbons to match her eyes.

'Come on.' She opened the gate and grabbed my hand, and I was through the looking glass into Marsaili's world before I even had time to think about it.

Marsaili's mum was a lovely woman who smelled of roses and spoke with a strange, soft, English accent that sounded almost musical to my ears. She had wavy brown hair and chocolate eyes, and was wearing a print apron over a cream woollen jumper and blue jeans. She had on a pair of green wellies, and didn't seem to mind them shedding dried mud all over the flagstone floor in the big farmhouse kitchen. She shooed two lively Border collies out into the yard and told us to sit at the table, and poured us tall glasses of cloudy home-made lemonade. She said she had seen me and my parents often at the church, although I didn't really remember seeing her. She was full of questions. What did my dad do? What did my mum do? What did I want to be when I grew up? I hadn't the faintest idea, but didn't like to admit that. So I said I wanted to be a policeman. She lifted her eyebrows in surprise and said that was a good thing to want to be. I could feel Marsaili's eyes on me the whole time, watching. But I didn't want to turn and look at her, because I knew I would only blush.

'So,' her mum said, 'will you stay for lunch?'

'No,' I said quickly, then realized that perhaps I had

sounded a little rude. 'I told my mum I'd be back by twelve. She said she'd have something ready. And then me and my dad are going out in a boat.' I was learning early that the telling of one lie often led to the telling of another. And then another. I started to panic in case she asked me something else I had to lie about. 'Can I have some more lemonade, please?' I tried to change the subject.

'No,' Marsaili said. 'Later.' And to her mum, 'We're going out to play in the barn.'

'Okay, just watch the mites don't bite.'

'Mites?' I said when we got out into the yard.

'Hay mites. You can't really see them. They live in the hay and bite your legs. Look.' And she pulled up the leg of her jeans to show me the tiny red bites on the leg underneath that she had scratched and made bleed.

I was horrified. 'Why are we going into the barn, then?'

'To play. It's alright, we've both got jeans on. And they probably won't bite you anyway. My dad says they only like English blood.' She took my hand again and led me across the farmyard. Half a dozen hens went skittering off across the cobbles as we headed for the barn. Away to the left stood a stone byre, where they fed and milked the cows. There were three large pink pigs snuffling about in a stye amongst scattered hay and chopped turnip. All they seemed to do was eat and shit and piss. The sweet, pungent smell of pig manure filled the air and made me screw up my face.

'This place stinks.'

'It's a farm.' Marsaili seemed to think it hardly worth commenting on. 'Farms always stink.'

The barn was huge inside, with baled hay piled up almost to the corrugated tin roof. Marsaili started clambering across the lower bales. And when she realized I wasn't following, turned and waved me up after her, irritated that I hadn't taken her lead.

'Come on!'

Reluctantly I followed her up towards the roof, to where a narrow opening took us into a space where the bales created an area the size of a small room, almost totally enclosed except for where the large hay-bale steps led up to it from below.

'This is my space. My dad made it for me. Of course, I'll lose it once we have to start using the hay to feed the animals. What do you think?'

I thought it was great. I had nowhere I could really call my own, except for the tiny attic bedroom my father had made, and you couldn't do anything in there without the whole house hearing. So I spent most of my time outdoors. 'It's brilliant.'

'D'you ever watch cowboys on telly?'

'Sure.' I tried to be nonchalant. I'd seen something called *Alias Smith and Jones*, but hadn't found it very easy to follow.

'Good, I've got a great game of cowboys and Indians for us to play.'

At first I thought she meant it was some kind of board game, until she explained that I was to be the cowboy, captured by a tribe of warriors, and that she would be the Indian princess who had fallen in love with me and was going to help me escape. It didn't sound like any of the games I had ever played with Artair, and I wasn't very keen. But Marsaili had it all worked out, and took charge in a way that left me little room for dissent.

'You sit here.' She led me into the corner and made me squat down with my back against the bales. She turned away for a moment to retrieve something from a little hidey-hole in the hay, before turning back with a length of rope and a large red handkerchief in her hands. 'And I'll tie you up.'

I didn't like the sound of that at all and started to get to my feet. 'I don't think that's a good idea.'

But she pushed me back down with an unexpected firmness. 'Of course it is. You have to be tied up so that I can come and untie you. And you can't tie yourself up, can you?'

'I don't suppose so.' I conceded the point with great reluctance.

Marsaili proceeded to tie my hands behind my back, and then looped the rope around to tie my ankles together, my knees folded up under my chin. I felt trussed and helpless as Marsaili stood back to survey her handiwork and smile her satisfaction. I was beginning to have serious doubts about the wisdom of having come to the farm at all. Whatever I had imagined we might get up to, it was not this. But worse was to come. Marsaili leaned over and began tying the red handkerchief around my head like a blindfold.

'Hey, what are you doing?' I pulled my head away to try to stop her.

'Hold still, silly. You have to be blindfolded, too. The Indians always blindfold their prisoners. And, anyway, if you were to see me coming, you might give the game away.'

By now I was beginning to doubt her sanity and panic was setting in. 'Give the game away to who?' I looked around the hay-bale room. 'There's no one here!'

'Of course there is. But they're all sleeping now. That's the only reason I can sneak up in the dark and set you free. Now, hold still while I tie the blindfold.'

I was hardly in a position to resist, since I had already allowed her to tie me up, so I sighed loudly and submitted with indignant resignation. She leaned over again, placing the folded handkerchief over my eyes and tying it behind my head. The world went black, except for where the light leaked in around the edges of the hanky, and then it was red.

'Okay, don't make a sound,' Marsaili whispered, and I heard the rustling of the hay as she moved away. Then silence. A very long silence. A silence so long that I began to be scared that she had run off and left me there as a joke, all tied up and blindfolded. At least she hadn't gagged me as well.

'What's going on?'

And from somewhere much closer than I had expected came an answering 'Shhhhh! They'll hear you.' Marsaili's voice was not even a whisper. More like a breath.

'Who will?'

'The Indians.'

I sighed and waited. And waited. My legs were beginning to seize up now, and I couldn't straighten them out. I wriggled to try to shift my position, and rustled the hay.

'Shhhhh!' Marsaili's voice came again.

Now I heard her moving, circling around me in her secret straw room. And then more silence, before suddenly I could feel her breath hot on my face. I had not realized she was so close. I almost jumped. I could smell the sweetness of the lemonade still on it. And then soft, wet lips pressed themselves against mine, and I could taste it, too. But I was so startled, I pulled my head back sharply and banged it against the bale at my back. I heard Marsaili giggling. 'Stop it!' I shouted. 'Untie me now!' But she just kept giggling. 'Marsaili, I mean it. Untie me. Untie me!' I was close to tears.

A voice came from somewhere down below. 'Hello-o . . . Everything alright up there?' It was Marsaili's mum.

Marsaili's voice thundered in my ear as she bellowed back, 'Everything's fine, Mum. We're just playing.' And she started untying me quickly. As soon as my hands were free I pulled off the blindfold and scrambled to my feet, trying to recover as much of my dignity as I could.

'I think you'd better come down for a minute,' Marsaili's mum called.

'Okay,' Marsaili shouted back. She bent down to untie my feet. 'Just coming.'

I wiped my mouth with the back of my hand and glared at her. But she just smiled sweetly back at me. 'That was fun, wasn't it? Pity the Indians woke up.' And she went leaping off down the bales to where her mother was waiting for us below. I dusted the hay out of my hair and followed.

I knew immediately from the look on Marsaili's mum's face that something was wrong. She seemed a little flushed. 'I think, perhaps, I've rather given the game away,' she said, looking at me with something like an apology in her chocolate-brown eyes.

Marsaili frowned. 'What do you mean?'

But her mum kept her eyes on me as she spoke. 'I'm afraid I phoned your folks to ask if you could stay for lunch, and to tell them I'd run you back home afterwards.' My heart sank, and I felt Marsaili turn a look of consternation in my direction. Her mum said, 'You didn't tell us that your folks had forbidden you to come to the farm on your own, Fin.' Aw, hell, I thought. The ba's in the slates! 'Your father's on his way over now to pick you up.'

The problem with telling plausible lies, is that when you do get caught, after that nobody believes you, even when you're telling the truth. My mother sat me down and told me the story about the boy who cried wolf. It was the first time I had heard it. And she had a talent for embellishment, my mother. She could have been a writer. I didn't really know what *woods* were then, because there weren't any trees where we lived. But she made them sound dark and scary, with wolves lurking behind every tree. I didn't know what wolves were either. But I knew Artair's neighbour's Alsatian dog, Seoras. It was a huge beast. Bigger than me. And my mother made me imagine what would happen if Seoras went wild and attacked me. That's what wolves are like, she told me. I had a vivid imagination, so I could picture the boy being told to be careful of the wolves in the woods and then shouting 'Wolf! Wolf!' as a joke and bringing everyone running. I could even imagine him doing it a second time, because of the reaction he'd got the first time around. I couldn't really believe he'd do it a third time, but I figured that, if he did, those who had come running the previous times would think he was just playing games again. And of course, my mother said, that was when there really were wolves. And they ate him.

My father was more disappointed than angry. Disappointed that I should have chosen to sneak off to see some girl on a farm, rather than take the boat we had worked on together all summer out on her maiden voyage. But he didn't take his belt to me because of his disappointment. It was for the lie. And the sting of leather on the backs of my thighs, and my mother's story

165

about the wolves, led me to decide there and then never to lie again.

Except, of course, by omission.

My father took the *Eilidh* out on his own that day, while I was sent to my room to cry myself dry and think about what it was I'd done. And I was grounded every Saturday for a month. I could play in the house, or the garden, but was not allowed to venture beyond. Artair was permitted to come to our house, but I couldn't go to his. And I had no pocket money for four whole weeks. At first Artair thought it was hilarious, and gloated over my misfortune – particularly because it involved Marsaili. But he soon got fed up. If he wanted to play with me, then he was restricted to my house and garden just the same as I was. And eventually he turned his annoyance on me and lectured me about being more careful next time. I told him there wasn't going to be a next time.

I stopped walking Marsaili home from school. Artair and I went with her only as far as the Mealanais road end, and then we left her to go the rest of the way on her own, and we took the single-track up the hill to Crobost. I was wary of Marsaili, too, since the incident with the rope and the blindfold, so usually I avoided her in the playground at playtimes and lunch breaks. I lived in terror that someone would find out about the kiss in the straw room. I could just imagine what fun the other boys would have at my expense.

*

It was some time after Christmas that I came down with the flu. The first time ever. And I thought I was going to die. I think, perhaps, my mother did, too. Because all I can really remember about that week was that every time I opened my eyes she was there, a cool, damp facecloth in her hand to lay across my forehead, whispering words of love and encouragement. Every muscle in my body was aching, and I seemed to flit between burning fevers, with temperatures running at a hundred and six, and spells of uncontrollable shivering. My seventh birthday came and went that week, and I barely noticed. At first I had nausea and vomiting and couldn't eat. It was nearly a week before my mother was able to persuade me to take some arrowroot mixed with milk and a little sugar. I liked the taste of it, and every time I have tasted it since, I think of my mother and her ever-present comfort during those dreadful days and nights of my first flu.

In fact it was, I think, the first time I had ever been ill. And it took it out of me. I lost weight and felt weak, and it was a full fortnight before I was fit enough to return to school. It was raining the day I went back, and my mother was concerned that I would get chilled and wanted to take me in the car. But I insisted on walking, and met Artair at the top of the path to his bungalow. He hadn't been allowed near while I was ill, and he peered at me now, warily.

'Are you sure you're okay?'

'Sure I'm sure.'

'You're not infectious or anything?'

'Of course not. Why?'

'Because you look bloody terrible.'

'Thank you. That makes me feel a whole lot better.'

It was early February. The rain was really no more than a smirr, so light you could hardly see it. But it made us very wet, blowing in on the edge of an icy north wind. It got in around my neck and my collar so that the fabric rubbed my skin, my cheeks were burning and my knees were red raw. I loved it. For the first time in two whole weeks I felt alive again.

'So, what's been happening while I was off?'

Artair waved a hand vaguely in the air. 'Not much. You haven't missed anything, if that's what you're worried about. Oh, except the times tables.'

'What's that?' It sounded very exotic. I imagined tables laden with clocks.

'Multiplication.'

I had no idea what that was either. But I didn't want to appear stupid, so all I said was, 'Oh.'

We were almost at the school before he told me. Very casually, as if it were nothing. 'I've joined the country dancing group.'

'The what?'

'Country dancing. You know ...' And he raised his arms above his head and made a funny little shuffle with his feet. 'The pas de bas.'

I was beginning to think he'd lost his marbles in my absence. 'Paddy Bah?'

'It's a dance step, stupid.'

I gawped at him in amazement. 'Dancing? You? Artair, dancing's for girls!' I couldn't imagine what had come over him.

He shrugged, making lighter of it than I could have imagined possible. 'Mrs Mackay picked me. I didn't have any choice.'

And I thought for the first time that, perhaps, I had been lucky to be off with the flu. Otherwise she might have picked me. I felt truly sorry for Artair. Until, that is, I discovered the truth.

We were walking up the road at three that afternoon with Marsaili. I hadn't been at all sure that she was pleased to see me back. She'd said a cool hello when I took my seat beside her in class, and then proceeded to ignore me for the rest of the day. At least, that's how it appeared to me. Every time I looked at her, or tried to catch her eye, she seemed to be studiously avoiding mine. In the playground at break times she stuck close to the other girls, skipping and chanting rhymes and playing peever. Now, as we headed towards the main road, other groups of primary kids strung out before us and behind us, she said to Artair, 'Did you get the date of the Stornoway trip from Mrs Mackay?'

He nodded. 'I've got a note for my parents to sign.'

'Me, too.'

'What Stornoway trip?' I was feeling distinctly left out. It's amazing how much you can miss in two short weeks.

'It's a dancing competition,' Marsaili said. 'Schools from all over the island are competing at the town hall.'

'Dancing?' For a moment I was confused, and then like the haar lifting along the northern coast on a warm summer's morning, all became clear. Marsaili was in the country dancing group. And that's why Artair had joined, even at the risk of ridicule from his male peers. I gave him a look that would have turned milk. 'Didn't have any choice, eh?'

He just shrugged. I caught Marsaili looking at me, and I could tell she was pleased by my reaction. I was jealous, and she knew it. She rubbed salt in the wound. 'You can sit beside me on the minibus if you like, Artair.'

Artair was a little self-conscious by now and so played it cool. 'Maybe. We'll see.'

We crossed the main road to the Mealanais road end, and I wondered if he had been walking her all the way home in my absence. But we stopped, and it was clear that she did not expect us to be going with her. 'See you on Saturday, then,' she told Artair.

'Yeh, okay.' He shoved his hands deep in his pockets as he and I turned away towards the Crobost road. As I glanced back, Marsaili was skipping off along the Mealanais road with a lightness in her step. Artair was walking much faster than usual, and I almost had to run to keep up with him.

'Saturday? Is that when the dancing competition is?'

He shook his head. 'No, that's on a schoolday.'

'So what's happening on Saturday?'

Artair kept his eyes fixed on a point somewhere on the road up ahead. 'I'm going to play at the farm.'

I couldn't believe it. I wouldn't have been able to identify them accurately then, but I was suffering from all the classic symptoms of jealousy. Anger, hurt, confusion, melancholy. 'Your parents won't let you!' I was grasping at straws.

'Yes, they will. My mum and dad and Marsaili's mum and dad are friendly from the church. My mum even gave me a lift over to Mealanais last Saturday.'

I think my mouth must have been hanging open. Had it been June, I'd have caught flies. 'You've been before?' I was almost incredulous.

'A couple of times.' He flicked me a look, a smug little smile on his face. 'We played cowboys and Indians in the barn.'

I had nightmarish images of Marsaili tying Artair up with the same length of rope, blindfolding him with the same red hanky. I asked, my mouth so dry I could hardly speak, 'Did she kiss you?'

Artair's head snapped around to look at me, an expression of pure disgust and incomprehension written across his face. 'Kiss me?' I could hear the horror in his voice. 'Why on earth would she want to do that?'

Which was, if nothing else, a crumb of comfort in the depths of my misery.

The wind was blowing in from the north-east on Saturday. A bitter February gale with sleet on its leading edge. I stood by our gate in my yellow oilskins and sou'wester and my black wellies watching for the Avenger going past. My mother called to me several times, saying I'd catch my death out there and that I should come and play in the house. But I was determined to wait. I think, perhaps, there was a part of me hoping that Marsaili and Artair had just been playing some kind of cruel joke. And I'd have stood out there happily all morning if only that car had never passed. But it did, just after nine-thirty. Artair's mum driving, and Artair's face pressed against the window in the back, blurred by the condensation, but clearly grinning. His hand gave a little triumphal wave, like royalty in training. I glowered at him in the wet, the sleet stinging my face red and disguising my tears. But I could feel the hot tracks they made down my cheeks.

On Monday morning I surprised Mrs Mackay by suggesting to her that since I was now almost self-sufficient in English I no longer needed a translator, and that she could rearrange our seating alphabetically as she had originally intended. The idea must have appealed to Mrs Mackay's sense of orderliness, because she readily agreed. I was shifted from the first row to the second and was now several desks removed from Marsaili. Her dismay was undisguised. She turned and lowered her head slightly, raising doe eyes to give me her injured animal look. I steadfastly ignored her. If her plan had been to make me jealous, then it had succeeded. But it had also backfired, because from now on I was going to have nothing to do with her. I caught Artair smirking his satisfaction from two desks away. From now on I wasn't going to have anything to do with him either.

I gave them both a wide berth at playtime, and when the bell rang for the end of school I was the first out of the door, and halfway up the road before Marsaili and Artair had even left the playground. At the main road I looked back and saw Marsaili hurrying to try to catch me up, with Artair trailing a little breathlessly behind her. But I turned determinedly away, and headed off up the Crobost road as fast as I could without actually running.

The trouble with jealous revenge is that while you might inflict hurt on the other party, it does nothing to lessen the effect of the hurt you are feeling yourself. So everyone ends up unhappy. And, of course, once you have adopted a certain attitude, it is hard to change it without losing face. I had never been as unhappy as I was through the next two days, and never more determined to stay that way.

On the Thursday at midday the country dancing group left for Stornoway in the school minibus. I watched from a window in the dining hall, rubbing a little clear patch in the misted glass so that I could see them standing by

173

the gate waiting for the minibus to come around from the garage. Four girls and two boys, Artair and Calum. Artair was talking animatedly to Marsaili, trying hard to hold her attention. But she was clearly distracted, peering towards the school, hoping to catch a glimpse of me watching. I felt a certain masochistic pleasure. I saw Artair fumble for his puffer and take two long pulls at it, a sure sign that he was under pressure. He was losing her focus.

But that was no consolation to me during what seemed like an interminable afternoon. The five of us left in class were set the task of copying out words from the blackboard. Capital letters then small letters. I kept gazing from the window at the low cloud blowing in off the Atlantic, tearing itself ragged along the coastline and throwing out squally little showers in between very occasional blinks of sunlight. And Mrs Mackay gave me a right rollicking for not paying attention. That was my problem, she told me, I had no concentration. I was a dreamer. Plenty of ability, but no will to work. In truth, I had no will to do much of anything. I was like some sad, lovesick little puppy locked away on its own in a cupboard. It is strange, looking back, to remember how early I was afflicted by such emotions.

By the time the bell went I was almost suffocating. I couldn't wait to get out into the blast of icy wind and fill my lungs with fresh salt air. I scuffed and dragged my feet all the way up the road and went into Crobost Stores to buy some tablet with the last of my pocket money. I felt the need of something sweet to comfort me. There is a gate there, just opposite the store, that takes you on to a tractor track leading up the hill to peat trenches which have been dug there by generations of Crobosters. I climbed over the gate and, with hands sunk deep in my pockets, trudged up the boggy track to the peat-cuttings. From there I had a view of the school in the distance, and I could look down on both the Mealanais and Crobost single-tracks. You could see the main road all the way up to Swainbost and beyond, and I would be able to see the minibus returning from Stornoway. I had been up here the previous May, cutting peats with my father and mother; hard, back-breaking work slicing down into the soft peat with a special spade, and then stacking the turfs in groups of five along the top of the trench to dry in the warm spring winds. You had to go back later and turn them, and when they were properly dried, you went with a tractor and trailer and took them back to the croft to build your great, humpbacked peat stack, herringboned for drainage. Once properly dried, the peats became impervious to the rain, and would fuel your fire throughout the long winter. The cutting was the worst bit, though, especially if the wind dropped. Because then the midges would get you. Tiny biting flies. The Scottish curse. The single midge is so small you can hardly see it, but they gather together in clusters, great black clouds of them, getting in your hair and your clothes and feeding on your flesh. If you were to be locked in a room filled with midges you would go insane before the day was out. And sometimes that's just how it was at the peat-cutting.

There were no midges now, though, in the depths of a Hebridean winter. Just wind blowing through dead grass, and the sky spitting its anger. The light was going fast. I saw the headlights of the minibus coming over the rise from Cross before I realized that's what it was. Where the road turned down to the school, it stopped, orange emergency lights flashing, to let off the kids from Crobost. It was just Marsaili, Artair and Calum. They stood talking for a moment after the minibus drove off, then Artair and Calum hurried off in the direction of the Crobost road, and Marsaili started up the farm road towards Mealanais. I sat on for a minute, sucking on the crumbling, sugary sweetness of my tablet, watching Marsaili on the single-track below. She looked tiny from here, lonely somehow in a way that it's hard to explain. Something in her gait, something leaden in her steps that suggested unhappiness. I suddenly felt unaccountably sorry for her and wanted to run down the hill and give her a big hug, and tell her I was sorry. Sorry for being jealous, sorry for being hurtful. And yet something held me back. That reluctance to give expression to my feelings which has dogged me most of my life.

She was almost out of sight, lost in the winter dusk, when for once something overcame my natural reticence and propelled me down the hill after her, arms windmilling for balance as I stumbled clumsily in my wellies across the squelching moor. I snagged my trousers on the barbed wire as I fell over the fence, sending sheep running off in a panic. I clopped along the road after her at a half-run. By the time I caught her up, I was breathing hard, but she didn't turn her head, and I wondered if she knew I had been on the hill watching her the whole time. I fell in beside her and we walked some way without a word. When, finally, I had got my breath back, I said, 'So, how did it go?'

'The dancing?'

'Yeh.'

'It was a disaster. Artair panicked when he saw all the people, and he had to keep puffing on his inhaler and couldn't go on stage. We had to go on without him. But it was hopeless, because we'd practised with six and it just didn't work with five. I'm never going to do it again!'

I couldn't help feeling a sense of satisfaction that verged on elation. But I kept my tone sombre. 'That's a shame.'

She flicked me a quick look, perhaps suspecting sarcasm. But I looked suitably saddened by her news. 'It's not really. I didn't like it, anyway. Dancing's for daft girls and soft boys. I only joined because my mum said I should.'

We lapsed into silence again. I could see the lights of Mealanais farm ahead of us in the hollow. It would be pitch-black on the road home, but my mother always made me carry a small torch in my schoolbag because there was so little daylight in winter that you never knew when you would need it. We stopped at the white gate and stood for a moment.

Eventually she said, 'Why have you stopped walking me up the road after school?'

I said, 'I thought you preferred Artair's company.'

She looked at me, blue eyes piercing the darkness, and I felt a sort of weakness in my legs. 'Artair's a pain in the neck. He follows me around everywhere. He even joined the dance class just because I was in it.' I didn't know what to say. Then she added, 'He's just a daft boy. It's you I like, really, Fin.' And she gave me a quick, soft kiss on the cheek, before turning and running down the track to the farmhouse.

I stood for a long time in the dark, feeling where her lips had touched my cheek. I could feel their softness and their warmth for a long time after she had gone, before putting my fingers up to touch my face and dispel the magic. I turned, then, and started running in the direction of the Cross–Skigersta road, happiness and pride swelling my chest with every breath. I was going to be in such trouble when I got home. But I couldn't have cared less.

EIGHT

Marsaili turned from the sink as Artair came in the kitchen door. There was a simmering anger in her eyes, words of rebuke on her lips, before she saw that he had company. Fin had not come yet into the light off the top step, and so she had no idea who it was, just a shadow in Artair's wake.

'Sorry I'm late. Ran into an old friend in town. Gave me a lift back. Thought you might want to say hello.'

The shock on Marsaili's face was clear for both men to see as Fin stepped into the harsh light of the kitchen. And beyond the shock was an immediate self-consciousness. She ran dishwater-red hands quickly down her apron, and one of them moved involuntarily to brush stray hairs away from her face. There was about her the sense of a young woman, not yet middle-aged, who had simply stopped caring about herself. Stopped caring, too, about what others might think. Until now.

'Hello, Marsaili.' Fin's voice sounded very small.

'Hello, Fin.' Just hearing her speak the name she had

given him all those years before filled him with sadness. At something precious lost and gone for ever. Marsaili's self-consciousness was giving way to embarrassment. She leaned back against the sink and folded her arms across her chest, defensive. 'What brings you to the island?' There was none of Artair's tone in a question that seemed prosaic in the circumstances.

Artair answered for him. 'He's investigating Angel Macritchie's murder.'

Marsaili nodded a perfunctory acknowledgement, but showed no interest. 'Are you here for long?'

'Probably not. A day or two, maybe.'

'Figure you'll catch the killer that fast, eh?' Artair said.

Fin shook his head. 'As soon as they rule out a connection to the Edinburgh murder, they'll probably send me back.'

'And you don't think there is one?'

'Doesn't look like it.'

Marsaili appeared to be listening, but still without curiosity. She kept her eyes on Fin. 'You haven't changed.'

'Neither have you.'

She laughed then, genuine mirth in her eyes. 'Same old bad liar.' She paused. Fin was still standing in the open doorway and did not look as if he intended to stay. 'Have you eaten?'

'I'll get a fish supper in Stornoway.'

'Will you fuck,' Artair grunted. 'The chippys'll all be shut by the time you get back.'

'I've got quiche in the oven,' Marsaili said. 'It'll only take fifteen minutes to heat up. I never know when Artair'll be home.'

'Aye, that's right.' Artair shut the door behind Fin. 'Good old unreliable Artair. Will he be early, will he be late? Will he be drunk, will he be sober? Keeps life interesting, that right, Marsaili?'

'It would be irredeemably dull otherwise.' Marsaili's tone was flat. Fin searched for some hint of irony but found none. 'I'll put the potatoes on.' She turned away to the cooker.

'Come and have a drink,' Artair said, and he led Fin through to a small living room made smaller by a huge three-piece suite and a thirty-two-inch TV set. It was switched on, with the sound turned down. Some awful game show. Poor reception, and the colour up too high, made it almost unwatchable. The curtains were drawn, and a peat fire in the hearth made the room cosy and warm. 'Sit down.' Artair opened up a cupboard in the sideboard to reveal a collection of bottles. 'What'll you have?'

'I won't, thanks.' Fin sat down and tried to see through to the kitchen.

'Come on, you need something to whet the appetite.'

Fin sighed. There was going to be no escaping this. 'A very small one, then.'

Artair poured two large whiskies and handed him one. '*Slàinte*.' He raised his glass in a Gaelic toast.

'*Slàinte mhath*.' Fin took a sip. Artair gulped down half his glass, and looked up as the door opened behind Fin.

Fin turned to see a teenage boy of sixteen or seventeen standing in the hall doorway. He wasn't particularly tall, five ten or eleven, and slight-built. He had straw-fair hair, shaved short at the sides but longer on top, gelled into spikes. A single loop of earring hung from his right ear and he wore a hooded sweatshirt over baggy blue jeans that gathered around chunky white trainers. He had his mother's cornflower-blue eyes. A good-looking boy.

'Say hello to your uncle Fin,' Artair said. And Fin stood up to shake the boy's hand. A good firm handshake, and direct contact from eyes that were too much like his mother's for comfort.

'Hey,' he said.

'We called him Fionnlagh.' It was Marsaili's voice, and Fin looked round to see her standing in the kitchen doorway watching, an odd expression on her face, colour in her cheeks where there had been none before.

It was a shock for Fin to hear his own name. He looked at the boy again and wondered if they had named him after him. But why would they? It was a common enough name on the island. 'I'm pleased to meet you, Fionnlagh,' Fin said.

'Are you going to eat with us?' Artair asked him.

'He's already eaten,' Marsaili said.

'Well, he can have a drink with us, then.'

'I'm still trying to sort out the problem with the computer,' Fionnlagh said. 'I think maybe the motherboard's blown.'

'Motherboard, you'll note,' Artair said to Fin. 'Never the father board. It's always the mothers that cause the trouble.' He turned to his son. 'So what does that mean?'

'Means it's buggered.'

'Well, can you not fix it?'

Fionnlagh shook his head. 'I'd need to replace it. And that would probably cost as much a buying a new computer.'

'Well, we haven't got the money to go buying another fucking computer,' Artair snapped. 'When you get a job you can save up for one yourself.'

Fin said to him, 'What kind of computer is it?'

'It's an iMac. G3. One of the old jellybeans.'

'And what makes you think it's the motherboard?'

Fionnlagh exhaled in frustration. 'The screen's gone blue and dark so you can hardly read it, and the image is all sort of squeezed up, like it's been compressed.'

'What system are you on?'

'Oh, I'm miles behind. I just upgraded from nine to Jaguar. Need a better computer to run Snow Leopard.'

Artair snorted. 'Jesus Christ, boy! Can you not speak a fucking language we can understand?'

'There's no need to talk like that, Artair,' Marsaili said quietly. Fin stole a glance at her across the room and saw her discomfort.

'You any idea what he's talking about?' Artair said to Fin. 'It's all double Dutch to me.'

'It's a degree in computer studies I'm doing at the Open University,' Fin said.

'Well, la-di-fucking-da. The boy who couldn't speak English can speak Computer now.'

Fin said to Fionnlagh. 'Is that when the problem started, when you installed the new system?'

The boy nodded. 'Yeh, the day after I did the upgrade. Cost a fortune for the memory card, too.'

'I should know, I bloody paid for it,' Artair growled and emptied his glass. He stooped to refill it.

'Where is the computer? In your room?' Fin said.

'Yeh.'

'Can I have a look at it?'

'Sure.'

Fin laid his glass on a coffee table and followed Fionnlagh out into the hall. A staircase led up to an attic room. 'Place has changed since your day,' Artair said, coming out after them. 'I put in a bedroom for the kid up in the attic. Me and Marsaili are in my parents' old room, and my mother's in mine. We keep my dad's study as a guest room.'

'Not that we ever have any guests,' Fionnlagh muttered as he reached the top of the stairs.

'What was that?' his father called after him.

'Just telling Fin to watch that loose carpet on the top stair.' Fionnlagh briefly caught Fin's eye, and in that moment it was as if they had become complicit in a subterfuge that only they would ever know about. Fin winked and got a tiny smile in return.

Fionnlagh's room ran from one side of the attic to the

other at the north end of the house. There was a dormer window at each side cut into the slope of the ceiling. The east dormer had an unrestricted view out across the Minch. The computer was on a table set against the north gable. It sat in a pool of light from an Anglepoise lamp that seemed to intensify the darkness in the rest of the room. Fin was only vaguely aware of posters stuck to the walls. Football players and pop stars. Eminem was whining at them from a stereo system Fin couldn't see.

'Turn that shit off.' Artair had come in behind them and was leaning on the door jamb, his drink still in his hand. 'Can't stand that rap. That's rap with a silent C.' He snorted at his own joke. 'Know what I mean?'

'I like Eminem,' Fin said. 'It's all in the lyrics. He's kind of like the Bob Dylan of his generation.'

'Jesus,' Artair exploded. 'I can see you two are going to get on just great.'

'I store most of my tracks in the computer,' Fionnlagh said. 'But since the screen went ...' He shrugged hopelessly.

'Are you online?' Fin asked.

'Yeh, we just switched to broadband a couple of months ago.'

'Can I take a look?'

'Go ahead.'

Fin sat in front of the iMac and moved the mouse, waking the computer from its sleep mode. The screen came up dark blue and distorted, just as Fionnlagh had described. The desktop was barely visible, with its Finder window and dock bar along the bottom. 'When you loaded in the new system, did the screen ever come up normal?'

'Yeh, it was working great that first night. It was when I opened up the next day it was like this.'

Fin nodded. 'Bet you didn't upgrade your firmware.'

Fionnlagh frowned. 'Firmware? What's that?'

'It's kind of like the stuff in the computer's brain that allows the hardware and the software to talk to one another. Apple really screwed up by not telling people that a system upgrade on a G3 required a firmware upgrade as well.' He saw the consternation on Fionnlagh's face and grinned. 'Don't worry, you've got about half the Mac-owning world for company. People were throwing away their computers when all they needed to do was download a simple firmware upgrade. There was a lot of anger about it out there.'

'And we can do that?' Fionnlagh asked, as if it were too good to be true. 'We can download a firmware upgrade?'

'Yep.' Fin opened up a squashed web browser and tapped in a URL address. A moment later he was on the Apple website clicking on the firmware download for a G3. It took less than two minutes to download, and when the icon appeared on Fionnlagh's screen, Fin double-clicked on it to install. 'Takes about thirty seconds. Then, hopefully, after we restart it's going to be working just fine.' When the installation was complete, he dropped down the Apple menu and selected restart. The screen went black, the iMac delivered its welcome chorus, and then began reloading its operating system. Half a minute later the desktop screen appeared, bright and sharp and undistorted. '*Et voilà.*' Fin sat back, pleased with himself.

'Aw, man, that's brilliant!' Fionnlagh could hardly contain his joy. 'That's just brilliant.' His delight was shining in his eyes.

Fin stood up to vacate his seat. 'It's all yours. Enjoy. It's a neat system. Any problems, just let me know.'

'Thanks, Fin.' Fionnlagh dropped himself into his chair and within moments had the arrow darting about the screen, opening up windows, pulling down menus, eager to explore all the possibilities he thought had been lost.

Fin turned to find Artair watching thoughtfully, still leaning on the door jamb. He had not said a word since the Eminem put-down. 'Pretty fucking smart,' he said quietly. 'I could never have done that for him in a million years.'

Fin shifted uncomfortably. 'It's amazing what you pick up on the Open University.' He cleared his throat self-consciously. 'I think I left my drink downstairs.'

But Artair didn't move, transferring his gaze, instead, to the quarter-inch of amber liquid in the bottom of his glass. 'You always were smarter than me, weren't you, Fin? My father knew that. Which is why he spent more time on you than he ever did on me.'

'We both spent a lot of time in that room down there,'

Fin said. 'I owe your dad a lot. I can't believe how generous he was, giving up all his spare time like that.'

Artair cocked his head and gave Fin a long, hard look. Searching for what? Fin felt discomfited by his gaze. 'Well, at least it worked for you,' Artair said finally. 'Got you off the island and away to university. Didn't get me any further than a dead-end job at Lewis Offshore.'

The silence between them was broken only by the clacking of Fionnlagh's keyboard. The boy seemed barely aware of them, lost in his own ether world of computer and internet. Marsaili called from downstairs that their quiche was ready, and the awkwardness of the moment passed. Artair snapped out of his dwam.

'Come on, we'll get your glass topped up, and some food in your belly.'

At the foot of the stairs, a voice called faintly from the far end of the hall. 'Artair . . . Artair is that you?' The feeble, tremulous voice of an old woman.

Artair closed his eyes, taking a deep breath, and Fin saw the muscles in his jaw working. Then he opened his eyes. 'Just coming, *mamaidh*.' And, under his breath, 'Shit! She always knows when I'm fucking home.' He pushed brusquely past Fin and headed towards the room at the end of the hall. Fin went into the living room to retrieve his glass, and then into the kitchen. Marsaili was sitting at a gateleg table she had opened up from the wall. There were three plates of quiche and potato, and three chairs pulled up around them.

'Has he gone to see her?'

Fin nodded and saw that there was just a trace of red on her lips now, and colour around her eyes. She had released her hair from its clasp and taken a brush through it. It had changed her. Not enough for comment, but enough to be noticed. She indicated the chair opposite and he sat down. 'So how have you been?'

There was a weariness in her smile. 'As you see.' She began eating. 'Don't bother waiting for Artair. He could be long enough.' She watched him take a mouthful of quiche. 'And you?'

Fin shrugged. 'Things could have been worse.'

She shook her head sadly. 'And we were going to change the world.'

'The world's like the weather, Marsaili. You can't change it. And you can't shape it. But it'll shape you.'

'Ah, yes, always the philosopher.' And unexpectedly she reached across the table and ran the tips of her fingers lightly down his cheek. 'You're still very beautiful.'

In spite of himself, Fin blushed. He half-laughed to cover his embarrassment. 'Isn't that what I'm supposed to say to you?'

'But you never could lie convincingly. And, anyway, you were always the beautiful one. I remember seeing you that first day at school and thinking I'd never seen anyone so beautiful. Why do you think I wanted to sit beside you in class? You've no idea how jealous the other girls were.'

And he hadn't. He had only ever had eyes for Marsaili.

'If only I'd known then what a shit you were, I could have saved us all a lot of heartache.' She popped another piece of quiche in her mouth and grinned, the same upward curl of her mouth at the corners that he remembered so well. The deep dimples in either cheek. The same mischief in her eyes.

'I was right,' Fin said. 'You *haven't* changed.'

'Oh, but I have. In more ways than you could ever know. Than you would ever want to know.' She seemed lost in contemplation of her quiche. 'I've thought about you often over the years. How you were. How we were, as kids.'

'Me, too.' Fin inclined his head, a tiny smile on his lips. 'I've still got that note you sent me.' She frowned, not remembering what note. 'Before the final year primary dance. You signed it, *The Girl from the Farm.*'

'Oh my God.' Her hand shot to her mouth as the memory came back from someplace she had buried it long ago to save herself the embarrassment of remembering. 'You've still got that?'

'It's a bit grubby, and torn around the folds. But, yes, I've still got it.'

'What have you still got?' Artair came into the kitchen and dropped himself heavily into his chair. The mood between Fin and Marsaili was broken immediately. Artair shoved a mouthful of food in his face and looked at Fin. 'Well?'

Fin summoned the strength for another lie. 'An old

school photograph from primary seven.' He glanced up to find Marsaili avoiding his eye.

'I remember that one,' Artair said. 'It's the only one I wasn't in. I was sick that year.'

'Yeh, that's right. You had a really bad asthma attack the night before.'

Artair shovelled more food into his mouth. 'Nearly died that time. Close-run fucking thing.' He glanced up from one to the other and grinned. 'Might have been better for all of us if I had, eh?' He washed his food down with whisky. Fin noticed that he had topped it up again. 'What? Nobody going to say, naw, Artair, it'd have been a terrible thing if you'd died back then. Life just wouldn't have been the same.'

'Well, *that's* true,' Marsaili said, and he shot her a look.

They ate, then, in silence until Artair had cleared his plate and pushed it away. His eyes fell on Fin's empty glass. 'You need topped up, son.'

'Actually, I'd better be going.' Fin stood up, wiping his mouth on the paper napkin Marsaili had laid out.

'Going where?'

'Back to Stornoway.'

'How?'

'I'll call a taxi.'

'Don't be fucking stupid, man. It'll cost you a bloody fortune. You'll stay over with us tonight, and I'll give you a lift to town in the morning.'

Marsaili stood up and lifted the empty plates away from the table. 'I'll get the bed in the spare room ready.'

By the time Marsaili came back in from the spare room, Artair had installed Fin and himself in the sitting room, glasses refilled, a football match playing on the television, the sound still down. Artair was well gone now, his eyes glazed and half-shut, slurring his words, relating some story from childhood about a bike accident of which Fin had no recollection. Fin had said he'd needed water in his whisky, and when he'd gone into the kitchen to get it, poured half of the whisky down the sink. Now he was sitting nursing his glass uneasily, wishing he had not given in so easily to Artair's insistence that he stay over. He looked up eagerly, hoping for rescue, when Marsaili came in. But she looked tired. She glanced at Artair, a strange, passive expression on her face. Resignation, perhaps. And then she went into the kitchen to turn off the lights. 'I'm going to bed. I'll clear up in the morning.'

Fin stood up, disappointed, as she left the room. 'Goodnight.'

She paused for just a moment in the doorway and their eyes met fleetingly. 'Goodnight, Fin.'

As the door closed, Artair said, 'And good fucking riddance.' He tried to focus on Fin. 'You know, I'd never have fucking married her if it hadn't been for you.'

Fin was stung by the vitriol in his voice. 'Don't be daft! You were chasing Marsaili from that first week at school.'

'I'd never even have fucking noticed her if she hadn't got her claws into you. I was never after *her*. I was only ever trying to keep her away from you. You were my pal, Fin

Macleod. We were friends, you and me, from just about the time we could walk. And from that first fucking day, there she was trying to take you away from me. Driving a wedge between us.' He laughed. A laugh without humour, corrosive and bitter. 'And fuck me if she isn't still doing it. Think I didn't notice the lipstick, eh? Or the mascara? You think that was for your benefit? Naw. It was her way of raising two fingers at me. 'Cos she knew I'd see it, and know why she'd done it. She's not wanted to make herself attractive to me for a very long time.'

Fin was shocked. He had no idea what to say. So he just sat clutching his watered-down whisky, feeling the glass warm in his hands, watching the peat embers dying in the hearth. The air in the room seemed suddenly to have chilled, and he reached a decision. He knocked back the remains of his whisky and stood up. 'I think maybe I'd better go to bed.'

But Artair wasn't looking at him. He was gazing off into some distant place in a whisky-fogged mind. 'And d'you know what the real fucking irony is?'

Fin didn't know, and didn't want to. 'I'll see you in the morning.'

Artair tilted his head up to squint at him. 'He's not even mine.'

Fin felt his stomach lurch. He stood frozen in suspended animation. 'What do you mean?'

'Fionnlagh,' Artair slurred. 'He's your fucking kid, not mine.'

*

193

The anaglypta wallpaper had been painted sometime recently. One of those whites with a hint of peach, or pink maybe. There were new curtains and a new carpet. And the ceiling had been painted, a plain matt white. But the water stain in the corner had come through it, insidious, invasive, and still in the shape of a gannet in flight. The crack was still there, too, in the plaster, running through the gannet and across the cornice. The cracked window pane had been replaced by double glazing, and a double bed was pushed against the wall where Mr Macinnes had had his desk. The shelves of the bookcase opposite still groaned with the same books Fin remembered from those long evenings of maths and English and geography. Books with exotic, distracting titles: *Eyeless in Gaza*, *The Case of the Black-eyed Blonde*, *Boys Will Be Boys*, *Smeddum*. And the even more bizarre names of their authors: *Aldous Huxley*, *Earl Stanley Gardner*, *Lewis Grassic Gibbon*. Mr Macinnes's old armchair was pushed into one corner, the fabric on the arms worn shiny by his elbows. Sometimes people leave their traces on this earth long after they are gone.

Fin was almost overwhelmed by a sense of melancholy. But, then, he thought, melancholy did not really describe it. Some great weight seemed to be bearing down on him, crushing him, making it difficult to breathe. The room itself felt like a dark and disturbing place. His heart was racing as if he were afraid. Afraid of the light. He turned off the bedside lamp. Afraid of the dark. He turned it on again and realized he was shaking. There was something he was trying to remember. Stirred by something Artair had said, or a look he had given him, or a tone in his voice. Leaning against the wall behind the door, he noticed for the first time, was the card table at which he had spent so many hours preparing for his exams. The Cyprus-shaped coffee stain. He was sweating now, and he turned off the light again. He could hear the thump of his heart, the pulse of blood in his ears. When he closed his eyes he saw only red.

How could Fionnlagh be his son? Why wouldn't Marsaili have told him she was pregnant? How could she have married Artair if she had known? Jesus! He wanted to scream and to wake up back home with Robbie and Mona and the life he had known until just four short weeks ago.

He heard voices raised in anger through the wall, and he held his breath to try to hear what they were saying. But the form of the words was lost in the brick. Only their tone made it through the mortar. Fury, hurt, accusation, denial. The sound of a door slamming, and then silence.

Fin wondered if Fionnlagh had heard any of it. Maybe he was used to it. Maybe it was a nightly occurrence. Or was tonight different? Because tonight a secret had escaped, and was moving amongst them like a ghost. Or was it just that Fin was the last to see it, the last to feel its cold fingers of uncertainty turning his world forever upside down?

NINE

It was early in the July of the year I sat my Highers. School was out and I was waiting for my results to confirm a place at Glasgow University. It was the last summer I would spend on the island.

I cannot begin to describe how I felt. I was elated. It was as if I had passed the last several years in the dark with a great weight pressed down upon me, and now that the weight had been lifted I was coming out, blinking, into the sunlight. It helped that the weather that year was sublime. They say that seventy-five and seventy-six were great summers. But the best summer I remember was that last summer before I left for university.

It was years since I had broken up with Marsaili. I can look back now and wonder at my cruelty, and can only console myself with the thought that I had been so very young at the time. But, then, youth is always a handy excuse for crass behaviour.

Of course, she continued to be in my class until the end of primary school, although she had become oddly invisible to me. During the first two years of secondary, still at Crobost, our paths crossed fairly frequently. But after we moved to the Nicolson in Stornoway I hardly ever saw her. The occasional glimpse in a school corridor, or wandering The Narrows with her classmates. I knew that she and Artair had been an item through third and fourth years, even though he was at a different school. I would see them together from time to time at dances in the town hall, or at parties. They broke up in fifth year, when Artair was repeating his O levels, and I was vaguely aware of Marsaili going with Donald Murray for a time.

I went out with a succession of girls all through secondary, but none of them lasted very long. Most of them were put off when they met my aunt. I suppose she must have seemed pretty weird. I had just got used to her. Like the crap you leave lying around your room when you're a kid, you just stop seeing it after a while. But as school finished I was footloose and fancy-free with no intention of tying myself down. Glasgow offered the prospect of boundless new possibilities, and I didn't want to be bringing any baggage with me from the island.

It was sometime during that first week in July that I remember Artair and me going down to the beach together at Port of Ness. We shared markedly contrasting moods. During the run-up to my Highers I had spent long, difficult hours locked away in his dad's study preparing for the exams. Mr Macinnes had been hard on me, driving me relentlessly towards success without let-up. After Artair's five failed O grades he had all but given up on his son, even though Artair had decided to go back for a fifth year to resit. It was as if Mr Macinnes was investing in me all the hopes and aspirations he had once harboured for Artair. It had created tension between Artair and me, born, I think, out of jealousy. We would meet up sometimes after my tutoring sessions and walk up through the village together in tense and difficult silence. I can remember us standing at the foot of the slipway at Crobost harbour throwing stones into the water for more than an hour without a word passing between us. We never talked about the tutoring. It lay between us like a silent shadow.

But all that was behind me now, and the day seemed to reflect my mood, brilliant sunshine coruscating across the still waters of the bay. Only the slightest of breezes ruffled the warm air. We had taken off our socks and sandshoes and rolled up our jeans, and ran barefoot along the gently sloping beach, splashing in and out of the small, briny waves breaking on the shore, leaving perfect footprints in virgin sand. We had one of those plastic sacks they use for bagging the commercial peat, and we were going to catch crabs in the pools left by the outgoing tide amongst the rocky outcrops at the far end of the beach. To me the summer seemed to stretch ahead, an endless succession of days like this, filled with the simplest pleasures of life, unhurried by age or ambition.

Artair, though, was gloomy and depressed. He had

been accepted for a welding apprenticeship at Lewis Offshore, starting in September. He saw his summer slipping away, like sand through his fingers. The final summer of his boyhood, with only the drudgery of a dead-end job and the responsibility of adulthood awaiting him at the end of it.

It was another world down there among the rock pools, hidden away from the realities of life. The only sound came from the gulls, and the sea rushing gently up to meet the shore. The water trapped in all the rocky crevices was crystal-clear and warming in the sun, filled with the colour of crustaceans clinging stubbornly to black rock, the gentle waving of seaweed the only movement apart from the scuttling of the crabs. We had collected nearly two dozen of them, dropping them into the sack, before we took a cigarette break. Although I had fair hair, I had my father's skin and took a fine tan. I had removed my T-shirt to roll up under my head, and lay draped across the rocks, sunning myself, eyes closed, listening to the sea and the birds that fed off it. Artair sat with his knees folded up under his chin, arms wrapped around his shins, puffing gloomily on his cigarette. Oddly, smoking didn't seem to affect his asthma.

'Every time I look at my watch,' he said, 'another minute's gone by. And then an hour, and then a day. Soon it'll be a week, then a month. And another one. And then I'll be clocking in on my first day.' He shook his head. 'And soon enough, I'll be clocking out on my last. And then they'll be putting me in the ground at Crobost cemetery. And what will it all have been about?'

'Jesus, man. We're talking sixty, seventy years. And you've just blown it all away in a heartbeat. You've got your whole life ahead of you.'

'It's alright for you. You're leaving. You've got your escape route all planned out. Glasgow. University. The world. Anywhere other than here.'

'Hey, look around you.' I raised myself up on one elbow. 'It doesn't come much better than this.'

'Yeh,' Artair said, his voice heavy with sarcasm, 'that's why you're in such a fucking hurry to leave.' I had no reply to that. He looked at me. 'Cat got your tongue?' He flicked his cigarette end off across the rocks, sending a shower of red sparks dancing in the breeze. 'I mean, what have I got to look forward to? An apprenticeship at a rig construction yard? Years stuck behind a mask firing jets of frigging flame at metal joints? Jesus, I can smell it already. And then there's all the years of travelling that fucking road from Ness to Stornoway, and a hole in the ground at the end of it all.'

'It's what my father did,' I said. 'It wasn't what he wanted, but I never heard him complain about it. He always told us we had a good life. And he crammed most of it into all those hours he wasn't working at the yard.'

'And a fat lot of good it did him.' The words were out before he realized it, and Artair turned quickly towards me, regret in his eyes. 'I'm sorry, Fin. I didn't mean it like that.'

I nodded. I felt as if the only cloud in the sky had just cast its shadow on me. 'I know. But you're right, I suppose.' I let my own bitterness creep in. 'Maybe if he hadn't devoted so much of his time to his God, he might have had more of it left for living.' But then I took a deep breath and made a determined effort to get out from under the shadow. 'Anyway, there's nothing definite yet about the university. It still depends on the exam results.'

'Aw, come on.' Artair was dismissive. 'You'll have walked it. My dad says he'll be disappointed if you don't get straight "A"s.'

It was then that we first heard the voices of the girls. Distant initially, chattering and laughing, and then getting closer as they came towards us along the beach. We couldn't see them from where we were, and of course they couldn't see us. Artair put a finger to his lips, then signalled me to follow. We scrambled barefoot over the rocks until we saw them, no more than thirty yards away, and we ducked down so as not to be seen. There were four of them, local girls from our year at school. We peered up over the edge of the rocks to get a better look. They were taking towels from baskets and laying them in the soft sand beneath the cliffs. One of them stretched out a reed mat and tipped bottles of ginger and packets of crisps on to it from her bag. And then they started stripping off T-shirts and jeans, to reveal white flesh and bikinis beneath.

I suppose I must have registered subconsciously that Marsaili was among them, but it wasn't until I saw her standing there in her bikini, arms raised, tying her hair up in a knot at the back of her head, that I realized she was no longer the little girl I had jilted in primary school. She had grown into a very desirable young woman. And the sight of soft sunlight shading the curve of her bottom at the top of long, elegant legs, and the swelling of breasts barely contained in her skimpy blue top, caused something to stir in my loins. We dropped down again behind the rocks.

'Jesus,' I whispered.

Artair was gleeful. Gone in an instant was his depression, to be replaced by mischievous eyes and a wicked smile. 'I've got a great fucking idea.' He tugged my arm. 'Come on.'

We picked up our T-shirts and the sack of crabs, and I followed Artair back over the rocky outcrop towards the cliffs. There was a path here that we sometimes used to climb down to the rocks without having to go around to the Port and then back along the beach. It was steep and shingly, a cleft cut deep into the cliff face by a glacial encroachment during some past ice age. About two-thirds of the way up, a narrow ledge cut diagonally across the face before doubling back on itself and leading up, finally, in a series of natural steps, to the top. We were thirty feet above the beach now, the turf soft and spongy underfoot, and liable to break away in treacherous peaty clumps if you got too close to the edge. We had achieved our goal of reaching the clifftop without being seen, and we made our way carefully along it until we reached a point above where we thought the girls were sunbathing. The edge sloped away steeply here, falling about twenty feet to a final sheer drop of around ten to the beach below. Grass grew in reedy patches on the thin layer of soil that clung to the rock. We couldn't see the girls, but we could hear them talking to one another as they lay side by side on their towels. The trick was going to be making sure we were directly above them before releasing the hard-won contents of our sack. Nothing short of a direct strike would be acceptable.

We got on to our backsides and began inching our way down the steep, grassy slope. I went first, clutching the sack, and Artair followed, and then acted as a kind of anchor, digging his heels into the crumbling earth and holding me with both hands by my left forearm, so that I could lean out and try to catch a glimpse of the girls. We had to go almost all of the way down to the final drop before I caught sight of four pairs of heels lying in a row. They were a little over to our left, and I signed to Artair that we had to move across a bit. As we did, some loose earth and pebbles freed themselves from the fringes and dropped on to the beach. The chatter stopped.

'What was that?' I heard one of them ask.

'A hundred million years of erosion.' It was Marsaili's voice. 'You don't think it's going to stop just because we're sunbathing below it?'

The heels were immediately beneath me now, like four sets of feet set out on a mortuary slab. I leaned out as far as I dared and saw that they were all lying on their fronts, bikini tops undone to avoid that tell-tale white line across the back. Perfect. I was probably twelve or fifteen feet above them. I grinned at Artair and nodded. I took the sack in my free hand, loosening the top, before shaking it out over the edge. Two dozen crabs went flying through space and out of sight. But their effect was immediate. Great shrieks of terror split the air, rising to us from below like rapturous applause for the success of our venture. Barely able to control our laughter, we inched a little lower, and I craned to catch a sight of the mayhem on the beach.

It was at that moment a great sod of dry earth chose to detach itself from the crumbling rock and send me sliding down the slope and over the edge, in spite of Artair's best efforts to hold on. Like the crabs before me, I hurtled through space, dropping the last ten feet to the beach and landing, fortunately enough, on my feet, although gravity promptly induced me to sit down heavily.

Panicked crabs were scuttling in every direction. I found myself looking up at four startled girls looking down at me. Four pairs of naked breasts bobbing in the sunlight. We all stared at each other for a moment, all of us speechless, frozen in a moment of mutual disbelief. Then one of the girls screamed, and three of them crossed their arms over their chests in extravagant gestures of false modesty, giggling now and feigning coy-ness. In truth, I think they were not entirely dismayed by my sudden and unexpected appearance.

Marsaili, however, made no attempt to cover herself up. She stood for several moments with her hands on her hips, breasts thrust out defiantly. Firm, pert breasts, I couldn't help noticing, with large, erect and very pink nipples. She took two steps forward and slapped me so hard across the face that I saw lights flashing. 'Pervert!' she spat contemptuously. And she bent down to retrieve her bikini top and strode away across the sand.

I didn't see Marsaili again for almost a month. We were into August now, and my exam results had come through. As Mr Macinnes had predicted, I got straight 'A's in English, art, history, French and Spanish. I had given up maths and science after my O grades. It was strange. I had an aptitude for languages, but never any inclination to use it. My acceptance for Glasgow University had been confirmed, and I was going to do an MA. I wasn't quite sure what that was, but anything to do with the arts interested me, and I never seemed to have to work as hard as I did with the more academic subjects.

I had long since recovered from Marsaili's slap, but it had left red weals on my face that I wore like a badge of honour for several days after. Artair had made me describe in great detail to him what I had seen when I landed on the beach. For his part, he had scrambled back up to the top of the cliff and not caught sight of so much as a nipple. The story spread like wildfire through the neighbouring villages, and I enjoyed a brief status as a cult hero among a whole generation of pubescent boys in Ness. But like the summer itself, the recollection was waning, and the day when Artair would clock in for the first time was approaching with unwelcome haste. He was becoming increasingly morose.

I found him in a black mood the day I called at his bungalow to tell him about the party on Eilean Beag. It was a tiny island just a few hundred yards off the north shore of Great Bernera, which was like the fire in a dragon's mouth just to the west of Calanais, where the sea had eaten deep into the south-west coastline of Lewis. I don't know who had organized it, but a friend of Donald Murray had invited him, and he invited us. There were to be bonfires and a barbecue, and if the weather was fine we would sleep on the beach under the stars. If it was wet, there was an old shieling where we could shelter. All we had to do was bring our own drink.

Artair shook his head grimly and told me he couldn't go. His father was away on the mainland for a few days, and his mother was not well. He was going to have to stay in with her. She'd had chest pains, he said, and her blood pressure was through the roof. The doctor thought perhaps she was suffering from angina. I had never heard of angina, but it didn't sound very pleasant. I was disappointed that Artair couldn't go. Disappointed for him. He needed cheering up.

But my concern for Artair didn't stay long in my mind. By the Friday it was already fading, and when Donald Murray arrived at my aunt's house to pick me up on that afternoon, all thoughts of Artair were blown away by the roar of Donald's exhaust, and the sulphurous cloud it emitted. From somewhere he had managed to acquire a red, soft-top Peugeot. It was old, and somewhat the worse for wear, but it was a wonderful, vivid red, and the roof was down, and Donald lounged behind the wheel looking like a film star with his bleached hair and his tanned face and his sunglasses.

'Hey, bro,' he drawled. 'Wanna ride?'

And I certainly did. I wasn't interested in where he had got it, or how. I just wanted to sit up there in the front beside him and cruise the island, and see the jealous looks on all the other kids' faces. An open-topped car on the Isle of Lewis was almost unheard-of. After all, when would you ever be able to use it with the roof down? On a handful of days in any given year, if you were lucky. Well, that year we were big-time lucky. The good weather had scorched the island brown through July, and it was still holding.

We loaded four boxes of beer into the boot from my aunt's lean-to, where I had been storing it. Donald's father would not have permitted such contraband to be kept at the manse. My aunt came out to see us off. When I think back now, I can see that perhaps she was not well, even then. Though she never said a word to me about it.

207

But she was pale, and thinner than she had been. Her henna-dyed hair was wispy and sparse, with half an inch of white at the roots. Her make-up was caked and pasty, crumbling in the creases of her over-rouged cheeks. Mascara was clogged in her lashes, and her mouth was a slash of pale pink. She was wearing one of her diaphanous creations, layers of different-coloured chiffon pinned into something resembling a cape, over cut-off jeans and pink open sandals. Her toenails were painted pink, too. Thick, horny nails in feet made ugly by arthritis.

She had been my mum's big sister. Ten years older than her. And two more different people it would be hard to imagine. She must have been in her thirties during the hippy days of the 1960s, but that was her defining era. She'd spent time in London and San Francisco and New York, the only person I ever met who had actually been at Woodstock. It's strange how little I know about her, really. The young are not curious about their elders, they just accept them for what they are. But I wish now I could go back and ask her about her life, fill in all those gaps. But, of course, you can't go back. She had never been married, I knew that, but there had been some big relationship with someone famous. And wealthy. And married. When she returned to the island she bought the old whitehouse overlooking Crobost harbour and lived there on her own. As far as I knew she never told anyone what happened. Perhaps she confided in my mother, but I would have been too young for my mother to have told me. I think there was only ever one great love in her life, a life on which she seemed simply to close the door when she moved into the old whitehouse. I have no idea how she lived, where her money came from. We could never afford the luxuries, but I never wanted for food or clothes, or anything that I really desired. When she died there was ten pounds in her bank account.

My aunt was an enigma, one of the great unexplored mysteries of my life. I lived with her for nine years, and yet I cannot say that I ever knew her. She didn't love me, I can say with some certainty. Nor I her. I would say she tolerated me. But she never had a harsh word. And she always took my part when the world was against me. There was – how can I put it? – a kind of unspoken, almost reluctant, affection between us. I don't think I ever kissed her, and the only time I can remember her holding me was the night my parents died.

She loved the car. I suppose it must have appealed to that long-lost free spirit in her. She asked Donald if he would take her for a ride, and he told her to jump in. I sat in the back as he tore up the cliff road and over to Skigersta, sparks flying from the cigarette my aunt insisted on trying to smoke. Her hair blew back from her face to reveal its fragile, bony structure, crêpe-like skin stretched tight over all its slopes and angles, like a death mask. And yet I don't think I had ever seen her so happy. When we got back to the house there was a radiance about her, and I think she almost wished she was going with us. When I looked back as the car slipped over the brow of the hill towards Crobost she was still standing watching us go.

We picked up Iain and Seonaidh and some more beer at the bottom of the hill and set off south for Great Bernera. It was a glorious drive down the west coast, with the warm wind battering our faces and the sun burning our skin. I had never seen the ocean so calm, glittering away towards a hazy horizon. A gentle swell, as if it were breathing slow and steady, was the only perceptible movement. Kids waved to us in village after village. Siadar, Barvas, Shawbost, Carloway, and some of the older folk stood and watched in amazement, figuring no doubt that we were tourists from the mainland, mad folk brought across the water in the belly of the *Suilven*. The standing stones at Calanais ranged in silent silhouette against the western sky, another of life's mysteries that we were unlikely ever to unravel.

By the time we found the jetty at the north-east point of Great Bernera, the sun was sinking lower in the sky and flooding the ocean with its dazzling liquid gold. We could see Eilean Beag sitting low in the water just a couple of hundred yards from the shore. It was no more than half a mile long, and maybe three or four hundred yards wide. The shieling sat close to the shore and there were several fires already burning at various points around it and along the beach, smoke hanging above the island in the still air. We could see figures moving about, and the sound of music carried as clear as a bell across the strait.

We unloaded the beer from the car and Donald parked it on the bank beside several dozen others. Seonaidh rang the bell on the jetty, and a few minutes later someone began rowing a boat across to fetch us.

Eilean Beag was fairly flat and featureless, summer grazing for sheep, but it had a fine, sandy beach along its southern fringe, and another shingle beach along the north-west flank. There must have been nearly a hundred people on the island that night. I knew hardly any of them. I supposed a lot of them must have come from the mainland. They were gathering in animated groups of those who knew one another, each with their own fire, each with their own music pounding out from their own ghetto blasters. The smell of barbecued meat and fish filled the air. Girls were wrapping food in tinfoil parcels to bury in the embers. Although I had no idea whose party it was, it did seem remarkably well organized. When we first got ashore, Donald slapped me on the back and said he'd catch me later. He had a rendezvous with a quarter-ounce of dope. Iain and Seonaidh and I stacked the beer with the rest of the booze at the shieling, and opened ourselves some cans. We found some kids we knew from school and spent the next couple of hours drinking and talking and eating fish and chicken straight from the fire.

Night seemed to fall suddenly, darkness catching us un-aware. The sky still glowed red in the west and fires were stoked and refuelled with driftwood to give more light. I don't know why, but a certain melancholy descended on me with the dark. Perhaps I was too happy and knew it couldn't last. Maybe it was because it was my last summer on Lewis, although I had no idea then that I would only ever return once, for a funeral. I opened a fresh can and wandered off among the fires strung out along the shore, animated faces gathered around them reflecting their light, laughing, drinking, smoking. Mixed now with the smell of woodsmoke and barbecue was the sweet, woody perfume of marijuana. From the water's edge, I looked up at a sky free from any light pollution, and felt myself filled with a sense of wonder at its vast, inky, starlit span. There are moments when you look at the sky and you feel that everything revolves around you, and other times when you just feel infinitesimally small. That night I felt like the merest speck of dust in the history of infinity.

'Hey, Fin!' I turned at the sound of my name to see Donald at the nearest fire with some other kids. He had his arm around a girl, and they appeared mostly to be paired off in couples. 'What the hell are you doing out there on your own in the dark? Come and join us.'

To be honest, I didn't really want to. I was wallowing a little in my melancholy, enjoying my solitude. But I didn't like to be rude. As I walked into the circle of light around the fire, Donald was snogging his girl, breaking off only as he became aware of me standing there. That was when I saw that the girl was Marsaili, and I felt a tiny jolt of jealousy, like electricity, passing through my body. I am sure my face must have flushed red, but the firelight disguised my embarrassment.

Marsaili smiled at me, superior, a look of cool calculation in her eyes. 'Well, well, if it isn't Peeping Tom.'

'Peeping Tom?' There was puzzlement in Donald's half-smile. He must have been the only kid in Ness who hadn't heard the story. Maybe he'd been away on the mainland fetching his red, soft-top Peugeot. So Marsaili told him, although not exactly the way I would have told it, and he laughed so much I thought he was going to choke.

'Man, that's priceless. Sit down for Chrissake. Have a joint with us and loosen up.'

I sat down, but waved aside the offer of a joint. 'Naw, I'll just stick with beer.'

Donald gave me a knowing look and cocked his head. 'A dope virgin, are we?'

'Every kind of virgin probably,' Marsaili said.

I blushed again, thankful for the darkness and the fire. 'Course not.' But I was. And, as Marsaili suspected, in more ways than one.

'So don't give me any of this shit about beer,' Donald said. 'You'll smoke with us, right?'

I shrugged. 'Sure.' And as I drank from my can I watched him carefully roll what these days they call a spliff, joining together four sheets of cigarette papers, sprinkling tobacco along the centre of the 'skin' and then crumbling the cooked resin along its length. He laid a strip of card at one end and rolled the joint around it into a long cigarette, licking along the sticky edge of the paper and then twisting the other end closed. That was the end he lit, taking a long pull on it, sucking a great cloud of smoke into his lungs and holding it there while he passed the joint to Marsaili. As Marsaili sucked on it, Donald exhaled deeply, smoke drifting into the night, and I could see the effect of it almost instantly, peace descending on him like a shroud out of the darkness. Marsaili passed it to me, its end wet with her saliva. I smoked the occasional cigarette, and so didn't think I would disgrace myself by choking on the inhalation. But I wasn't expecting the smoke to be so hot, and a fit of coughing exploded from my lungs into my throat. When I regained control, I found Donald and Marsaili looking at me with knowing little smiles. 'Caught the back of my throat,' I said.

'You'd better take another drag, then,' Donald told me, and I had no option but to try again. This time I managed to keep the smoke in my lungs for about ten seconds, passing the joint back to Donald, before exhaling slowly.

Of course, I should have known that I would give myself away as a first-timer by giggling. I spent the next fifteen minutes laughing at anything and everything. It's amazing how funny things were. A comment, a look, a shriek of laughter from the neighbouring bonfire. Any one of these would set me off. Donald and Marsaili watched me with the laid-back detachment of experienced smokers, until finally my giggles subsided. By the time we had smoked a second joint I was feeling supremely mellow, staring into the flames and seeing all sorts of answers there to those questions about life that the young always like to ask. Answers that were as elusive as the flames themselves, and never there the next morning when you woke up.

I was only vaguely aware of someone calling from the beach and Donald getting to his feet and padding away across the sand. When I looked around, I saw that most of the other kids around our fire had drifted away too, and only Marsaili and I were left sitting there. We were not within touching distance, but she was looking at me with a very odd expression.

'Come here.' She patted the sand beside her.

Like an obedient little dog, I shuffled around until my backside filled the dent she had made in the beach with her hand. I felt my thigh touching hers, and the heat of her body next to mine.

'You're a complete bastard, you know that?' But her voice was soft, and without rancour. Of course, I knew that I was, so I didn't dare contradict her. 'You stole my heart when I was too young to know any better, and then you dumped and humiliated me.' I tried a smile, but I'm sure it must have come out like some ghastly grimace. She looked at me earnestly and shook her head. 'I don't know why I still have these feelings for you.'

'What feelings?'

She leaned over, and with the same hand she had used to slap me, turned my face towards her and kissed me. A long, soft, open-mouthed kiss that sent tremors running through me, and blood rushing to my loins.

When finally she had finished with me, she said, 'Those feelings.' She sat for a minute looking at me, then stood up and reached for my hand. 'Come on.'

We walked hand-in-hand among the fires, faces passing in a blur, music mixing one song into another, voices murmuring softly in the night, the occasional peal of laughter. I had a sense of heightened awareness of everything around me: the sound of the sea, the density of the night, the closeness of the stars, like the tips of white-hot needles that you could reach up and touch and prick your fingers. I was aware, too, of the warm touch of Marsaili's hand in mine, the softness of her skin as we stopped repeatedly to kiss, her breasts pushing gently into my chest, my penis swelling now and straining at my jeans, pressing into her abdomen. I felt her hand slipping down to close itself around my hardness.

The main room in the shieling was empty when we got there, its earthen floor strewn with empty beer cans and stacked with boxes of booze and binbags filled with the detritus of the barbecue. Marsaili seemed to know where she was going, and led me to a door at the back of the room. As we reached it, the door opened and a couple, not much older than we were, came out giggling, brushing past us, oblivious to our presence. The back room was much smaller, lit by candles placed around the wall. The air was heavy with the scent of dope and burning wax and the smell of human bodies. A tarpaulin had been thrown across the floor and was covered with travelling rugs and cushions, and sleeping bags which had been unzipped and opened out like quilts.

Marsaili squatted down on one of the rugs, still holding my hand, and pulling on it so that I would sit beside her. Almost before my backside hit the floor, she had pushed me over, rolling on top of me, kissing me with a ferocity I had never experienced. Then she sat astride me, straightening up to pull off her top, and those fine, pink-nippled breasts I had seen on the beach swung free. I cupped their gentle firmness in my hands, and felt the nipples harden against my skin. She reached down and unzipped my jeans, releasing me from their constraint, and a tiny spike of fear shot through my dope-induced torpor.

'Marsaili, you were right,' I whispered.

She looked at me. 'What do you mean?'

'I've never done this before.' It was not a confession I would ever have made in the cold light of day.

She laughed. 'Don't worry. I have.'

Unaccountably, I was filled with indignation and sat upright. 'Who with?'

'It's none of your business.'

'Was it Artair?' Somehow it seemed very important to me that it shouldn't have been Artair.

She sighed. 'No, it wasn't Artair. If you must know, it was Donald.'

Somehow I was both startled and relieved. Also confused. I suppose the beer and the dope, and everything else that was happening to me that night, had combined to rob me of my reason. Even my jealousy. And I submitted to Marsaili's greater experience. I don't really remember very much about that first time. Only that it seemed to be over very quickly. But, as it turned out, there were many more opportunities for us that summer to practise and perfect our technique.

As we struggled back into our clothes afterwards, the door suddenly burst open, and Donald was standing there grinning, a girl on each arm. 'For Christ's sake, have you two not finished yet? There's a bloody queue out here.'

TEN

The clacking of the keyboard filled the silence in the darkened bedroom. The screen reflected its light on Fin's pale face, concentration gathered in the frown around his eyes and across the bridge of his nose. These exams were so important. Everything depended on them. The rest of his life. Focus, focus. Concentrate. A movement in his peripheral vision made him turn, and he felt goosebumps raising themselves across his arms and shoulders. He was there again. That impossibly tall man in the hooded anorak, greasy hair dragged down over his ears. Just standing in the doorway, like before, head bowed against the ceiling, big hands hanging loosely at his sides. This time his lips were moving, as if he were trying to say something. Fin strained to hear, but there were no words coming from his mouth, just the rank, bitter smell of stale tobacco on a breath whose foulness seemed to fill the room.

Fin woke, startled, with the stink of stale alcohol breath in his face. Daylight was streaming through thin curtains, seeping in around all their edges. Artair's weary, bloated face hovered over him, a hand shaking his shoulder. 'Fin, for fuck's sake, wake up, Fin.'

Fin sat bolt upright, breathing hard, disorientated, still afraid. Where the hell was he? Then his eye fell on the card table folded against the wall and the Cyprus coffee stain. He raised his eyes to the ceiling and saw the gannet in flight. 'Jesus.' He was still gasping for breath.

Artair stood back, looking at him curiously. 'Are you alright?'

'Yeh. Fine. I'm fine. Just a nightmare.' Fin drew in a deep lungful of warm, sour air. 'What time is it?'

'Six.'

He had barely slept, turning frequently to look at the digital display on the bedside table. Two. Two forty-five. Three fifteen. Three fifty. The last time he had looked it was almost five o'clock. He could only have been dozing for an hour or so.

'We have to go right now,' Artair said.

Fin was confused. 'At this time?'

'Fionnlagh and me have to get down to Port of Ness before I leave for work. We're helping the boys load the lorry with supplies for An Sgeir.'

Fin pushed the quilt aside and swung his legs out of the bed. He rubbed tired eyes. 'Give me a minute to get dressed.'

But Artair made no move to go. Fin glanced up to find his old schoolfriend watching him intently, an odd expression in his eyes. 'Listen, Fin. What I said last night . . . I was drunk, okay? Just forget it.'

Fin returned his gaze. 'Was it true?'

'I was drunk.'

'*In vino veritas.*'

Artair lost patience. 'Look, I was fucking pissed, alright? It hasn't mattered for seventeen years, why the fuck should it matter now?' Fin heard the phlegm crackling in his throat as he turned away and abruptly left the room. And he heard him sucking twice on his puffer out in the hall before his footsteps receded angrily towards the living room.

Fin got dressed, and in the bathroom slunged his face with cold water, and found bloodshot eyes staring back at him from the mirror. He looked terrible. He squeezed some toothpaste on to his finger and rubbed it around his teeth and his gums, swilling out his mouth to try to get rid of the bad taste from the night before. He wondered how he was going to be able to face Fionnlagh in the cold light of day, knowing what he knew now. He glanced at himself in the mirror and looked quickly away again. He hardly knew how to face himself.

The Astra was idling on the road above the house. The growl of the engine through the exhaust sounded as rough as Fin felt. Artair was sitting sullenly behind the wheel, Fionnlagh in the back in his hooded sweatshirt, clasped hands resting on the seat between his legs, his face puffy from lack of sleep. Yet, still, he seemed to have found time to gel his hair into spikes. Fin slipped into the passenger seat and glanced in the back. 'Hi,' was all he said, turning in his seat to face front, and feeling hopelessly inadequate as he snapped the seatbelt into its clasp.

Artair crunched into first gear and released the handbrake, and they lurched off down the road. Fin was quite sure that if he were stopped, Artair would not pass a breathalyser.

The sky was leaden, but it did not look like rain. Somewhere away on the ocean, sun slanted through a break in the cloud that you couldn't see, like an invisible spotlight casting a circle of illumination on the water. A strong wind tugged at the summer grasses. As they passed the church, they could see all the way across to the Port, and the Astra bumped its way down the single-track towards the main road.

Fin found the silence in the car almost unbearable. Without turning he said to Fionnlagh, 'So how did you get on with the computer?'

'Great.' Fin waited for him to go on. But that was it.

Artair said, 'He's not looking forward to going to An Sgeir.'

Fin craned round to look at the boy. 'Why?'

'Not my scene. I'm not much into killing things.'

'The boy's soft,' Artair said scornfully. 'It'll be good for him, make a man of him.'

'Like it did us?'

Artair cast Fin a look of disdain, then fixed his eyes

again on the road. 'Rite of passage, that's what it's all about. Boys becoming men. No one said it had to be easy.'

There was no policeman on duty in Port of Ness. Maybe they thought it was no longer necessary, or perhaps they did not believe that anyone would be up this early. The crime-scene tape at the shore road had been drawn aside and wrapped around an orange traffic cone. The narrow road twisted down to the harbour, and they saw a lorry drawn up on the quay, and seven or eight vehicles pulled up alongside the boatshed. The shed was still marked off by black-and-yellow tape fluttering in the wind, and as they parked and walked past it, they each glanced in. A man had been murdered here. A man they knew. And each of them was touched by the sense that somehow Angel Macritchie still lingered there in the shadows, like a ghost unable to rest until his killer had been found.

His presence was there, too, among the ten men gathered around the lorry, if only through his absence. He had been one of them for eighteen years, and should have been among them today, helping to load the supplies stacked up along the quayside: bags of peat to fuel the fires, drinking water in metal casks, mattresses, tarpaulins, boxes of food, tools, a car battery to power the radio link, more than forty sacks of curing salt piled a metre high against the harbour wall.

Fin found that he knew many of the faces of the men on the quay. Some of them were in their fifties, veterans from the year when Fin and Artair had gone out to the rock, still making the annual pilgrimage. There were one or two of Fin's contemporaries from school, and younger men in their twenties whom Fin did not know. But there was an unspoken bond between them all. It was a very exclusive club whose membership extended to a mere handful of men going back over five hundred years. You only had to have been out to An Sgeir one time to qualify for membership, proving your courage and strength, and your ability to endure against the elements. Their predecessors had made the journey in open boats on mountainous seas because they had to, to survive, to feed hungry villagers. Now they went out in a trawler to bring back a delicacy much sought after by well-fed islanders. But their stay on the rock was no less hazardous, no less demanding than it had been for all those who had gone before.

Fin said his hellos and solemnly shook all their hands. The last of them took Fin's in both of his. A thickset man of medium height, heavy black eyebrows beneath a head of dense black hair touched only here and there by grey. Physically he was not a big man, but he was a huge presence. Gigs MacAulay was in his early fifties. He had been out to the rock more often than anyone else on the team. He had already made some fourteen or fifteen trips to An Sgeir by the time Fin and Artair were initiated into the ancient rite. He was recognized then as the unspoken team leader. And he was still. There was an additional firmness and warmth in his handshake, and he fixed Fin with sharp, deeply blue Celtic eyes. 'Good to see you, Fin. You've done well, I hear.'

Fin shrugged. 'I suppose.'

'If we do our best, God can't ask that we do any more.' His eyes flickered away towards Artair and then back to Fin. 'It's been a long time.'

'It has.'

'Must be, what? Seventeen, eighteen years?'

'Must be.'

'Artair's boy's coming with us for the first time.'

'Aye, I know.'

Gigs looked at the boy and grinned. 'Though he'll not be needing his hair gel out on the rock, will you, son?' The others laughed, and Fionnlagh blushed, turning his head away to stare mutely out across the ocean. Gigs clapped his hands together. 'Right, we'd better get this lot on the lorry.' He looked at Fin. 'Are you going to give us a hand?'

'Sure,' Fin said, and he took off his parka and his jacket, tossing them on to a stack of empty creels, and rolled up his sleeves.

They worked methodically, in a chain, like any good team, passing the sacks and the boxes one to the other, and up to the men stacking them on the lorry. Fin found himself watching Fionnlagh, looking for something of himself in the boy, some sign that this was, indeed, his flesh and blood. They had similar colouring, but then Marsaili was fair, too. And they were his mother's pale blue eyes that he had. Fin's were green. If he had anything of Fin in him, perhaps it wasn't physical. More like something in his demeanour, in his quiet reticence.

Fionnlagh caught Fin watching him, and Fin immediately turned away, embarrassed. Gigs heaved a bag of salt into his arms. It was heavy, and Fin grunted. 'It was easier in my day,' he said, 'when you just had to load straight on to the trawler here at the Port.'

'It was that.' Gigs shook his head gravely. 'But with the damage to the harbour the trawlers can't get in any more, so we've got to haul it all to Stornoway now.'

'But you guys still leave from here?'

'Most of us do, aye. In the small boat.' Gigs nodded towards an open boat tied up at the quay, her outboard motor tipped clear of the water. 'We motor out to meet the trawler there in the bay and haul the wee boat aboard. We still need her to ferry everything on to the rock at the other end.'

'So, are you any nearer to catching Angel's killer?' one of the younger men suddenly asked Fin, his curiosity getting the better of him.

'I'm not leading the investigation,' Fin said. 'I don't really know how things are going.'

'Aye, well, they seem to think this DNA test's going to get him,' one of the others said.

Fin was surprised. 'You know about that already?'

'Sure do,' said Gigs. 'I think every man in Crobost got a call yesterday from the incident room. Got to go into the police station in Stornoway, or the doctor's surgery up at Crobost sometime today to give a sample.'

'It's voluntary, though,' Fin said.

Artair said, 'Aye, but do you really think anyone's not going to do it? I mean, it would look fucking suspicious, wouldn't it?'

'I'm not doing it,' Fionnlagh said, and they all stopped and looked at him.

'Why not?' Artair demanded.

'Because it's the thin end of the wedge.' Fionnlagh's face flushed with a strange passion. 'The beginnings of a police state. We're all going to end up on a database somewhere, identified by a DNA barcode, and we're not going to be able to do anything or go anywhere without someone knowing why, or where we've come from, or where we're going to. You'll end up getting turned down for a mortgage, or life insurance, because the insurance company thinks you're a bad risk. It'll all be there on the DNA database. Your grampa died of cancer, or maybe there's a history of heart disease on your mother's side. You'll get knocked back for a job because your prospective employer's discovered that your great grandmother spent time in a mental institution, and your barcode looks a hell of a lot like hers.'

Artair looked at the faces gathered around listening open-mouthed. The loading of the lorry had ground to a halt. 'Will you hark at him. He sounds like one of these left-wing radicals. Karl fucking Marx. I don't know where the hell he gets it from.' His eyes darted momentarily towards Fin, then he turned to Fionnlagh. 'You'll take the test and lump it.'

Fionnlagh shook his head. 'No,' he said with a quiet resolution.

'Look . . .' Artair took a more conciliatory tone. 'We're all going to do it, right?' He looked around for support. Everyone nodded and murmured their agreement. 'So it's going to look pretty fucking suspicious if you don't. Is that what you want? Is it? You want them to think it was you?'

A look of sullen resignation fell across Fionnlagh's face. 'Well, whoever did it should get a medal.' Fin did not miss the echo of Artair's words. Fionnlagh took in all the faces turned in his direction. 'The man was a brute and a bully, and I'll bet there's not a single one of you standing on this jetty who doesn't think he got everything he deserved.'

No one said a word. And a few moments' silence stretched into half a minute, tempered only by the sound of the wind rushing through the grasses on the cliff. Finally, as if just to break it, one of the men said, 'So does it hurt, this DNA test?'

Fin smiled and shook his head. 'No. They take a thing like a big cotton bud and scrape it down the inside of your cheek.'

'Not your bum cheek, I hope,' a thin man with ginger hair and a cloth cap said, and they all laughed, glad to be able to release the tension. "Cos nobody's sticking a big cotton bud up my arse!'

The laughter was a cue to begin loading again, and they restarted the passing of salt sacks along the chain to the lorry.

'How long before they get the results of the DNA tests?' Artair asked.

'Don't know,' Fin said. 'Two or three days, maybe. Depending on how many samples they take. When are you hoping to leave for the rock?'

'Tomorrow,' Gigs said. 'Maybe even tonight. Depends on the weather.'

Fin blew air through clenched teeth as he took another sack, and felt the sweat breaking out across his forehead. He was going to have to shower and change when he got back to Stornoway. 'You know, what I don't understand is why you kept taking him.'

'Angel?' Gigs asked.

Fin nodded. 'I mean, you all hated him, didn't you? I haven't come across a single person since I got here who's had one good word to say for him.'

The comedian with the ginger hair said, 'Angel was the cook. He was good at it.' And there was a mumble of accord.

'So who have you asked to stand in for him?' Fin said.

'Asterix.' Gigs nodded towards a wee man with a big, whiskery moustache. 'But we didn't ask him. We never ask anyone, Fin. We let it be known that there's a place available, and if someone wants to go, then they come and ask us.' He paused, a sack of salt weighing heavily in his arms. But he didn't seem to notice. 'That way no one can lay the blame at our door if anything goes wrong.'

When they had finished loading the lorry, they took a break for a smoke, a quiet moment together before this unlikely assembly of weavers and crofters, electricians, joiners and builders, headed off to crofts and workplaces. Fin wandered away along the jetty, past rusting capstans and tangles of green fishing net. There was fresh concrete around the walkway and the wall where work had recently been carried out to repair the damage caused by ferocious seas. A great grassy rock rose from the water in the inner harbour. As a boy, Fin had gone out to it at low tide and climbed up to the top, sitting there to survey all around him. King of the harbour. Until the tide came in and trapped him there. He'd had to wait until the tide went out again before he could get off the rock. For like most island boys of his generation, he had never learned to swim. There had been hell to pay when eventually he got home.

'You know, we've never spoken properly about what happened that year.' Gigs's voice close at his shoulder startled him. Fin turned and saw that the others were still gathered around the lorry at the far end of the jetty, smoking and talking. 'When we got back, you were in no condition to talk. Didn't remember much, anyway. And then you left for the university and never came back.'

'I don't know that there was anything much for us to say,' Fin said.

Gigs leaned against the lifebelt hanging from the harbour wall and gazed across at the breakwater quay, smashed now by the sea, where the trawler used to berth to land the harvest from An Sgeir. 'In the old days, hundreds of people gathered on the quay there, queuing up the road to the village, just to be sure of at least one guga.' The wind whipped the smoke of his cigarette from his mouth.

'I remember it,' Fin said, 'from when I was a boy.'

Gigs tilted his head and cast him a searching look. 'What else do you remember, Fin – from the year you came with us?'

'I remember that I nearly died. It's not something I'm likely to forget.' He felt Gigs's eyes piercing him, like searchlights seeking illumination in some dark place deep inside, and he was discomfited by it.

'A man did die.'

'I'm hardly likely to forget that either.' Emotion welled up in Fin like water in a spring. 'There's hardly a day goes by that I don't think about it.'

Gigs held his eye for a moment then looked away again towards the shattered quay. 'I've been out to the rock more than thirty times, Fin. And I remember every single trip. Like songs in a hymn book, they're all different.'

'I suppose they are.'

'You'd think maybe one year would begin to seem like all the others after thirty-odd years, but I can recall every detail of every one like it was the last.' His pause was laden. 'I remember the year you came with us as if it was yesterday.' He hesitated, seeming to consider his words carefully. 'But outside of those of us who were there, it's never been discussed.'

Fin shuffled uncomfortably. 'It was hardly a secret, Gigs.'

Gigs's head swivelled again in his direction, the same look in his eyes. Searching. And then he said, 'Just so you know, Fin. It's an unwritten rule. Whatever happens on the rock stays on the rock. Always did, always will.'

ELEVEN

The news that Artair and I were to join that year's team going out to An Sgeir ruined my last summer on the island. It came out of the blue, literally, and sent me into a deep, black depression.

There were only six weeks left before I was due to leave for university in Glasgow, and I wanted to spend them as I had the last two. Marsaili and I had passed nearly every day together since our encounter on Eilean Beag. I had begun to lose count of the number of times we had made love. Sometimes with the ferocity and passion of people who fear they might never have the chance again – it had been like that the time we made love in the barn, high up among the bales, where Marsaili had stolen that first kiss all those years before. Other times with a slow, languid indulgence, as if we believed that these idyllic days of summer, sun and sex would never end.

It did not seem possible, then, that they would. Marsaili, too, had been accepted for Glasgow University, and four more years together stretched ahead of us. We had gone to Glasgow the previous week to search for digs. I told my aunt that I was going with Donald, not that she would have cared much who I went with. Marsaili's folks thought she was going with a group of schoolfriends. We shared a B & B for two nights, lying in together all morning, wrapped around each other until the landlady threw us out. We imagined how each and every day would be like this once we started university, sharing the same bed, making love every night. Such happiness seemed almost impossible. Of course, I know now that it was.

We trailed around the West End for hours, following up ads in the paper, working through a list we had been given by the university, checking out tip-offs from other students encountered in the bars of Byres Road the previous night. We struck lucky. A room of our own in a large Edwardian flat in Highburgh Road, sharing with six others. First floor, red sandstone tenement, stained glass, wood panelling. I had never seen anything like it. It was all so extraordinarily exotic. Late-opening pubs; Chinese, Italian, Indian restaurants; delicatessens open till midnight; mini-markets open twenty-four hours; shops, pubs, restaurants open on a Sunday. It hardly seemed credible. I could imagine how deliciously illicit it would feel to buy a Sunday newspaper on a Sunday and read it over a pint in a pub. Back then, back on the island, you never saw a Sunday newspaper before Monday.

When we returned to Lewis the idyll continued, although now there was an edge of impatience to it.

While both of us would have been happy for the summer to last for ever, we could hardly wait for the time to come when we would leave for Glasgow. Life's great adventure lay ahead of us and we were almost wishing away our youth in our haste to embark upon it.

The night before I received the news about An Sgeir, Marsaili and I went down to the beach at Port of Ness. We picked our way in the dark through the rocks at the south end of it, to a slab of black gneiss worn smooth by aeons, hidden away from the rest of the world by layers of rock that appeared to have been cut into giant slices, stood on end, then tipped over to lie in skewed stacks. Cliffs rose up above us to a night sky of infinite possibilities. The tide was out, but we could hear the sea breathing gently on the shore. A warm breeze rattled the sun-dried heather that grew in ragged, earthy clumps on shelves and ledges in the cliff. We laid out the sleeping bag we had brought with us and stripped naked to lie on it in the starlight and make love in long, slow strokes, in time with the beat of the ocean, in harmony with the night. It was the last time there was real love between us, and its sweet intensity was nearly overpowering, leaving us both limp and breathless. Afterwards we slipped naked over the rocks to the hard flat sand left by the receding tide, and ran across it to where the water spilled moonlight upon the shore, and we high-danced through the breaking waves, hand-in-hand, shrieking as the cold water burned our skin.

When we got back to the sleeping bag, we rubbed each other down and got dressed, chittering in the cold. I took Marsaili's head in my hands, her tangle of golden hair still dripping, and gave her a long, slow kiss. When we broke apart I looked deep into her eyes and frowned, noticing for the first time that there was something missing.

'Whatever happened to your glasses?'

She smiled. 'I got contacts.'

It is hard to remember now just why I reacted so violently against the notion of joining the trip to An Sgeir to harvest the guga, although I can think of many reasons why I would not have wanted to go.

I was not a particularly physical boy, and I knew that life on An Sgeir would be unremittingly hard, physically gruelling, full of danger and discomfort.

I did not relish the prospect of slaughtering two thousand birds. Like most of my peers, I enjoyed the taste of the guga, but had no desire to see how it reached my plate.

It would mean being separated from Marsaili for two whole weeks, or even longer. Sometimes the weather kept the hunters trapped on the rock for several more days than they intended.

But there was more to it than that. It seemed somehow like falling back into that black hole from which I had only just emerged. I can't really explain why. It's just how it was.

I had gone down to Artair's to see how his mother was

doing. I had seen very little of him in the last few weeks. And I found him sitting on an old tractor tyre out by the peat stack staring across the Minch towards the mainland. I hadn't noticed before, but the mountains of Sutherland stood sharp and clear against the pastel blue of the sky, and I knew then that the weather was about to break. From the look on Artair's face I feared the worst for his mother. I sat on the tyre beside him.

'How's your mum?'

He turned and gave me a long, vacant look, as if he were staring clean through me.

'Artair . . . ?'

'What?' It was as though he had just woken up.

'How's your mum?'

He shrugged dismissively. 'Oh, she's okay. Better than she was.'

'That's good.' I waited, and when he said no more, added, 'So what's wrong?'

He took his puffer from his pocket, clutching it in that distinctive way he had, half-covering his face, pressing down on the silver cartridge and sucking on the nozzle. But he had no time to tell me before I heard a door closing behind us and his dad's voice calling from the step. 'Fin, has Artair told you the good news yet?'

I turned as Mr Macinnes approached. 'What news?'

'There are two vacancies on the trip to An Sgeir this year. I've persuaded Gigs MacAulay that you two should come with us.'

If he had slapped my face with all the power he possessed, I doubt if I could have been more stunned. I didn't know what to say.

Mr Macinnes's smile faded. 'Well, you don't look too pleased about it.' He glanced at his son and sighed. 'Just like Artair.' And he shook his head in vigorous irritation. 'I don't understand you boys. Have you any idea what an honour it is to be allowed to go out to the rock? It's a time of great comradeship and togetherness. You'll go out there as boys and come back as men.'

'I don't want to go,' I said.

'Don't be ridiculous, Fin!' Artair's dad was utterly dismissive. 'The village elders have agreed, the team has accepted you. Of course you're going. What kind of fool would I look if you cried off now? I went out on a limb to get you boys accepted. So, you'll go. And that's that.' He turned and stormed off towards the house.

Artair just looked at me, and there were no words needed to know that we shared the same feelings. Neither of us wanted to hang around, in case Mr Macinnes came out again, so we headed off up the road out of the village towards my aunt's house, and the tiny harbour below it. It was a favourite spot, usually quiet, punts pulled up along one side of the steep slipway, the small jetty at the foot of it overlooking the clear green waters below the fold of cliffs that protected the harbour. We sat together on the edge of the jetty by the winching angle and watched the movement of the water distort the crabs in their creels, kept there underwater by the crabbers until the price picked up. I don't know how long we sat in silence, just as we had after my tutoring sessions, listening to the rise and fall of the water sucking at the rocks that rose out of it, black and glistening, and the plaintive cries of the gulls on the clifftops. But, finally, I said, 'I'm not going.'

Artair turned to me, a look of pain in his eyes. 'You can't leave me to go on my own, Fin.'

I shook my head. 'I'm sorry, Artair, that's up to you. But I'm not going, and no one can make me.'

If I had expected an ally in Marsaili, then I was to be sorely disappointed.

'Why *don't* you want to go?'

'I just don't.'

'Well, that's not exactly a reason, is it?

I hated the way Marsaili always applied logic to situations that were purely emotional. The fact that I didn't want to go should have been reason enough. 'I don't need a reason.'

We were in the barn, high up among the bales. There were blankets and a stash of beer, and we were expecting to make love again that night, haymites or not.

'There are boys your age all over Ness who would kill for the chance to go out to the rock,' she said. 'The one thing everyone has for those guys is respect.'

'Yeh, sure. Killing a lot of defenceless birds is a great way of earning respect.'

239

'Are you scared?'

I hotly denied it. 'No, I'm not scared!' Although that was not, perhaps, entirely true.

'It's what people will think.'

'I don't care what people think. I'm not going and that's an end of it.'

There was an odd mix of sympathy and frustration in her eyes – sympathy, I think, at the clear strength of my feeling, frustration at my refusal to say why. She shook her head gently. 'Artair's dad . . .'

'. . . is not my father.' I cut her off. 'He can't make me go. I'll find Gigs and tell him myself.' I stood up, and she quickly grabbed my hand.

'Fin, don't. Please, sit down. Let's talk about it.'

'There's nothing to talk about.' The trip was only a matter of days away. I had thought to get moral support from Marsaili, to bolster me in a decision which would have repercussions. I knew what people would say. I knew that the other kids would whisper behind their hands that I was a coward, that I was betraying a proud tradition. If you had been accepted for An Sgeir, you had to have a damned good reason for backing out. But I didn't care. I was leaving the island, escaping the claustrophobia of village life, the petulance and pettiness, the harbouring of grudges. I didn't need a reason. But obviously Marsaili thought I did. I headed towards the gap in the bales, then stopped suddenly, struck by a thought. I turned. 'Do *you* think I'm scared?'

She hesitated a little too long before replying. 'I don't know. I only know that you're behaving very strangely.'

Which tipped me over the edge. 'Well, fuck you, then.' And I jumped down to the lower bales and hurried out of the barn into the gathering twilight.

Gigs's croft was one of several on the lower slopes below Crobost, a narrow strip of land running down to the cliffs. He kept sheep and hens, and a couple of cows, and planted root vegetables and barley. He did a bit of fishing, too, though more for personal consumption than any kind of commerce, and would not have made ends meet had it not been for his wife's part-time job as a waitress at a hotel in Stornoway.

Darkness had fallen by the time I got back from Mealanais, and I sat up on the hill above the MacAulay crofthouse looking down on the single light shining out from the kitchen window. It fell in a long slab across the yard, and I saw a cat moving through it, stalking something in the dark. Someone with a sledgehammer was trapped inside my chest and trying to break out. I felt physically sick.

There was still light in the sky away to the west, long, pale strips of it between lines of purple-grey cloud. No red in it whatsoever, which was not a good sign. I turned and watched the light as it faded and felt cold for the first time in weeks. The wind had turned. The warm, almost balmy south-westerly had swung around and carried on its edge now a chill straight down from the Arctic. The pace of the wind was picking up, and I could hear it whistling through the dry grasses. Change was on the way. When I looked down towards the crofthouse again, I could see the shadow of a figure in the kitchen window. It was Gigs. He was washing dishes at the sink. There was no car in the drive, which meant his wife was not yet back from town. I closed my eyes and clenched my fists and made my decision.

It took me only a few minutes to get down the hill to the croft, but as I reached the road a pair of car head-lights swung up suddenly over the rise and raked across the moor in my direction. I ducked down by the fence, crouching amongst the reeds, and watched as the car turned into the drive and parked outside the crofthouse. Gigs's wife got out. She was young, maybe twenty-five. A pretty girl, still in her white blouse and black skirt. She looked tired, a drag in her gait, as she pushed open the kitchen door. Through the window I saw Gigs taking her in his arms and giving her a long hug and then a kiss. My disappointment was acute. This was not something I could discuss with Gigs when his wife was around. I stood up from the long grass, leaped over the fence and pushed my hands deep into my pockets, heading off then towards the bothan on the Habost road.

There were very few bothans still operating after the big crackdown by the police. I never really saw what the problem was. They might have been unlicensed, but they were never run for profit. They were just places where men gathered together for a drink. But even though they were illegal, I was still underage, and would not be allowed in. There was an odd morality that still operated. Which did not mean, however, that I could not get my hands on a drink. I found a small gathering of my contemporaries in the stone shed behind the bothan, sitting around on the skeletons of old agricultural machinery, tipping cans of beer into their faces. For cash and cigarettes, some of the older boys would slip out from time to time with drink for the kids in the shed, turning it into a kind of baby bothan. Somebody had acquired half a dozen six-packs, and the air was thick with the smell of dope, and manure from the neighbouring byre. A tilley lamp hung from the rafters, so low that you would bang your head on it if you did not take care.

Seonaidh was there, and Iain, and some other boys I knew from school. I was seriously depressed by now, and intent only on getting drunk. I began pouring beer down my throat like there was no tomorrow. Of course, they had heard that Artair and I were going out to the rock. Word, in Ness, spreads like fire on a dry peat moor, fanned by the winds of speculation and rumour.

'You lucky bastard,' Seonaidh said. 'My dad was trying to get me on the trip this year.'

'I'll swap you.'

Seonaidh pulled a face. 'Aye, right.' Naturally, he thought I was joking. I could have made a necklace from the eye teeth everyone there that night would have given to take my place on the team. The irony was, they could have had it for nothing. Any one of them. Of course, I couldn't tell them that. They would never have taken me seriously or, if they had, they'd have thought I was insane. As it was, my lack of enthusiasm seemed to signal to them that I was merely playing it cool. Their jealousy was hard to take. And so I just drank. And drank.

I didn't hear Angel coming in. He was older than us, and he'd been drinking in the bothan most of the night. He'd brought out some beers in return for a joint. 'Well, well, if it isn't orphan boy,' he said when he saw me. His face was round and yellow in the light of the tilley lamp and floated through the dark of the shed like some luminous balloon. 'You'd better get as much drink down you as you can, son, 'cos you'll get none out on An Sgeir. Gigs is unre-fucking-lenting about that. No alcohol on the rock. Smuggle out so much as a dram and he'll throw you off the fucking cliff.' Someone handed him a rolled-up joint and he lit it, pulling the smoke deep into his lungs and holding it there. When, finally, he blew it out he said, 'You know I'm the cook this year?' I didn't. I knew he'd been out before, and that his father, Murdo Dubh, had been the cook for years. But I also knew that his father had been killed in an accident on a trawler during a stormy February that year. I suppose, if I'd thought about it, it would have been logical for Angel to follow in his father's footsteps. It's what men in Ness had done for generations. 'Don't worry,' Angel said, 'I'll make sure you get your fair share of earywigs in your bread.'

After he'd gone, another joint was lit and handed around. By now, I was feeling sick, and after a couple of drags, the suffocating claustrophobia of the shed began spinning my world around and around. 'I've got to go.' I pushed out of the door into the cold night air and immediately threw up in the yard. I leaned against the wall, pressing my face against the cool stone, wondering how on earth I was going to get myself home.

The world seemed to pass me by in a blur. I have no idea how I even managed to get as far as the Crobost road. The lights of a large vehicle caught me full-beam, and I froze like a rabbit, wobbling on the verge until it passed with a whump of air that knocked me over into the ditch. It might not have rained in weeks, but the residual water held by the peat still drained in a thick, brown sludge into the bottom of the ditch. It covered me like slurry, clinging to my clothes, running down my face. I gasped and cursed and pulled myself out to roll over on to the spiny verge. I lay there for what seemed like hours, although it was probably only minutes. But it was long enough for that cold edge on the fresh north wind to chill me through. I struggled on to my hands and knees, teeth chattering now, and looked up as another vehicle came down the road towards me, illuminating my misery in the glare of its lights. As it approached, I turned my head away and shut my eyes. The car stopped, and I heard a door opening, and then a voice. 'In the name of God, son, what are you doing there?' Big hands lifted me almost bodily to my feet, and I found myself looking up into Gigs MacAulay's frowning countenance. He took his forearm across my face to wipe the mud off on the sleeve of his overalls. 'Fin Macleod,' he said, recognizing me finally. He sniffed the alcohol on my breath. 'For Heaven's sake, son, you can't go home in this state!'

It took me some time to warm up again, huddled on a chair by the peat fire, a blanket over my shoulders, a mug of hot tea cupped in my hands. There was still a tremor ran through me each time I took a sip from it. The mud had dried now and was caked and cracking like shite on my skin and my clothes. God knows what I must have looked like. Gigs had made me leave my trainers at the door, but there was still a trail of dried mud between it and the fire. Gigs sat in his chair on the other side of the hearth and watched me carefully. He smoked an old, blackened pipe, and blue smoke curled from it into the light of the oil lamp on the table. It smelled sweet as a nut, a pitch higher than the toasty scent of the peat. His wife had taken a damp towel to my face and hands before brewing the tea and then, on some unspoken signal, retired to bed.

'Well, Fin,' Gigs said at last, 'I hope this is you getting it out of your system before you go out to the rock.'

'I'm not going,' I said in a voice so small it was little

more than a whisper. I was still drunk, I suppose, but the shock of falling in the ditch had sobered me up a little, and the tea was helping, too.

Gigs did not react. He puffed gently on the stem of his pipe and watched me speculatively. 'Why not?'

I have no recollection now of what I said to him that night, how it was that I expressed those feelings of deep, dark dread that the very thought of going out to the rock had aroused in me. I suppose, like everyone else, he must have assumed that it was fear, pure and simple. But while others might have displayed contempt for my cowardice, Gigs appeared to understand in a way that seemed to lift that enormous weight which had been bearing down on me from the moment Artair's dad had given me the news. He leaned towards me across the fire, holding me steady in the gaze of those Celtic blue eyes of his, his pipe smoking gently in his hand. 'We are not twelve individuals out there, Fin. We are twelve together. We are a team. Each one of us is reliant on the other and supports the other. It's hard, aye. It's fucking hard, boy. And it's dangerous. I don't pretend otherwise. And the Lord will test us to the very edge of our endurance. But you'll be richer for it, and you'll be truer to yourself. Because you'll know yourself in a way that you never have before, and maybe never will again. And you'll feel that connection that we all feel with every one of those men who've been out there before us, reaching back through the centuries, joining hands with our ancestors, sleeping in the places they have slept, building cairns by the cairns they have left.' He took a long pause, sucking on his pipe, allowing the smoke to eddy around his lips and nostrils, rising into the stillness in blue wreaths around his head. 'Whatever your blackest fear, Fin. Whatever your greatest weakness. These are things you must face up to. Things you must confront, or you'll spend the rest of your life regretting it.'

And so with a heart full of dread I went on the trip to An Sgeir that year, although I wish, today, with every fibre of my being that I had not.

In the days before we left, I kept myself to myself. The wind had swung further round, to the north-east, and a storm that seemed to mark the end of summer hammered the island for two days. Force-ten winds blew the rain in horizontally off the Minch, and the land drank it thirstily. I had not made up with Marsaili after our last exchange in the barn, and I avoided going to Mealanais. I stayed indoors, reading in my room, listening to the rain battering against the windows and the wind lifting tiles on the roof. On the Tuesday night Artair came to the door to say that we were leaving for the rock the next day.

I couldn't believe it. 'But the weather's coming from the north-east. They always say you can't land on the rock if there's any kind of easterly.'

Artair said, 'There's a new front coming in. A north-westerly. Gigs thinks we've got a twenty-four-hour window for getting on to the rock. So we go tomorrow night. We've to load the trawler at the Port tomorrow afternoon.' He didn't seem any happier about it than I was. He sat on the edge of my bed in silence for a long time. Then he said, 'So you're going?'

I couldn't even bring myself to speak. I acknowledged with a tiny nod of my head.

'Thanks,' he said. As if somehow I was doing it for him.

It took several hours the next day to load the *Purple Isle* berthed at the breakwater quay at Port of Ness. All the supplies required to maintain twelve men on a rock in the middle of the ocean for a fortnight. There was no natural spring on An Sgeir, so all of our water was taken in old beer casks. We had boxes and boxes of food, two tons of pickling salt in sacks, tools, waterproofs, mattresses to sleep on, a fifteen-foot aerial lashed together to pick up a signal for the radio. And, of course, the peat for the fires that would warm us and feed us. The hard graft involved in passing everything from the quay to the trawler and stowing it in the hold took my mind off our imminent departure. Although the storm had abated, there was still a heavy swell, and the trawler rose and fell against the harbour wall, making the transfer of supplies a difficult and sometimes perilous task. We got soaked, too, as the sea broke again and again over the wall, sending spray cascading down upon us as we worked. The previous day waves had been smashing into the breakwater and exploding fifty feet into the air, sending their spume arcing over the harbour to obliterate it from view at each pulse of the ocean.

We left on the midnight tide, diesel engines thudding as we slipped out into the bay from the relative shelter of the harbour, facing into the huge swell, waves breaking over the bow to pour in foaming rivers across the deck. It seemed no time at all until the lights of Ness were swallowed by the night as we yawed and pitched into open seas beyond the Butt of Lewis. The last thing to vanish was the comforting flash of the lighthouse on the clifftop at the Butt, and when that was gone there was only the ocean. Untold stormy miles of it. If we missed the rock the next stop would be the Arctic. I gazed out into the blackness in what I can only describe as abject terror. Whatever my greatest fear, I figured I was facing it right now. Gigs tugged on my oilskins and told me to go below. There was a berth reserved for Artair and me and we should get some sleep. The first day and the last on the rock, he said, were always the hardest.

I don't know how I slept, squeezed into that narrow berth right up on the port side of the bow, shivering and wet and miserable. But I did. We had crashed through eight hours of mountainous seas to cover fifty miles across some of the most notorious waters in the world, and I had slept through it all. I think it was the change in the pitch of the engines that wakened me. Artair was already scrambling up the ladder to the galley. I wiped the sleep from my eyes and climbed out to drag on my boots and my oilskins, and then follow him up on deck. It was broad daylight, the sky above us torn and shredded by the wind, periodically obscured by the squally showers of fine rain that blew in our faces.

'Jesus,' I said, 'what's that stink?' It was a high-pitched acrid stench, a porridge of shite and ammonia.

'That's the guano, orphan boy.' Angel grinned at me. He actually seemed to be enjoying this. 'Ten thousand years of accumulated bird shite. Get used to it. You're going to be living with it for the next two weeks.'

That was how we knew we were close to the rock. The stink of bird shit. We couldn't see it yet, but we knew it was there. The *Purple Isle* had slowed to only a few knots. The swell of the ocean had dropped dramatically, and we were going with it now rather than fighting it.

'There she is!' someone shouted, and I peered through the mist and rain to catch my first sight of this legendary place. And there she was. Three hundred feet of sheer black cliff streaked with white, rising straight out of the ocean in front of us. Almost in that same moment, as the mist cleared, splinters of sunlight fell through fissures in the cloud, and the glistening rock was thrown into an instant projection of sharply contrasting light and shade. I saw what looked like snow blowing in a steady stream from the peak before I realized that the snowflakes were birds. Fabulous white birds with blue-black wingtips and yellow heads, a wingspan of nearly two metres. Gannets. Thousands of them, filling the sky, turning in the light, riding turbulent currents of air. This was one of the world's most important surviving gannet colonies, and these extraordinary birds returned in ever-increasing numbers year after year to lay their eggs and raise their chicks in this forbidding place. And that in spite of the annual harvest by the men of Crobost, and the two thousand chicks we were about to take from their nests this year again.

An Sgeir lay along a line that ran approximately south-east to north-west. The towering spine of the rock dropped from its highest point in the south to a bleached curve of two-hundred-foot cliffs at the north end, like a shoulder set against the prevailing weather of lashing gales and monstrous seas that rose out of the south-west to smash upon its stubborn gneiss. Three promontories on its west side jutted into the ocean, water breaking white and foaming furiously in rings all around them as they dipped down into undersea ravines.

The nearest rib of rock was called Lighthouse Promontory, because of the automatic lighthouse built at its conjunction with the rest of the island – the highest point of which loomed over us as we approached. Beyond it, the second and longest of the promontories formed an inlet that cut deep into the heart of the island, open to the east, but providing shelter from the west and the north. It was the only place on An Sgeir where it was possible to land our supplies. Here, time and the relentless assault of the elements had carved out caves in the rock so deep that finally they had cut clean through to the sheer cliffs at the far side. It was possible, Gigs said, to paddle through them in a punt, or a rubber dinghy, great natural cathedrals rising forty and fifty feet into blackness, before emerging on the other side of the island. But only ever when the sea was flat calm, which was almost never.

An Sgeir was barely half a mile long, its vertebral column little more than a hundred yards across. There was no soil here, no grassy banks or level land, no beaches. Just shit-covered rock rising straight out of the sea. I could hardly have imagined anything more inhospitable.

The skipper steered the *Purple Isle* gently into the inlet they called Gleann an Uisge Dubh, Black Water Creek, and dropped anchor in the bay, a great rattling of rusted chain as it left its locker. With the cutting of the engines, I became aware for the first time of the noise of the birds, a deafening cacophony of screeching, calling, chattering creatures that filled the air along with the stink of guano. Everywhere you looked, on every ledge and stack and crack in the rock, birds sat in nests or huddled in groups. Gannets and guillemots and kittiwakes and fulmar petrels. The bay around us was alive with young shags, their long, snakelike necks dipping in and out of the water in search of fish. It was extraordinary to think that a place so hostile and exposed could play host to so much life. Gigs slapped my back. 'Come on, son, we've got work to do.'

A punt was lowered on to the gentle swell, and we began the process of transferring our supplies from boat to rock. I went out with the first load, Gigs gunning the outboard and motoring us in to the landing place, cutting the motor at the last moment and turning broadside to allow the swell to lift us gently up against the rock. It was my job to jump out with the rope on to a ledge no more than two feet wide and secure it to a large metal ring set into the stone. I nearly went on my arse as my feet slithered under me on a slimy skin of sulphur lichens. But I kept my balance and slipped the rope through the ring. The punt was secured and we began unloading. We balanced boxes and kegs and sacks precariously on ledges and outcrops until it looked as if everything we had brought with us had been dropped from a great height on to the lower reaches of the cliffs. With each return of the boat, more of the team arrived and leapt ashore. Just beyond our landing point, the rock folded away into one of its cathedral caves. It was dark and creepy, with the eerie sound of water sucking on rock echoing from somewhere deep within its blackness like the rasping breath of some living creature. It was easy to imagine how legends of sea monsters and dragons had grown out of such places.

After four hours the last of the supplies was brought

ashore, and the rain began again, misty wet sheets of it, soaking everything, making every algae-covered surface of every rock treacherous underfoot. The last thing we took on to the island was a small rubber dinghy, which four of the team dragged up the slope to secure about fifty feet above the bay. It was to be used for emergencies, although I could not think what kind of emergency would make me want to put to sea in it. To my astonishment, I saw that Angel had crouched down in a shallow cleft in the cliff, and using his body as shelter had built a small fire of peats. He had a kettle close to boiling on it. The *Purple Isle* blew her foghorn out in the bay, and I turned to watch her pull anchor and head towards the open sea. It was a dreadful feeling watching her slip away like that, the skipper's mate waving from the stern as she went. She was our only link with home, our only way back. And she was gone, and we were left here on our own on this barren lump of rock fifty miles from the nearest landfall. For better or worse, I was here, and all that remained now was to get on with it.

Miraculously, Angel was now passing around mugs of hot tea. Tins of sandwiches were opened, and we crouched there on the rock, the smell of peat smoke in our nostrils, the sea snapping at our feet, and drank to warm ourselves, and ate to restore our energy. For now, all these boxes and barrels and sacks had to be man-handled two hundred and fifty feet to the top of the island.

What I had not expected was the ingenuity of the guga hunters. On some previous expedition, they had brought out wooden planking and constructed a chute, two feet wide and nearly two hundred feet long. It was built in ten-foot sections, which they wrapped in tarpaulin and stored on the rock for each successive year. Piece by piece the sections were retrieved and slotted together, braced against the rock by stout legs and stays. It looked like one of the old wooden flumes you would see in black-and-white photographs from the goldrush days of the Klondike. A dolly on castors came thundering down from the top at the end of a length of rope, and the process of hauling up kegs and sacks and rolled-up mattresses began. Smaller boxes were passed hand to hand in a chain of men all the way up to the top of the rise. Artair and I passed boxes between us in silence, and then up the chain to Mr Macinnes, who kept up a constant commentary, explaining how the chute would be kept in place for the two weeks we were on the rock, and used at the end of it to slide the gugas – plucked, singed, gutted and cured – one by one to the boat below. All two thousand of them. I could not begin to imagine how we could kill and process so many birds in just fourteen days.

It was mid-afternoon by the time we had transferred all our supplies to the top of the rock, and Artair and I climbed our way wearily up to join the others. There we saw for the first time, crouched among the rocks and the boulders, the remains of an old blackhouse, built more than two centuries before, and maintained each year by the guga hunters to provide their shelter. It comprised just four walls, and the sun- and salt-bleached struts of a non-existent roof. I could not believe that this was to be our home for the next two weeks.

Mr Macinnes must have seen our faces. He grinned. 'Don't worry, boys. In an hour we'll have her transformed. She'll be a lot cosier than she looks now.' In fact the transformation took less than an hour. To reach the blackhouse we had to stumble across the chaos of rocks on the top of the island, slipping and sliding in the spinach of lichen, guano and mud that covered them, trying to avoid the nesting fulmar petrels tucked into nearly every crevice. The whole crown of the rock seemed alive with birds, nests woven from frayed scraps of coloured string, the debris of broken and discarded fishing nets scavenged from the sea. Green, orange, blue. Entirely incongruous in this most primeval of places. As we blundered among them it was impossible to escape the vomit of the fledgling petrel chicks, an involuntary response to our sudden and unexpected presence. Their vile green bile spattered over our boots and oilskins as we passed, the stink of it almost as bad as the shite that coated every treacherous surface.

Within the walls of the blackhouse, great sheets of corrugated iron wrapped in tarpaulin were recovered and unwrapped, and we set about nailing them in place between the angled beams of the roof. Then we threw the tarpaulins over them, and fishing net weighed down by boulders that were left to hang all around the walls. Now our blackhouse was weathertight and waterproof. Inside was dark and damp, the smell of guano almost overwhelming. The floor was strewn with discarded nesting materials, and our first task was to clear it out, and remove the nests built into every nook and cranny of wall space, carefully re-siting them somewhere out among the rocks. Half a dozen peat fires were lit in open-hearthed barrels to dry out rain-soaked walls, and we transferred all our supplies into a room at the far end of the blackhouse where, in a traditional home, the animals would have been kept.

Thick, choking smoke quickly filled the place, a fumigation, driving out the smell of shit, and forcing streams of earwigs out from every crack and crevice in the walls. Our eyes were streaming. Artair dashed outside, airways reacting to the smoke. He was gasping for breath. I followed him out to find him sucking desperately on his puffer, panic subsiding as his tubes reopened and oxygen flooded his lungs.

Gigs said, 'Go and make yourself familiar with the rock, boys. There's nothing more you can do here just now. We'll give you a shout when grub's up.'

And so, with the wind whipping around our legs, and the rain running in sheets off our oilskins, we made our way slowly and carefully across the rock, heading north to the third promontory, a huge arc of smooth rock almost severed from the mother island by a deep gully.

We had seen the stacks of cairns there, silhouetted against the grey sky, piles of stones laid meticulously one on the other to create columns three feet high and more, like gravestones. Out there on the promontory, next to the cairns, we found the remains of a small beehive-like dwelling, its roof long since caved in. We found flat rocks to sit on and with some difficulty lit ourselves cigarettes. Still, it seemed, there was nothing for us to say to each other. So we sat in silence and looked back across the length of An Sgeir. We had a marvellous view of the rock from here, rising up to its peak at the lighthouse, a short, squat, concrete structure with a maintenance hatch, and a strangely structured glass roof to protect the light. Seabirds gathered around it in their thousands. Next to it was the only flat and level place on the island. A square of concrete laid into the rock to provide a landing pad for the helicopters that brought out maintenance crews twice a year. We could see the ocean all around us, grey-green and leaden, breaking against the rock in wreaths of creamy foam, rising and falling into a distance obscured by rain. Despite the presence of ten other men on the island, and my best friend sitting beside me, I cannot ever remember feeling so alone. Depression fell over me like a shroud.

In the distance, we saw a figure approaching across the rock. As he got nearer we realized it was Artair's dad. He called and waved and began climbing up towards us. Above the sound of wind and rain battering my hood I heard Artair say, 'Why the fuck can't he just leave us alone!' I turned to see if the remark had been directed to me. But he was staring straight ahead at his approaching father. I was startled. I had never heard Artair speak like that about his dad before.

'You shouldn't smoke, Artair,' were Mr Macinnes's first words when he reached us. 'Not with your condition.' Artair said nothing, but continued smoking all the same. Mr Macinnes sat down beside us. 'You know the story behind the ruined dwelling?' He pointed to the collapsed beehive. We shook our heads. 'It's the remains of a twelfth-century monastic cell inhabited, some say, by St Ronan's sister, Bruinhilda. There's another just like it on a rock called Sula Sgeir ten miles or so west of here, close to North Rona. Legend has it that her remains were found in one of them, whether or not it was here or on Sula Sgeir I don't know. But her bones were bleached as white as driftwood by the elements, and there was a cormorant nesting in her ribcage.' He shook his head. 'Hard to believe that anyone could live out here on their own.'

'Who built the cairns?' I asked. From our position I could see now that there were dozens and dozens of them, stretched across the curve of the promontory like a cemetery.

'The guga hunters,' Mr Macinnes said. 'Every one of us has our cairn. Each year we add another stone, and when we have been for the last time, they are the reminder to all those who follow that we have been before.'

A shout from the direction of the blackhouse drew our attention, and we saw someone waving us back.

'They must be ready for us to eat,' Mr Macinnes said.

By the time we got to the blackhouse, there was smoke billowing out of the hole in the roof left for its escape. The interior was surprisingly warm now, and less smoky than it had been. Angel had his cooking fire burning in an open keg in the middle of the floor, a pot hanging over it from a chain in the roof, a mesh grill set over the flames for making toast, a large frying pan bubbling with oil set on top of it. Gone was the stink of guano and bird vomit, to be replaced by the smell of kippers cooking in the pan. There were potatoes boiling in the pot, and Angel had made a stack of smoky toast for us to mop up the juices. There were two big pots of tea to wash it all down.

Three-foot-wide stone ledges all around the walls had been covered with tarpaulins and laid with the big mattresses we had dragged up the rocks earlier in the day. Our beds. By the flickering yellow light of candles set at intervals around the room, I could see beetles and earwigs crawling all over them. I shuddered at the thought of spending one night here, let alone fourteen. Or more.

Before we ate, we washed our hands in water preserved from last year's trip, a brown, cloudy soup in a cut-down keg, and then gathered around the fire, squatting on the floor, as Gigs opened his bible and read to us from it in Gaelic. I barely listened to the monotonous drone of his voice. For some reason I was filled with a sense of dread, of anticipation, premonition perhaps. Somewhere, programmed into the time–space continuum, it may be that deep down I knew what was going to happen. I began shaking, and when Gigs had finished reading, ate my fish with trembling fingers.

I don't remember there being much talk around the fire that first night. We were a solemn group, battered and bruised by the weather, calling on reserves of fortitude and stamina to face the days ahead. We could hear the wind howling around our ancient stone shelter, and the rain hammering on the roof. I don't even remember going to bed, but I can recall very clearly lying on a damp mattress on that unyielding stone shelf, fully dressed and wrapped in blankets, wishing that I was young enough to weep with impunity. But big boys don't cry. So I held my peace and drifted away on the tide of a shallow, troubled sleep.

I felt better the next day. It's amazing what a few hours' sleep can do to restore a broken spirit. Sunshine slanted through the tarpaulin draped across the doorway, blue peat smoke hanging in the light. I tumbled out of bed, blinking matter from my eyes, and squeezed into the circle of men gathered around the fire. The warmth of the glowing peats was almost soporific. Someone spooned me out a bowl of porridge and I dunked thick chunks of smoky toast into the hot goo of it and filled my mouth. I poured scalding tea into my mug and thought I had never tasted anything so good. I guess the first night is the worst, like maybe your first night in a prison. After that, you know the worst, and you just get on with it.

A hush fell on the group as Gigs opened his bible, a well-worn tome scarred and tashed from constant use. His voice rose and fell in soft Gaelic incantations as he read from it and we listened in the solemn first light of the day. 'Right, then,' he said as he closed it. And it was his signal, or so I thought, that the first killing spree of the trip was to begin. 'Fin, Donnie, Pluto, you're with me.' I felt a great sense of relief that I would be with Gigs that first day. Artair was with another team. I tried to catch his eye across the fire and give him a smile of encouragement, but he wasn't looking my way.

I had expected that we would make straight for the cliffs to begin the harvest, but in fact we spent most of the morning constructing a bizarre network of struts and cables across the top of the rock, from the killing grounds to the processing areas up by the cairns and down again to the top end of the chute. These aerial wireways, in hundred-metre lengths, were mounted on crude wooden tripods and cranked up to the correct tension with a jockey-winch. Operated by pulleys, this ingenious network would allow sacks of dead birds, suspended from hooks, to be whizzed across the island from one place to the next with minimum effort. Everything was dependent on the angle and tension of the cables, so that gravity would do most of the work, and Gigs was meticulous in getting each of these factors just right. Each bird weighed around nine pounds, and each sack carried ten birds. To have attempted to manhandle such cumbersome loads across this treacherous and uneven rocky moonscape would have been madness. And yet, before Gigs came up with his idea for pulleys and cables, that is just what the guga hunters must have done for all the centuries they had been coming here.

At midday, we were out near Lighthouse Promontory when I saw Angel making his way over the rock towards us, performing an extraordinary balancing act. In one hand he carried a large black kettle of hot tea, in the other, dangling from a plastic box of cake and sandwiches, were our mugs, tied by their handles to the ends of twelve lengths of string. Each day at noon, and at five, we would look for his lumbering form picking its way across the island with hot tea and sandwiches to keep us going. Much as I disliked Angel Macritchie, I had no complaints about his food. He was punctilious in everything he did, as all the veterans said his father was before him. He had something to live up to, and he made certain that he did. And I suppose that is why, although nobody liked him, he succeeded, at least, in earning their respect.

We sat around the lighthouse then, eating sandwiches and cake and washing it all down with mouthfuls of hot tea. Cigarettes were rolled and smoked, a comfortable silence among the group as sunlight flitted in and out of low, broken cloud, taking the cold edge off the wind that still blew out of the north-west. In a few minutes the slaughter would begin, and the taking of all those lives was, I think, the subject of quiet reflection. It is hard to start the killing, easier once it has begun.

We commenced among the colonies on the east-facing cliffs of the Lighthouse Promontory, two teams of four starting at either end and working towards each other in a pincer movement. A third team of three worked its way across the top. As soon as we climbed down on to the cliffs, the parent birds rose in their thousands from the nests, shrieking and wheeling overhead as the killing of their chicks got under way. It was like working in the midst of a snowstorm, the flashing white of gannet feather filling your eyes, your ears full of their anger and anguish and the beating of their wings against the wind. And you had to be careful, as you climbed level with the nests, that the chicks did not take your eye out, a reflex jab of the beak if you startled them.

Gigs led our group along ledges and cracks and shelves of rock, examining each nest for its contents. He carried a catching pole, more than six feet long with a sprung metal jaw at one end. He reached out with it to pluck the chicks from their nests, quickly passing them back to the second in the group. Donnie was a veteran of more than ten years, a quiet man probably well into his fifties, always with a cloth cap pulled down over his brow, silver whiskers bristling on a face ravaged by time and weather.

He carried a stout stick, and when a bird was swung round to him on the end of the pole he seized it and killed it with a single, well-practised blow. I was next in the chain. Gigs had decided to blood me in the truest sense of the word. I carried a machete, and it was my job to decapitate the birds and hand them back to Pluto, who arranged them in piles for us to collect on the return. At first I was sickened by my task, and slow at it. I was squeamish about the blood that ran over my hands and spattered my overalls. I felt warm splashes of it on my face. But they started coming so fast that I had to let go of my reserve, to free my mind of all thought and fall into a rhythm, both mechanical and mindless. Thousands of gannets and fulmars screamed and wheeled in endless eddies about our heads, and two hundred feet below the sea boiled and thrashed against the green collar of algae on the lowest rocks. Gradually my blue overalls turned black with blood.

At first I had thought that Gigs was selecting the chicks at random. Some he took, others he left in the nest. It was Donnie who explained to me that the fledgling gannet went through three stages of development. The downy young chicks of the first stage produce very little meat, and so Gigs would leave them to grow to adulthood. The slim, black, young birds at the third stage of development were harder to catch. It was the second-stage chicks that were the real prize, easily identified by the three remaining clumps of down on the head, back and legs. Fine and meaty and easy to catch. Gigs had years of practice in identifying them at a glance.

We moved across the cliff with astonishing speed, in a wave of killing, leaving piles of dead gugas in our wake. Until finally we met up with the second group. It had taken just over ten minutes, and Gigs signalled that the carnage was over for the day. And so we retraced our steps, carrying back as many gugas as we could, piling them up, and then forming a chain to pass them one by one to the top. There, the heap of dead birds harvested by the three groups mounted, and Gigs took out a pencil and a small notebook and carefully counted their number and noted it in his book. I looked back across the cliffs at where we had been, blood streaking red against the black, and realized that I had not even had time to be afraid. Only now did I become aware of how one slip, one careless move, would have led to almost instant death.

Gigs turned to me, and as if giving up some great secret handed down to him across generations, said simply, 'Well, Fin, that's what we do.'

'Why?' I said to him. 'Why do you do it?'

'It's the tradition,' Donnie volunteered. 'None of us wants be the one to break it.'

But Gigs shook his head. 'No. It's not the tradition. That might be a part of it, aye. But I'll tell you why I do it, boy. Because nobody else does it, anywhere in the world. Just us.'

Which, I supposed, made 'us' special in some way. Unique. I looked at the pile of dead birds on the rock and wondered if there was not, perhaps, some better way to be special.

We bagged the birds in hessian sacks, and I watched the strange spectacle of sack after sack swooping across the rock, dipping to a halt at the lowest point, and then being hauled on ropes up to the area by the cairns where eventually they would be plucked. There they were tipped out on to tarpaulins and left to dry in the wind.

I slept that night the sleep of the dead, and woke to find that the weather had changed again. Rain beat steadily against the rock on the leading edge of a blustering south-westerly, and it was mid-morning before an edgy Gigs decided that we could not afford to sit around any longer waiting for a break in the rain. So with silent resignation we got into our oilskins and headed out again on to the cliffs, with poles and sticks and machetes, feeling the icing of guano slippery beneath our boots as we worked our way through the colonies tucked away in the lower reaches of the Lighthouse Promontory.

The pile of birds grew, covered now to save them from a soaking. The process of plucking them did not begin until the rain was by. Which was not until the Sunday, but since the guga hunters would not work on the Sabbath, all we could do was remove the tarpaulins and let the sun and the wind labour at drying the birds while we took our leisure.

It was strange. During that whole two weeks on the rock, I was never once on the same team as Artair. Hardly ever saw him, in fact. It was almost as if they were keeping us apart, although I cannot imagine why. Even on the two Sundays I barely saw him. Or his dad. When I think back I can't really remember Mr Macinnes at all. But I suppose that wasn't really surprising. We were never on a team together, and the factory process of plucking, singeing, gutting and curing meant that groups of us worked on different parts of the process in different places at different times. The only time we were all together was when we ate, squeezed around the peats in the gloom of the blackhouse, too tired some nights even to talk. We were just faces in the firelight. It was not unheard-of for Gigs to insist that we went back out after our evening meal to catch up on that day's plucking. There were occasions when we were out there by the cairns until midnight, pulling out fistfuls of feathers by the light of a tilley. We had little inclination to talk, and not much to say if we did.

Still, it was odd that Artair and I did not get together on that first Sunday, even if just to share our misery in silence. I climbed down to a spot near where we had landed our supplies. It was more sheltered from the wind here, and seawater trapped in pools among the rocks warmed gently in the August sunshine. Several of the men who had been before sat around the pools with their boots and socks lined up along a ledge of rock, trousers rolled up to the knees, bare feet dangling in the tepid water. There was some idle banter and smoking of cigarettes, but the men seemed to clam up when I arrived, and so I didn't stay long. I climbed instead towards the top of the promontory where I found a slab of flat stone, angled towards the south, on which I could lie out in the sunshine and close my eyes, escaping, at least in my mind, to the summer idyll I had been forced to abandon so prematurely.

It was wonderful just to do nothing, simply to lie there and relax aching muscles and let the sun warm your bones. Later I went back to the blackhouse to drag out my mattress and try to get the dampness out of it, but it was so deep inside that it would have taken days of constant sun to dry it out completely.

All too soon our day of rest was over, and we were crawling back on to our shelves after an evening meal of bacon and eggs and fried bread, and Gigs's nightly reading from the Gaelic Bible. I caught Artair watching me from his mattress on the other side of the blackhouse. I smiled and called goodnight, but he just turned his face to the wall without a word.

We began the plucking on the Monday. The birds had dried off nicely in the Sabbath sunshine and we sat up amongst the cairns with the wind blowing around our ankles to do the job. It was a messy business. Gigs showed me how it was done. First he placed a bird between his knees and plucked the neck, leaving only a narrow collar of feathers. Then he turned to the breast, pulling out handfuls of feathers all the way down to the tail. He ripped off the new primaries from the upper wing and pinched off the leading edge quills. Then the bird was turned over and the back and the legs were plucked until only the finest white down remained. Gigs could pluck a guga in under three minutes. It took me more than twice that long.

It was relentlessly hard and competitive. We stopped every hour to count and call out the tally of how many birds we had plucked. Gigs had always plucked the most, Artair and myself the fewest. And then we would start again.

By the end of that first morning, my hands had all but seized up, every muscle and joint aching to the point where I could hardly hold a single feather between thumb and forefinger. And the feathers got everywhere. In your eyes and up your nose, in your ears and mouth. They clung to your hair and stuck to your clothes. At the height of the plucking, with the wind whistling around us, it was as if we were trapped in a blizzard of feathers and down. Artair's asthma reacted badly to it, and after two hours he could scarcely breathe. Gigs excused him from further plucking, and he was sent to light the fires for the singeing.

The fires were lit in low, metre-square chimney stacks built of loose stone in an area almost directly above where we had first come ashore. It had been discovered decades, perhaps centuries, earlier that this was an ideal spot for providing the strength and direction of draught the fires needed to burn at their fiercest. And so the stacks were always assembled at the same spot. As we sent the plucked birds in sacks of ten screaming nearly two hundred yards down the wire to what Gigs called *the factory*, I saw Artair carrying glowing peats in makeshift tongs from the blackhouse to get the fires started. By the time the birds had been successfully transferred, and we had climbed down to join him, Artair had a fire blazing in each chimney. He and Pluto were delegated to do the singeing. I watched as Pluto showed Artair how. He took a bird and snapped its wing joints across his chest. Then, with a wing in each hand, and the guga hanging limply between them, he lowered it into the flames to singe away the remaining down. I watched as the flames licked up around the dead bird, turning it for a moment into a fiery angel, before Pluto withdrew it sharply from the fire. The down had dissolved to a fine, black ash, its webbed feet burned to a curled crisp. It was important not to scorch the skin and ruin the flavour, but it was equally important to leave it free of quills, because these would ruin the texture. Artair and Pluto began working their way through all the birds we had plucked that day, creating in turn dozens of their own fiery angels on that gusty Monday afternoon.

From the fire they went to Old Seoras, a wiry skeleton of a man with a head like a skull. Protective goggles increased the illusion. He scrubbed the ash off the birds before handing them on to Donnie and Malcolm, who exercised a kind of quality control, burning off anything missed by the flames with blowtorches.

They went then to John Angus, who hacked off the wings with a hand-axe and passed the birds for splitting to Gigs and Seumas, where they sat facing each other astride a thick oak beam raised up on two low cairns. The splitting beam had served its bloody purpose over decades, seasoned and weathered by all its years on the rock. On it, with knives as sharp as razors, the gugas were split from end to end and the tail removed. Three careful cuts were made above the ribs, and with one deft movement, fingers thrust between flesh and bone plucked out the ribcage and entrails. It was my job to take those entrails from the growing pile and drape them over the edge of the chimneys where Pluto and Artair were forging their angels. The fat immediately ran down into the flames, spitting and popping and fuelling their ferocity.

The final stage followed the splitting. Gigs and Seumas made four neat slashes in the flesh of the birds with their knives, creating pockets into which fistfuls of salt were thrust to begin the curing.

On ground as flat as they could make it, right next to the top of the chute, the two men spread out tarpaulins and laid the salted birds in a large circle, feet turned towards the centre, the outside flap of skin folded up to prevent leakage of the pickling fluids created by the salt. A second circle overlapped the first, and a third overlapped the second, moving closer to the centre until the entire first layer had been formed. A huge wheel of dead birds. Then another layer began on top of that, and another, and another, until it stood nearly five feet high. By the end of the two weeks, there were two huge wheels like that, each comprised of a thousand birds. All around us their wings lay scattered across the rocks, to blow away in the autumn gales on a final flight to freedom.

And that's how it was on the rock for two stultifying weeks. Working our way across all the cliffs, through all the colonies. Ever-repeating cycles of killing, plucking, singeing, splitting. Until those wheels were completed. It was a numbing experience which after a while became wholly mechanical. You got up in the morning and you worked your way through the day until you crawled back on to your mattress at night. Some of the men even seemed to enjoy it. A kind of silent camaraderie, punctuated by the cracking of the odd joke and the relief of laughter. Something inside me just shut down, and I retreated into myself. I was not a part of the camaraderie. I don't think I laughed once in fourteen days. I just gritted my teeth and counted them off one by one.

By the second Sunday the job was almost done. The weather had been reasonably favourable, and we had made good progress. It was dry, although not as sunny as the previous week. I made my way up to the lighthouse and stood on the concrete apron of the helipad and looked back across the island. The whole of An Sgeir was laid out beneath me, the prickly curvature of its spine, its promontories like three broken ribs, all that remained after an eternity of erosion. I could see, just off the northwest tip, stacks of black rock rising out of a deep green sea that frothed angrily against them, clouds of seabirds around their peaks, riding the thermals in endless, effortless circles. I turned and made my way to the edge of the cliff. It fell away sheer, in a three-hundred-foot drop. But it was cut through by cracks and splits and deep chimneys, and was transected in several places by ledges, white-caked by guano which had been worn smooth by the wind and the rain. There were thousands upon thousands of nests on the cliff. The richest pickings on the island. And the most inaccessible. Tomorrow we would climb down to the ledges below and reap our final harvest. A sickening little knot of fear tightened itself in my stomach and I looked away. Just one more day to get through, and then on Tuesday we would begin the process of decamping in time for the arrival of the *Purple Isle*, weather permitting, on Wednesday. I could hardly wait.

That night we had the finest meal of our stay. We ate the first of that year's gugas. By now our supplies were running low. The bread was stale and sometimes mouldy, and always crawling with earwigs. The meat was all eaten, and we seemed to be living on porridge and eggs. The only constant at every meal was the diet of scripture and psalms served up from Gigs's bible. So the guga was manna from Heaven, a reward perhaps for all our piety.

Angel spent the afternoon preparing. He took three gugas from the first wheel and washed and scraped them clean. Then he divided each into four and plunged them into a large pot of water boiling over the fire. While they boiled he peeled the last of our tatties and set them in water over a second fire. By the time they were near the boil, he was ready to change the water in which the gugas were cooking. He carefully removed the pieces of bird, tipped the greasy, salt-clouded brown water away over the rocks, and refilled it with fresh to bring back to the boil. Then the birds were returned to the pot for a final half-hour.

The sense of anticipation in the blackhouse that evening as we sat down around the fire, clutching our plates, was very nearly palpable. The tin box of irons that was usually passed around for us to select our cutlery was kept stowed in its place. You only ever ate the guga with your fingers. Angel served a piece of bird on to each of our plates and we helped ourselves to liberal portions of potato. And the feast began, there in the blue smoky light of the fire, skin and meat and tattie filling hungry mouths, savoured in silence. The flesh was firm, but tender, the colour and texture of duck, but with a taste that lay somewhere between steak and kipper.

A quarter bird was more than enough, along with the tatties, to leave us sated and sleepy, and listening in an almost trancelike state to Gigs reading from the Bible. And then bed, and the welcome mist of sleep. I doubt if there was a man in the blackhouse that night who gave a single thought to the dangers he would face on the final cliffs tomorrow. If he had he would almost certainly not have slept.

Yet again the wind had changed. Coming down from the north-west now, with a spit of rain on its cutting edge. It was a lot colder, too. Up by the lighthouse, where I had stood only yesterday with a warm breeze blowing in my face, you could lean into the wind without falling over. It was going to make the job of working the cliffs below all the harder. At first I could not see how we could possibly get down to the ledges I had seen the day before. The cliff fell away in a perpendicular drop of ninety feet to the first of them. But off to the left, Gigs led us down a steep gully, almost hidden by the fold of the rock. It developed into a deep chimney, cracks and fissures creating steps on one face, and you could ease your way down it by bracing your back against the opposite wall. The chimney was little more than three feet across, narrowing at the foot, so that finally you simply squeezed out on to the first of the ledges. And as we did, thousands of gannets took to the air, shrieking their alarm, wings beating around our faces. The ledge was thick with nests. The guano here filled every crevice in the rock, smoothing out its textures and hollows. Blasted by the wind and the salt, it had hardened to a smooth, white surface, like marble, and was treacherous underfoot. We were fortunate at this point to be in the lee of the wind, and the rain flew past us and above us. The sea thrashed against the rock at the foot of the cliff two hundred feet below. Gigs signalled that we should move quickly, and so we set off along the ledge, little more than four feet at its widest, killing as fast as we could, birds heaping up behind us, scarlet pooling around us on the white guano marble. Off to our right, a second team was working another ledge. I had no idea where the third team was.

The way it happened was wholly unexpected. There is something about killing that dulls the senses, but even now I don't know how I could have been so stupid. We had returned to the chimney, piling up dead birds at the foot of it. Pluto climbed back to the top and lowered a rope, and we tied four birds at a time to the end of it so that he could haul them up. Gigs was exploring a possible route down to the next ledge, when I turned, startling a chick nesting in a crevice. With a screech and a flutter of down and wings, it was in my face. I felt its beak gouging my cheek. I raised my arms to fend it off and took a single step back into space. In that split second I almost believe now that I could have recovered my balance. I have thought about it so many times. But at that time, in that moment, it was just as though the cliffs had let me go, releasing me to my fate. There was air beneath my feet, my hands grabbing hopelessly for something to hold. But there was nothing. I can remember thinking how Gigs had told me that there had never, within living memory, been an accident on the cliffs. And I felt like I was spoiling the record. I heard the birds laughing as I fell, taking pleasure in my plight. Unlike them, I could not fly. Served me right for killing their children. I went silently, too surprised to feel fear and give vent to it. Like a dream, I suppose, I thought perhaps it wasn't really happening. Not to me.

Then the first impact went through me like a hammer blow from a mallet. Somewhere about my left arm or shoulder. The pain was intense, prompting me at last to break my silence. I screamed. But I suppose it was that impact which saved my life. There were several other blows, more glancing than the first, before I came to a sudden stop. I heard my skull cracking, but consciousness was snuffed out in an instant, like the flame of a candle, and I felt no pain.

The first thing I remember hearing was the voices. Shouting. I had no idea what they were shouting, because as something like awareness returned it brought pain. They say that you cannot feel pain in two places at the same time. But I was conscious of it in my shoulder, searing, like something sharp cutting through flesh and muscle and tendon, all the way to the bone. And also in my head, which felt as if someone had clamped it in an iron vice and was slowly turning the screw. I must have been hurting elsewhere, pain I would become aware of much later, but at that moment all my senses were engulfed by those two centres of it. I couldn't move, and through the mist of my suffering I wondered if I had broken my back. As I forced my eyes open, I found I was looking straight down at the sea, perhaps a hundred and fifty feet below, smashing itself furiously over the rocky outcrops. Waiting for me, urging me into its arms, cheated by this ledge of the chance to suck my shattered body down into its seething darkness.

With an enormous effort I rolled away from the precipice and on to my back. I bent my leg at the knee, and somewhere in the fog of my distress I found relief at the thought that, after all, my spinal cord might still be intact. The ledge was narrow, two feet or less. Miraculously it had stopped my fall and held me there, cradled in the bosom of the cliff. I could see blood on my hands, panicking briefly before I realized it was the blood of the gugas we had been slaughtering in the minutes before my fall. The frayed end of a green plastic rope dangled just above my head, and some fifty feet higher up I saw the heads and shoulders of men leaning out into the void as far as they dared, peering down to try to catch a sight of me. Even in my state of confused semi-consciousness I could see that there was no way to climb down. The rock was sheer and smooth and coated with guano. If they were to reach me, someone would have to come down on the end of a rope.

They were still shouting. At first I thought it was to me. I saw Artair leaning right out from the cliff, his face pale and shocked. He was shouting, too, but I couldn't make out his words. And then a shadow fell across my face, and I turned my head as Mr Macinnes pulled himself up on to the ledge beside me. He looked terrible. Unshaven, his face liverish-yellow, eyes sunk deep in his skull. He was sweating and shaking, and it seemed it was all he could do to find a handhold to keep himself from falling, kneeling in that narrow space, pressed hard against the face of the cliff. 'It's going to be okay, Fin.' His voice sounded hoarse and thin. 'You're going to be okay.' And with that he grabbed the green rope, winding it several times around his wrist, before swinging out from the rock and turning himself around so that he ended up sitting on the ledge right beside my head. He pushed himself back against the cliff, eyes closed, breathing deeply. Somehow he had climbed up from down below to reach me. To this day I have no idea how he got there. But I could almost smell his fear. It's odd, in that moment I can remember, even through all my pain, feeling sorry for him. I reached up a hand and he grabbed it and squeezed it.

'Can you sit up?'

I tried to speak, but no words would come. I tried again. 'I don't think so.'

'We need to get you sitting up, so I can tie the rope under your arms. I can't do it on my own, I'll need your help.'

I nodded. 'I'll try.'

With one hand still clutching the rope, he put his

other arm around my waist to try to pull me upright. The pain that shot through my arm and shoulder was excruciating and I cried out. I paused for several minutes, gasping for breath, hanging on to him like grim death. He kept muttering words of encouragement, words that were just sounds blown away in the wind. But still, I took comfort from them. And courage. With my good arm I clutched his and held on, bracing myself with the leg I had been able to bend, and heaved with all my might until I had dragged myself up into a half-sitting position. I cried out again, but now I was propped against his legs, and he was able to thread the rope quickly under both arms, around my back, and start tying it in a big, secure-looking knot on my chest.

When he had finished, we both sat breathing hard, trying not to look down, and trying harder not to anticipate the moment when he would release me from his grasp and swing me free of the ledge. For then I would be suspended on the end of this length of frayed green plastic, my life dependent upon his knot and the strength of those above to pull me to safety. In some ways, I think I might have settled then for the fall, the few seconds the drop would take, a swift death on the rocks below putting an end to my pain.

'You're bleeding,' he said. And even as he spoke I felt the blood running warm down my neck from a head wound somewhere above my ear. He searched for a handkerchief and wiped fresh blood from my face. 'I'm so sorry, Fin,' he said. And I wondered why. It was not his fault I had fallen.

He tipped his head back and shouted up to the others that he was ready, giving three sharp tugs on the rope. There was a responding pull, and all the slack was taken up.

'Good luck,' Mr Macinnes said. The rope jerked me up and I screamed again from the pain. He let go of me, then, and I swung free of the rock, spinning crazily in the wind, rising in a series of short, painful bursts. Twice I smacked against the cliff face before swinging out again into the updraught from the sea. And all the while, the gannets flew around my head, shrieking their fury, willing me to fall. *Die, die, die*, they seemed to be calling.

I was barely conscious by the time they got me on to the ledge I had fallen from, concerned faces crowding around me. And Gigs's voice. 'Hell, son, I thought you were a goner.'

And then someone shouted, and the alarm in his voice was chilling, commanding. I turned my head in time to see Mr Macinnes sailing through the air, arms stretched out like wings, as if he thought he could fly. It seemed to take for ever for him to reach the rocks below, where his flight ended abruptly. For a moment, he lay face down, his arms pushed out to either side, one leg bent at the knee, like a parody of Christ on the cross. And then a huge wave washed over him and dragged him off, white foam turning pink as he vanished for ever into its bottomless green depths.

There was the strangest hush then, as if all the birds had answered some call for a moment's silence. Only the wind continued with its mournful whine until rising, even above that, I heard Artair's howl of anguish.

TWELVE

I

The mountains of Harris rose up before them, piercing low black cloud, and tearing great holes in it to reveal startling shreds of blue, and ragged scraps of white. Fragments of sunshine fell upon the spangling waters of a loch that cut deep into the hills. At the bend, on the curve of the hill, they flashed past an old, abandoned shieling with a view as timeless as the island itself.

'And some people choose to sit in traffic on the M25 for two hours every day,' George Gunn said. 'More bloody fool them, eh?'

Fin nodded his agreement and supposed that he was one of those fools. How many hours of his life had he wasted sitting in traffic jams in Edinburgh? The road to Uig, winding through some of the bleakest, most beautiful country anywhere on earth, was a reminder that life did not have to be like that. But as the mountains approached, wreathed in cloud and mist, blue and purple and darkest green, their brooding quality was infectious, and in the shadow of their sullen splendour Fin found himself sinking back into the depression with which he had awakened.

On his return to Stornoway he had stood under hot water in the shower in his hotel room for a long time, trying to wash away the memories of the night before. But stubbornly they had stayed with him, and he was haunted by the image of the young Fionnlagh, like the young Fin, troubled and unhappy at the prospect of his trip to An Sgeir. Shocked, too, by the change in his oldest friend. The fresh-faced Artair, once so full of life and mischief, overweight now, foul-mouthed and hard-drinking, trapped in a loveless marriage, with a crippled mother and a son who was not his. And Marsaili. Poor Marsaili, ground down by life and the years, weary and washed out.

Yet, in those few moments across the kitchen table, he had seen again in her the young Marsaili, still there in the flash of her eyes, in her smile, the touch of her fingers on his face. And that old, sarcastic wit that he had once adored.

Gunn was aware of his distraction, glancing across the car at his passenger. 'Penny for them, Mr Macleod.'

Fin shook himself out of his reverie and forced a smile. 'I wouldn't waste my money if I were you, George.'

They turned into a long gully, cut through solid rock by the relentless force of water over millions of years. A once huge river reduced now to a trickle amongst the boulders. And as they emerged from the shadows, they caught their first glimpse of Uig beach through a cleft in the land. Acres of white sands. They could not even see the ocean.

Gunn swung away from the shore, following a single-track road over a cattle grid and up into the hills, running alongside a broad, swift-moving shallow river, which tumbled and smashed itself over jagged chunks of stone that rose in steps and clusters from the river bed.

'Do you get much wild salmon in Edinburgh, Mr Macleod?'

'No, we don't. All we seem to get these days is the farmed stuff.'

'Aye, hellish, isn't it? All those bloody chemicals and antibiotics, and them making the poor wee things swim in circles. The flesh is that soft you can just poke your fingers right through it.' He glanced across at the river rushing past them. 'I suppose that's why some folk'll pay so much money to come and catch the real thing.'

'And why others'll risk so much to poach it.' Fin avoided looking at Gunn. 'You had much of the real thing recently, George?'

Gunn shrugged. 'Och, you know, a wee taste of it now and then, Mr Macleod. My wife knows someone who can get us the odd bit of it from time to time.'

'Your wife?'

'Aye.' Gunn sneaked a glance across the car. 'I never ask, Mr Macleod. What you don't know can't hurt you.'

'Ignorance is no excuse in the eyes of the law.'

'Aye, and sometimes the law's an ass. God didn't put the world's finest salmon in our rivers, Mr Macleod, so that some Englishman could come here and charge other Englishman a bloody fortune to take them away.'

'And if you knew someone was poaching them?'

'Oh, I'd arrest them,' Gunn said without hesitation. 'That's my job.' He kept his eyes on the road ahead. 'Maybe you'd like to eat with me and my wife tonight, Mr Macleod. I daresay she might be able to dig up a piece of the real thing from somewhere.'

'A tempting offer, George. I might take you up on it. But let's see how the day pans out first. You never know, they might be putting me on a plane home this afternoon.'

They came up over a rise in the road, and there below them, nestling on the shore of a tiny scribble of grey loch, was Suainaval Lodge, a cluster of Scots pines growing around it, carefully cultivated in the shelter of the surrounding hills. The lodge was based upon what must once have been an old farmhouse, extended and built out and up. It was an impressive property, freshly painted, a brilliant white that stood out in the gloom of this tenebrous place. A metalled road ran down to a parking area at the side of the house and a landing stage where a cluster of small boats bobbed on the ruffled surface of the loch. There was only one vehicle parked there, a battered-looking Land Rover. Gunn pulled in beside it and they stepped out on to the tarmac. A big man in blue overalls and a tweed jacket, a matching peaked cap pulled down over his ruddy, round face, came hurrying out of the lodge.

'Can I help you folks?' To Fin he appeared to be in his forties, but it was hard to tell. His face was weathered and broken-veined. What hair could be seen beneath his cap was gingery, flecked with white.

'Police,' Gunn said. 'From Stornoway.'

The man breathed a sigh of relief. 'Well, I'm right glad to hear it. I thought you were from the ministry come a day early.'

'What ministry is that?' Fin asked.

'Agriculture. They come and count the sheep to calculate the subsidy. They were at Coinneach Iain's place yesterday, and I haven't had a chance to move his beasts over to my place yet.' He nodded towards a small croft-house on the opposite shore, a strip of land marked off on the hill above it, white sheep dotted amongst the heather.

Fin frowned. 'There are sheep there already.'

'Oh, aye, they're mine.'

'So why would you want to bring Coinneach Iain's sheep here?'

'So the man from the ministry'll think I've twice as many as I have, and give me twice the subsidy.'

'You mean the same sheep get counted twice?'

'Aye.' The man seemed surprised by Fin's slowness.

'Should you be telling us this?'

'Och, it's no secret.' The man was dismissive. 'Even the fella from the ministry knows. If the sheep are here when he arrives, he'll count them. It's the only way any of us gets to make a living. That's how I've had to take this job at the lodge.'

'What job's that?' Gunn asked.

'Caretaker. I look after the place while Sir John's not here.'

'Sir John who?' Fin said.

'Wooldridge.' The caretaker chuckled. 'He tells me just to call him Johnny. But I don't like to, him being a Sir and all.' He thrust out a big hand. 'I'm Kenny, by the way.' He grinned. 'Another Coinneach, so folk just call me Kenny. Big Kenny.'

Fin withdrew his crushed hand from the iron grip of Kenny's monstrous paw. 'Well, Big Kenny,' he said, flexing his fingers, 'is *Johnny* around?'

'Oh, no,' Big Kenny said. 'Sir John's never here in the summer. He always brings a party in September. The autumn's best for the hunting.'

Gunn drew a folded sheet of paper from his pocket and opened it up. 'What about a James Minto?'

Big Kenny's face clouded, the broken veins around his nose turning a dark purple. 'Oh, him. Aye, he's around. He's always around.'

'You don't sound particularly pleased about that,' Fin said.

'I've no beef with the man myself, sir. But no one likes

him very much. Someone's got to put a stop to the poaching, and he's done a good enough job of it, I suppose. But there's ways of doing things, and ways of doing things. If you get my meaning.'

'And you don't like his way of doing things,' Gunn said.

'No, sir, I do not.'

'Where can we find him?' Fin asked.

'He's in an old crofthouse among the doons on the south side of Uig beach.' He stopped, mid-flow, as if suddenly remembering who he was talking to. He frowned. 'What's he done? Killed someone?'

'Would it surprise you if he had?' Fin said.

'No, sir, it would not. It wouldn't surprise me at all.'

Minto's crofthouse was a former holiday let set amongst the dunes at the end of the shore road. It looked out over the whole expanse of Uig beach, from the distant ocean in the west to Uig Lodge in the east, an impressive hunting lodge that stood in splendid isolation on a bluff overlooking the sands, mountains rising behind it in layer upon undulating layer of pastel purple and blue, like paper cut-outs laid one behind the other. Immediately opposite, on the far side of the beach, was a collection of white-painted buildings at Baile-na-Cille, the birthplace of the Scottish prophet Kenneth Mackenzie.

'Of course,' Fin's father had told him, 'we know him in the Gaelic as Coinneach Odhar, and the world knows him as the Brahan Seer.' Fin remembered as clear as day sitting on the edge of the machair as his father assembled their kite, hearing the story of how a ghost, returning to her grave at Baile-na-Cille one night, had told Coinneach's mother to look for a small, round, blue stone in a nearby loch. 'She was told that if she gave this stone to her son and he held it to his eye he would be able to see the future.'

'And did she?' a wide-eyed Fin had asked his father.

'Aye, son, she did.'

'And could he really see the future?'

'He predicted many things, Fionnlagh, that have come true,' his father told him, and he reeled off a whole list of prophecies that meant nothing to the young Fin. But as the adult Fin stood now and gazed off towards the gravestones on the far machair he recalled one prophecy that his father had never lived to see fulfilled. The Brahan Seer had written, *When men in horseless carriages go under the sea to France, then shall Scotia arise anew, free from all oppression.* The Channel Tunnel had been the merest twinkle in Margaret Thatcher's eye when he and his father were flying kites on the beach, and not even the most ardent nationalist could have predicted then that a Scottish parliament would be sitting again in Edinburgh before the end of the century. Coinneach Odhar had been burned to death for witchcraft nearly three hundred years before any of it.

'It's a kind of magical place, this,' George Gunn said, raising his voice to be heard over a wind that rippled like water in undulating waves through the long machair grasses.

'Aye, it is.' And Fin thought about the crofter who had discovered, buried in the sands of Uig, the Lewis Chessmen, carved from walrus tusks by twelfth-century Norsemen. And he could imagine how it was possible, as legend had it, for that crofter to think that they were really elves and gnomes, the pygmy sprites of Celtic folk-lore, and to turn on his heels and flee for his life.

A man came out from the front door of the crofthouse as they slammed the car doors shut. He wore moleskin trousers tucked into knee-high black boots, and a thick woollen jumper under a jacket with leather patches at the shoulders and elbows. He had a shotgun broken over one arm, and a canvas satchel hanging from his shoulder. His black hair was cropped short and his face lean. But even a deep summer tan could not hide the yellow remains of bruising around it, and there were several healing scars on badly split lips. He had striking pale-green eyes, and Fin decided that he was about the same age as himself. The man paused for a moment, then closed the door behind him and sauntered towards them with the hint of a limp in his gait. 'Can I be of any assistance to you gentlemen?' He was soft-spoken, his gentle cockney cadences barely audible above the racket of the wind. But his voice did not reflect the wariness in his strange green eyes, or the tension Fin could see in the way he held his body, something of the cat about him, all wound up and ready to spring.

'James Minto?' Fin said.

'Who wants to know?'

'Detective Inspector Finlay Macleod.' Fin nodded towards Gunn. 'And Detective Sergeant George Gunn.'

'Identification?' Minto was still eyeing them cautiously. They both showed him their warrant cards, which he examined, and then nodded. 'Okay, you've found him. What do you want?'

Fin cocked his head towards the shotgun. 'I take it you've got a licence for that?'

'What do you think?' Wariness was turning towards hostility.

'I think I asked you a question which you haven't answered.'

'Yes, I've got a licence.'

'What are you thinking of shooting?'

'Rabbits, if it's any of your business, Detective Inspector.' He bore all the hallmarks of a soldier in the ranks displaying his contempt for a senior officer.

'Not poachers.'

'I don't shoot poachers. I catch them and I hand them over to you people.'

'Where were you on Saturday night between eight and midnight?'

For the first time Minto's confidence wavered. 'Why?'

'I'm asking the questions.'

'And I'm not answering unless I know why.'

'If you don't answer I'll put you in handcuffs in the back of that car and take you to Stornoway where you'll be charged with obstructing a police officer in the course of his duties.'

'Fucking try it, mate, and you'll end up with two broken arms.'

Fin had read Gunn's printout on Minto. Ex-SAS, serving in the Gulf and Afghanistan. And something in Minto's tone told him that he meant what he said. Fin kept his voice level. 'Threatening a police officer is also an offence, Mr Minto.'

'So handcuff me and throw me in the back of your car.'

Fin was surprised by the quiet menace in Gunn's voice at his side. 'I think you'd better answer Mr Macleod's questions, Mr Minto, or it's you who'll have the broken arms, and it's me who'll break them while I'm putting them in cuffs.'

Minto flicked him a look of quick appraisal. Hitherto, he had paid little attention to Gunn. If he had dismissed him as a junior officer of no consequence, he was now clearly rethinking. He reached a decision. 'I was at home Saturday night. Watching the telly. Not that you get a very good picture down here.' He dragged his eyes away from Gunn and back to Fin.

'Can anyone verify that?' Fin said.

'Yeh, like I've got a lot of mates round Uig. They're always dropping by for a beer and a chat.'

'You were on your own, then?'

'You're quick for a copper.'

'What programmes did you watch?' Gunn asked with the authority of someone who had probably been watching TV himself on Saturday night.

Minto threw him another wary glance. 'How the fuck should I know? Bloody telly's the same every night. Crap.' He looked from one to the other. 'Look, the sooner you ask me what it is you want to know, the sooner I'll tell you, and we can put an end to this little game, okay?'

'Maybe we should do this indoors,' Fin said. 'And you could make us a cup of tea.' It seemed like a good way of defusing hostilities.

Minto thought about it for a few moments. 'Yeh, okay. Why don't we do that?'

For a man who lived alone, Minto kept his house in perfect order. The tiny sitting room was spartan and clean, devoid of pictures or ornaments, except for a chessboard on a table by the window, opposing chessmen in various stages of conflict across the black and cream ivory squares. Fin could see into the kitchen as they sat waiting for Minto to come through with the tea. There wasn't a dirty dish in sight. Cutlery hung in neat racks on the wall, and dish towels hung drying, carefully folded above a heater. Minto carried in a tray with a pot of tea and three cups and saucers, a small jug of milk and a crock of sugar cubes. Fin had been expecting mugs. There was something faintly manic in Minto's fastidiousness, a tidiness and discipline dinned into him perhaps by years in the army. Fin wondered what motivated a man to come to a place like this to live on his own. His job, by its nature, would not lead him to make many friends. But he seemed to go out of his way to make enemies. Nobody liked him much, Big Kenny had said. And Fin could see why.

As Minto poured, Fin said, 'Not easy to play chess with yourself.'

Minto glanced across the room towards his chessboard. 'I play by telephone. My old commanding officer.'

'You have the Lewis Chessmen, I see.'

Minto grinned. 'Yeh, not the originals, unfortunately. Ain't figured out how to break into the British Museum yet.' He paused. 'Beautiful things, aren't they?'

Beautiful was not a word Fin had expected to hear passing Minto's lips. If he had suspected for a moment that Minto might have been aware of life's aesthetics, he would not have thought him likely to appreciate them. But the one thing Fin had learned from his years in the police was that however much you believed you had them figured out, people invariably surprised you. 'Have you ever seen the originals? They keep a few of them at the National Museum of Scotland in Edinburgh.'

'Never been to Edinburgh,' Minto said. 'In fact, I haven't been anywhere in Scotland except here. And I haven't been off the island since I arrived fifteen months ago.' Fin nodded. If that were true, it would rule Minto out of any connection with the Leith Walk murder. 'I thought at first maybe you'd come to tell me you'd got the bastards who did this to my face.'

'Afraid not,' Gunn said.

'Nah,' Minto drawled. 'Don't know what I was thinking. Like every other bugger round here, you're more interested in looking after your own. Right?' He sat down and dropped two lumps of sugar in his tea and stirred in some milk.

'A lot of your poachers turn up pretty badly marked themselves,' said Gunn.

'A lot of my poachers don't like getting caught.'

Fin said, 'Do you work alone?'

'Nah. There's a couple of other guys on Sir John's payroll. Locals, you know, probably out poaching themselves when they're not out with me.'

'Sir John's payroll must be quite hefty then,' Fin said. 'Three of you on a salary just to catch poachers.'

Minto laughed. 'A drop in the bloody ocean, mate. You know, there's consortiums of fishermen come up here, stay in the lodge, and pay ten grand a week just for one beat. Over a season that's a lot of dosh, know what I mean? And these guys ain't too happy paying that kind of money if there ain't no fish in the river. A hundred years ago, over on Grimersta Estate, they was catching more than two thousand salmon a year. Back then, they say the guy who owned the place caught fifty-seven of the buggers off the same rod in one day. These days we're lucky if we pull a few hundred in a season. The wild salmon's a dying breed, Detective Inspector. It's my job to see they don't become extinct.'

'By beating the living daylights out of anyone you catch taking them illegally?'

'You said that, I didn't.'

Fin sipped reflectively on his tea, momentarily startled by the unexpected perfume of Earl Grey. He glanced at Gunn and saw that the detective sergeant had put his cup back on the table, the tea undrunk. Fin refocused on Minto. 'Do you recall a man called Macritchie? You caught him poaching on the estate here about six months ago. Handed him over to the police, in a bit of a state apparently.'

Minto shrugged. 'I've caught a few poachers in the last six months, mate. And every one of them's been a Mac-something-or-other. Give me a clue.'

'He was murdered in Port of Ness on Saturday night.'

For a moment, Minto's natural cockiness deserted him. A frown gathered itself around his eyes. 'That's the guy that was in the paper the other day.' Fin nodded. 'Jesus Christ, and you think I had something to do with that?'

'You got beaten up pretty badly a few weeks ago. By an assailant or assailants unknown.'

'Yeh, unknown because you bloody people haven't caught them yet.'

'So they weren't just poachers that you stumbled on?'

'Nah, they was out to give me a doing. Lying waiting for me they were.'

'And you couldn't identify them, why?' Gunn asked.

'Because they was wearing bloody masks, wasn't they? Didn't want me to see their faces.'

'Which means they were probably faces you knew,' Fin said.

'Well, knock me down with a feather. I'd never have thought of that.' Minto took a large gulp of tea as if to wash away the bad taste of his sarcasm.

'Must be a lot of folk around here who're not too fond of you, then,' Fin said.

And finally Minto saw the light. His green eyes opened wide. 'You think it was this guy Macritchie. You think I knew it was him and killed him for it.'

'Did you?'

Minto's laugh was mirthless. 'Let me tell you something, mate. If I'd known who did this to me,' he pointed to his face, 'I'd have dealt with it quickly and quietly. And I wouldn't have left any marks.'

Outside, the wind was still bending the long grasses. The shadows of clouds raced across miles of compacted sand, and they saw that the tide had turned and was rushing across the flats with indecent haste. At the car they stopped and Fin said, 'I'd like to go up to Ness, George, and talk to a few folk.'

'I'll need to go back to Stornoway, sir. DCI Smith keeps us on a tight leash.'

'I suppose I'll have to ask him for a car.'

'Oh, I wouldn't do that, Mr Macleod. He'd probably just say no.' Gunn hesitated. 'Why don't you drop me off at the station and take my car. Better to be forgiven than forbidden, eh?'

Fin smiled. 'Thanks, George.' He opened the car door.

Gunn said, 'So what do you think?' He nodded towards the crofthouse. 'About Minto.'

'I think if it wasn't for the drive down and back, we'd have been wasting our time.' Gunn nodded. But Fin had the impression it was a nod of acknowledgement rather than of agreement. 'You don't agree?'

'No, I think you're probably right, Mr Macleod. But I didn't like the fella much. Gave me the willies. With his kind of training he'd know how to use a knife alright, and I don't believe he'd think twice about using it.'

Fin ran a hand back through the fine, tight curls of his hair. 'They're pretty highly trained, these SAS types.'

'Aye, they are.'

'And you think you could have broken his arms?'

Gunn shot him a look and blushed, a tiny smile stretching his lips. 'I think he could have probably broken every bone in my body before I even got near him, Mr Macleod.' He inclined his head slightly. 'But he wasn't to know that.'

II

The Pottery had been there at the foot of the hill for as long as Fin could remember. When he had first taken over the old croft, Eachan Stewart had been a long-haired, wild-eyed man of about thirty who had seemed very old to all the children of Crobost. Fin and the other boys in the village had thought him a wizard, and for once had obeyed parental advice and stayed away from the Pottery, fearing that he might cast an evil spell on them. He did not belong to the island, although his grandfather was said to have come from Carloway, which was the Lewis equivalent of the Wild West. Born somewhere in the north of England, he had been christened Hector, but returning to his roots had called himself Eachan, its Gaelic equivalent.

As he pulled Gunn's car on to the grass verge opposite, Fin saw Eachan sitting outside the front door of his cottage. He was well into his sixties now. The hair was just as long, but pure white, and the eyes a little less wild, dulled like his brain by years of smoking dope. On the peeling white gable of the house, the red-painted legend, *The Pottery*, was still visible where he had daubed it across the wall thirty years before. A shambolic garden, filled with the accumulated detritus of decades of beachcombing, was festooned with green fishing nets draped between rotting fenceposts. Stakes of bleached driftwood flanked a rickety wooden gate. A cross-beam was tied to them by lengths of frayed rope and hung with buoys and floats and markers – orange, pink, yellow, white – blowing and rattling in the wind. Stunted and wind-blasted shrubs clung stubbornly to the thin, peaty soil where Eachan had planted them when Fin was still a boy.

A great attraction, then, for the kids on their way to school, had been the mysterious earthworks which Eachan Stewart had begun shortly after his arrival. Over a period of nearly two years, he had laboured in amongst the reedy and unproductive bog that surrounded his house, digging, and wheeling barrows of soil across the moor to pile in great heaps, like giant molehills, thirty or forty feet apart. Six of them altogether. The kids would sit up on the hill and watch him at work from a safe distance as he levelled them off and seeded them with grass, only realizing belatedly that he had built himself a mini, three-hole golf course, with tees, and greens with flagpoles stuck in the holes. They had gawped in amazement the first day he appeared with his chequered pullover and cloth cap, a golf bag slung across his shoulder, to tee up on the first hole and christen the course by playing his first round of golf. It took him only fifteen minutes, but from then on it became a routine that he followed with religious fervour every morning, rain or shine. After a while, the novelty of it wore off for the kids, and they found other things to engage their interest. Eachan Stewart, eccentric potter, had stitched himself into the fabric of life there and become, to all intents and purposes, invisible.

Fin saw that the golf course the mad potter had laboured so hard to create all those years before was drowning now amongst a sea of long grasses, neglected and left to grow wild. Eachan glanced up when his gate scraped across an overgrown path. His eyes narrowed quizzically as Fin approached. He was threading pottery windchimes to hang amongst the two dozen or more already lined up along the front of the cottage. The dull pitch of colourfully glazed terracotta pipes rattling in the wind filled the air around him. He looked Fin up and down. 'Well, from the look of those shoes you're wearing, lad, I'd say you were a policeman. Am I right?'

'You're not wrong, Eachan.'

Eachan cocked his head. 'Do I know you?' His Lancashire accent had never left him, even after all these years.

'You did once. Whether you'll remember me is another matter.'

Eachan looked hard into his face, and Fin imagined he could almost hear the wheels of his memory creaking and grinding. But he shook his head. 'You'll need to give me a hint.'

'My aunt used to buy, shall we say, some of your more unusual pieces.'

Lights appeared in the old man's eyes. 'Iseabal Marr,' he said. 'Lived in the old whitehouse up by the harbour. Got me to make her those big pots in primary colours for her dried flowers, and she was the only local ever to buy one of my pairs of fucking pigs. An eccentric creature she was, right enough. God rest her soul.' Fin thought it was rich, Eachan calling his aunt eccentric. 'And you must be Fin Macleod. Jesus, lad, the last time I saw you was when

I helped carry you from the *Purple Isle* the year old man Macinnes died on the rock.'

Fin felt his face redden, stinging as if from a slap. He'd had no idea that Eachan was one of the men who'd carried him from the boat that year. He had no recollection at all of the journey back from An Sgeir, or the ambulance dash across the moor to Stornoway. The first things he recalled were the starched white sheets of his hospital bed, and the concerned face of a young nurse hovering over him like an angel. He remembered thinking for a moment that he had died and gone to Heaven.

Eachan stood up and pumped his hand. 'Good to see you, lad. How are you?'

'I'm fine, Eachan.'

'And what brings you back to Crobost?'

'The murder of Angel Macritchie.'

Eachan's bonhomie dropped quickly away, and he became suddenly wary. 'I've already told the coppers everything I know about Macritchie.' He turned abruptly and went into his cottage, a shambling figure in denim dungarees and a grubby-looking long-sleeved grampa shirt. Fin followed him inside. The cottage was one big room that served as workshop, showroom, living room, kitchen and dining room. Eachan lived, worked and sold his wares here. Every available space on every table and shelf was crowded with his pots and goblets and plates and figurines. Where there was no pottery, there were piles of dirty dishes and laundry. Hundreds of windchimes hung from the rafters. The kiln was in a lean-to out back, and he had an outside toilet in a broken-down shed in the garden. A dog slept on a settee that looked as if it doubled as Eachan's bed, and smoke leaked from a small cast-iron stove where he burned his peats, misting the light that fell through crowded windows into the room.

'I'm not here officially,' Fin said. 'And there's only me and you to know what passes between us. All I'm interested in is the truth.'

Eachan lifted an almost empty whisky bottle from a shelf above the sink, swilled the tea leaves out of a dirty cup and poured himself a measure. 'Very subjective thing, the truth. You want one?' Fin shook his head and Eachan emptied the cup in a single draught. 'What do you want to know?'

'Macritchie was supplying you with dope, right?'

Eachan's eyes opened wide in amazement. 'How do you know that?'

'The Stornoway police suspected for some time that Macritchie was dealing dope. And everyone in the world, Eachan, knows that you enjoy the odd spliff or three.'

Eachan's eyes opened wider. 'They do? I mean, even the police?'

'Even the police.'

'So how come I never got arrested?'

'Because there are bigger fish to fry than you, Eachan.'

'Jesus.' Eachan sat down abruptly on a stool, as if the

knowledge that everyone knew, and had always known, that he smoked dope took away all the illicit fun of it. Then he looked up at Fin, suddenly alarmed. 'You think that gives me a motive for killing him?'

Fin almost laughed. 'No, Eachan, I think it gives you a motive for lying for him.'

The old man frowned. 'What do you mean?'

'The Donna Murray rape. The animal rights activist that he beat up right on your doorstep.'

'Aw, now, wait a minute.' Eachan's voice rose in pitch. 'Right. Okay. I admit it. Big Angel kicked the living shit out of that lad. I saw him do it, right on my doorstep, just like you said. But a lot of other people saw it, too. And I might have felt sorry for the boy, but he was asking for it. There was nobody in Crobost who'd have grassed on Angel for that.' He poured the dregs of the whisky bottle into his cup with a shaking hand. 'But that wee Donna Murray, she was just telling lies.'

'How do you know that?'

'Because I went up to the Social that night for a pint before closing time, and I saw her coming out into the car park and then heading up the road.' He knocked back his whisky.

'Did she see you?'

'No, I don't think she did. She seemed right pre-occupied. I was on the other side of the road, and that street light up there's been out for months.'

'And?'

'And then I saw Angel coming out. Or should I say staggering out. Man, he was pissed. Even if he'd had the inclination he'd never have had the wherewithal. The cold air hit him like a bloody sledgehammer and he threw up all over the pavement. I gave him a wide berth, I can tell you. I didn't want him to see me. He could be bloody aggressive when he'd had a drink in him. So I stood in the pool of darkness by the street light that doesn't work and watched him for a couple of minutes. He leaned against the wall, getting his breath back, and then he wobbled off down the road towards his house. The opposite direction from Donna Murray. And I went and had my pint.'

'You didn't see anyone else out there?'

'Nope. Not a soul.'

Fin was thoughtful. 'So why do you think she accused him of raping her?'

'How the hell should I know? Does it matter? He's dead now. Doesn't make any difference.'

But somehow Fin thought that it might. 'Thanks, Eachan. I appreciate your frankness.' He moved away towards the door.

'So what really happened out on the rock that year, then?' Eachan had lowered his voice again, but it couldn't have had more impact if he had shouted.

Fin stopped and turned in the doorway. 'What do you mean?'

'Well, everyone said it was an accident. But nobody ever talked about it. Not in all the years since. Not even

Angel, and he couldn't keep a secret for five minutes.'

'That's because there was no secret to keep. I fell on the cliff. Mr Macinnes saved my life and lost his own in the process.'

But Eachan just shook his head. 'No. I was there, remember, when the boat came in. There was more to it than that. I've never known so many men say so little about so much in my life.' He squinted through the gloom at Fin and took a few unsteady steps towards him. 'Go on, you can tell me. There's only me and you here to know what passes between us.' There was something unpleasant in his smile.

Fin said, 'You any idea where Calum Macdonald lives?'

Eachan frowned, disconcerted by the sudden change of subject. 'Calum Macdonald?'

'He's about my age. We were at school together. I think he works a loom these days.'

'The cripple?'

'That's him.'

'Squirrel, they call him.'

'Do they? Why?'

'I've no idea. He's in the pebbledash cottage at the top of the hill. The last one in the village, on the right.' Eachan paused. 'What's he got to do with what happened on An Sgeir?'

'Nothing,' Fin said. 'I just want to look up an old friend.' And he turned and ducked through the windchimes out into a freshening north wind.

III

Calum Macdonald's pebbledash bungalow sat amongst a cluster of three houses just over the brow of the hill. When Fin was last in Crobost it had been semi-derelict, an old single-storey, tin-roofed whitehouse left to rot. Someone had spent a lot of money on it since then. A new roof, double-glazing, a kitchen extension built on the back. There was a walled garden, the wall sprayed with the same pebbledash as the house. And someone had spent a lot of time taming the wilderness, laying lawns and planting flowerbeds. Fin knew that there had been some kind of compensation paid, although no amount of money could compensate for a lifetime in a wheelchair. He assumed that the money had gone on the house, or that at least a part of it had.

Calum's mother had been widowed before Calum was born – another fatality at sea – and the two of them had lived in a row of council houses near the school. Fin knew that Calum had never told her about the bullying, or about what happened the night he broke his back. They had all lived in terror of what would happen when the full story came out. But it never did. Like everything else in his life, his fears, his dreams, his secret desires, Calum kept it to himself, and the expected storm never broke.

Fin parked by the gate and walked up the pavings to the kitchen door. There was a ramp there in place of a step. He knocked and waited. There were two houses behind Calum's, and a large breezeblock garage with rust-red doors. An overgrown yard was littered with the remains of cannibalized tractors and broken-down trailers. A stark contrast with the neat and tidy garden on this side of the wall. Fin turned, as the door opened, to find an elderly woman standing at the top of the ramp. She was wearing a print apron over a woollen jumper and tweed skirt. When he had last seen Calum's mother her hair had been the purest black. Now it was the purest white. But it was carefully arranged in soft curls around a face almost as colourless, a face scarred by a tracery of fine criss-crossing wrinkles. Her eyes were a pale, watery blue, and they peered at him without recognition. Fin was almost startled to see her. He could never quite get used to the fact that people his age had parents who were still alive.

'Mrs Macdonald?'

She frowned, wondering if she should know him. 'Aye.'

'It's Fin Macleod. I used to live up near the harbour with my aunt. I was at school with Calum.'

The frown faded, but there was no smile. Her mouth set itself in a hard line. 'Oh,' she said.

Fin shuffled awkwardly. 'I wondered if it might be possible to see him.'

'Well, you've taken your time coming, haven't you?' Her voice was hard, the Gaelic giving it a steely edge. It also had the rasp of an inveterate smoker. 'It's almost twenty years since Calum broke his back, and none of you even had the decency to visit. Except for Angel, poor boy.'

311

Fin was torn between guilt and curiosity. 'Angel came to see Calum?'

'Aye, every week. Regular as clockwork.' She paused to draw a wheezing breath. 'But he'll not be coming any more, will he?'

Fin stood for a moment, uncertain how to respond, before deciding there was no adequate response he could make. 'Is Calum there?' He looked beyond her into the house.

'No, he's not. He's working.'

'Where can I find him, then?'

'In the shed, round the other side of the house. Angel built it for the loom.' She took a packet of cigarettes from the pocket of her apron and lit one. 'You'll hear it when you go round. Just knock.' She blew out a cloud of smoke and closed the door in his face.

Fin followed the path around the bungalow. The paving stones had been carefully laid and cemented to smooth out the passage for the wheelchair, and Fin wondered if Angel had been responsible for that, too. He ducked under a clothesline heavy with washing blowing in the wind, and saw the shed in the lee of the house. It was a simple breezeblock structure, harled to protect it from the rain, and had a steeply pitched tin roof. There was a window in each face, and a door facing out to a hump of peat stack and the moor beyond. Sunlight reflected in momentary flashes on fragments of water gathered in all its hollows.

As he approached the door he heard the rhythmical clacking of the loom, the turning of wheels turning wheels, sending wooden shuttles shooting back and forth across lines of spun wool almost faster than the eye could see. When he'd been a boy, it was nearly impossible to walk down any street in Ness without hearing a loom in action somewhere, in someone's shed or garage. Fin had always wondered why tweed woven on Lewis was called Harris Tweed. Whatever it was called, its weavers had never made much money at it. Harris Tweed was not Harris Tweed unless woven by hand, and at one time islanders had laboured at home in their thousands to produce the stuff. The mills in Stornoway paid them a pittance for it before selling it on to markets in Europe and America for a handsome profit. But now the bottom had fallen out of those markets, tweed replaced by more fashionable fabrics, and only a handful of weavers remained, still earning a pittance.

Fin raised his hand to knock on the door and hesitated, closing his eyes, and feeling again a surge of the guilt that had haunted him through all the years since it happened. For just a moment he wondered if Calum would remember him, before dismissing the thought as foolish. Of course he would remember. How could he forget?

313

THIRTEEN

It might seem like stating the obvious, but the Lews Castle School in those days was in Lews Castle. Many of the students and staff lodged at the school, in accommodation created amidst the castle's rabbit warren of corridors and landings. I only mention it, because the year that Calum and I climbed up on the roof was the last year that the school was actually in the castle. The building was in a poor state of repair and deteriorating fast, and the education authority couldn't afford the upkeep. So the school moved elsewhere, even though it was still called the Lews Castle School.

Oddly enough, the place it moved to was the Gibson Hostel in Ripley Place, where I lodged during my first year at the Nicolson, which was my third year of secondary school.

Because of his poor results at Crobost, Artair had been sent to the Lews Castle for vocational studies, and found himself in the delightful company of such old friends as Murdo Ruadh and his big brother, Angel. Calum had the good fortune to be sent to the Nicolson. He never said anything, but it must have been a huge relief for him to escape the endless bullying and beatings he had suffered through all the years at Crobost.

I never had very much time for Calum at school. He sort of tagged around after us, I think in the hope that he might pick up some of our cast-off girlfriends. Calum wasn't very good with girls. He was crushingly shy and would blush to the roots of his ginger curls if one even spoke to him. The only way he would get to meet any girls was if he was part of a crowd. And that way he would never have to make a fool of himself by making his own introductions. It's hard for teenage boys. Girls don't realize it. You have to put yourself out there, vulnerable to rejection if a girl turns you down when you ask for a dance, or offer to buy her a fish supper in The Narrows. All those hormones that flood a teenage boy's system force him into risking such rejection, then leave him frustrated as well as humiliated when it comes. I am happy not to be fifteen any more.

We were all at the St Valentine's Day dance that year in Stornoway town hall. Usually we would go back to Ness for the weekend, but because of the dance everyone was staying over at the hostels. There was a band playing the latest songs from the charts. It's funny how at that age music provides your memory markers. Usually it's olfactory, a scent associated with some place or moment in your life, that catches you by surprise and transports you

315

back through space and time, evoking with startling resonance a memory you had all but forgotten. But it's mostly music that takes you back to your teens. I have always associated certain songs with certain girls. I remember a girl called Sine (her name was pronounced like the English *Sheena*). It was Sine I took to the dance that February. Whenever I hear the Foreigner single 'Waiting for a Girl Like You', maybe just a fragment of it caught on some golden oldies show on the car radio, or some TV repeat of an old *Top of the Pops*, I think of Sine. She was a pretty wee girl, but a bit too keen. I can remember jumping about at the dance like an idiot to XTC's 'Senses Working Overtime', and Meat Loaf's 'Dead Ringer for Love'. But 'Waiting for a Girl Like You' was the Sine song. As I recall, that night I didn't wait for her at all. I abandoned her and left early with Calum to get back to the hostel before they closed the doors. That was my excuse, anyway.

Artair was still going out with Marsaili at the time, and they went to the St Valentine's dance together. There was a song in the charts then called 'Arthur's Theme (Best That You Can Do)'. I thought it was really weird, because the lyrics seemed to fit Artair so well. All about just having a good time and not caring about other people's aspirations for you. Artair's Song, I called it. When they played it that night, Artair and Marsaili were dancing together, kind of close and smoochy. I was dancing with Sine, but I couldn't help watching them over her head. I hadn't listened to the first verse before, which wasn't the verse about Arthur. But I caught it that time. It was about finding a girl who turns your heart around, and then losing her and not really knowing quite how you managed it. And those words stirred something inside me, some latent sense of jealousy or regret, and I found myself dancing with Sine and wishing it was Marsaili. Of course, it passed. Hormones again. They played havoc with my head in those days.

Calum was having a frustrating night. He'd been dancing with a demure little dark-haired girl called Anna. But only when it suited her. He asked her for every dance. Sometimes she would say yes. Other times she turned him down. He was completely smitten, and she knew it and was playing games with him.

About halfway through the night, a group of us was standing shivering out in the street, smoking, and drinking from cans of beer that someone had planked outside. The thump of music and the rabble of voices from the dance followed us out into the wet February night, along with Calum. Murdo Ruadh and Angel were there in the crowd and saw an opportunity to do a little Calum-baiting.

'Aye, you're on for a bit of nookie the night, son,' Murdo said, leering at the miserable Calum.

'That'll be fucking right,' Angel said. 'She's a wee prick-teaser that one.'

'What would you know about her?' Calum said moodily.

317

'What do I know about her?' Angel guffawed. 'Everything, boy. Been there, done it.'

'Liar!' Calum shouted. In other circumstances, Angel might have taken offence and given Calum a doing, but for some reason he was in a benevolent mood that night and seemed more intent on taking Calum under his wing than doing him any harm. I know now, of course, that he had already formed a plan.

'Anna works up at Lews Castle,' he said. 'She's a maid at the school. Maid Anna, they call her.'

Murdo Ruadh slapped Calum on the back. 'Aye, boy, and you've never lived until you've made Anna. Everyone else has.' And he fell about laughing at his own joke.

Calum went for him. Like a cat. All claws and flailing arms. Murdo was so taken aback he dropped his can, and beer fizzed out of it all over the pavement. Artair and I pulled Calum off, and I really thought then that Murdo was going to kill him. But Angel stepped in, pushing a big hand into his wee brother's chest. 'Lay off, Ruadh. Can't you see the boy's smitten?'

Murdo was fuming. This was a serious loss of face. 'I'll fucking kill him.'

'No, you won't. The boy's just not thinking right. I remember the first time you got all soppy over some lassie. God, it was pathetic.' Murdo's humiliation increased with every word his brother uttered. 'You need to . . . what's the word . . . empathize.' He grinned. 'There's maybe a wee favour we could do the boy.'

Murdo looked at Angel as if he thought he had lost his senses. 'What're you on about?'

'Bath night.'

A look of complete incomprehension scrawled itself on Murdo's face. 'Bath night? For Christ's sake, Angel, we're not sharing that with a wee shite like him.'

Calum struggled to free himself from my grip and straighten his jacket. 'What do you mean?' Out in the bay a foghorn sounded, and we turned to see the lights of the *Suilven* as she ploughed her way out into the Minch on the start of her three-and-a-half-hour crossing to Ullapool.

Angel said, 'The staff at the school have got rooms up at the top of the castle. They share a bathroom up in the gods, and because the window looks out on to the roof, they never pull the blind. Wee Anna takes her bath every Sunday night, ten o'clock on the dot. I don't think there's a boy in the school who hasn't been up there for a peek. She's got a great wee body on her, that right, Murdo?'

Murdo just glowered at his brother.

'We could arrange a private viewing for you if you want.'

'That's disgusting!' Calum said.

Angel shrugged. 'Suit yourself. We've made the offer. You don't take us up on it, that's your loss.'

I could see that Calum was torn, but I was relieved when at length he said, 'No way,' and went strutting off back into the dance.

'That's pretty shitty,' I said, 'winding him up like that.'

Angel made a great show of extravagant innocence. 'Nobody's winding him up, orphan boy. You get a view into that bathroom up there as clear as day. You fancy a wee peek yourself?'

'Fuck off,' I said. I was good at the witty comeback in those days. And I went back into the dance in search of Sine.

I was pleased to see that Calum was dancing with Anna when I went in, but over the next hour or so she must have knocked him back seven or eight times. On a couple of occasions I saw him sitting on one of the seats along the wall, all on his own, watching miserably as she danced with other boys. She even danced with Angel Macritchie, the two of them chatting animatedly and laughing together, and I saw her rubbing her body against him and glancing over to see if Calum was watching. Of course, he was. He was a poor soul, really, and I couldn't help feeling sorry for him.

And then I forgot about him, and started working on how to extricate myself from the Sine situation. Every time I sat down she was all over me. She even put her tongue in my ear, which I thought was disgusting. Ironically, it was Calum who rescued me in the end. He came up to us with his hands thrust deep in his pockets. I remember the band was playing the Stranglers' song 'Golden Brown'.

'I'm going.'

I made a great show of looking at my watch. 'Oh, my

God, is it that time already? We'll never get back to the Gibson before they lock the doors.' Calum opened his mouth to say something, but I cut him off before he got me into trouble. 'We're going to have to run.' I jumped to my feet and turned to Sine. 'Sorry, Sine. See you next week.' I saw her jaw drop in amazement before I took Calum by the arm and hurried him away across the dance floor. 'But not if I see you first,' I muttered under my breath.

'What's going on?' Calum said.

'Just getting myself out of a tight corner.'

'Lucky you. I can't even get *into* a tight corner.'

The smell of the sea was strong on the wind that night. An icy February blast that would have cut you in two. The rain had stopped, but the streets were all shiny under the streetlamps, like wet paint. The Narrows were jammed, and Calum and I pushed our way through to the inner harbour and along Cromwell Street to Church Street, before climbing the hill to Matheson Road.

It was only when we turned into Robertson Road that Calum told me he was going to do it.

'Do what?'

'I'm going up to the castle tomorrow night.'

'What?' I couldn't believe him. 'You're kidding.'

'It's all arranged. I spoke to Angel before we left the dance. He's going to fix it for me.'

'Why?'

'Because Angel was right. She's just a wee prick-teaser.

It'll be like getting my own back on her, getting to see her naked in the bath.'

'No, I mean why would Angel fix it for you? All he's ever done is beat the living crap out of you. Why would he suddenly be your best pal?'

Calum shrugged. 'He's not as bad as you think, you know.'

'Aye, right.' I was unable to conceal my scepticism.

'Anyway, I was wondering . . .' He hesitated. From up here we could just see, over the rooftops, the crenellated towers of the castle, floodlit on the hill across the bay.

'What were you wondering, Calum?'

'I was wondering if you would come with me?'

'What? You've got to be joking! No way.' Not only would it be a Sunday, and we'd get hell if we were caught sneaking out at that time of night, but I was highly suspicious of the whole thing. Calum was being set up. For what, I had no idea, but I was pretty sure that Angel had not suddenly discovered a philanthropic side to his nature.

'Oh, please, Fin. I can't do it on my own. You don't have to go up on the roof or anything. Just come to the castle with me.'

'No!' But I already knew I would. Reluctantly. It was certain that they were planning something for the poor wee bugger. And someone had to look out for him. If I went along maybe I could stop him from getting into too much trouble. I wish now that I hadn't. Maybe things would have turned out differently.

*

It was a bitterly cold night, a stiff wind sweeping frequent squally showers of sleet and hail in off the Minch. I really did not want to leave the dry, warm security of the hostel to embark on some insane adventure, nature unknown, outcome uncertain. But I had, in the end, promised Calum, and so we ducked out into the night just before nine-thirty, waterproofs turned up around our necks, and baseball caps pulled down low on our heads, peaks obscuring faces in case we were spotted. We had left a window open on a first-floor corridor at the back of the hostel, accessible by rone pipe, so that we could get back in. Although I did not relish the climb on a night like this.

Stornoway was like a ghost town, streetlamps casting feeble pools of light in dark, empty streets. The God-fearing people of the town were locked up cosy in their homes behind drawn curtains, watching TV and supping cups of hot cocoa before heading for bed. In the inner harbour, the rattle and creak of trawlers tied up at the quayside fought to be heard above the wind. The icy black waters were choppy, slapping against the concrete stanchions of the quay and breaking white on the shores of the Castle Green on the other side of the bay. We hurried along the deserted Bayhead, turning off at the Bridge Community Centre and scampering quickly over the bridge into the trees beyond. Up the hill, then, in a fearful sleety squall, and on to the road above the golf club. As we reached the road, the sky opened up, and the most extraordinary silver moonlight spilled down across the manicured expanse of golf course, so bright you might almost have expected to see golfers pitching up the hill to the fifth hole.

Lews Castle was built in the 1870s as a mansion house for Sir James Matheson. He bought the Isle of Lewis in 1844 with the proceeds from the opium he and his partner William Jardine had imported into China, turning six million Chinese into hopeless addicts in the process. It's strange to think that the misery of millions led to the transformation of a tiny Hebridean island thousands of miles away on the other side of the world, or that people and their land can just be bought and sold. Matheson built a new harbour, and gas and waterworks in Stornoway, as well as a brickworks at Garrabost. He created a chemical factory to extract tar from peat, and a yard to build and repair ships. He transformed the forty-five miles of dirt tracks across the island into two hundred miles of coach-bearing roads. And, of course, he razed the old Seaforth Lodge on the hill overlooking the town, to build his mock-Tudor castle.

It is an extraordinary building of pink granite, with turrets and towers and crenellated battlements. It dominates the hill above the harbour, and is probably the most unlikely thing you will see on any of the islands that make up the Hebridean archipelago.

Of course, in those days, I didn't know the full history. Lews Castle was just there, as if it had always been there. You accepted it, the same way you accepted the cliffs that ringed the Butt, or the fabulous beaches at Scarasta and Luskentyre.

It loomed dark that night amongst the trees at the top of the hill, lights showing in just a few of its windows. Calum and I skirted the main entrance, a huge vaulted porch leading to enormous double doors, and made our way around the back to where Angel had told Calum they would meet him, next to the single-storey annexe that housed the boiler room. Right enough, as we arrived in the long, narrow courtyard between the boiler room and the laundry, a figure moved in the shadows and an arm waved us forward.

'Come on, hurry up!' I was taken aback to find that it was Artair. He was surprised to see me, too. 'What are you doing here?' he hissed in my ear.

'Looking out for Calum,' I whispered back.

But he just shook his head. 'You daft bastard!' And my sense of foreboding deepened.

Artair opened a red door into a short, gloomy corridor. It smelled of old cabbage. I soon realized why, as Artair put a finger to his lips and led us through the kitchens in the semi-dark and then out into what they called the Long Hall. It ran almost the full length of the front of the castle, night lights glowing faintly all along it. As we slipped past what had originally been the library, and then the ballroom, I realized that if we were going to be caught, it would most likely be here. There was nowhere to hide in the nearly two hundred feet of hallway. Any one of the doors along either side, or at either end, might open at any minute, trapping us in full view.

So it was with some relief that we reached the main staircase at the far end of the hall, and followed Artair up the wide stone steps two at a time to the first floor. A narrow spiral stairway took us up to the second floor. Artair led us through further dark halls and doorways into a corridor leading to a tall window at the north end of the castle. There, in the shadows, a group of boys stood waiting in impatient anticipation. More than half a dozen of them. Torches flashed in our faces and I caught a glimpse of theirs. Some I knew, some I didn't. Murdo Ruadh and Angel were among them.

'What are you doing here, orphan boy?' Angel growled in a low whisper, an echo of Artair.

'Just making sure Calum doesn't come to any harm.'

'Why would he?'

'You tell me.'

'Listen, smart boy.' Angel grabbed the lapels of my jacket. 'That wee bitch'll be getting into her bath in less than five minutes. So you've not got much time.'

'I'm not going up on the roof with him.' I pulled myself free of his grasp.

'Aye, you fucking are,' Murdo breathed in my face. 'Or it might just come to the attention of the janitor that there's an intruder in the castle. Know what I'm saying?'

'So call the janitor,' I said. 'Then whatever it is you've got planned will be well and truly screwed.'

Murdo glared at me, but I'd called his bluff and he had no comeback.

Angel slid the window open and stepped out on to the fire escape. 'Come on, Calum. Get out here.'

'Don't, Calum,' I said. 'They're setting you up.'

'Fuck off, orphan boy!' There was murder in Angel's eyes as he peered back at me through the window. Then his frown relaxed into a smile and he turned it on the wavering Calum. 'Come on, son. We're not setting you up for anything. Except an eyeful. If you don't hurry up you'll miss her.' Calum turned away from my disapproval and climbed on to the fire escape. It rattled noisily as I climbed out after him. There was still a chance of persuading him not to do it.

From the second-floor platform of the fire escape, steps ran down to a half-landing, and doubled back to the first-floor platform immediately below. From there steps led up and on to the roof of the entrance porch, and in the other direction down and around the wall to the front of the castle. An extending ladder leaned against the wall outside the window. Angel unhooked the extension and slid it up, almost to its full length, re-hooked it and leaned it against the wall again, adjusting the angle to make it easier to climb.

'There you go.'

Calum looked up. The ladder reached just beyond a ledge nearly three feet below the crenellations around the roof. I saw the panic in his eyes. 'I can't do it.'

'Course you can.' Angel's voice was almost soothing.

Calum gave me a frightened rabbit look. 'Come with me, Fin. I'm not good with heights.'

'You should have fucking thought of that before you came,' Murdo whispered through the window.

'You really don't have to do this, Calum,' I said. 'Let's just go home.'

I wasn't prepared for the violence with which Angel slammed me up against the wall. 'You go up there with him, orphan boy. Make sure he doesn't come to any harm.' I felt his spittle in my face. 'That's what you came for, isn't it?'

'I'm not going up on the roof!'

Angel leaned in close and whispered, almost intimately, 'Either you go up, orphan boy, or you go down. The hard way.'

'Please, Fin,' Calum said. 'I'm too scared to do it on my own.'

I didn't see that I had any choice. I pulled myself free of Angel's grip. 'Alright.' I looked up towards the roof wishing I had never agreed to come. In fact it looked a fairly simple matter to climb the ladder and then swing yourself up through one of the crenellations on to the roof. It had to be flat up there, and once you were up there was no danger of falling, with the battlements creating a retaining wall.

'We're running out of time,' Angel said. 'And the longer we're out here the more chance we have of getting caught.'

'Go on, Calum,' I said. 'Let's get it over with.'

'You are coming with me?'

'I'm right behind you.' I glanced back through the window at Artair, and he just shrugged, as if to say that it wasn't his fault that I had chosen to come with Calum.

Angel said, 'Once you're up, you'll see the pitched roof of the attic. It's a skylight window into the bathroom. You'll know which one when the light comes on.'

And all the time I kept wondering what the trick would be. What we were really going to find up there. But there was no way of backing out now. At least the rain was off for the moment, and the moonlight made it easy to see where we were going.

Calum set off up the ladder, making it tremble beneath him, the rattle of it transferring to the fire escape. 'For Christ's sake keep the noise down,' Angel called after him in a stage whisper, grabbing the ladder to hold it steady. Then he turned to me. 'Right, orphan boy, on you go.' He grinned, and I just knew this was all going to end in tears.

As I had thought, it was relatively easy getting on to the roof from the ladders. Even for Calum. I joined him, crouching on the flat, tarred surface, and we could see, through the crenellations, all the way down to the harbour below. The trawlers looked unreal, toy boats lined up against the quay, the town spreading itself up over the hill behind, necklaces of light tracing the lines of the streets as they criss-crossed each other in a traditional grid pattern. Somewhere, away out in the Minch, we saw the lights of a tanker making its way steadily north through a heavy swell.

In the moonlight I could see the pitch of the attic roof quite clearly. There were a couple of skylights, but no light in either of them.

'Where now?' Calum whispered.

'Let's just sit tight and wait to see if a light comes on.'

We crouched down with our backs to the battlements, knees pulled up to our chests to try to keep warm, and waited. I checked my watch. It was nearly five past ten. I heard some rattling and giggling from the fire escape below, and was tempted to give up right there and then and climb back down. But the thought of Angel waiting for us at the foot of the ladders was enough to make me decide to give it another few minutes.

Suddenly a light went on in the nearer of the two skylights, and an elongated square of yellow fell out across the roof. Calum's eyes positively gleamed with anticipation. 'That must be her.' He was suddenly emboldened. 'Come on.' And he scuttled across the roof to the skylight. Since I was there, I thought, I might as well have a look, too. So I followed him, and we crouched for a minute or more below the level of the window, plucking up the courage to raise our heads into the light and peer in. We could hear the sound of water running, and someone moving about below the window.

'You go first,' I said. 'Better hurry up, before the

window gets all steamed up and we can't see anything.'

A look of worry flitted across Calum's face. 'I hadn't thought of that.' Slowly he eased himself up the pitch of the roof until he was pushing up on his tiptoes, and I could see him peering in the window. I heard a loud hiss, and then he was crouching down beside me again, a face like thunder. I don't think I'd ever seen him so angry. 'Bastards! Fucking bastards!' I hadn't heard him swear like that either.

'What is it?'

'See for yourself.' He drew another deep indignant breath. 'Bastards!'

So I pushed myself up the angle of the roof until my face was level with the window. Just as someone on the other side took it off the latch and pushed it out. I found myself face to face with a big, round, white-faced woman wearing a pink bath cap and nothing else. The startled look on her face could only have been a reflection of my own. I'm not sure if it was my scream or hers that I heard, but we both screamed, of that I am certain, and she went staggering backwards and fell into her bath, great mountains of juddering white flesh displacing gallons of hot water all across the floor. For a moment I was paralysed, staring in shock at the fat, naked woman floundering in the bath. She was sixty if she was a day. My face must have been clearly visible in the bathroom light, because she was staring back at me, her legs still in the air. I had no wish to see what they revealed, but found my eyes drawn in horrified fascination. She took a deep tremulous breath that sent her mountainous pink breasts quivering, and she screamed the scream of the dead. I thought she was going to burst my eardrums. I slithered back down the roof and almost landed on top of Calum.

His eyes were like headlamps. 'What happened?'

I shook my head. 'It doesn't matter. We've got to get the hell out of here!'

I could hear her screaming, 'Help!' And, 'Rape!' And thought that now she was just indulging in wishful thinking. Lights were going on all across the roof. I ran back over to where we had climbed up from the ladder, and I could hear Calum pattering along behind me. I squeezed between the crenellations, turning and dropping a leg down to find the top rung, before I realized it wasn't there.

'Shit!'

'What is it?' Calum looked terrified.

'The bastards have taken the ladder away.' So that had been their plan. To trap us up on the roof. They must have known Anna would not be taking a bath that night. She might even have been in league with them. What none of them could have foreseen, however, was that we would be spotted by the fat lady who was. Now the ladder was gone, we were stuck on the roof, and the whole castle had been alerted. It could only be a matter of time before they found us, and then there would be hell to pay. I climbed back on to the roof, anger fighting with anticipation of the humiliation to come.

'Well, we can't just stay here.' Calum was panicking. 'They'll find us.'

'We've got no choice. There's no way down unless you've suddenly grown wings.'

'We can't be caught! We *can't*!' He was becoming hysterical. 'What'll my mother say?'

'I think that's the least of our worries, Calum.'

'Oh God, oh God,' he said again and again. 'We've got to do something.' He started climbing through the crenellations.

I grabbed him. 'What are you doing?'

'If we get on to the ledge, we can jump down on to the fire escape from there. It's only about ten feet.' This from the boy who only ten minutes earlier had been claiming a fear of heights.

'Are you mad? Calum, it's too dangerous.'

'No, we can do it, we *can*.'

'Jesus, Calum, don't!' But there was nothing I could do to stop him. He braced himself with a hand on either side of the gap, and slid down until his feet found the ledge. There were lights coming on now in the north tower. The woman was still screaming, but her voice had become distant. I had a mental image of her running naked along a corridor somewhere, and I shuddered.

I saw Calum glance down, and when he turned back again his face was sheet-white in the moonlight. There was an odd look in his eyes, and I felt my stomach lurch. I just knew something bad was going to happen. 'Fin, I was wrong. I can't do it' His voice was quivering and breathless.

'Give me your hand.'

'I can't move. Fin, I can't move.'

'Yes, you can. Just give me your hand and we'll get you back on the roof.'

But he was shaking his head. 'I can't do it. I can't. I *can't*.' And I watched in disbelief as he just let go and slipped backwards out of view. I could not move. It was as if I had been turned to stone. There was a yawning silence, and then a dreadful clatter on the fire escape below. Calum never made a sound.

It must have been a full half-minute before I could bring myself to look. He had missed the second-floor platform completely, falling another whole floor to land on his back on the handrail and slide down on to the metal grille. His body was twisted at an unnatural angle, and he was not moving.

Right then felt like the worst moment of my life. I closed my eyes and prayed fervently that I would wake up.

'Macleod!' My name came up to me from below, and I heard a clatter on the fire escape. I opened my eyes and saw Angel on the platform. He had the ladder out there again, and was fumbling to slide the extension up the rungs. The top of the ladder scraped across the wall just beneath the crenellations. 'Macleod! For fuck sake, get down here now!'

I was still stone, the same granite as the walls, a part of them, locked there for eternity. I couldn't drag my eyes away from the prone, twisted form of poor Calum thirty feet below.

'Macleod!' Angel almost bellowed my name. Blood rushed back through my frozen veins and I began shaking almost uncontrollably. But, still, I could move again. And with jelly legs, I clambered like an automaton through the crenellations and on to the ladder, going down it faster than was safe, my hands burning on the cold metal. I had barely reached the platform when Angel grabbed my jacket. His face was inches from mine. I could smell the stale tobacco on his breath and for the second time that night felt his spittle in my face. 'You don't say a word. Not a fucking word. You were never here, right?' And when I said nothing, he pushed his face even closer. 'Right?' I nodded. 'Okay, go. Down the fire escape. Don't even look back.'

He let go of me and starting climbing back through the window, leaving the ladder where it was, leaning up against the wall. I could see washed-out frightened faces in the darkness beyond. Still I didn't move. Angel glared back at me from inside. And for the first time in my life I saw fear in his face. Real fear.

'Go!' He slid the window shut.

I turned then and ran down the rattling steps of the fire escape until I reached the first-floor platform. There I stopped. I would have to step over Calum's body to reach the next flight of stairs. I could see his face now. Pale and passive, just as if he were sleeping. And then I saw the blood seeping slowly across the metal from behind his head, thick and dark, like molasses. There were voices coming from somewhere in the grounds below, and outside lights came on at the front door. I knelt down and touched his face. It was still warm, and I saw the rise and fall of his chest. He was breathing. But there was nothing I could do for him. It could only be a matter of minutes before they would find him. And me, too, if I didn't go. I stepped carefully over him and ran down the final flight of steps as fast as I could, jumping the last half-dozen and then sprinting for the cover of the trees. I heard someone shout, and footsteps running on gravel. But I didn't look back. And I didn't stop running until I reached the bridge at the Community Centre. In the distance I heard the wail of a siren and saw the blue light of an ambulance flashing up through the trees towards the castle. I leaned over the rail, holding on to it to stop my legs from buckling, and threw up into the Bayhead River. The tears were streaming down my face in the freezing February wind, and I turned and hurried across the main road to begin the long, slow jog up Mackenzie Street to Matheson Road. The lights were out in most of the windows now, and I felt like I was the only person still alive in the whole of Stornoway.

By the time I got to Ripley Place, I could hear the distant siren of the ambulance on its return journey from the castle to the hospital. If I had believed in miracles, I would have asked God for one right there and then. Maybe it's my fault that I didn't. Maybe if I had, Calum would have been okay.

That was the last time I saw him, and I have lived with the memory of that final moment ever since. The spattering of freckles in a chalk-white face. The tight, carrot curls. The blood like treacle on the metal beneath him. The impossible twist of his body as it lay in the moonlight.

He was airlifted to a specialist unit in Glasgow. We heard through the grapevine that he had broken his back and wouldn't walk again. He never returned to school, staying on the mainland during those first months for intensive therapy. It's amazing how quickly time grows new skin over open wounds. As it became clear that the true circumstances surrounding what really took place that night were not going to surface after all, new memories replaced old, raw ones, like healing skin, and poor Calum gradually receded from the forefront of all our minds. An old wound that only hurt if you thought about it, and so you didn't. At least, not consciously. Not if you could help it.

FOURTEEN

I

He knocked on the door, but the clackety-clack of the loom continued uninterrupted. Fin drew a deep breath and waited until there was a pause for a change of shuttle. Then he knocked again. There was a moment's silence, then a voice told him to enter.

The inside of the shed was a dumping ground for almost everything imaginable. An old bicycle, a lawnmower and strimmer, garden tools, fishing net, electric cable. The loom itself was set in the corner, the walls behind it lined with shelves of tools and stacks of different-coloured spun wool, all within easy reach of the weaver. There was a clear passage to it for the wheelchair, and Calum sat behind the loom, large metal handles jutting up at either hand from the mechanism below.

Fin was shocked. Calum had put on a huge amount of weight. His once-delicate frame was round-shouldered and gross. A great collar of flesh propped up his chin, and his ginger hair was all but gone. What was left of it had been cropped, although it still kept its colour. Pale skin that never saw the sun looked bleached, almost blue-white. Even the once vivid spattering of freckles seemed to have faded. Calum squinted at Fin standing in the light of the doorway, his green eyes wary and suspicious.

'Who's that?'

Fin moved away from the door so that the light was no longer behind him. 'Hello, Calum.'

It was a moment or two before Fin saw recognition in Calum's eyes. There was surprise there, too, for just a second before a dull glaze passed across them like cataracts. 'Hello, Fin. I've been expecting you for twenty years. You took your time.'

Fin knew there were no excuses he could make. 'I'm sorry.'

'What for? It wasn't your fault. My stupid idea. And as you see, I didn't have wings after all.'

Fin nodded. 'How have you been?' Even as he said it he knew it was a stupid thing to ask. And he only did because he had no idea what else to say.

'How do you think?'

'I can't imagine.'

'I bet you can't. Unless it's happened to you, how can you possibly imagine what it's like to have no control of your bowels or your bladder? To have to be changed like a baby when you soil yourself? You wouldn't believe the sores you get on your arse when you have to sit on it all day. And sex?' A tiny bitter breath of laughter forced its way between his lips. 'Well, of course, I'm still a virgin. Can't even have a wank. Couldn't find the damned thing even if I wanted to. And the irony of it is, that's what it was all about in the first place. Sex.' He paused, lost in some distant memory. 'She's dead, you know?'

Fin frowned. 'Who?'

'Maid Anna. Killed in a motorbike accident years ago. And here's me, a big lump of lard stuck in a wheelchair, still going strong. Doesn't seem right, does it?' He dragged his eyes away from Fin and finished rethreading the shuttle before slipping it back into the empty slot in its drum. 'Why are you here, Fin?'

'I'm a cop now, Calum.'

'I'd heard.'

'I'm investigating Angel Macritchie's death.'

'Ah, so you didn't just call for the pleasure of my company.'

'I'm on the island because of the murder. I'm here because I should have come a long time ago.'

'Putting old ghosts to rest, eh? Rubbing salve on a troubled conscience.'

'Maybe.'

Calum sat back and looked at Fin very directly. 'You know, the biggest irony of all is that the only real friend I've had in all the years since it happened was Angel Macritchie. Now there's a fucking turn-up for you.'

'Your mother told me he'd built the shed for the loom.'

'Oh, he did more than that. He refitted the whole house, made every room accessible for the chair. He made that garden out there, and laid the path so I could sit out if I wanted.' He shrugged. 'Not that I ever wanted.' He grabbed the handles on either side of him. 'He adapted the loom so that I could work it by hand, a clever extension to the foot pedals.' He started working the levers backwards and forwards, and the shuttles flew across the weave of the cloth, wheels and cogs interlocking to drive the whole complex process. 'Smart man.' He raised his voice above the clatter of the machine. 'Much smarter than we ever gave him credit for.' He released the levers and the loom came to a halt. 'Not that I make much from the weaving. Of course, there's my mother's pension, and the little money that's left from the compensation we got. But it's hard, Fin, making ends meet. Angel made sure we never went short. He never came empty-handed. Salmon, rabbit, deer. And, of course, he always had half a dozen gugas for us each year. Cooked them himself, too.' Calum lifted another shuttle from a wooden bin hooked over the arm of his chair and played with it distractedly. 'At first, when he started coming, I suppose it was guilt that made him do it. And I think he expected I would blame him.'

'Didn't you?'

Calum shook his head. 'Why should I? He didn't force me to go up on the roof. Sure, he was trying to make a fool of me, but I was the one who made the fool of myself. He might have taken the ladder away, but he didn't push me off the roof. I panicked. I was stupid. I'm the only one to blame.' Fin saw his knuckles turning white as his fingers tightened around the shuttle before he released it into its box. 'Then when he realized I didn't bear him any ill-will, I suppose he might just have stopped coming. Conscience clear. But he didn't. If you'd told me all those years ago that I'd end up being friends with Angel Macritchie I'd have told you you were off your head.' He shook his head as if he still found it hard to believe himself. 'But that's what we became. He'd come up every week to work in the garden, and he'd sit in here for hours, just talking. About all sorts.'

He broke off, and sat lost in a silence that Fin did not dare to break. Then tears welled up suddenly in his eyes, blurring green, and Fin was shocked. Calum glanced up at his old school friend. 'He wasn't a bad man, Fin. Not really.' He tried to wipe the tears away. 'He liked folk to think he was some kind of hard case, but all he did was treat people the way life treated him. A kind of sharing out of the misery. I saw another side to him, a side I don't think anyone else ever saw, not even his own brother. A side he wouldn't have wanted anyone else to see. A side to him that showed how he might have been in other circumstances, in another life.' And more tears trembled on the rims of his eyes before spilling over to roll down his cheeks. Big, silent, slow tears. 'I don't know what I'm going to do without him.' He made a determined effort to blink them away and took out a handkerchief to dry his face. He tried to force a smile, but it looked more like a grimace. 'Anyway . . .' A bitter edge crept back into his voice. 'It was good of you to drop by. If you're ever passing, call again.'

'Calum . . .'

'Go, Fin. Just go. Please.'

Fin turned reluctantly towards the door and pulled it gently shut behind him. He heard the loom start up inside. Clackety-clack, clackety-clack. The sun was shining across the moor beyond the peat stack, a mocking sun that only heightened Fin's depression. He found it hard to imagine what Angel and Calum had talked about together all those years. But one thing was certain. Whoever had murdered Angel Macritchie, it wasn't Calum. The poor, crippled weaver was probably the only person on earth to spill a tear over Angel's passing.

II

As he drove back down the hill, there was more and more blue in the sky, torn in ragged patches from the swathes of cloud blowing in off the Atlantic. The land, falling away below him, was an ever-changing patchwork of sunlight and shadow, one chasing the other across a machair peppered with crofts and cottages, fences and sheep. The ocean, away to his right, was a hard, bright, steely reflection of the sky.

He passed his parents' croft and felt a gut-wrenching sadness at the sight of the collapsed roof. Only a few moss-covered tiles clung to the remains of it. The once white walls were streaked with mould and algae. The windows were gone. The front door lay ajar, opening into a dark, abandoned shell of a house. Even the floorboards had been stripped out. Just a trace of peeling purple paint remained, clinging stubbornly to the door jamb.

He dragged his eyes away from it, back to the road, and pushed his foot down on the accelerator. It was no good looking backwards, even if you had no notion of where it was you were going.

There was someone in the garden beyond Artair's bungalow, bent over beneath the raised bonnet of an old Mini. Fin slipped his foot across to the brake and drew in at the top of the drive. The figure straightened up, turning at the sound of car tyres sliding on gravel. Fin had thought for a moment that the person in the boiler suit might have been Marsaili, but he was not disappointed when he saw that it was Fionnlagh. He turned off the ignition and stepped out on to the path. In the dark, the night before, he had not seen the car wrecks piled up in the garden, and not noticed them when he had left in a rush that morning. Five of them, rusted and stripped down for their parts, bits and pieces of them strewn across the grass like the old bones of long-dead animals. Fionnlagh had a toolkit open on the ground beside him. He was holding a spanner in oil-blackened hands, and there were oily smears on his face. 'Hi,' he said, as Fin approached.

Fin nodded towards the Mini. 'Got her going yet?'

Fionnlagh laughed. 'Naw. I think maybe she's been dead for too long. I'm just trying to get her on life support.'

'It'll be a while before she's back on the road, then?'

'It'll be a miracle.'

'They're all the rage again these days, Minis.' Fin peered at it more closely. 'Is she a Mini Cooper?'

'An original. I got her for a fiver from a car graveyard in Stornoway. It cost more to get her here than it did to buy her. My mum said if I could get her going she would pay for my driving lessons.'

As he spoke Fin had the opportunity to look at him more closely. He was a slight-built boy, like his mother, the same intensity in his eyes. But there was the same mischief there, too.

'Caught your killer yet?'

'Afraid not. Is your mum at home?'

'She's gone down to the store.'

'Ah.' Fin nodded, and there was a moment of awkwardness between them. 'Have you been to the surgery yet, to give your DNA sample?'

A surly expression fell across the boy's face, like a shadow. 'Yeh. Wasn't any way I was going to get out of it.'

'How's the computer?'

The shadow passed and his face lit up again. 'Brilliant.

345

Thanks, Fin. I'd never have figured that firmware thing out for myself. System Ten's brilliant. I've spent half the day copying my CDs into iTunes.'

'You'll need an iPod to download them to.'

The boy smiled ruefully. 'You seen the price of them?'

Fin laughed. 'Yeh, I know. But the Shuffle's pretty cheap.' Fionnlagh nodded, and the two of them fell into another uneasy silence. Then Fin said, 'How long d'you think your mum'll be?'

'Dunno. Half an hour maybe.'

'I'll hang on, then.' He hesitated. 'You fancy going down to the beach? I feel like I need a good blast of sea air to blow away the cobwebs.'

'Sure. I'm getting nowhere fast with this anyway. Give me two minutes to clean up and get out of this boiler suit. And I'll have to let my gran know where I'm going.' Fionnlagh gathered his tools back into their box and took them into the house with him. Fin watched him go and wondered why he was torturing himself like this. Even if he was Fin's biological son, Fionnlagh was still Artair's boy. Artair had said to him that morning, *It hasn't mattered for seventeen years, why the fuck should it matter now?* And he was right. If it had always been that way, why should knowing about it make any difference? Fin kicked at a spiny turf of grass with the toe of his shoe. But somehow it did.

Fionnlagh appeared in jeans and trainers and a fresh white sweatshirt. 'Better not be too long. My gran doesn't like being left on her own.'

Fin nodded and the two of them set off along the top of the cliffs to the gully that Artair and Fin used as boys to get down to the shore. Fionnlagh made easy work of it, not even taking his hands out of his pockets until he jumped the last four feet on to the flat, slightly angled slab of gneiss where the young Fin had once made love to Marsaili. Fin found climbing down to the rocky out-crop a little harder than when he had last done it eighteen years before, and fell behind as Fionnlagh skipped sure-footedly over the slippery black wedges of rock to the beach. He waited on the sand for Fin to catch him up.

'My mum said you two used to go out together.'

'That was a long time ago.'

They headed down to the water's edge and started walking towards the Port. 'So why did you break up?'

Fin found himself slightly embarrassed by the boy's directness. 'Oh, you know, people do.' He laughed at a suddenly returning memory. 'Actually, we broke up twice. First time, we were only eight.'

'Eight?' Fionnlagh was incredulous. 'You were going out when you were eight?'

'Well, I wouldn't really call it going out. We had a kind of thing between us. Had done ever since we started school. I used to walk her home to the farm. Are her folks still there?'

'Oh, sure. But we don't see very much of them these days.' Fin was surprised and waited for Fionnlagh to elucidate, but he didn't. Instead, he said, 'So why did you break up when you were eight?'

'Oh, it was all my fault. Your mum turned up at school one day wearing glasses. Awful things. Blue, with wings, and lenses so thick they made her eyes look like golf balls.'

Fionnlagh laughed at the image Fin had conjured up. 'Jees, that must have made her attractive.'

'Well, exactly. And, of course, everyone in the class made fun of her. *Four eyes*, and *goggle eyes*, all that kind of stuff. You know how merciless kids can be.' His smile faded into sadness. 'And I wasn't any better. I was embarrassed to be seen with her. Avoided her in the playground, stopped walking her home from school. I think she was devastated, the wee soul. Because she was a pretty little girl, your mum. Very self-confident. And a lot of the boys in the class were dead jealous of me. But all that went when she got the glasses.' And even as he remembered it, he felt a stab of guilt and melancholy. Poor Marsaili had gone through hell. And he had been so cruel. 'Kids. They have no idea how hurtful they can be.'

'And that was it? You just stopped being an item?'

'More or less. Your mum pursued me for a while. But if I saw her coming towards me in the playground, I made sure I was suddenly involved in a conversation with someone or joining in a game of football. I was always out of the school gate ahead of her so I wouldn't have to walk her up the road. Sometimes I would turn around in class and find her just looking at me with big doe eyes, glasses discarded on the desk in front of her. But I always pretended I didn't notice. And Jesus . . .' Suddenly something came back to him that he hadn't thought about in more than twenty years. 'There was that time in church.' The memory returned in unexpectedly vivid detail.

Fionnlagh was intrigued. 'What? What happened in church?'

'Oh God . . .' Fin shook his head, smiling remorsefully. 'Except, I'm sure God didn't have much to do with it.' The incoming tide forced them to step smartly up the beach to avoid getting their feet wet. 'In those days my parents were still alive, and I had to go to church every Sunday. Twice. I always used to take a tube of sweets with me. Polo Fruits or something. It was a kind of game to relieve the boredom. To see if I could get them out of the packet and into my mouth without being caught, and then suck them away to nothing without being seen. I suppose it was a kind of small, secret victory against the power of religious oppression if I could work my way through a whole packet without them ever knowing. Although I doubt if I thought about it quite like that at the time.'

Fionnlagh grinned. 'Couldn't have been too good for the teeth.'

'It wasn't.' Fin ran his tongue ruefully around his fillings. 'I'm sure the minister knew what I was up to, he just never caught me. There were times he would fix me with a steely eye, and I would just about choke on the saliva gathering in my mouth as I tried not to swallow until he looked away. Anyway, there was this one Sunday when I was trying to slip a sweet in my mouth during a prayer. You know, one of those long, maundering prayers that the elders deliver from the front of the church. And I dropped the tube of sweets on the floor. Bare floorboards, loud clatter, and the bloody thing rolled right out into the middle of the aisle. Of course, everyone in the church heard it, including all those up in the gallery, which used to be full in those days. And everyone opened their eyes. And there was hardly a soul in the church who didn't see that tube of Polo Fruits lying there. Including the elders, and the minister. The prayer stopped mid-sentence, and hung there like a big question mark. You know, I've never known a silence to last as long in my life. And I knew that there was no way I could get those sweets back without admitting to them being mine. That's when a little figure darted out from the pews on the other side of the aisle and snatched them up.'

'My mum?'

'Your mum. Wee Marsaili took those sweets in full view of the entire congregation so that she would get the blame instead of me. She must have known the trouble she would be in. I caught her eye about ten minutes later. Big, golf-ball eyes peering at me through those awful lenses, looking for some hint of gratitude, some recognition from me for what she had done. But I was just so relieved to have escaped a leathering, I looked away as quickly as I could. I didn't even want to be associated with her.'

'What a bastard.'

Fin turned to find Fionnlagh looking at him, half serious, wholly in earnest. 'Yes, I suppose I was. I'm ashamed to admit it, but I can't deny it. And I can't go back and change it, or do anything different. It's just how it was. Poor Marsaili. She must really have been in love with me, that wee girl.' Unaccountably, and to his acute embarrassment, the world became suddenly blurred. He turned away quickly to look out over the bay, furiously blinking away the beginnings of tears.

'It's a sad story.'

Fin took a moment or two to recover himself. 'I spent the next four years more or less ignoring her.' He was lost now in a childhood world he had all but buried. 'To the point where I'd almost forgotten that there had ever been anything between us. Then there was a dance at the end of our last year of primary, and I asked a girl from the lighthouse called Irene Davis to go. I was at an age when I wasn't that interested in girls, but I had to ask someone, so I asked Irene. It never even occurred to me to ask your mum, until I got a letter from her. It arrived in the post a couple of days before the dance.' He could still see the big, sad scrawl, dark-blue pen on pale-blue paper. 'She couldn't understand why I had asked Irene instead of her. She suggested it wasn't too late to change my mind and ask her instead. Her solution to the problem of Irene was that your dad could take her. She signed it, *The Girl from the Farm*. But, of course, it was too late. I couldn't unask Irene, even if I'd wanted to. In the final event it was your dad who took your mum.'

They had reached the end of the beach, standing almost in the shadow of the boatshed where Angel had been murdered.

'Which only goes to show how much you know when you're eleven years old. Just five years later your mum and I were madly in love and going to spend the rest of our lives together.'

'So what happened that time?'

Fin smiled and shook his head. 'Enough. You've got to leave us a few secrets.'

'Aw, come on. You can't let it go at that.'

'Yes, I can.' Fin turned around and started heading back along the sand towards the rocks. Fionnlagh hurried to catch him up, falling in step beside him, following the footsteps they had left on the way out. Fin said, 'So what are your plans, Fionnlagh? Are you finished with school?'

Fionnlagh nodded glumly, kicking a shell along the compacted sand. 'My dad's trying to get me a job at the yard.'

'You don't sound very enthusiastic.'

'I'm not.'

'So what do you *want* to do?'

'I want to get off this bloody island.'

'Then why don't you?'

'Where would I go? What would I do? I don't know anyone on the mainland.'

'You know me.'

Fionnlagh glanced at him. 'Aye, for five minutes.'

'Listen, Fionnlagh. You might not think so now, but this is a magical place.' And when Fionnlagh gave Fin a look, he said, 'The thing is, you don't appreciate that until you've been away.' It was something he was only just beginning to realize himself. 'And if you don't go, if you stay here all your life, sometimes your view of the world gets skewed. I've seen it in a lot of people here.'

'Like my dad?'

Fin glanced at the boy, but Fionnlagh was keeping his eyes facing front. 'Some people just never get the chance to go, or don't take it if it comes.'

'You did.'

'I couldn't wait to get away.' Fin chuckled. 'I won't deny it, it's a great place to get away from. But it's good to come back to.'

Fionnlagh turned to examine him closely. 'So you're coming back, are you?'

Fin smiled and shook his head. 'Probably not. But that doesn't mean I wouldn't want to.'

'So, if I went to the mainland, what would I do?'

'You could go to college. If you get the qualifications you could go to university.'

'What about the police?'

Fin hesitated. 'It's a good job, Fionnlagh. But it's not for everyone. You get to see things you would never choose to. The very worst side of human nature. And its consequences. Things you can't really do anything to change, but still have to deal with.'

'Is that a recommendation?'

Fin laughed. 'Maybe not. But someone's got to do it. And there are some good people in the force.'

'Is that why you're leaving it?'

'What makes you think I'm leaving?'

'You said you were doing an OU course in computing.'

'You don't miss much, do you?' Fin smiled pensively. 'Let's say I'm looking at alternatives.'

They were nearly back at the rocks now. Fionnlagh said, 'Are you married?' Fin nodded. 'Kids?'

Fin took a long time to reply. Too long. But a denial would not roll off his tongue as glibly as it had with Artair. Finally he said, 'No.'

Fionnlagh clambered up over the rocks and turned back to give Fin a hand up. Fin grasped the proffered hand and pulled himself up alongside the teenager. 'Why would you not tell me the truth about something like that?' Fionnlagh said.

And, again, Fin was taken aback by his directness. A characteristic he had inherited from his mother. 'What makes you think I didn't?'

'Did you?'

Fin looked at him squarely. 'Sometimes there are

things about yourself that you just don't want to talk about.'

'Why?'

'Because talking about them makes you think about them, and thinking about them hurts.' There was an edge to Fin's voice. He saw the boy reacting to it and relented. He sighed. 'I had a son. He was eight years old. But he's dead now.'

'What happened?'

Fin's will to keep it pent up inside was cracking under the boy's relentless questions. He squatted down at the edge of a pool in the rocks, sunlight flashing on its glassy surface, and trailed his fingers through the tepid salt water sending ripples of light off to its miniature shores. 'It was a hit and run. My wife and Robbie were just crossing the road. It wasn't even a busy street. This car came round the corner and, bang. Hit the two of them. She went up in the air and landed on the bonnet. That's probably what saved her life. Robbie went right under the wheels. The driver stopped just for a second. We figure he'd probably been drinking, because the next thing, he put his foot down and was gone. No witnesses. No number. We never did get him.'

'Jesus,' Fionnlagh said softly. 'When did that happen?'

'Just over a month ago.'

Fionnlagh squatted down beside him. 'Fin, I'm so sorry. And I'm sorry I put you through the pain of it all over again.'

Fin waved aside the apology. 'Don't be daft, son. How could you have known?' And at his own use of the word, *son*, he felt his heart miss a beat. He glanced at Fionnlagh, but the boy seemed lost in thought. Fin let his gaze fall back on the water, and he saw, beneath the reflection of the sky, just a hint of movement. 'There's a crab in there. Your dad and I used to catch dozens of them down here.'

'Yeh, he used to bring me here a lot when I was wee.' Fionnlagh pulled up his sleeves in preparation for thrusting his hands into the water to catch the crab. Fin was shocked to see that both forearms had nasty purple-yellow bruising along the line of the bone. He grabbed Fionnlagh's wrist.

'Where on earth did you get bruises like that?'

The boy winced, pulling his arm away from him. 'That was sore.' He pulled his sleeves down to cover the bruises and stood up.

'I'm sorry.' Fin was distressed. 'It looks nasty. What happened?'

Fionnlagh shrugged. 'It was nothing. Did myself a bit of damage when I was putting the new engine in the Mini. Shouldn't have been trying to do it on my own.'

'No, you shouldn't.' Fin got to his feet. 'You need the proper equipment and help for that kind of thing.'

'Guess I know that now.' Fionnlagh jumped lightly over the rocks and started up the gully. Fin followed him, feeling that somehow he had managed to sour things between them. But when they got to the top of the cliffs it was as if nothing had happened. Fionnlagh pointed towards the road. A silver Renault was making its way up the hill. 'That's Mrs Mackelvie. She gave mum a lift down to the store. Looks like that's them back. Race you.'

Fin laughed. 'What? I must be twice your age.'

'I'll give you a sixty-second start, then.'

Fin looked at him for a moment, and then grinned. 'Okay.' And he took off, sprinting along the edge of the cliff before turning up the hill towards the bungalow. That's when it got hard, his legs becoming quickly leaden, lungs rasping in their attempt to drag in more oxygen. He could see the peat stack, and hear the engine of the Renault idling at the top of the path. He was nearly there. As he got to the peat stack, he saw Marsaili coming down the drive, bags of shopping in each arm, and the Renault pulling away up the hill. She saw him at almost the same moment, and stopped, staring in astonishment. He grinned. He was going to beat the boy. He was going to get to the house first. But at the last moment, Fionnlagh cantered past him, laughing, hardly out of breath, and turned on the path, as Fin had to stop and bend over to support himself on his thighs, gasping for breath.

'Come on, old man. What kept you?'

Fin glared up at him, and saw Marsaili smiling. 'Yes, old man. What kept you?'

'About eighteen years,' Fin said, panting.

The phone started ringing in the house. Marsaili

glanced towards the kitchen door, and Fin saw concern in her eyes.

'I'll get it,' Fionnlagh said. He ran to the kitchen door, mounting the steps in two leaps, and disappeared inside. After a moment the ringing stopped.

Fin found Marsaili looking at him. 'What are you doing here?'

Fin shrugged, still trying to recover his breath. 'Just passing. I was up seeing Calum.'

She nodded, as if that explained everything. 'You'd better come in.' He followed her down the path and up the steps to the kitchen. She put her bags on the kitchen table, and they could hear Fionnlagh's voice from the sitting room, still talking on the phone. Marsaili filled the kettle. 'Cup of tea?'

'That would be nice.' He stood awkwardly, watching her plug in the kettle and take two mugs down from a wall cabinet. His breathing was returning to something like normal.

'Just teabags, if that's okay.'

'Fine.'

She dropped a bag in each cup and turned to look at him, leaning back against the worktop. They heard Fionnlagh hanging up the phone, and then his footsteps on the stairs up to his room. And still she kept looking at him, blue eyes searching, probing, violating. The kettle growled and hissed as its element began heating the water. The kitchen door was not properly closed, and Fin could hear the wind whistling around its edges.

'Why didn't you tell me you were pregnant?' he said.

She closed her eyes, and for a moment he felt released from their hold. 'Artair said he'd told you. He had no right.'

'I had a right to know.'

'You had no right to anything. Not after . . .' She broke off, gathering her calm, drawing it in around her. 'You weren't here. Artair was.' She fixed him with her eyes again, and he felt trapped by them, naked in their gaze. 'I loved you, Fin Macleod. I loved you from that first day you sat next to me in school. I even loved you when you were being a bastard. I've loved you all the years you weren't here. And I'll still love you when you're gone again.'

He shook his head, at a loss for what to say, until at length he asked lamely, 'So what went wrong?'

'You didn't love me back enough. I'm not sure you ever loved me.'

'And Artair did?'

Tears welled up in her eyes. 'Don't, Fin. Don't even set foot on that road.'

He crossed the kitchen in three steps and put his hands on her shoulders. She turned her face away from him. 'Marsaili . . .'

'Please,' she said, almost as if she knew that he was going to tell her he had always loved her, too. 'I don't want to hear it. Not now, Fin, not after all these wasted years.' And she turned to meet his eye. Their faces were inches apart. 'I couldn't bear it.'

They had kissed before either of them realized it. There was no conscious decision behind it, just a reflex action. A small meeting of their lips before breaking apart again. A breath, and then something much more intense. The kettle was shaking and rattling in its holder as it brought the water to a boil.

The sound of Fionnlagh on the stairs forced them apart, recoiling as if from an electric shock. Marsaili turned quickly to the kettle, flushed and flustered, to pour boiling water into their mugs. Fin thrust his hands in his pockets and turned to stare, unseeing, from the window. Fionnlagh came through from the living room carrying a large holdall. He had changed out of his sweat-shirt into a heavy woollen jumper and wore a thick, waterproof jacket. If their guilt made them self-conscious, Fin and Marsaili need not have feared that Fionnlagh would notice. He was in a black mood, pre-occupied and agitated.

'We're going tonight.'

'To the rock?' Fin asked. Fionnlagh nodded.

'Why so soon?' All Marsaili's embarrassment had been stripped away in a moment by a mother's concern.

'Gigs says there's bad weather on the way. If we don't go tonight it could be another week. Asterix is picking me up at the road end. We're going in to Stornoway to load up the boat and leave from there.' He opened the door, and Marsaili crossed the kitchen quickly to catch his arm.

'Fionnlagh, you don't have to go. You know that.'

He gave her a look layered with meaning which only his mother could interpret. 'Yes, I do.' And he pulled his arm away and slipped out the door without so much as a goodbye. Fin watched from the window as he hurried up the path, slinging his holdall over one shoulder. He turned to look at Marsaili. She stood, frozen, by the door, staring down at the floor, looking up only as she became aware of Fin's eyes on her.

'What happened on the rock the year you and Artair went?'

Fin frowned. It was the second time he had been asked that today. 'You know what happened, Marsaili.'

She shook her head almost imperceptibly. 'I know what you all said happened. But there had to be more to it than that. It changed you. Both of you. You and Artair. Things were never ever the same after that.'

Fin gasped his frustration. 'Marsaili, there *was* no more to it. God, wasn't it bad enough? Artair's dad died. And I nearly died, too.'

She inclined her head to look at him. There was something like accusation in her eyes. As if she believed he was not telling her the whole truth. 'There was more than Artair's dad died. You and I died. And you and Artair died. It was like everything we'd all been before, died that summer.'

'You think I'm lying to you?'

She closed her eyes. 'I don't know. I really don't know.'

'Well, what does Artair say?'

She opened her eyes and her voice dropped in pitch. 'Artair doesn't say anything. Artair hasn't said anything in years.'

A voice called from somewhere in the depths of the house. Feeble, yet still imperative. 'Marsaili! Marsaili!' It was Artair's mother.

Marsaili raised her eyes to the ceiling and let go of a deep, quivering sigh. 'I'll be there in a minute,' she called.

'I'd better go.' Fin moved past her to the door.

'What about your tea?'

He stopped and turned, and their eyes met again, and he wanted to run the back of his hand gently across the softness of her cheek. 'Some other time.' And he went down the steps to the path and hurried up it to where he had left Gunn's car at the side of the road.

III

A sense that they had all wasted their lives, that they had somehow missed their chances through stupidity or neglect, lay heavy on his shoulders, pulling him down into deep dejection. His mood was not helped by the bruising clouds gathering themselves on the Minch, nor by the Arctic breath carried on a stiffening breeze. He turned the car and drove up the hill and out of Crobost to the turnoff that led down to the harbour, drawing in beside the old whitehouse where he had lived with his aunt for nearly ten years. He got out of the car and stood breathing deeply, facing into the wind, the sound of the sea breaking on the pebble beach below.

His aunt's house was all closed up, neglected, willed to a charity for cats which had been unable to sell it, and then ignored it. He felt as if he ought to have some emotional response to the place, considering how long he had lived there. But it left him cold. His aunt had never treated him badly, and yet still he could only associate it with unhappiness. No single memory. Just a dark, amorphous cloud of despondency that he found hard to explain, even to himself. It stood looking out across the bay, where fishing boats had once brought their catch for processing in the salt houses built into the hill above the shore. Only the stony remains of their foundations provided testimony now to the fact that they had ever existed. Out on the headland stood three tall cairns. They had fascinated Fin as a boy, and he had visited them often, replacing stones occasionally displaced by unusually ferocious storms. Three men returning from the Second World War had built them there, his aunt had told him. No one knew why, and the men were long dead. Fin wondered if anybody bothered to repair them now.

He walked down the hill to the tiny Crobost harbour, where he and Artair had sat so often throwing stones into deep, still water. A stout steel cable snaked down the slipway from the winchhouse above the harbour, a large hook on the end of it. The winchhouse was a square, harled box of a building with two openings at the front and a door in the side. Fin pushed the door open, and the big, green-painted diesel motor sat in silent witness to the thousands of boats it had lowered into the water, or pulled from it. The key was in the ignition, and from impulse he turned it and the motor coughed but wouldn't start. He adjusted the choke and tried again, and it spat and spluttered and caught this time, thundering away in the dark enclosed space. Someone was still maintaining it in good order. He switched it off, and the silence seemed deafening in the aftermath of its roar.

Outside, half a dozen small boats were pulled up along the edge of the slipway, angled against the foot of the cliff, one behind the other. Fin recognized the faded sky-blue of the *Mayflower*. Hard to believe it was still in use after all these years. Above the winchhouse, the skeleton of a boat long since fallen into desuetude lay tipped over, keelside up. The last flakes of purple paint lay curling along her spine. Fin stooped down to wipe away the green slime covering the remaining planks on her bow and saw there, in faded white letters, his mother's name, *Eilidh*, where his father had carefully painted it the day before he launched her. And all the regrets of his life rose up inside him like water in a spring, and he knelt beside the boat and wept.

*

Crobost cemetery was out on the machair above the west shore beyond the school, where the village had buried its dead in the sandy soil for hundreds of years. Gravestones rose up like prickly spines over the brow of the hill. Thousands of them. Generations of Niseachs with a last and eternal view of the sea which had both given them life and taken it away. Rings of white foam broke upon the shore below as Fin picked his way through all the names of those who had gone before. All the Macleods and Mackenzies, Macdonalds and Murrays. The Donalds and Morags, Kenneths and Margarets. It was exposed here to the full fury of the Atlantic gales, and little by little the sea had eaten away at the machair until it had been necessary for the villagers to build defences against it to stop the bones of their ancestors being washed away with the soil.

Fin finally found the graves of his parents. John Angus Macleod, thirty-eight years old, loving husband of Eilidh, thirty-five. Two flat stones laid in the grass side by side. He had never been back since the day they were put in the ground and he had stood and watched the first spades of earth rattling across the coffin lids. He stood now with the wind blowing full in his face and thought what a waste it had been. So many lives had been touched by their deaths. Changed by them. How very different everything might have been.

FIFTEEN

Usually I slept the sleep of the dead. But that night I was restless. Not that I could claim in any way to have had a premonition of what was to come. It was more likely to have been the bed. It was my old bed, where I had slept the first three years of my life, before my father made the attic rooms. It was built into a recess of the wall in the kitchen where we spent most of our lives. It was a kind of wooden stall with cupboard space below it to store linens, and a curtain that pulled over to screen it off from the rest of the room.

I had always felt warm and secure there, hearing the murmur of my parents' voices in the room beyond the curtains before I went to sleep, and waking to the smell of the peats, and toast, and the sound of porridge bubbling on the stove. It had taken me a long time to get used to the cold isolation of my new room in the roof of the house, but now that I had, I found it hard to sleep again in my old bed. But that is where I was that night, because my aunt was babysitting, and she did not want to have to run up and down stairs all evening.

I must have been drifting in and out of sleep, because the first thing I remember was the sound of voices out in the hall, and a cold draught that found its way through the house and into my stall from an open door somewhere. I slipped barefoot out of bed, wearing only my pyjamas. The room was lit by the glowing embers in the hearth, and by a strange blue light that flashed around the walls. It took me a moment to realize it was coming from outside. The curtains weren't drawn, so I padded to the window to peer out, and saw a police car sitting on the road, blurred by rain running down the glass. The blue flashing light on its roof was almost mesmeric. I saw figures in the path, then heard the sound of a woman's voice, wailing as if in pain.

I had no idea what was happening, still half asleep and disorientated when the door opened. Lights came on in the room, nearly blinding me. My aunt was there, pale as a ghost, and chill air rushed in behind her to wrap itself around me like a big cold blanket. I saw a police officer, and a woman in uniform behind her. But these are just fragments of recollection. I can give you no really clear account of what happened. I remember only the sudden soft warmth of my aunt's breasts as she knelt in front of me and clutched me to her, and the sobbing that punctuated her breathing as she said, over and over, 'The poor laddie. The poor wee laddie.'

It was really the next day before I understood that my parents were dead. If an eight-year-old can ever understand what death is. I knew that they had been to a dance in Stornoway the night before, and I knew now that they weren't ever coming back. It is a difficult concept to handle at that age. I recall being angry with them. Why weren't they coming back? Didn't they know I would miss them? Didn't they care? But I had spent more than enough time in church to have a decent grasp of the notion of Heaven and Hell. They were places you went when you died. Either to one or the other. And so when my aunt told me my parents had gone to Heaven, I had a sort of rough idea where that was, somewhere beyond the sky, and that once you went there it was for ever. The only thing I couldn't grasp was why.

Looking back, I'm amazed my aunt told me any such thing, given her feelings about God and religion. I suppose she thought that maybe it was the best way of breaking it to me gently. But there is no way that the death of your parents can be broken to you gently.

I was in shock. All that day the house seemed full of people. My aunt, some distant cousins, neighbours, friends of my parents. A succession of faces fretting and fussing over me. It is the only time I ever heard any explanation of what happened. My aunt never spoke to me about it once in all the years I lived with her. Someone said – I have no idea who, just a voice in a crowded room – that a sheep had jumped up from the ditch, and that my father had swerved to avoid it. 'By that shieling on the Barvas moor, you know, the one with the green roof.' Voices were lowered, and in a hush of whispers I could barely make out, I heard someone else say, 'Apparently the car turned over half a dozen times before it caught fire.' There was a gasp, and another voice said, 'Oh my God, what a way to die!'

I think sometimes there are folk who take an unhealthy interest in death.

I spent a lot of time alone in my room, barely aware of the comings and goings downstairs, cars drawing up at the path and then driving off again. I had heard people time and again saying how brave I was, and my aunt telling them how I hadn't spilled a single tear. But I know now that tears are a kind of acceptance. And I was not ready for that yet.

I sat on the edge of my bed, numbness insulating me from the cold, and looked around the room at all the familiar things that filled it. The panda that shared my bed, a snow globe with a santa and reindeer that I had got in my stocking the previous Christmas. A big box of toys dating back to the days when I could barely crawl, coloured plastic shapes and disconnected pieces of Lego. My Scotland football shirt with *Kenny Dalglish* and the number 7 on the back. The football my father had bought me in the sports shop in Stornoway one Saturday afternoon. A rack full of board games. Two shelves laden with children's books. They might not have had much money, my mother and father, but they had made sure that I never wanted for anything. Until now. And the one thing I wanted most they couldn't give me.

It occurred to me, sitting there, that one day I would die too. It was not something I had ever thought about before, and it nudged up against my grief for space in my little locker of horrors. But you can't dwell on the thought of your own death for long, and very soon I had banished it altogether by deciding that since I was only eight it was a very long way off, and I would deal with it only when I had to.

And still I couldn't cry.

The day of the funeral, the weather was like a reflection of the anger and despair with which I had not yet come to terms. Rain tipped down, verging on sleet. December gales blew it in off the sea, under our umbrellas and into our faces. Stinging and cold.

I remember only black and grey. There was a long, sanctimonious service in the church, and I am haunted still by the sound of the Gaelic psalm-singing, those plain, unaccompanied voices such a potent evocation of my grief. And afterwards, outside the house, with the coffins placed side by side on the backs of chairs set in the middle of the road, more than a hundred people gathered in the rain. Black ties and coats and hats. Black umbrellas fighting with the wind. Pale, sad faces.

I was too small to help carry a coffin, and so I took my

place at the head of the procession immediately behind it, Artair at my side. I could hear his distress in the phlegm that crackled when he breathed. And was unaccountably moved when his cold, wee hand slipped into mine and squeezed, a silent expression of friendship and sympathy. I clung on to it tightly for all the length of that walk to the cemetery.

Only men are allowed to accompany the dead to their place of burial on the Isle of Lewis, and so the women lined the road to watch us go as we left the house. I saw Marsaili's mum, her face a picture of misery, and I remembered how she had smelled of roses that first day when I had gone to the farm. Marsaili stood beside her, clinging to her coat, black ribbons in the bunches of her hair. I noticed that she wasn't wearing her glasses that day. She reached out to me in the rain with her soft blue eyes, and I saw such pain in them that I had to look away.

That was when the tears came, hidden by the rain. The first time I cried for my parents. And I suppose it was then that I accepted that they really were gone.

I had not thought beyond the funeral, or even wondered what would happen next. If I had, I doubt if I could ever have imagined how brutally my life would change.

Barely had the last person left the house, than my aunt took me upstairs to pack a suitcase. All my clothes were stuffed unceremoniously inside it. I was permitted a small bag to carry a selection of toys and books. We would come back another time, she said, and go through what was left. I didn't really understand that this was no longer to be my home, and as it happened we never did come back for the rest of my things. I have no idea what happened to them.

I was hustled out to my aunt's car which was standing in the road, engine running, wipers scraping the rain from the windscreen. It was warm inside, but smelled damp, and the windows were all misted. I never even thought to look back as we drove away up the hill.

I had been in my aunt's house before, and always thought it a cold, miserable place, for all the colourful pots of plastic flowers and fabrics she draped around. There was a chill damp in that house that got into your bones after a while. There had been no fire on all day, and so it seemed even more wretched than usual when she pushed open the door to let us in. The naked bulb in the hall was harsh and bright as we struggled up the stairs with the bag and the case.

'Here we are,' she said, opening the door to an attic room at the end of the hall, sloping ceilings, damp-stained wallpaper, condensation on rusted windows. 'This is your room.' There was a single bed pushed against one wall, draped with a pink candlewick bedspread. A wartime utility wardrobe stood with its doors open, empty hangers and bare shelves awaiting the contents of my case. She hefted the suitcase on to the bed. 'There you are.' She threw open the lid. 'I'll leave you to put away your things in the wardrobe the way you like. It'll just be kippers for tea, I'm afraid.'

She was almost out the door when I said, 'When will I be going home again?'

She stopped and looked at me. And although there was pity in her eyes, I'm sure there was a degree of impatience there, too. 'This is your home now, Fin. I'll call you when tea's ready.'

She closed the door behind her, and I stood in the cold, cheerless room that was now mine. My sense of desolation was very nearly overwhelming. I found my panda in the bag of toys and sat on the edge of the bed, clutching him to my chest, feeling the damp of the mattress coming through my trousers. And I realized for the first time that day, that my life had changed inexorably and for ever.

SIXTEEN

I

The car rumbled over the cattle grid and into the car park. Fin parked it at the foot of the steps to the manse. All light had been squeezed out of the late afternoon sky by those ominous clouds which had been gathering earlier over the ocean. Now they were rolling in from the north-west, contused and threatening, and casting a deep gloom over the north end of the island. There were lights on in the front room of the minister's house, and as he climbed the steps, Fin felt the first spits of rain.

He rang the bell and stood on the doorstep, wind tugging at his jacket and trousers. The door was opened by a young woman in her mid-thirties. She was a head shorter than Fin, with cropped dark hair, a white T-shirt tucked loosely into khaki cargo pants and white trainers. Somehow she was not what he had expected of Donald Murray's wife. And she was oddly familiar. He looked at her blankly, and she tilted her head.

'You don't remember me, do you?' There was no warmth in her question.

'Should I?'

'We were at secondary school together. But I was a couple of years behind you, so you probably didn't notice me. Of course, we all had a crush on you.'

Fin felt himself blushing. So she was thirty-three, maybe thirty-four, which meant she was perhaps only seventeen when she'd had Donna.

'I can almost hear the wheels turning.' There was a seam of sarcasm in her voice. 'Don't you remember? Donald and I went out for a while at the Nicolson. Then we met up again in Glasgow after I left school. I went to London with him. He still hadn't found God in those days, so marriage was something of an afterthought. After I got pregnant, that is.'

'Catriona,' Fin said suddenly.

She raised her eyebrows in mock surprise. 'Well done.'

'Macfarlane.'

'You do have a good memory. Is it Donald you want to see?'

'Actually it's Donna.'

An invisible shutter came down. 'No, it's Donald.' She was emphatic. 'I'll go and get him.'

As he waited, the rain started to fall, and by the time Donald Murray came to the door Fin was already drenched. The minister looked at him impassively. 'I didn't know we had anything more to say to each other, Fin.'

'We don't. It's your daughter I want to talk to.'

'She doesn't want to speak to you.'

Fin glanced up at the sky, screwing up his face against the rain. 'Look, can I come in? I'm getting soaked out here.'

'No. If you want to talk to Donna, Fin, you're going to have to make it official. Arrest her, or whatever it is you people do when you want to question folk. Otherwise just leave us alone, please.' And he closed the door.

Fin stood for a while on the step, choking back his anger, before pulling up his collar and making a dash for the car. He started the engine and set the blower going, and struggled out of his wet jacket, throwing it onto the back seat. He slipped into first gear and was lifting the clutch when the passenger door opened. Catriona Macfarlane got in, slamming the door shut behind her. Her hair was wet and plastered to her head. Her T-shirt had become almost see-through, a lacy black bra clearly visible beneath it. Fin couldn't help noticing, and reflecting on how little God seemed to have changed Donald's predilections over the years.

She sat staring straight ahead, her hands clasped in her lap, fingers interlocked. And she said nothing.

Fin broke the silence. 'So did you find him, too?'

She turned to look at him, frowning. 'Find who?'

'God. Or was that just Donald's idea?'

'You've never seen him like we have. When he's angry.

With God on his side. Full of sound and fury and right-eous indignation.'

'Are you scared of him?'

'I'm scared of what he'll do when he finds out the truth.'

'And what is the truth?'

Her hesitation was momentary. She rubbed a clear patch in the condensation on the passenger window and peered up at the manse. 'Donna lied about being raped by Macritchie.'

Fin grunted. 'I'd already worked that one out. And I wouldn't be surprised if Donald has, too.'

'Maybe he has.' Another glance up at the manse. 'But he doesn't know why.'

Fin waited, but Catriona said nothing. 'Well, are you going to tell me or not?'

She was wringing her hands now. 'I wouldn't have known myself if I hadn't found the open pack in her room and confronted her with it.' She glanced at him self-consciously. 'A pregnancy-testing kit.'

'How far gone?'

'Then, just a matter of weeks. But she's three months now and starting to show. She was terrified of what Donald would do if he found out.'

'And that's why she made up the story about Macritchie?' Fin was incredulous. Catriona nodded. 'Jesus Christ. Didn't she know that paternity could be established by a simple DNA test?'

'I know, I know. It was stupid. She was panicking. And she'd had too much to drink that night. It was a really bad idea.'

'You're right.' Fin watched her closely for several moments. 'Why are you telling me this, Catriona?'

'So you'll leave us alone. It doesn't matter about the rape claim any more. The poor man's dead. I want you to stop bothering us so we can work this out for ourselves.' She turned to meet his gaze. 'Just leave us in peace, Fin.'

'I can't make any promises.'

She glared her hatred and fear at him, and then turned to open the car door.

As she stepped out into the rain, Fin said, 'So who's the father?'

She stooped to look back at him, the rain pouring down her face, dripping from her nose and chin. 'Your pal's son.' She nearly spat it out. 'Fionnlagh Macinnes.'

II

He had very little recollection of the drive back to town. He drifted between confusion and uncertainty, an oppressive sky bearing down on him, reducing the mountains of Harris to a grey smear in the distance, rain blurring his windscreen. The wind drove it laterally across the Barvas moor, and he had to focus his attention on the road until he reached the summit, just beyond the tiny Loch Dubh, and saw the lights of Stornoway spread out below him in the gloomy early evening, the town crouching in the shelter of the hills, cradled in the protective arms of its harbour.

Rush hour over, Bayhead was all but deserted in the rain, but as he turned into the harbour car park he was surprised to see a large crowd caught in lurid technicolor by the lights raised on stands by the television crew come to video them. Mostly they were just curious spectators braving the rain in the hope of getting their faces on TV. At their core were a dozen or more banner-toting protesters in red and yellow waterproofs. Hand-scrawled banners with slogans like *Save the Guga*, *Murderers*, *Strangled and Beheaded*, *Bird Killers*. Ink running in the wet. All a little cheap and nasty, Fin thought, and not very original. He wondered who funded these people.

When he got out of the car he heard them chanting, *Kill-ers, Kill-ers, Kill-ers*. There were one or two familiar faces on the periphery of the crowd, reporters whom Fin recognized from national newspapers. A couple of grim-faced uniformed police officers stood watching from a discreet distance, rain falling like veils from the peaks of their chequered caps.

On the quayside was the lorry they had loaded that morning at Port of Ness. It was empty now, standing idling amongst the empty creels and heaps of fishing net. A bunch of men in oilskins and sou'westers stood looking down into the hold of the *Purple Isle*, the same trawler which had taken Fin out to An Sgeir all those years before.

Thick coats of fresh paint had been applied to rusted rails and weathered planking. Her deck was blue, the wheelhouse a recently lacquered mahogany. She looked like an old whore trying hard to hide her age.

Fin put his head down and pushed through the crowd on to the quay. He caught a glimpse of Chris Adams leading the chants of the protesters, but he had no time for him right now. He spotted Fionnlagh beneath one of the sou'westers, and grabbed his arm. The boy turned. Fin said, 'Fionnlagh, I need to talk to you.'

'Hey, my man!' It was Artair's voice, full of good-natured bonhomie. He slapped Fin on the back. 'You're just in time to join us for a pint before we set sail. Are you game?' Fin looked round to find Artair grinning at him from beneath another dripping sou'wester. 'Jesus, man, have you not got a fucking coat? You're soaked to the skin. Here ...' He jumped up into the cab of the lorry and pulled out a yellow oilskin jacket and threw it over Fin's head. 'Come on, we'll get pissed together. I need some drink in me before we go. It's going to be a rough ride out.'

McNeil's was heaving, the air filled with steam, the smell of stale alcohol, and the sound of voices animated by drink. All the tables were full, and a crowd three or four deep was gathered around the bar. The windows were all steamed up, like most of the men who had been there for the past couple of hours. The twelve guga hunters and Fin forged a path to the bar, and those among the drinkers who recognized them raised their voices in loud toasts to the guga. The crew of the *Purple Isle* had stayed on board to prepare for their departure, and maintain their sobriety for what was likely to be a stormy passage.

Fin found a half-pint of heavy thrust into one hand, and a measure of whisky into the other. Artair grinned maniacally. 'A half and a half. Just what you need to set you on your feet.' It was the fastest way to get drunk. Artair turned away to the bar again. Fin closed his eyes and knocked the whisky back in a single pull, then chased it down with a long draught of beer. For once, he thought, maybe getting drunk was not such a bad idea. But in his peripheral vision, he caught a glimpse of Fionnlagh making his way to the toilet, and he put both glasses on the bar and pushed his way through the crowd after him.

By the time he got there, Fionnlagh was washing his hands at the sink, and two men at the urinals were zipping up their flies. Fin waited for them to go. Fionnlagh was watching him warily in the mirror. It was obvious from his eyes that he knew something was wrong. As the door swung shut, Fin said, 'Are you going to tell me about those bruises?' He saw the colour wash itself out of the boy's face.

'I told you this afternoon.'

'Why would you not tell me the truth about something like that?' And the echo of his own words made Fionnlagh turn to face his accuser.

'Because it's none of your fucking business, that's why.' He tried to push past, but Fin caught him and swung him around, grabbing the sweater beneath his waterproof jacket and yanking it up to expose a chest covered in yellowing purple bruises.

'Jesus!' He pushed the teenager face-first up against the wall and pulled up the sweater to reveal his back. Ugly bruising marred the pale, ivory skin. 'You've been in some fight, boy.'

With a determined effort, Fionnlagh pulled himself free, and swung around. 'I told you, it's none of your fucking business.'

Fin was breathing hard, fighting to control emotions that threatened to choke him. 'I'll be the judge of that.'

'No, you won't. We haven't been any of your business for eighteen years. And all you've done is come here and upset my mum. And my dad. And me. Why don't you just go away, back to where you came from?'

The door opened behind them, and Fionnlagh's eyes flickered beyond Fin to see who it was. His face coloured slightly, and he pushed past Fin and out of the toilet. Fin turned to find Artair standing there, a bemused smile on his face. 'What's going on?'

Fin sighed and shook his head. 'Nothing.'

He made to follow Fionnlagh, but Artair thrust a big hand in his chest to stop him. 'What have you been saying to the boy?' There was real menace in his voice, and all the warmth had leached out of his eyes.

Fin found it hard to remember that this was the little boy who had held his hand all those years ago at his parents' funeral. He met his old friend's eye and held it. 'Don't worry, Artair, your secret's safe with me.' And he looked down at the hand still pressed into his chest. Slowly Artair removed it, and a smile crept back into his eyes. But it was a smile without humour.

'That's alright, then. I'd hate for your boy to come between us.'

Fin brushed past him and back out into the pub. He searched among the faces, looking for Fionnlagh. The guga hunters were still at the bar, and he saw Gigs watching him with dark, thoughtful eyes. But he couldn't see Fionnlagh. A thump on his back almost took his breath away. 'Well, if it isn't the fucking orphan boy.' Fin spun around. For one bizarre, surreal moment, he almost expected to see Angel Macritchie. Or his ghost. Instead he found himself confronted by the leering red face of his brother. Murdo Ruadh seemed just as big to Fin as he had that first day at school. Only now he was carrying a lot more weight, like his older brother, and his ginger hair was darker, oiled back across an enormous flat head. He wore a donkey jacket over a grubby white T-shirt, and baggy jeans with a crotch that dragged halfway down his thighs. Big callused hands looked as if they could crush a cricket ball. 'What the fuck are you doing back here polluting the place?'

'Trying to find your brother's killer.'

'Oh, aye, like you'd fucking care.'

Fin felt his hackles rise. 'You know what, Murdo? Maybe I don't fucking care. But it's my job to put killers behind bars. Even if they've murdered scum like your brother. Okay?'

'No, it's not fucking okay!' Murdo was shaking with anger, his jowls quivering. 'You fucking smarmy little bastard!' And he lunged at Fin, who stepped quickly aside and watched Murdo's momentum carry him smashing into a table laden with glasses that went crashing across the floor. Angry, startled drinkers jumped to their feet cursing him, alcohol darkening crotches and thighs. Murdo ended up on his knees, as if in prayer, hands and face baptized by beer. He roared like some great angry bear and clambered to his feet, swivelling around, looking for Fin.

Fin stood, slightly breathless, surrounded by a circle of men screaming encouragement, baying for blood. He felt an iron grip on his arm and turned to see Gigs, his face set and intense. 'Come on, Fin, let's get you out of here.' But Murdo was already charging, a fist like a Belfast ham swinging through the air. Gigs pulled Fin aside, and the fist connected with a big, bald bruiser of a man with a walrus moustache. His nose seemed to burst open like soft fruit. His knees folded under him and he dropped to the floor like a sack of coal.

There was uproar in the pub, and a single, high-pitched voice rose above all the others, shrill and commanding. A woman's voice. 'Out! Get out! The lot of you, before I call the police.'

'They're here already,' some joker quipped, and those who knew Fin, laughed.

The manageress was a lady in her middle years, not unattractive, soft blond curls around an elfin face. But she had been in this game a few years and knew how to handle men with a drink in them. She rapped a stout wooden stick on top of the bar. 'Out! Now!' And no one was going to argue with her.

Several dozen men spilled out into The Narrows. The street was deserted. Rain lay in pools and puddles under streetlamps that barely cut the twilight gloom. Gigs still had Fin by the arm, and the guga hunters crowded around to hustle him away towards the quay. Murdo's voice roared above the howl of the wind. 'Ya yellow wee bastard! Running away with yer fucking pals. Just like you always fucking did!'

Fin stopped and yanked his arm free of Gigs's grip. 'Leave it,' Gigs said.

But Fin turned to face the rage of the dead man's brother, a large crowd gathering behind him in silent expectation.

'So come on then, you wee shit. What are you waiting for?'

Fin stared at him with the hatred of thirty years burning inside, and knew that this was wrong. He let all the tension drain out of him. He sighed. 'Why don't we shake on it, Murdo? Fighting's not going to solve anything. Never has, never will.' He walked warily towards the big man with his hand outstretched, and Murdo looked at him in disbelief.

'You're not fucking serious?'

'No,' Fin said. 'I'm not. I just wanted to get close enough to make sure I didn't miss.' And he swung his boot solidly into the sweet spot between Murdo's legs, taking him completely by surprise. A look of sheer astonishment was replaced almost immediately by one of excruciating pain. As he doubled over, Fin brought a knee up squarely into his face, and saw blood spurting from his mouth and nose. Now Murdo staggered backwards into the crowd, which parted like the Red Sea to let him through. Fin followed him, balled fists like pistons hammering into his great soft midriff, one after the other, forcing grunts from between bloody lips. Each blow a payback. For that first day in the playground, banged up against the wall and saved only by the intervention of Donald Murray. For the night they stole the tractor tyre. For poor Calum condemned to life in a wheelchair. For all the brutality meted out by this gutless bully through all the years. Fin was losing count now of the number of times he had hit him. He had also lost all reason, overtaken by a mindless frenzy. And he just kept hitting and hitting. Murdo was on his knees, eyes rolling, blood bubbling between his lips, pouring from his nostrils. The roar of voices in the street was deafening.

Fin found strong hands catching his arms, pinning them to his sides and lifting him bodily away. 'For fuck's sake, man, you're going to kill him!' He turned his head to see the perplexed look on George Gunn's face. 'Let's get you out of here before the cops come.'

'You are the cops.'

'The uniforms,' Gunn said through clenched teeth. 'If you're still here when they arrive your career's dead in the water.'

Fin went limp, then, and let Gunn pull him away through the jeering crowd. He caught the merest glimpse of Fionnlagh among all the faces. The boy seemed shocked. And he saw Artair laughing, delighted to see Murdo Ruadh finally get his comeuppance.

As they hurried away along The Narrows towards the Crown, they heard the wail of a police siren, a signal for the crowd to disperse. Two of his friends had pulled Murdo to his feet and were dragging him hurriedly away. It was all over.

Fin was still shaking as they sat at the bar. He placed his hands flat on the counter to stop them trembling. They were largely undamaged. He knew not to risk his hands on bone that could just as easily damage him. He had concentrated his punches in the soft, well-padded upper body, the stomach and ribs, bruising his opponent, eroding his stamina, hurting him without hurting himself. The real damage had been done by his boot and his knee in the first two strikes, all the pent-up rage and humilia-tion of thirty years fuelling his assault. He wondered why it hadn't made him feel any better, why he felt sick and depressed and defeated.

The lounge bar of the Crown was deserted, except for a young couple deep in intimate conversation in the far corner. Gunn sat up on a stool beside Fin and slipped a fiver to the barmaid for their drinks. He said in a low, con-trolled voice, 'What the hell were you doing, Mr Macleod?'

'I don't know, George. Making a complete bloody idiot of myself.' He looked down and saw Murdo Ruadh's blood on his jacket and trousers. 'Literally.'

'The DCI's already pissed off because you never checked in after Uig. You could be in big trouble, sir. Big trouble.'

Fin nodded. 'I know.' He took a long drink from his pint glass until he felt the beer-buzz bite. He closed his eyes tightly. 'I think I might know who murdered Macritchie.'

Gunn was silent for a long time. 'Who?'

'I'm not saying he did. Just that he's got a damned good motive. And a bunch of bruises to go with it.' Gunn waited for him to go on. Fin took another pull at his beer. 'Donna Murray made up the story about Macritchie raping her.'

'I think we all knew that, didn't we?'

'But we didn't know she was pregnant. That's why she did it, George. So that she could have someone to blame. So that she wouldn't have to face her father with the truth.'

'But as long as her father believed she'd been raped, that always put him in the frame, always gave him a motive.'

'Not her father. Her boyfriend. The one who got her pregnant. If he thought she'd really been raped, he'd have had just as strong a motive.'

'Who's the boyfriend?'

Fin hesitated. Once he'd said it, it was out. And there was no way to put the genie back in the bottle. 'Fionnlagh Macinnes. My friend Artair's son.' He turned to look at Gunn. 'He's covered in bruises, George. Like he's been in a helluva fight.'

Gunn was silent for a long time. 'What are you not telling me, Mr Macleod?'

'What gives you that idea, George?'

'Because it's cost you a lot to tell me what you have already, sir. Which makes it personal. And if it's personal, then you haven't told me everything.'

Fin smiled grimly. 'You know, you'd make a good cop. Ever thought about taking it up as a career?'

'Naw, I hear the hours are terrible. My wife would never stand for it.'

Fin's smile faded. 'He's my son, George.' George frowned. 'Fionnlagh. I never knew until last night.' He let his head fall forward into open palms. 'Which makes the kid that Donna Murray's carrying my grandchild.' He blew a long jet of air out through pursed lips. 'What a God-awful mess!'

Gunn sipped thoughtfully at his beer. 'Well, I can't do

anything about your personal life, Mr Macleod, but maybe I can put your mind at rest about the boy.'

Fin turned sharply to look at him. 'What do you mean?'

'I've never felt good about that minister. I know his wife said he was at home with her on Saturday night, but wives have been known to lie for their husbands.'

Fin shook his head. 'It's not Donald.'

'Hear me out, sir.' Gunn drew a deep breath. 'I did a bit of checking today. There's all these different denominations here on the island. Well, you know that. Donald Murray's with the Free Church of Scotland. They have their General Assembly every year at St Columba's Free Church in Edinburgh. Turns out it was held in May this year, the same week as your murder in Leith Walk. Which puts Donald Murray at the scene of both crimes. And like all experienced coppers, Mr Macleod, neither you nor I believe in coincidence. Do we?'

'Jesus.' Fin had not expected this.

'The DCI sent two uniforms to Ness to bring him in for questioning about an hour ago.'

Fin slipped off his stool. 'I'm going to the station to talk to him.'

Gunn grabbed his arm. 'With all due respect, sir, you've been drinking. If Mr Smith smells alcohol on your breath, you'll be in even bigger trouble than you already are.'

They heard the distant chanting of protesters on the quayside. *Kill-ers, Kill-ers, Kill-ers.*

'That must be the *Purple Isle* leaving port,' Fin said, and he crossed to the window. But he couldn't see the Cromwell Street Quay from there.

'Are they going to An Sgeir tonight?'

Fin nodded. 'And Fionnlagh's with them.'

'Well, then, he's not going anywhere fast in the next two weeks, is he? And you can talk to Donald Murray in the morning. I don't think he's going anywhere very fast either.'

Out in The Narrows Fin said, 'Thanks, George. I owe you.'

Gunn shrugged. 'The reason I came looking for you tonight, sir, was to say that my wife was able to get her hands on a bit of wild salmon, just like I thought. Plenty for the three of us. She said she would grill it for us if we wanted.'

But Fin was distracted. 'Maybe another night, George. Tell her thanks, anyway.'

Gunn looked at his watch 'Aye, well, it was getting a bit late, right enough. And to tell you the truth, sir, I prefer my salmon poached.'

Fin caught his twinkle. 'Me too.' He handed Gunn his car keys. 'She's in the Cromwell Street car park.' He walked with him down to North Beach, where they shook hands and Fin watched him head off towards the car park. The *Purple Isle* had already turned south at the end of North Beach Quay and was out of sight somewhere between the Esplanade and Cuddy Point. Fin retraced his steps over Castle Street, across The Narrows and down to

South Beach. Streetlamps shone miserably in the rain all the way along the front to the deserted bus station at the far end, and the lights of the new ferry terminal. The old pier at the near end was shrouded in darkness.

Fin stuck his hands deep in his pockets, hunching his shoulders against the wet and the cold, and walked out on to the deserted pier. There was a tanker tied up on her east side, but not a soul in sight. He saw the lights of the *Purple Isle* as she motored into view, ploughing her way through the choppy swell and into the bay towards Goat Island. He could see figures moving about on deck, but it was impossible to tell who they were, just yellow and orange smudges.

He had no idea what to feel any more. What to believe or to think. But he knew that the boy who was his son was taking with him a secret on board that trawler, sailing through treacherous seas to a desolate rock in the North Atlantic where eighteen years earlier Fin had almost died.

And it troubled him to think of the boy on the rock, amongst the slaughter and the fiery angels and the wheels of dead meat. Whatever his secret might be.

SEVENTEEN

I

Low cloud shaved the tops of the hills, propelled across the island by a strong westerly. Baskets of colourful hanging flowers all along the front of Stornoway police station swung dangerously in the wind. Litter blew about the street in gusts and eddies, and folk leaned into the breeze, hunched against the unaccustomed August chill.

Fin made the weary hike up Church Street from the harbour, a woollen sweater beneath his parka in place of the bloodstained shirt he had left soaking in the washbasin of his hotel room. He had dozed off and on through the hours of darkness, but sleep had eluded him. Real sleep. The kind that wraps all thoughts in black and lowers them gently to the bottom of a deep, dark well. Several times he had considered calling Mona. But what could he have told her? That they had no need to grieve any longer for the loss of Robbie? Because he had found another son he didn't even know he had?

He went through the car park and entered the police station by its back door. The duty sergeant was leaning on the charge bar filling in forms. The pervasive institutional perfume of toilets and disinfectant that lingered in police cells everywhere was ameliorated by the smell of toast and coffee. Fin glanced up at the CCTV camera above the charge bar and showed the sergeant his ID.

'Is the Reverend Murray still here?'

The sergeant nodded down the hall. The gate to the cells was lying open, and most of the doors were ajar. 'First on the right. It's not locked.' He saw Fin's surprise. 'He's still helping us with our inquiries, sir. Hasn't been officially detained. Would you like some coffee?'

Fin shook his head and walked down the hall. Everything was clean and freshly painted. Cream walls, beige doors. He pushed open the door of the first cell on the right. Donald was squatting on a low wooden bench below a small window high in the wall. He was eating toast, and a mug of steaming coffee sat on the bench beside him. He was still wearing his dog collar beneath a jacket that was crumpled now and creased. A little like his face. He looked as if he had slept as much as Fin. There were dark shadows around panda eyes, hair uncombed and unkempt, falling forward across his forehead. He took in Fin at a glance, and barely acknowledged him.

'You see that?' He tipped his head towards the corner of the cell to Fin's left. Fin looked down and saw a white arrow beside a capital letter *E*, painted on the dark-red concrete floor. 'Points east. To Mecca. So that Muslim prisoners will know what direction to pray in. The sergeant tells me he can't ever remember a single Muslim prisoner in here. But it's regulation. I asked him if he could give me a bible so that I might find comfort in the midst of this hell. He apologized. Someone had misplaced the bible. But he could give me a copy of the Koran and a prayer mat if I wanted.' He looked up, his face full of contempt. 'This used to be a Christian island, Fin.'

'Aye, with Christian values, like truth and honesty, Donald.'

Donald met his eye very directly. 'I didn't kill Angel Macritchie.'

'I know that.'

'So why am I here?'

'It's not my call.'

'They say I was in Edinburgh at the same time as some other murder. So were half a million others.'

'Can you account for your movements that night?'

'Several of us were staying at the same hotel. I think we had dinner together. They're checking it out with the rest. Of course, that doesn't account for my movements after I went to bed – since I was on my own.'

'I'm glad to hear it. They say the number of prostitutes in Edinburgh increases every time there's a General Assembly.' Donald gave him a sour look. 'Anyway, it doesn't really matter. Your DNA sample will clear you of killing Macritchie when the results come through. God's bar code.'

'Why are you so sure I *didn't* do it?'

'I've been thinking about that all night.'

'Well, I'm glad I'm not the only one who hasn't had any sleep. So what conclusion did you come to?'

Fin leaned against the door frame. He felt weak and tired. 'I always thought you were one of the good guys, Donald. Always standing up for what you believed in, never giving in to the bullies. And I never once saw you raise so much as a finger to anyone. Your power was psychological, not physical. You had a way of dealing with people without ever resorting to violence. I don't think you're capable of killing anyone.'

'Well, thank you for the vote of confidence.'

Fin ignored his tone. 'But what you *are* capable of is a great, stubborn, self-serving pride.'

'I knew there had to be a catch.'

'Standing up to bullies, risking yourself for others, defying your father, playing the rebel. All part of the same reason you ended up turning to God.'

'Oh, yes, and what's that?'

'Your all-consuming desire to be the centre of attention. It's always been about image with you, Donald, hasn't it? Your own self-image. The image you wanted others to have of you. The red car with the soft top, the succession of pretty girls, the drugs, the drink, the high life. And now the minister. You don't get to be much more centre-stage than that. Not on the Isle of Lewis. And in the end, it all boils down to one thing. And do you know what that is?'

'Why don't you tell me, Fin?' For all his defiance, Fin's words were having their effect. Colour had risen high on Donald's cheeks.

'Pride. You're a proud man, Donald. And your pride comes before everything else. Which is funny, because I always thought pride was a sin.'

'Don't lecture me on the Bible.'

But Fin wasn't about to let up. 'And something, they say, that comes before a fall.' He pushed himself away from the door frame and slipped his hands into his pockets, stepping into the middle of the cell. 'You know perfectly well that Macritchie never raped Donna. And I also think you know why she claimed he did.'

For the first time, Donald looked away, his gaze falling to the floor, focused on something only he could see. Fin saw his fingers tighten around his coffee mug.

'You know she's pregnant, don't you? But you'd rather turn a blind eye to the truth, have the world believe it was Macritchie's fault. Because what would it do to your image? Your precious sense of self. If the minister's daughter got herself pregnant, not because she was raped, but because she had consensual sex with her boyfriend. What a stain on your reputation. What a blow to your pride.'

Donald was still staring at the floor, the muscles of his jaw working in silent anger.

'Think about it, Donald. Your wife and your daughter are scared of you. Scared! And I'll tell you something else. Angel Macritchie wasn't worth much. But he wasn't a rapist. He didn't have many redeeming features, but he doesn't deserve a stain like that on his memory.'

Fin hurried down the stairs from the charge bar, wrapped up in the same thoughts which had kept him awake most of the night. Not one of them included DCI Tom Smith, so it took him a moment to register his voice.

'Macleod!' The voice was terse and thick with Glasgow accent. When Fin failed to react it came again, louder. '*Macleod!*' Fin turned and saw him standing in the open doorway of an interview room. 'In here.'

Gone was the smooth, manicured image cultivated by the Glaswegian CIO. He was unshaven, his shirt crushed and roughly rolled up at the elbows. His Brylcreemed hair fell in greasy loops down each side of his wide, flat brow, and the scent of Brut had been replaced by a faintly unpleasant body odour, which was only marginally worse. He, too, had clearly been up all night.

He shut the door behind them and told Fin to sit at the desk. It was strewn with papers, and an ashtray was full to overflowing. But he did not sit himself. 'You've been in talking to Murray.' It wasn't a question.

'You've got the wrong man.'

'He was in Edinburgh the night of the Leith Walk murder.'

'So was every other Free Kirk minister on the island.'

'But they didn't have a motive for killing Macritchie.'

'Neither does Murray. He knows Macritchie never raped his daughter. Her boyfriend got her pregnant, so she made up the story.'

Uncharacteristically, Smith seemed at a loss for words. But it was only temporary. 'How do you know this?'

'Because I know these people, Chief Inspector. I'm one of them, as you were so pleased to point out when you described them to me as *unsophisticated* the day I got here.'

Smith bristled. 'I'll not take any cheek from you, Macleod.'

'But I should turn the other cheek when you choose to be insulting? Is that how it works?'

Smith bit back a response. 'If you're so fucking clever, Macleod, then obviously you'll know who it was who killed Macritchie.' He paused. 'Do you?'

'No, sir. But I think you were right from the beginning. There is no Edinburgh connection. Just someone trying to lead us up a blind alley.'

'I'm honoured to have your endorsement, Detective Inspector. And when exactly did you come to this conclusion?'

'At the post-mortem, sir.'

'Why?'

Fin shook his head. 'It just didn't feel right. Too many

things that didn't correspond. Small things. But enough to make me think we were probably looking at two different killers.'

Smith wandered to the window, short arms folded across his chest. He turned to face Fin. 'And you were going to share this with me, when?'

'It wasn't a conclusion, sir. Just a feeling. But if I'd shared it with you, you'd have put me on the first plane back to Edinburgh. And I felt that my local knowledge gave me something to offer the investigation.'

'And you thought that was a decision you had the power to make?' Smith shook his head in disbelief. He leaned his weight on the desk, knuckles glowing white, and sniffed the air. 'I don't smell any alcohol. Did you rinse your mouth out before coming in this morning?'

Fin frowned. 'I don't know what you're talking about, sir.'

'I'm talking about an officer under my command getting involved in a drunken brawl in the Narrows last night. I'm talking about an officer who is only going to remain under my command for as long as it takes him to board the first available flight out of here. I want you off the island, Macleod. If you can't get a plane, get a ferry.' He drew himself up to his full height, which wasn't great. 'I've already spoken to your division head in Edinburgh. So I imagine you can expect a warm reception when you get home.'

*

His abortive return to the island was over. All those painful encounters with the ghosts of his past. It was almost a relief. And Fionnlagh was right. They had been none of his business for eighteen years, he had no right coming back and involving himself in their lives now. A man had been murdered, and his killer was still free. But that was no longer his responsibility. He was going home, if that's what it still was. If Mona was still there. He could simply draw the curtain again, and forget. Look forward instead of back. So why did the prospect fill him with such dread?

Fin brushed past the relief map of Lewis and Harris in the hallway and pushed open the firedoors into reception. The duty officer behind the glass glanced up, CCTV pictures flickering on a bank of screens behind him. There were two solitary figures sitting waiting patiently on plastic chairs pushed back against the wall opposite the window, but Fin didn't notice them. He was almost out of the front door before one them called his name and got to her feet.

Catriona Macfarlane, or Murray, as Fin supposed she now was, stood clasping her hands in front of her. She looked pale and defeated. And sitting like some little rag doll propped up on the empty row of seats behind her was a young girl who looked barely more than twelve years old, hair drawn back from a bloodless face without a trace of make-up. With a shock, Fin realized that this must be Donna. She seemed so young. It was hard to believe that she could be three months pregnant. Perhaps with make-up the girl looked older. She was not unattractive, in a plain sort of way. She had her father's colouring, the same delicate ivory skin and sandy hair. She was wearing jeans, and a pink blouse beneath a quilted anorak that drowned her.

'Bastard!' Catriona said.

'I had nothing to do with it, Catriona.'

'When are you going to let him go?'

'As far as I'm aware, he can leave any time he likes. I'm being sent back to Edinburgh. So you'll get your wish. I won't be bothering you again.' Their lives were no longer his concern.

He pushed open the swing door and hastened down the stairs out into the blustery wind. He had already crossed Kenneth Street, and was passing the fish and chip shop, before he heard footsteps on the pavement behind him. He looked round to see Donna chasing down Church Street after him. Her mother was standing on the steps of the police station. She called her daughter's name. But Donna ignored her. The girl reached Fin and pulled up, breathless. 'I need to talk to you, Mr Macleod.'

A waitress chewing gum brought two coffees to them at their table in the window. A constant stream of traffic rumbled along Cromwell Street on the other side of the glass. It was still gloomy out there, sea the colour of pewter blowing in white-crested arcs across the harbour.

The girl toyed with her spoon. 'I don't know why I ordered coffee. I don't even like it.'

'I'll get you something else.' He raised a hand to call the waitress.

'No, it's alright.' Donna continued to play with her spoon, and turned her cup around in the coffee which had slopped into the saucer. Fin sugared his, and stirred it patiently. If she had something to tell him, he would let her do it in her own time. He took a sip. It was barely tepid. Eventually she looked up at him. 'I know my mother told you the truth about what happened with Mr Macritchie.' For a girl who had falsely accused a man of rape, there was an extraordinary candour in her eyes. 'And I'm pretty sure my dad knows it was all a lie, too.'

'He does.'

She seemed surprised. 'So you must know that my dad didn't kill him.'

'I never thought for a minute that your dad killed anyone, Donna.'

'So why are you holding him?'

'He's not being held. He's helping with inquiries. It's just procedural.'

'I never meant to cause all this trouble.' She bit her lip, and Fin saw that she was trying hard not to cry.

'What did you tell Fionnlagh?'

And suddenly the tears were put on hold. She looked at him warily. 'What do you mean?'

'Does he know you're pregnant?'

She lowered her head and shook it, and returned to playing with her spoon. 'I . . . I haven't been able to tell him. Not yet.'

'So there was no reason for him not to believe your story about Macritchie. Unless you told him otherwise.' She said nothing. 'Did you?' She shook her head. 'So he believed you'd been raped by him.'

She looked up, her eyes full of indignation. 'You can't believe that Fionnlagh killed him! I've never known a gentler person in my whole life.'

'Well, you've got to admit, you gave him a pretty strong motive. And he's got a lot of bruises on him that he's very reluctant to explain.'

She looked perplexed now rather than indignant. 'How could you even think that about your own son?'

For a moment, all Fin's cool deserted him. He replayed what she had said, hardly able to believe he had heard it. His voice was hoarse. 'How do you know that?'

She knew that she had turned the tables on him. 'Because Fionnlagh told me.'

It simply wasn't possible. 'Fionnlagh *knows*?'

'All his life. Or, at least, as far back as he can remember. Mr Macinnes told him years ago that he wasn't his son. I mean, Fionnlagh doesn't even remember when. He's just always known.' She had that look in her eyes again. 'He was in tears when he told me. And it made me feel like I must be really special to him. 'Cos he's never told anyone else. Ever. And I'm like, wow, he's only ever shared this

404

with me.' The brightness in her face at the memory of the moment, faded. 'We're both pretty sure that's why his dad beat him up all these years.'

Fin was stunned. His throat was dry. He felt sick. 'What do you mean?'

'He's a big man, his dad. And Fionnlagh, well, even now he's not exactly Mr Universe, is he? So it's still going on.'

'I don't understand.' He must have misunderstood.

'What don't you understand, Mr Macleod? Fionnlagh's dad beats him up. He's been doing it for years. Never so you can see it. But poor Fionnlagh's had cracked ribs, a broken arm once. Bruises all over his chest and his back and his legs. Like his dad was taking out the sins of the father on the son.'

Fin closed his eyes and wished that he would wake up from the nightmare. But she wasn't finished yet.

'Fionnlagh always covered it up. Never told a soul. Until the night he and I, you know, did it. And I saw for myself. That's when he told me. His dad – well, he's not really his dad at all, is he? – he's a monster, Mr Macleod. A complete monster.'

EIGHTEEN

It ruined the rest of the summer, the accident on the rock. I'm not sure it didn't ruin the rest of my life. I was in the hospital for almost a week. They said I was suffering from severe concussion, and I had headaches for months afterwards. They suspected a fractured skull, although nothing showed up on the X-ray. My left arm was broken in two places and they put it in plaster for more than a month. My whole body was black and blue, and I could hardly move when I first regained consciousness.

Marsaili came to see me every day, but I didn't really want her there. I don't know why, but I found her presence disturbing. I think she was hurt by how cold I was, and all her warmth was lost on me. My aunt came a couple of times, but she wasn't very sympathetic. She must have known by then that she was dying. I'd had a close encounter with death, but they said I would make a full recovery. Why should she waste her sympathy on me?

Gigs came, too. Just the one time. I vaguely remember him sitting at my bedside gazing at me with concern in those deep, blue eyes of his. He asked me how much I remembered of what happened. But it was still very hazy then. My memory of events was fragmented. Dislocated images. Artair's dad climbing on to the ledge beside me. His fear. His body lying on the rocks beneath the cliff, the sea reaching out foaming fingers to drag him off. The whole fortnight was a blur, as if I were peering back at it through gauze. That was the concussion, they said. Only with the passage of time did the gauze dissolve and the focus sharpen.

The thing that I remember most clearly about my spell in hospital was that Artair never came to see me once. It was not something I was aware of during the first few days, but as my recovery continued and they began to talk about sending me home, I realized he had not been to visit. I asked Marsaili about it, and she said his mother had been in a terrible state. There had been a funeral. Without a body. An empty coffin carried all the way to Crobost cemetery, containing only a handful of treasured belongings. They say that closure is hard without a body. Since it was certain that the sea would never give him up, I could not see how closure would ever be possible on the death of Mr Macinnes, and I began to think that perhaps Artair blamed me. Marsaili said she didn't think it was a question of blame. Just the pain of coming to terms with the death of a parent. I, of all people, should know about that. And, of course, I did.

The hardest time was between going home from the hospital and leaving for university. It was a dead time, full of long, empty days. We were into September now, and the summer was all but gone. I was hugely depressed, by what had happened to me on the rock, by the death of Artair's dad. My enthusiasm for going to Glasgow had diminished, but I held on to the hope that leaving for the mainland would mark a change in the way I felt, that I would somehow be able to put everything behind me and start again with a clean slate.

I found myself avoiding Marsaili, regretting that we had ever arranged to share a room in Glasgow. Somehow she seemed like a part of that everything I needed to leave behind. And I simply avoided the issue of Artair. If he couldn't bring himself to visit me in hospital, then I certainly wasn't going to see him.

On the days when it wasn't raining, I would go for long walks along the cliffs, heading south down the east coast, past the ruins of the ancient village and church at Bilascleiter, to the long, silver beach at Tolastadh where I would sit among the doons and watch the sea for hours. The only souls you ever saw were walkers on holiday from the mainland, the only company the thousands of seabirds that swooped and dived about the cliffs spotting for fish in the Minch.

It was when I got back one day from one of my walks

that my aunt told me that Artair's mother had suffered a stroke. She was in a bad way, my aunt thought. And I knew then that I couldn't avoid him any longer. My arm was still in plaster, and I couldn't ride my bike, so I walked. A journey that you would rather never end always passes quickly. It took no time at all to walk down the hill to Artair's bungalow. Which made it all the more absurd that I had not done it before now.

His dad's car was sitting in the drive where he had left it before setting off for An Sgeir. A potent reminder that he had not come back. I knocked at the back door and stood on the step with my heart in my mouth. It seemed like an age before it opened. Artair stood there looking down at me. He was terribly pale, dark shadows smudged beneath his eyes. He had lost weight. He looked at me impassively.

'I heard about your mum.'

'You'd better come in.' He held the door wide and I stepped up into the kitchen. The smell of his dad's pipe tobacco still lingered in the house. Another reminder of his absence. There was, too, an unpleasant smell of stale cooking. Dirty dishes were piled up at the sink.

'How is she?'

'It would probably have been better for her if she'd died. She's paralysed down one side. Lost a lot of her motor functions. Her speech is affected. Although the doctors think that might improve. If she survives. When she gets home from the hospital I'm told I'll have to feed her with a spoon. She almost certainly won't walk again.'

'Jesus, Artair. I'm so sorry.'

'They say it was the shock of my father's death.' Which made me feel even worse, if such a thing were possible. But he just shrugged and glanced at my plaster. 'So how are you?'

'Still getting headaches. The plaster's coming off next week.'

'Just in time for shooting off to Glasgow, then.' There was an acid edge to his voice.

'You didn't come to see me in the hospital.' I didn't frame it as a question, but we both knew I was asking why.

'I've been busy.' He was tetchy. 'I had a funeral to arrange. A thousand administrative things to take care of. Do you have any idea how much bureaucracy there is in death?' But he wasn't expecting an answer. 'No, of course you don't. You were only a kid when your parents died. Someone else took care of all that shit.'

His prickliness made me angry. 'You blame me, don't you, for your dad's death?' I just blurted it out.

He gave me such an odd look that I was completely discomfited. 'Gigs says you don't remember much about what happened out there on the rock.'

'What's to remember?' I said, still off-balance. 'I fell. Okay, so I don't remember exactly how. Something stupid, probably. And your dad climbed on to that ledge and saved my life. If that makes me responsible for his

410

death, then *mea culpa*. I'm sorry. I've never been more sorry about anything in my life. He was great, your dad. I remember him on the ledge telling me everything was going to be alright. And it was. Only not for him. I'll always be grateful to him, Artair. Always. Not just for saving my life. But for giving me a chance at life. For all those hours he put into getting me through my exams. I could never have done it without him.' It just poured out of me. All my misery and guilt.

I can recall Artair staring at me, still with that strange look in his eyes. I suppose he must have been weighing up just how much blame I deserved, because he seemed to come to a decision, and all the tension and anger suddenly drained out of him, like poison from a boil that's been lanced. He shook his head then. 'I don't blame you, Fin. I don't. Really. It's just . . .' And his eyes filled up. 'It's just hard dealing with the death of your dad.' He sucked in a deep, tremulous breath. 'And now this.' He lifted his hands hopelessly, and then let them drop back to his sides.

I felt so sorry for him that I did something I had never done before. Something that big, macho Lewismen just don't do. I gave him a hug. I sensed his initial surprise, and a momentary hiatus, before he hugged me back, and I felt the bristle of his unshaven face against my neck and the sobs that shook his body.

Marsaili and I left separately for Glasgow at the end of September and met up at the Curlers bar in Byres Road.

We had each been to the flat in Highburgh Road to drop off our bags, but there were issues to be settled. For my part I had to confront and deal with my feelings, or lack of them, for Marsaili. I could not explain it then, and I cannot explain it now. I had escaped from An Sgeir with my life, but something of me had died on the rock, just as Marsaili said all those years later. And Marsaili was somehow connected with that part of me that had gone. I needed to rebuild and regrow, and I was not certain where Marsaili fitted into that process, if at all. For Marsaili, the issue was simple. Did I want us to be together or not? I have to confess to my cowardice. I am not good at ending relationships. When there is a chance for the break to be swift and clean, I am likely to dither, afraid of causing hurt. In the final event, of course, it always gets messy, and you end up hurting people even more. So I didn't have the heart, or maybe was it the courage, to tell her it was over.

Instead we had a few drinks and went for a meal at a Chinese restaurant in Ashton Lane. We had wine with the meal, and several brandies to finish, and were drunk by the time we got back to the flat. Our bedsit was a large room at the front of the apartment, originally the sitting room I think. It had high ceilings with moulded cornices, and a gas fire in an elaborately carved wooden fireplace. Spectacular stained-glass oriel windows looked through trees on to the road below. Up a short flight of stairs was a shared bathroom, and at the back of the flat a large communal kitchen with a huge dining table and a television by a window overlooking the back court. We could hear the other students talking and playing music in the kitchen when we went in, but we weren't feeling very sociable that night. We went straight into our room and locked the door. Light from the streetlamps outside filtered through the leaves and fell among dappled shadows across the floor. We did not even bother drawing the curtains before unfolding the bed settee and stripping off our clothes. I suppose if anyone was looking, we might have been seen from the flats across the road. But we didn't care. A cocktail of alcohol and hormones spurred us into a bout of furious sex, brief and intense.

It seemed like a long time since we had last made love, on the beach at Port of Ness. That first night in Glasgow fulfilled some physical need, but when it was over I lay on my back staring at the ceiling, watching the reflected light move with the breeze among the leaves outside. It was not like it had been before. And it left me feeling empty, and knowing then that it was over, and that it could only be a matter of time before we would both have to face it.

Sometimes when you don't want it to be your fault, you engineer situations where fate, or even the other party, can be blamed for the break-up of a relationship. It was like that with me and Marsaili that first term at Glasgow University. I look back now, and I'm not sure who the person was who inhabited my body during those autumn weeks leading into our first winter in the city. But he was a truculent bastard, moody and difficult. He drank too much. He smoked too much dope. He made love to Marsaili when he felt like it, and treated her like shit the rest of the time. I am ashamed to say that I knew him, or was associated with him in any way.

I discovered lots of things about myself. I discovered that I wasn't really interested in the arts, or getting a degree. In fact, I wasn't interested in studying, full-stop. When I think of the hours that poor Mr Macinnes wasted on me! All that time and effort squandered. I discovered that I was what Lowlanders call a *teuchter*, a hick Highlander, immediately identified by my ugly island accent, and I made a determined effort to iron it out. It seemed that Gaelic sounded absurd to the non-Gaelic-speaking ear, and so I stopped speaking it to Marsaili, even when we were alone. I discovered that I was attractive to girls, and there appeared to be no shortage of them willing to sleep with me. Those were in the days before AIDS had made its first big impact, and sex was still very casual. I would go to a party with Marsaili and leave with someone else. When I got back to the flat, I would find her on her own in the dark. She would never confess to spilling tears over me, but I saw the mascara stains on her pillow.

It all came to a head towards the end of our first semester. There were two girls who shared the room across the hall from us. One of them had a fancy for me. She had never made any secret of it, even when Marsaili was around, and Marsaili hated her for it. Her name was Anita. She was a good-looking girl, but for all her encouragement I had never really taken an interest. She was *too* keen. Like Sine. And I had always backed away from that.

I got in early one day from university. I had skipped lectures and gone to the pub. I had already spent most of my grant for the year, but I just didn't care. I was hell-bent on a course of self-destruction. It was bitterly cold, a heavy sky over the city pregnant with snow. The shops were full of Christmas. My parents had died exactly two weeks before Christmas, and every one of them since had been miserable and depressing. Compounded by my aunt, who had never attempted to make it special for me. While all the other kids had looked forward to the Christmas holiday each year with great excitement, I only ever contemplated it with a sense of dread. And all the commercially motivated ersatz gaiety of the big city, the lights and trees and garish window displays, the endlessly repeating Christmas songs in shops and pubs, seemed only to heighten my sense of dislocation.

I was gently tipsy and consumed by self-pity when I got into the flat. Anita was in the kitchen on her own. She was rolling a joint and looked up, pleased to see me.

'Hi, Fin. I just scored some great dope. You wanna smoke?'

'Sure.' I turned on the TV, and there was some God-awful animation dubbed into Gaelic, buried away in

415

the afternoon schedules on BBC2. It was odd hearing it spoken again. Even although they were cartoon voices, they made me feel homesick.

'Jesus,' Anita said, 'I don't know how you can understand that stuff. It sounds like Norwegian on speed.'

'Why don't you go fuck yourself?' I said to her in Gaelic.

She smiled. 'Hey, what did you say?'

'I said I'd like to fuck you.'

She raised a coy eyebrow. 'What would Marsaili say?'

'Marsaili's not here.'

She lit her joint and took a long, slow pull at it, before passing it to me. I watched the smoke slowly leak from her mouth as I filled my lungs. When eventually I blew it out, I said, 'Has anyone ever made love to you in Gaelic?'

She laughed. 'In Gaelic? What do you mean?'

'If they had, you wouldn't need to ask.'

She stood up and took the joint from me and filled her mouth, pressing it then to mine so that we could share the smoke. I felt her breasts pushing up into my chest and she slipped her free hand down between my legs. 'Why don't you show me?'

If we had gone to her room instead of mine, things might have been different. But between the drink and the dope, and a girl with her hand down my trousers, I didn't really care. The bed hadn't been made from the morning. I turned on the gas fire, and we stripped off and climbed between the same sheets Marsaili and I had shared the night before. It was cold, and we pressed ourselves together for warmth, and I spoke to her softly in Gaelic.

'It's like you're casting a spell on me,' she said. And in a way I was. Making magic with the language of my father. And his father. Coaxing, cajoling, promising her stuff I could never deliver. Slipping inside her to give her my seed. Of course, she was on the pill, and so it was a seed that would fall on stony ground. But for a moment it was an escape. Not for her, for me. A chance to connect again, with the Fin Macleod I had once been. Free to be the boy who had once spoken only Gaelic. Free to touch my ancestors and be with them again. But, really, I think it was just the dope.

I'm not sure when I became aware of Marsaili standing in the doorway. But when I did, I looked up sharply. Her face was chalk-white.

'What is it?' Anita said, and then she saw her, too.

'Why don't you just pick up your clothes and get out,' Marsaili told her very quietly.

Anita looked at me, and I nodded. And with a great show of petulance, Anita climbed out of the bed, gathered up her things from the floor and stomped across the hall to her room. Marsaili closed the door behind her. She had the look in her eyes of a dog that has just been kicked by its master. Betrayal, hurt, shattered trust. I knew there wasn't anything I could say.

'You know, I never told you,' she said. 'The only reason I applied for a place at university was because I knew you had.' And I realized that must have been before our encounter on the island at Great Bernera. And I thought about the letter she had sent imploring me not to take Irene Davis to the final year dance at primary school. Signed, *The Girl from the Farm*. And I knew then that she had never stopped loving me, for all those years. I had to look away, no longer able to meet her eye. For I understood what I had done, in the end, with my cruelty and my selfishness. I had robbed her of hope. The hope that one day she would get me back. That she would find the old Fin again. I didn't know where that Fin was any more than she did, and I'm not sure that I had any hope of finding him myself.

I wanted to say sorry. To hold her, to tell her that everything would be alright. Just like Mr Macinnes had told me on that ledge on the cliff. But I knew it wouldn't be, and I wondered if he had known that, too.

Marsaili didn't say anything else. She took her suitcase down from the top of the wardrobe and started packing her clothes into it.

'Where are you going?'

'Home. I'll get the train to Inverness tomorrow, and then the bus to Ullapool.'

'Where'll you stay tonight?'

'I don't know. Not in this house, that's for sure.'

'Marsaili—'

'Don't, Fin!' She cut me off abruptly. Then more softly, with a catch in her throat, 'Just don't.'

I sat down on the edge of the bed, still naked and chittering with the cold, and watched her pack her case. When she had finished, she slipped on her coat and dragged the case out into the hall. She pulled the door shut behind her without a word, and after a moment I heard the front door open and close.

I went to the window and watched her as she struggled off down the street towards Byres Road. The little girl who had sat beside me that first day at school and offered to translate for me. The same little girl who had stolen a kiss from me high up among the bales in the barn at Mealanais Farm, and taken the blame for me when I dropped my sweets in church. After all these years, finally, I had hurt her beyond repair and driven her from my life. Big, fat snowflakes started falling, then, obscuring her from view before she reached the traffic lights.

I only ever returned to the island once after that, when my aunt died suddenly the following April. I say suddenly, only because the news came to me out of the blue. But, in fact, it had been a long, slow decline over several months. I'd had no idea she was ill, although it turned out that she had been diagnosed with terminal cancer the previous summer. She had refused the chemotherapy, telling doctors that she had lived a long and happy life, drinking the finest wines, and smoking the best cigarettes, sleeping with the most eligible men (and a few women), and spending their money with great abandon.

Why spoil the last six months? As it turned out, it was nearer nine months, most of which had been spent in pain, alone, in the freezing cold of her final winter.

I took the bus out to Ness, and walked up the hill through Crobost to the old whitehouse by the harbour. It was a blowy spring day, but there was a softness to the wind cutting through the dead grasses, and a warmth in the watery sunlight that broke periodically through the racing hordes overhead.

The house still had the chill of winter about it, a smell of damp and disinfectant. All the colourful vases of dried flowers, the purple-painted walls, the pink and orange fabrics of her heyday, were sad and tawdry now. Somehow she had given them their vibrancy, and without her they just seemed cheap and nasty. She had always been a huge presence in the house, and it was hugely empty without her.

The grate in which she had lit her final fire still contained its ash and burned-out embers, grey and impossibly cold. I sat for a long time in her seat, staring at the fire and thinking about all the years that I had lived with her. It was extraordinary how few memories of her I had collected in that time. What a strange, cold childhood I'd had.

In my bedroom I found all my old toys that she had stuffed in boxes and piled up in the wardrobe, a sad reminder of a past I was only too anxious to leave behind. I thought about Paul's letter to the Corinthians. *When I*

was a child, I spake as a child, I understood as a child, I thought
as a child: but when I became a man, I put away childish things.
All those Sabbath hours spent in the Crobost Free Church
had left their traces. I took the boxes of toys downstairs
and piled them up at the bin.

I had no idea what to do with my aunt's things. I went
into her bedroom and opened the wardrobe. Her clothes
hung in silent rows, colours obscured by the shadow of
her death. She had kept trousers and skirts and blouses
years beyond her ability to wear them. It was as if she had
harboured somewhere the hope that one day she might
find again the person she had been in the sixties. Young,
slim, attractive, her whole life ahead of her.

I did not want to spend a single night in this house.
But I had nowhere else to stay, and so as night fell I lit a
fire, wrapped myself in a blanket and slept on the settee
in front of it, flitting in and out of strange dreams in
which my aunt and Mr Macinnes were dancing together
across an empty dancefloor.

I wakened to the sound of banging. It was broad daylight. I looked at my watch and saw that I had slept for
nearly ten hours. There was someone knocking at the
door. I answered it, still wrapped in my blanket, screwing
my eyes up against the glare of sunshine to find myself
squinting at a woman called Morag. She was a second
cousin, I think, but much older than me. I'm not sure
that I had seen her since my parents' funeral.

'Fin. I thought it must be you. I could smell the peat

421

smoke, so I knew there was someone at home. I've got a key, but I didn't like to use it if there was somebody in. You know the funeral's today?'

I nodded blearily, and remembered that my aunt had never had a good word to say for Morag. But as it turned out it was Morag, in the absence of anyone else, who had organized everything to do with the funeral. 'You'd better come in.'

And it was Morag who solved the problem of my aunt's things. There was stuff, she said, that her family could use, and what they couldn't, she would take to the charity shop in Stornoway. 'You know, someone's thrown out all your old toys.' She was indignant. 'I found them at the bin. I've put them in the boot so they don't go to waste.' And some other kid, I thought, would build a new set of memories around them. I just hoped they would be happier ones than mine.

There weren't many people at the church. A few distant relatives, a few diehard villagers who went to every funeral, a handful of nosy neighbours, curious perhaps to learn a little more about the weird old woman who had lived in splendid isolation in the whitehouse by the harbour. It wasn't until the end of the service when I rose and turned towards the door, the Gaelic psalms still ringing in my ears, that I saw Artair and Marsaili slipping out together from a pew at the back. They must have known I was up there at the front, and yet they turned away quickly through the door, almost as if they were trying to avoid me.

But then they were there among the group of mourners outside the house fifteen minutes later when a dozen of us gathered on the cliff to take the frail remains of my aunt on her final journey. Artair acknowledged me with a nod and a shake of the hand, and we found ourselves shoulder to shoulder when we lifted the coffin off the backs of the chairs placed out on the tarmac. I'm sure the coffin was heavier than my aunt was. I saw Marsaili standing in black among the group of women who watched as the men began the long walk to the cemetery. This time I caught her eye, but only for a moment. She glanced quickly down towards the ground, as if overcome by grief. She had known my aunt only a little, and liked her even less. So it couldn't have been my aunt she mourned.

It wasn't until we had put my aunt in the ground, and left the gravediggers to cover her over, that Artair spoke to me for the first time. A small group of us straggled back through the headstones towards the gate of the cemetery, battered by the wind shearing in off the Atlantic. He said, 'How's university?'

'Not what it's cracked up to be, Artair.'

He nodded as if he understood. 'You like it down there, in Glasgow?'

'It's alright. Better than here.'

We were at the gate before anything more was said. We let the others through, and I hung back with him as he closed it. He turned to look at me, and it felt like a very long time before he spoke. 'Something you should know, Fin.' He took a deep breath and I heard the rattle of phlegm in his tubes. 'Marsaili and I got married.'

I don't know why – I mean, I had no right – but I felt a hot flush of anger and jealousy. 'Oh? Congratulations.'

Of course, he knew I didn't mean it. But what else could I have said? He nodded acknowledgement. 'Thanks.' And we set off across the machair to catch up with the others.

NINETEEN

I

Marsaili was out at the peat stack filling a bucket. She wore jeans, and wellingtons and a thick woollen jumper. For once her hair was unclasped and was blowing all around her face. With the wind driving down from the north she did not hear Fin's car pulling in at the top of the drive. A tiny Daewoo, the colour of vomit, which he had rented in town on a cheap one-day hire. All along the line of the coast below her, the sea broke in angry white wreaths, winding itself up for the storm gathering in the north-west like an invading army.

'Marsaili.'

She stood up, startled by his voice at her shoulder, and she wheeled around, surprised to see him, and then alarmed by what she saw in his face. 'Fin, what is it?'

'You must have known that he was beating the boy.' And she closed her eyes and let the bucket drop to the ground, spilling its peats all over the turf.

'I tried to stop it, Fin. I did.'

'Not hard enough.' His tone was harsh, accusing.

She opened her eyes and he saw the tears collecting there, preparing themselves to spill. 'You can't imagine what he's like. At first, when Fionnlagh was wee, and I saw the bruising, I couldn't believe it. I thought it must have been an accident. But there's a limit to the number of accidents you can have.'

'Why didn't you take him and leave?'

'I tried, believe me, I did. I wanted to. But he told me if I ever left, he would come after us. Wherever we went he would find us, he said. And he would kill Fionnlagh.' Her eyes desperately sought Fin's understanding. But he was like stone.

'You could have done *something*!'

'I did. I stayed. And I did everything I could to stop the beatings. He would never do it if I was around. So I tried always to be there. To protect him, to keep him safe. But it wasn't always possible. Poor Fionnlagh. He was wonderful.' The tears ran freely down her face now. 'He took it all like it was something to be expected. He never cried. He never complained. He just took it.'

Fin found himself shaking. With rage and pain. 'Jesus, Marsaili, why?'

'I don't know!' She almost shouted it at him. 'It's like he was doing it to get at me for some reason. Whatever it is that happened out on that bloody rock, whatever it is you're not telling me, either of you, it changed him beyond recognition.'

'You *know* what happened, Marsaili!' Fin lifted his arms in a hopeless gesture, and then let them fall again in frustration.

She shook her head. 'No, I don't.' And she looked at him long and hard, baffled by his obduracy. 'It changed all of us, you know that, Fin. But Artair was the worst. I wasn't aware of it at first. I think he was hiding it from me. But then, after Fionnlagh was born, it just started coming out of him, like poison.'

Fin's mobile started ringing in his pocket. 'Scotland the Brave'. Cheerful and jaunty. Ludicrously inappropriate in the circumstance. They stood staring at each other, the ridiculous ring-tone fibrillating in the wind. 'Well, aren't you going to answer the stupid thing?'

No one on the island knew his number. So it had to be someone from the mainland. 'No.' He waited for the answering service to pick it up, and was relieved when the ringing stopped.

'So what now?' She wiped the tears from her face with the back of her hand, and left a dirty, peaty smudge across her cheek.

'I don't know.' He saw the weariness in her eyes, the life ground out of her by all the years with Artair, and the guilt for all the beatings her son had been forced to endure, beatings that she had been unable to prevent. His phone started ringing again. 'Jesus!' He snatched it from his pocket, punched the phone symbol and slapped it to his ear. It was his answering service calling him back to let him know that he had one new message. He listened impatiently and heard a familiar voice, but so out of context that it took him several moments to identify it.

'Too busy to answer your bloody phone, eh? Out catching our killer, I hope.' It was the pathologist. Professor Angus Wilson. 'If not, I've got a little something for you that might help. It'll be in my report, but I thought I might give you a little advance notice. That wee ghost pill that we found in the killer's vomitus? It contains an oral form of the steroid cortisone, known as prednisone. Commonly used to treat painful skin allergies. But also very effective in reducing inflammation in the airways, so it's frequently prescribed for asthma sufferers. I suggest, therefore, that you keep your eyes peeled either for someone with a nasty rash, or an habitual asthmatic. Happy hunting, amigo.' The answering service told him there were no more messages.

Fin wondered why the ground had not swallowed him up. Everything else about his world had just fallen apart. So why should the earth still support him? He disengaged the phone and slipped it back in his pocket.

'Fin?' Marsaili was scared. He could hear it in her voice. 'Fin, what is it? You look like you've seen a ghost.'

He looked at her without seeing her. He was in the boatshed at Port of Ness. It was Saturday night, and it was dark. There were two men there. One of them was Angel Macritchie. The other one moved into the moonlight. It was Artair. Fin had no idea why they were there, but when Macritchie turned away, he saw something like a metal tube or a wooden pole flash through the light of the small open window and crash down on Angel's head. The big man dropped to his knees before falling forward on to his face. Artair was excited, breathing rapidly. He got down on his knees to pull the big man over on to his back. The dead weight was heavier to move than he had expected. He heard something, sounds from the village. Was it voices? Maybe it was just the wind. He began to panic, and with the panic he felt his airways start to close. His stomach reacted by heaving its contents out through his mouth. A reflex response. All over the unconscious Macritchie. Artair fumbled in his pocket for his pills and swallowed one and sucked on his puffer while he waited for it to work, still on his knees, breath rasping in the dark. Slowly his breathing became easier again, and he listened for the sound which had sparked his attack. But he heard nothing, and returned then to his task, slipping thick fingers around the big man's throat. And pressing. An urgency now about everything he would do.

Fin closed his eyes tight to try to squeeze the images out of them, and then opened them again to see Marsaili's consternation. 'Fin, for God's sake talk to me!'

His voice, when he found it, sounded small and caught phlegm in his throat. 'Tell me about Artair's asthma.'

She frowned. 'What do you mean, tell you about his asthma?'

'Just tell me.' He was finding strength in his voice. 'Is it worse than it used to be?'

She shook her head in frustration, wondering why he was asking her such stupid questions. 'Yes,' she said. 'It was becoming a nightmare. The attacks were getting worse and worse, until they put him on new medication.'

'Prednisone?'

Her head tilted in surprise, and something darkened the blue of her eyes. Premonition, perhaps. 'How did you know that?'

He took her arm and started pulling her towards the house. 'Show me.'

'Fin, what's this all about?'

'Just show me, Marsaili.'

They went into the bathroom, and she opened a mirrored cabinet on the wall above the washbasin. The bottle was on the top shelf. Fin lifted it down and opened it. It was nearly full.

'Why doesn't he have these with him?'

Marsaili was at a loss. 'I've no idea. Maybe there's another bottle.'

Fin did not even want to think about it. 'Is there somewhere he keeps his private papers? Stuff he never lets you see?'

'I don't know.' She thought about it, distracted, finding

concentration difficult. 'There's a drawer in his father's old desk that he always keeps locked.'

'Show me.'

The desk was pushed up under the window in Mr Macinnes's former study, buried beneath an avalanche of papers and magazines, and wire trays overflowing with paid and unpaid bills. Fin had slept in here the other night, but not even noticed it. The captain's chair that originally went with the desk was nowhere in evidence. An old dining chair was tucked between the pedestals. Fin pulled it out and sat down. He tried the left-hand drawer. It slid open to reveal a concertina folder full of household papers. Fin flicked quickly through it, but there was nothing to interest him. He tried the right-hand drawer and it was locked.

'Do you have a key?'

'No.'

'A heavy screwdriver, then. Or a chisel.'

She turned without a word and left the room, return-ing a few moments later with a large, heavy-duty screw-driver. Fin took it, driving it between the top of the drawer and the pedestal, levering it upwards until the wood splintered and the lock broke. The drawer slid open. Suspension folders hung from a built-in rack. Yellow, blue, pink. He went through them one by one. Bills, in-vestments, letters. Newspaper articles, downloaded from the internet. Fin stopped and heard himself breathing. Short, shallow breaths. He tipped the articles out on to the desktop. The *Herald*, the *Scotsman*, the *Daily Record*, the *Edinburgh Evening News*, the *Glasgow Evening Times*. All dated late May or early June. *Disembowelled Corpse Found in Leith. The Edinburgh Ripper. Strangled and Mutilated. Death in the Shadow of the Cross. Police Issue Appeal over Leith Walk Murder.* More than two dozen of them over a three-week period, when reporting of the murder was at its most frenzied, and before news of an impending increase in council tax took over the front pages.

Fin slammed his fist down on the desk, and a pile of magazines slid on to the floor.

'For Christ's sake, Fin, tell me what's going on!' A hint of hysteria was creeping into Marsaili's voice.

Fin dropped his head into his hands and screwed his eyes tight shut. 'Artair killed Angel Macritchie.'

There was a hush in the room so thick that Fin could almost feel it. Marsaili's voice, small and frightened, forced its way through it. 'Why?'

'It was the only way he could be sure of getting me back to the island.' He scuffed his hand through the printouts of the articles, sending several of them fluttering through still air. 'The papers were full of the murder in Edinburgh. All the gory details. The fact that I was in charge of the investigation. So if another body turned up here on Lewis, same weird MO, what was the betting I'd get involved at some stage? Especially when the victim was someone I was at school with. A gamble, maybe. But it paid off. Here I am.'

'But why? Oh, Fin, I can't believe I'm even hearing you say these things. Why would he want you here?'

'To tell me about Fionnlagh. So that I would know he was my son.' He thought about what Donna Murray had said. *Like he was taking out the sins of the father on the son.*

Marsaili sat heavily on the edge of the bed and put her hands to her face. 'I don't understand.'

'You said you thought he beat Fionnlagh to get at you. It wasn't you he was getting at. It was me. All those years, beating that poor kid, and all the time it was me he was punching, me he was kicking. And it was important to him that I knew that before . . .' And he broke off, frightened even to give voice to the thought.

'Before what?'

Fin turned slowly to look at her. 'He wasn't bothered about giving a DNA sample to the police. He knew he'd be on the rock by the time we figured out it was him. Too late to stop him.'

Marsaili stood up abruptly, as suddenly it occurred to her where all this was leading. 'Stop it, Fin! Stop it!'

He shook his head. 'That's why he didn't bother taking his pills with him. After all, why would he need them if he wasn't coming back?'

He checked his watch and stood up, scooping the newspaper articles back into their folder. Outside the wind was picking up. He could see all the way down to the shore, waves smashing across the rocks, retreating in foam. He turned towards the door, and Marsaili caught his arm.

'Where are you going?'

'I'm going to try and stop him killing our son.'

She bit down hard on her lip and tried to stop the sobs that threatened to choke her. Tears coursed down her cheeks. 'Why, Fin? Why would he do that?'

'Because for some reason he wants to hurt me, Marsaili. To inflict more pain on me than I can bear. He must know I've already lost one son.' And he saw a look in her eyes that told him she had not known. 'What better way to turn the screw than to kill the other?' He pulled himself free of her grasp, but she followed him to the door and grabbed him again.

'Fin, look at me.' There was something compelling in her voice. He turned to meet her intensity. 'Before you go . . . there's something you need to know.'

II

Rain battered against the window of the incident room, obliterating the view over harbour rooftops to the semi-derelict Lews Castle across the bay. There were nearly two dozen officers at desks around the room. All of them were turned towards Fin. Except for George Gunn and a couple of others who were still speaking on the phone. DCI Smith was flushed and exasperated. He had showered, and changed. His hair was smoothly Brylcreemed back from his face, and he smelled of Brut again. He might hold centre stage in the incident room, but he had been up-staged in his investigation by Fin. He was not a happy man, but he was being squeezed into a corner.

He said, 'Okay, so I accept that this Artair Macinnes probably is our killer.'

'His DNA'll confirm it,' Fin said.

Smith glanced irritably at the newspaper articles spread across the nearest desk. 'And you think he copied the Leith Walk murder to lure you back to the island.'

'Yes.'

'To tell you that his son is really your son.'

'Yes.'

'And then kill him.' Fin nodded. Smith let the moment hang. Then, 'Why?'

'I told you what happened on An Sgeir.'

'His father died rescuing you on the cliffs eighteen years ago. Do you really think that's sufficient motivation for him to commit two murders all these years later?'

'I can't explain it.' Fin's frustration bubbled into anger. 'I just know he's beaten that boy black and blue all his life, and now that he's told me I'm his father he's going to kill him. He's killed once to get me here. On the evidence, I don't think anyone can deny that.'

Smith sighed and shook his head. 'I'm not going to risk the lives of my officers by sending them off to a rock fifty miles out in the Atlantic in the middle of a storm.'

Gunn hung up and swivelled around in his chair.

'Latest weather report from the coastguard, sir. Storm-force winds in the vicinity of An Sgeir, and getting worse.' He glanced almost apologetically at Fin. 'They say there's no way they can land the chopper on the rock in these conditions.'

'There you are, then.' Smith sounded relieved. 'We'll have to wait until the storm passes.'

Gunn said, 'The harbourmaster's confirmed that the *Purple Isle* is back from An Sgeir. She docked about an hour ago.'

'I'm not asking a boat to go out in these conditions either!'

A uniformed sergeant came into the room. 'Sir.' His face was chiselled from grim, flinted rock. 'We can't raise the guga people on the CB.'

Fin said, 'Then there's something far wrong. Gigs always keeps a channel of communication open. Always.'

Smith looked to the sergeant for confirmation, and he nodded. The CIO sighed and shrugged. 'There's still nothing we can do about it before tomorrow.'

'The boy could be dead by tomorrow!' Fin raised his voice and felt an immediate hush fall across the room.

Smith raised a finger and touched it to the end of his nose. A strange, threatening gesture. His voice was a low growl. 'You're in serious danger of crossing a line here, Macleod. You are no longer involved in this case, remember?'

'Of course I'm involved. I'm at the very fucking centre

436

of it.' And he turned and pushed through the swing doors out into the corridor.

By the time he reached the foot of Church Street and turned left into Cromwell Street, Fin was soaked. His parka and hood had protected his upper body, but his trousers were plastered to his legs, and his face had stiffened and set under the assault of the freezing rain that drove in off the moor. He turned into the doorway of a green-painted gift shop for some respite, and found foot-high replicas of the Lewis Chessmen staring at him with curious expressions from beyond the glass, almost as if they empathized. He fumbled for his mobile phone and dialled the number of the incident room two hundred yards up the road. One of the uniforms answered.

'I want to speak to George Gunn.'

'Can I tell him who's calling?'

'No.'

A brief pause. 'One moment, sir.'

And then Gunn's voice. 'DS Gunn.'

'George, it's me. Can you talk?'

A moment's silence. 'Not really.'

'Okay, just listen. George, I need you to do me a favour. A big favour.'

III

The trawler rose and fell with the swell in the inner harbour, creaking and straining at its ropes. A red plastic bucket rolled back and forth across the forward deck. Heavy chains swung and rattled and chafed, and every piece of rigging on the boat's superstructure vibrated and whined in the wind. Rain hammered the windows of the wheelhouse, and Padraig MacBean sat up on a pilot's seat that had been worn and torn by years of use, duct tape fighting to contain thick wads of stuffing that seemed determined to escape it. He had one foot up on the wheel, and was puffing thoughtfully on the stump of a hand-rolled cigarette. He was young for a skipper, not much more than thirty. The *Purple Isle* had been his father's boat, and it was his father who had taken Fin out to the rock eighteen years ago, when Padraig could have been only twelve. Old MacBean had carried the guga hunters on their annual pilgrimage to An Sgeir for thirty years. After his death his sons had taken up the tradition. Padraig's younger brother, Duncan, was the first mate. There was only one other member of crew, a young lad called Archie. He had been unemployed, and joined them on a six-month work experience attachment two years ago. He was still attached.

'That's a helluva story you're telling me, Mr Macleod,' Padraig was saying, in the long slow Niseach drawl of a native of Ness. 'I have to tell you, I never much liked that

438

Artair Macinnes. And his lad's a quiet boy.' He took another pull at the remains of his cigarette. 'But I can't say I noticed anything untoward on the trip out.'

'Will you take me?' Fin asked him patiently. He knew it was a big ask.

Padraig lowered his head and peered out from beneath the roof of the wheelhouse. 'It's a hoor of a storm out there, sir.'

'You've been out in worse.'

'Aye, I have that. But never by choice.'

'We're talking about a boy's life, Padraig.'

'And I'm thinking about my boat, and the lives I'd be putting at risk by taking her out.'

Fin said nothing. He knew that the decision was in the balance. He had asked. He could do no more. Padraig sucked on the last half-inch of his cigarette, but it had gone out. He looked at Fin.

'I can't ask the boys to go.' Fin felt hope leaking out of every pore. 'But I'll put it to them. It'll be their decision. And if they say yes, then I'll take you.' Hope gathered itself again in Fin's heart.

He followed the young skipper out through the galley. Oilskins hung from hooks along one wall, above a row of yellow wellies. Dirty dishes slopped about in cloudy water in the sink, a skin of grease reflecting the harsh electric light. There was a kettle on the gas hob, beneath a row of chipped porcelain mugs hanging on pegs.

Rungs set into a riveted metal shaft took them down to

cramped living quarters in the rear of the trawler. Six berths were set into the hull around the stern of the boat, and a triangular table with benches along each side took up most of the available space. Duncan and Archie were sitting with mugs of tea and cigarettes watching a snowy picture on a tiny TV set mounted on the wall high up in one corner. Anne Robinson was being rude to some miserable contestant and insisting that they *were* the weakest link. A middle-aged woman with a face like fizz stormed towards the camera on her walk of shame. Padraig turned off the television and quelled the protestations of his crew with a look. He had something about him for a young man, a quiet, powerful presence that made itself felt.

In a low voice, in the insipid yellow electric light in the hold of the rusted old trawler, he told them what Fin was asking of them. And why. The two young men sat in their ragged pullovers and torn jeans, broken nails ingrained with oil and dirt, pale, mean faces born of generations of island poverty, listening to Padraig's story. Glancing occasionally at Fin. They barely made a living, these boys. And it was not much of a life, eating, sleeping, shitting aboard this old, painted whore of a trawler twenty-four hours a day, five, sometimes six days a week. Day after day they risked their lives, in order that they might live like this. When Padraig had finished, they sat in silence for a moment. Then Archie said, 'Well, it's cheaper than going to the pub, I suppose.'

IV

It was after seven when they left port, tipping past Cuddy Point into the outer harbour and facing into the rising swell that drove in off the Minch. By the time they had cleared Goat Island and motored out into deeper water, the sea was rising and breaking about them as they ploughed their way through the advance regiments of the storm. Padraig stood at the wheel, his face furrowed in concentration, green in the reflected phosphor of the battered radar screens that flashed and beeped all around the console. There was a little light left in the sky, but it was impossible to see anything. Padraig was guiding them by instruments and instinct. 'Aye, she's wild, right enough. Not so bad here in the lee of Lewis. It'll be a lot worse when we round the Butt.'

Fin could not imagine anything much worse. He had thrown up twice by the time they passed the Tiumpan Head Lighthouse, and he declined Archie's offer of fried egg and sausage that the boy was somehow managing to conjure in a galley that no longer had any fixed point of reference.

'How long's it going to take?' he asked Padraig.

The skipper shrugged. 'Took us just under eight hours last night. Could be nine or more tonight. We'll be heading right into the teeth of the storm. It'll be well into the early hours before we get to An Sgeir.'

Fin remembered how it had felt eighteen years before

when they had rounded the Butt of Lewis, and the beam of the lighthouse had finally faded into darkness. The security of the island behind them, they had set out into the vast wilderness of the North Atlantic, kept safe and dry only by a few tons of rusting trawler and the skills of her skipper. He had felt scared then, lonely, incredibly vulnerable. But none of that prepared him for the fury with which the ocean would fling itself upon them this time as they rounded the northern tip of Lewis. Diesel engines hammering in the dark, they fought against seemingly impossible odds, water rising sheer all around them, like black, snow-capped mountains, crashing over the bow and hammering into the wheelhouse. He hung on to whatever he could, wondering how Padraig could remain so calm, and tried to imagine how it might be possible to survive, sanity intact, another seven or eight hours of this.

'Before my father died,' Padraig had to shout above the roar of the engines and the anger of the storm, 'he bought another boat to replace the *Purple Isle*.' He nodded and smiled to himself, keeping his eyes fixed on the screens in front of him and the blackness through the glass. 'Aye, she was a right beauty, too. The *Iron Lady* he called her. He spent a lot of time and money making her just the way he wanted her.' He flicked a glance at Fin. 'There are times you wish it was that easy with a woman.' He turned and grinned back into the darkness, and then his smile faded. 'He was going to sell this old dear when he got the chance. Only he never did. Cancer of the liver. He was gone in a matter of weeks. And I had to step into his shoes.' He took a crumpled-looking cigarette one-handed from a Virginia tobacco tin and lit it. 'Lost the *Iron Lady* first time I took her out. A ruptured pipe in the engine room. By the time we got to it, there was more water coming in than we could pump out. I told the rest of them to get the dinghy out, and I tried everything I could to save her. I was up to my neck in the engine room before I finally baled out. Just made it, too.' Smoke swirled from his mouth in the turbulent air of the wheel-house. 'We were lucky, though. The weather was good, and there was another trawler within sight. I watched her go down. Everything that my father had put into her. All his hopes, all his dreams. And all I could think was, how was I going to tell my uncles I'd lost my father's boat? But I needn't have worried. They were just glad that we were safe. One of them said, "A boat's just a bunch of wood and metal, son. The only heart it has is in those who sail her."' He took a long pull at his cigarette. 'Still, I get goose-bumps every time I go over the spot where she went down, and I know she's just lying there on the seabed, right beneath where we last saw her. All my father's dreams, gone for ever, just like him.'

Fin felt the young skipper's intensity like a third presence in the wheelhouse. He looked at him. 'We just went over that spot, didn't we?'

'Aye, Mr Macleod, we did that.' He snatched a quick

look at the policeman. 'You should go and lie down in one of the berths for a while. You never know, you might get a bit of sleep. It's going to be a long haul.'

Duncan took his place in the wheelhouse as Fin went below and pulled himself up into the same berth he had occupied the only other time he had made the journey. He had no expectation of sleep, just the knowledge that in the long, slow hours ahead of them he would have plenty of time in which to turn over, again and again in his mind, all the unanswered questions that plagued him. Questions he knew would not be answered until they got to An Sgeir. And even then, there was no guarantee. Artair and Fionnlagh might already be dead, and he would never know. And never forgive himself for not having had at least some inkling of what was to come.

He was surprised, then, when Archie shook him awake. 'Nearly there, Mr Macleod.'

Fin slid out from his berth, startled, disorientated, and sat rubbing his eyes with the heels of his hands. The steady, rhythmic pounding of the engines seemed to have become a part of him, thudding inside his head, jarring his soul. The trawler was tipping and pitching wildly, and it was all he could do to climb back up into the galley without falling. Duncan was at the wheel, his face a study of concentration. Padraig sat beside him staring bleakly into the darkness. He was a bad colour. He saw Fin's reflection in the glass and turned. 'I've been trying to get them on the radio for the last hour, but all I'm getting is white noise and static. I don't like it, Mr Macleod. It's not like Gigs.'

'How long?' Fin said.

'Ten minutes, maybe less.'

Fin peered into the black but could see nothing. Padraig, too, was straining to see in the dark. 'Where's the fucking lighthouse?' He flicked a switch, and all the *Purple Isle*'s lights blazed into the night. The three hundred feet of cliff on which Fin had so nearly perished rose out of the sea almost immediately ahead of them, black and glistening and slathered in streaks of white guano. He was startled by how close they were.

'Jesus!' he said involuntarily, taking a step back and clutching the door frame to steady himself.

'Fuck sake, pull her round!' Padraig screamed at Duncan. His brother swung the wheel hard left, and the *Purple Isle* yawed dangerously, careening side-on through the waves that pounded and broke all around them. 'There's no light!' he bellowed. 'No bloody light!'

'Was she working last night?' Fin shouted.

'Aye. You could see her for miles.'

Duncan had control of the trawler again, setting her into the wind once more, and they ploughed around the southern tip of the rock, circumventing Lighthouse Promontory and cruising finally into the comparative shelter of Gleann an Uisge Dubh. Here there was a noticeable respite from the wind. But the rise and fall was still ten feet or more, and they could see the swell breaking white at the point where usually they would land supplies, smashing and splintering all around the entrance to the caves that cut deep into the underbelly of An Sgeir.

Padraig shook his head. 'There's no way you're going to get the dinghy in there tonight, Mr Macleod.'

'I didn't come all the way out here,' Fin shouted above the thud of the engines, 'to sit in a bloody boat while that man murders my son.'

'If I take the *Isle* in close enough to put you down in a dinghy, there's every chance we'll all get smashed to pieces on those rocks.'

'I saw your father back a trawler up to the quay at Port of Ness in a storm one year,' Fin said. 'In the days when they brought the guga back to Ness.'

'You remember that?' Padraig's eyes were shining.

'Everyone remembers that, Padraig. I was just a boy then. But folk talked about it for years.'

'He had no fear, my father. If he thought he could do something, then he just did it. Folk said he must have nerves of steel. But that wasn't true. He didn't have any nerves at all.'

'How did he do it?'

'He dropped the anchor first, and then reversed in. He figured if he got into trouble he would just slip gear and haul anchor, and it would pull him straight out to safety.'

'So, how much of your father do you have in you, Padraig?'

Padraig gave Fin a long, hard stare. 'Once you're in that dinghy, Mr Macleod, you're on your own. There's not a damned thing I can do for you.'

Fin wondered if he had ever been more frightened. Out here, with a monstrous sea smashing itself over the rocks all around them, he had never felt less in control. It was a raw confrontation with nature at its most powerful, and he seemed tiny and insignificant by comparison. And yet they had got themselves there in one piece, across fifty miles of storm-lashed ocean, and now there were only a few hundred feet still to cover. Duncan attached a line to the inflatable and kept her pulled tight to the stern as Padraig inched the *Purple Isle* backwards into the creek, keeping her anchor chain taut. The cliffs on the two promontories closed in around them, dangerously close now, and the trawler bucked and slid on the swell, one way, then the other. They could hear the sea snapping and slurping at the rock, as if it were trying to devour it.

Padraig signalled that he had taken her in as far as he dared, and Duncan nodded to Fin. Time to go. The rain was coming at him horizontally as he slid down the rungs of the ladder, wet fingers stiff in the freezing cold. Somehow he was still dry beneath his oilskins, but he knew that would not last long. His lifejacket seemed ludicrously flimsy. If he fell in the water, it would probably keep him afloat just long enough for the sea to tear him apart on the rock. The inflatable dinghy was swinging wildly, rising and falling beneath him, impossible to step into. He took a deep breath, as if about to duck below water, and let go of the *Purple Isle*, allowing himself to drop into the dinghy. As it gave way beneath his weight, his hands searched desperately for the rope that ran around the inflated perimeter. They found nothing but smooth, wet fabric. He felt himself slipping away, falling through space, the dinghy vanishing below him, and he braced himself for impact with the water. But at the last moment, the abrasive plastic of the rope burned the palm of his right hand, and he closed his fingers around it. The dinghy was there beneath him once more, and this time, clutching the rope, he rose and fell with it, securing himself by grabbing the line on the left-hand side.

He glanced up and saw Duncan's white face a long way above him. He seemed to be shouting something, but Fin couldn't hear what. He pulled himself towards the back of the dinghy and tipped the outboard over the stern. He opened the choke and pulled the starter cord. One, two, three, four times. Nothing. On the fifth, it coughed and spluttered and caught, and he gunned it furiously to stop it stalling. It was the moment of truth. Attached only by the umbilical of the rope, he was about to leave the safety of the mother ship.

The rope played out behind him as he swung the dinghy around, and her nose rose up through the swell towards the landing point. He twisted the accelerator, and the tiny orange vessel ploughed at a surprising speed towards the rocks. By the lights of the trawler, he saw the great black mouth of the cave opening up above him, and he could hear the cathedral roar and rush of the sea from deep within the belly of the island. A creamy-white frenzy of foam boiled all around him, and he felt the dinghy lifted by the swell and propelled towards the rocks. He yanked at the rudder and cranked up the motor to maximum power, pulling himself out of a collision at the last second, and the sea sucked him back out into the bay. The roar in his ears was deafening. He did not even dare to look back at the trawler.

He swung the dinghy around and faced the rocks again. They dipped up and down below the level of the swell, as if sizing him up, and then hiding in preparation for ambush. He hung there on the rise and fall for a full minute, gathering together all the broken pieces of his courage. He realized that timing was everything. He could not afford to run in with the swell as he had the first time. It was much more powerful than his tiny outboard and would dash him on to the rocks in a moment. He had to motor in as the swell receded, using his forward momentum against its retreat, to prevent a collision. Easy! He almost laughed at his ludicrous attempts to intellectualize his way through this. The truth was, if God existed, then Fin's life was well and truly in His hands now. He took deep breaths, waiting for the sea to break again on the rocks, and then accelerated hard into the retreating rush of white water. Again the mouth of the cave closed around him, and it seemed as if he were making no progress at all, just holding his own in the mist of froth and spume, before suddenly he was propelled forward at a speed he could not control. He tried to pull the rudder around, but the propeller was out of the water, blades screaming through air that offered no resistance. The whole of An Sgeir seemed to be throwing itself at him. He shouted his defiance, as the sea held him in its palm and lifted him clear out of the dinghy and up on to the rocks with a force that knocked all the breath from his body. He could taste blood in his mouth, and felt the jagged edges of the gneiss tearing at his flesh. The boat was gone, and he was pinned to the rock by the force of the water. And then almost immediately the pressure that held him there dissipated, and the sea started sucking him back. He felt himself sliding down the glistening black surface of rock worn smooth by millions of years. He scrabbled for a handhold, but the green collar of algae all around An Sgeir squeezed through his fingers like slime, and he was aware of the power of the sea drawing him down into a cold, dark place where he knew that sleep was for ever.

And then he felt it. The cold bite of iron, the movement of the ring as his fingers closed desperately around it, and held. And held. Almost dislocating his shoulder as the sea pulled and jerked, before finally, reluctantly letting go. For a moment he lay still, clutching the mooring ring, washed up on the rock like a beached sea creature. And then he scrambled for a foothold, and then a handhold, and the strength to propel himself upwards before the sea returned to reclaim him. He could sense it snapping at his heels as he found the ledge of rock on which Angel had built a fire of peats and made them tea on the day they landed there eighteen years before. He'd made it. He was on the rock, safe from the sea. And all that it could do now was spit its anger in his face.

He became aware for the first time that the rain had stopped, and huge tears in a black sky overhead released sudden and unexpected shards of moonlight to strike down across the island. He saw the *Purple Isle* in a pool of dazzling silver light motoring back out into the safety of the bay, still dipping and yawing on a sea furious at her complicity in Fin's escape.

Fin fumbled for the torch clipped to his belt, hoping that it would still work. Its light flashed into his face, and he waved it in the dark to let the crew know that he was safe. Then he pulled his knees up to his chest, his back to the cliff, and huddled there for a full five minutes, trying to regain his breath and his composure, and his will to tackle the climb to the top. He flashed the torch at his watch. It was after 4 a.m. In under two hours, dawn would break in the east. He was almost afraid to contemplate what daylight might bring.

The rain stayed off, fragments of moon flitting in and out between scraps of breaking sky. Fin wondered if he was imagining that the wind had dropped just a little. He got unsteadily to his feet and shone his torch up the incline. There, caught in its beam, smooth and glistening in the light, was the chute the guga hunters used to haul their supplies up to the top of the rock. Still in use after all these years. Fin raised his torch and followed its angled progress up the steepest sections of the slope, and he saw the rope that they used snaking down across the jumble of rock and boulders. He climbed up until he was able to grab the end of it, and he pulled hard. It held fast. He tied it around his waist, and began the long climb to the top, using the rope to guide him in the dark, to pull himself up the steepest gradients, stopping frequently to wind it around his waist, a safety measure against the possibility of a fall.

It took him a full twenty minutes to haul himself up to the roof of the island and unravel himself from the rope. He looked back, gasping for breath, battered and buffeted by the wind that swept unimpeded across the chaos of rock and stone, and saw the lights of the *Purple Isle* winking out in the bay. As he turned, an almost full moon emerged from the ragged remnants of the storm cloud overhead, and spilled its light all over An Sgeir. He saw the squat silhouette of the lighthouse, bracing itself in darkness at the highest point of the island, and a hundred yards away across the shambles of boulders and nests, the dark, huddled shape of the old blackhouse. There was no light, no sign of life. But the smell of peat smoke carried to him on the edge of the wind, and he knew that there must be someone inside.

V

Petrel chicks puked on his feet as he stumbled across the rocks by the light of his torch, overturning nests and sending birds squawking off into the night. The tarpaulin hanging across the entrance to the blackhouse had been weighted down with heavy boulders. He yanked it free and pushed his way inside.

He could see the embers of the peat fire in the centre of the room glowing still in the dark, and he could smell the sour perfume of human sweat, a pitch above the pervasive smell of peat smoke. He flashed his torch around the walls, cutting through blue, smoky air, and saw the shapes of men lying hunched on mattresses all along the stone shelf. Several of them were already stirring, and his torchlight caught a pale, sleepy face full in its beam. It was Gigs. He raised a hand to shade the light from his eyes. 'Artair? Is that you? What the hell's going on?'

'It's not Artair.' Fin let the tarpaulin drop again behind him. 'It's Fin Macleod.'

'Jesus,' he heard someone say. 'How in God's name did you get here?'

They were all awake now. Several men sat up and swung their legs around and slid down to the floor. Fin made a quick head count. There were ten of them. 'Where's Artair and Fionnlagh?' Someone lit a tilley lamp, and by its spectral light, Fin could see all their faces through the smoke, staring back at him as if he were a ghost.

'We don't know,' Gigs said. Another lamp was lit, and someone stooped to rake the fire and pile on fresh peats. 'We were working almost until dusk setting up the pulleys. Artair and Fionnlagh left our group, and we all thought they'd come back to the blackhouse. But when we got here, there was no sign of them. Their kit was gone, and the radio smashed.'

'And you don't know where they went?' Fin was incredulous. 'There aren't exactly many places to hide on An Sgeir. And they wouldn't have lasted long out there in this weather.'

One of the other men said, 'We think they must be somewhere down in the caves.'

'But we've no idea why.' Gigs fixed his eyes on Fin. 'Maybe *you* can tell *us*.'

'How in the name of the wee man did you get here, Fin?' It was Asterix. 'I didn't see any wings on you yesterday.'

'Padraig brought me.'

'In this weather?' Pluto peered at Fin through the gloom. He had been with the hunt the year that Fin was with them. 'Are you insane?'

Fin's sense of urgency grew to something approaching panic. 'I think Artair is going to kill Fionnlagh. I've got to find them.' He pulled aside the tarpaulin to head back out into the storm. Gigs crossed the blackhouse in three strides and grabbed his arm.

'Don't be a bloody fool, man! It's pitch out there. You'll

kill yourself before you'll find them.' He pulled him back inside and dragged the tarpaulin across the doorway. 'There's no one going out there looking for anyone until we've got light to see by. So why don't we all sit down and brew ourselves some tea, and we'll hear you out?'

Flames were licking up around the dry slabs of peat as the guga hunters gathered around the fire and Asterix lowered a pot of water over the heat. Some of the men had blankets wrapped around their shoulders. Others pulled on flat caps or baseball caps. Several lit cigarettes to breathe more smoke into air already thick with it. And they sat in a strange, tense silence, waiting for the water to boil, and for Asterix to fill the pots. Fin found an odd reassurance in their quiet patience, and he tried to let a little of the tension drain out of muscles screwed taut by the events of the last hour. It seemed barely possible to him that he was here at all.

When the tea had masked, Asterix filled their mugs, and the tins of dried milk and sugar were passed around. Fin made his tea sweet, and took big gulps of the syrupy, milky liquid. It did not taste much like tea, but the heat of it was comforting, and he felt a kick as the sugar hit his bloodstream. He looked up and found them all watching him, and he had the strangest sense of déjà vu. He had sat around the fire in this shelter on the rock every night that he had been on the island eighteen years ago, but this was different. This had the quality of a dream. Of something not quite real. And the dark spectre of apprehension began clouding his thoughts. He had been here before, but not in any way that he remembered.

'So . . .' Gigs broke the silence. 'Why is Artair going to kill his son?'

'Two nights ago he told me that Fionnlagh was *my* son.' The wind outside seemed like a distant cry. The air in the blackhouse was as still as death, and smoke was suspended in it almost without movement. 'And for some reason—' Fin shook his head, '—I don't know why, he seems to hate me beyond reason.' He breathed deeply. 'It was Artair who murdered Angel. He did it by copying a murder in Edinburgh that I had been investigating, to try and draw me back to the island. I'm pretty sure he wanted me to know that Fionnlagh was my son, so that by killing him he could make me suffer.'

There was a stirring of unrest around the fire. Fin saw several of the men glancing at each other, dark looks laden with meaning. Gigs said, 'And you can't think of a single reason why Artair might hate you so much?'

'I can only think that somehow he must blame me for the death of his father.' Fin had a sudden sense that perhaps there were others around the fire who might also think that. 'But it wasn't my fault, Gigs. You know that. It was an accident.'

And still Gigs stared at him intently, a look of incomprehension in his eyes. 'You really *don't* remember, do you?'

Fin was aware of his breath coming fast and shallow

456

now, fear beginning to wrap itself around him with long, cold fingers. 'What do you mean?'

Gigs said, 'I was never sure if it was the knock on the head. You know, the concussion. Or if it was something deeper. Something in your mind. Something psychological that was making you blank out the memory.' Fear flooded every locker in Fin's mind. He had a sense of some long-forgotten wound being opened up to recover a piece of hidden shrapnel, and he could hardly bear it. He wanted to scream for Gigs to stop. Whatever it was, he didn't want to know. Gigs rubbed his unshaven jaw. 'At first, when I came to see you at the hospital, I thought you must be faking it. But I'm pretty sure now that you weren't. That you genuinely don't remember. Maybe that was a good thing, maybe not. Only you'll know that in the end.'

'For God's sake, Gigs, what are you talking about?' The mug was trembling in Fin's hand. Something unspeakable hung above them in the smoke.

'Do you remember that night I found you drunk at the side of the road? Babbling about not wanting to go to the rock?' Fin nodded mutely. 'You don't remember why?'

'I was scared, that's all.'

'Scared, yes. But not of the rock. When I got you back to the croft, you told me something that night that caused you pain that I can't imagine. You sat in the chair in front of my fire and cried like a baby. Tears like I've never seen a young man cry. Tears of fear and humiliation.'

Fin sat wide-eyed. It was someone else Gigs was talking about. Not him. He was there that night. There were no tears. He was drunk, that was all.

Gigs let his gaze drift darkly around all the faces circling the fire. 'Some of you were out on the rock that year, so you know what I'm talking about. Some of you weren't. And to them, I'll say now what I said then. Whatever happens on this rock, whatever passes between us, stays here. On the island. It'll be in our heads, but it'll never pass our lips. And if any man here breathes a word of it to another living soul, then he'll answer to me before he answers to his maker.' And there was not a single man around the fire who did not believe that to be true.

As the flames devoured the peats, so the shadows of the men assembled there danced on the walls like silent witnesses to an oath of silence, and the dark beyond the light seemed to draw the blackhouse tight in around them. Eyes turned back towards Fin, and they saw a man lost in a trance, trembling in the dark, all blood drained from a face as white as bleached bone.

Gigs said, 'He was the devil himself, that man.'

Fin frowned. 'Who?'

'Macinnes. Artair's father. He did unimaginable things to you boys. In his study. All those years of tutoring, shut away behind a locked door. First Artair, and then you. Abuse the like of which no child should ever have to suffer.' He stopped to pull in a breath, almost suffocated by the silence. 'That's what you told me that night, Fin.

You never talked about it, you and Artair. Never acknowledged it. But each of you knew what was going on, what the other was suffering. There was a bond of silence between you. And that's why you were so happy that summer. Because it was over. You were leaving the island. You never had any reason to see Macinnes ever again. It was an end to it once and for all. You'd never told a soul. How could you have faced the shame of what it was he'd done to you? The humiliation. But now you would never have to. You could put it behind you. Forget it for ever.'

'And then he told us we were going to the rock.' Fin's voice was the merest whisper.

Gigs's face was set grim in deeply etched shadow. 'Suddenly, after the relief, you were faced by two weeks with him here on An Sgeir. Living cheek by jowl with the man who had ruined your young life. And God knows, we're in one another's pockets here. There's no escape. Even if he couldn't lay a finger on you, you would have had to suffer the man nearly twenty-four hours a day. For you it was unthinkable. I didn't blame you then, and I don't blame you now, for how you felt.'

Although Fin's eyes were closed, they were open wide for the first time in eighteen years. The sense that he had had all his adult life, of something that he could not see, something just beyond the periphery of his vision, was gone. Like removing blinkers from a horse. The shock of it was physically painful. He was rigid with tension. How could he not have remembered? And yet all his conscious thoughts were awash now with memories, like the vivid recollection of scenes from a nightmare in the moments of waking. He felt bile filling the emptiness inside him, as images flickered across his retinas, like a faded family video out of sync with its playhead. He could smell the dust off the books in Mr Macinnes's study, the stink of stale tobacco and alcohol on his breath as it burst hot on his face. His could feel the touch of his cold, dry hands, and recoiled from them even now. And he saw again the image of the funny man with the impossibly long legs who had haunted his dreams ever since Robbie's death, like the harbinger of his returning memory. That figure who stood silently in the corner of his study, head bowed by the ceiling, arms dangling from the sleeves of his anorak. And he recognized him now for the first time. He was Mr Macinnes. With his long, grey hair straggling over his ears, and his dead, hunted eyes. Why had he not seen it before?

He opened his eyes now to find tears streaming from them, burning his cheeks like acid. He scrambled to his feet and staggered to the door, pulling the tarpaulin aside and emptying his stomach into the storm. He dropped to his knees then, retching and retching until his stomach muscles seized and he could not draw a breath.

Hands lifted him gently to his feet and steered him back into the warmth. A blanket was placed around his shoulders, and he was guided again to sit sobbing at his place by the fire. His trembling was uncontrollable, as if he were in a fever. A sheen of fine sweat glistened on his brow.

He heard Gigs's voice. 'I don't know how much you remember of it now, Fin, but that night, when you told me, I was so angry I wanted to kill him. To think that a man could do something like that to children! To his own son!' He drew in a deep, scratching breath. 'And then I wanted to go to the police. To have charges brought. But you begged me not to. You didn't want anyone to know. Ever. Which was when I realized that the only way to deal with it was here on the rock. Among ourselves. So that no one else *would* ever know.'

Fin nodded. He didn't need Gigs to tell him the rest. He remembered now as clearly as if it had happened yesterday, a film of obfuscation peeled away from every year which had passed since. He remembered the men gathered around the fire on that first night, and Gigs laying his bible down after the reading and shocking them all by confronting Artair's father with his crimes. A ghastly silence, a denial. And Gigs badgering and threatening like an advocate in the High Court, physically menacing, evoking God's wrath, facing him with everything Fin had told him, until finally the older man cracked. And it all poured out of him like poison. Prompted by fear and by shame. He couldn't explain why he had done it. He had never meant it to happen. He was so, so sorry. It would never happen again. He would make it up to the boys, both of them. Mr Macinnes had simply disintegrated in front them.

Fin remembered, too, the look that Artair had given him across the fire, the sense of hurt and betrayal in his eyes. Fin had broken their bond of silence. He had shattered the only thing which had allowed the Macinnes family still to function. Denial. If you denied it, it never happened. And Fin realized now, perhaps for the first time, that Artair's mother must have known, and that she too had been in denial. But Fin's confession to Gigs had meant that denial would no longer be an option. And every other alternative was unthinkable.

Gigs let his gaze wander around the faces at the fire, flames reflecting the horror in their eyes. He said, 'We sat in judgement on him that night. A jury of his peers. And we found him guilty. And we banished him from the blackhouse. His punishment was to live rough on the rock for the two weeks that we were here. We would leave him food out by the cairns, and we would take him back with us when we were finished. But he would never return to the rock. And he would never, ever, lay a hand on either of those boys again.'

Fin realized why Mr Macinnes had never reckoned in his memory of their two weeks on the rock. But now he saw again the fleeting glimpses of the ghostlike figure of Artair's father climbing up from the caves below to collect the food left for him up by the cairns. A shambling figure stooped by shame. Although he had never said anything, Gigs must have sensed Artair's hostility towards Fin after his confession, and kept them always on separate work gangs.

Fin looked across the peats at the flames throwing their light in Gigs's face. 'The day I had the accident on the cliffs. After Mr Macinnes had tied me to the rope. He didn't fall, did he?'

Gigs shook his head sadly. 'I don't know, Fin. I really don't. We didn't know how we were going to get down to you. And then someone spotted him climbing up from below. He must have heard the commotion from the caves down there. I guess he was trying to redeem himself somehow. And in a way he did. He probably saved your life. But whether he fell, or whether he jumped, well that's anyone's guess.'

'He wasn't pushed?'

Gigs canted his head just a little to one side and stared back at Fin. 'By who?'

'By me.' He had to know.

Outside, the storm was blowing itself out. But the wind still whistled and screamed in every crack and crevice in the rock, through all the gullies and caves, among all the cairns left by the generations of guga hunters who had gone before. Gigs said, 'We'd hauled you up fifty feet by the time he went, Fin. No one pushed him, except maybe the hand of God.'

TWENTY

I

He heard someone call his name. Bright, hard and clear. *Fin. Fin Macleod.* But distant. From somewhere beyond the fog. He rose swiftly, as if from the darkness of the seabed, and broke the surface of consciousness, startled and blinking in pain at the light that blinded him. Shapes and shadows were moving around him. Someone had pulled back the tarpaulin, flooding the blackhouse with the soft, yellow light of sunrise. Smoke from the smouldering fire swirled and eddied in the wind that sneaked in with it.

When Gigs had said they should try to get some sleep before dawn, Fin had been unable to imagine how that might be possible. And yet now he could not even remember curling up on the stone shelf along the far wall. Some self-protective mechanism had simply shut him down. The same mechanism, perhaps, which had hidden all his troubled memories in a dark and inaccessible corner of his mind for eighteen years.

'Fin Macleod!' The voice called again, but this time Fin detected the wheeze in it. Artair. Fear slid through him like a frozen arrow. He jumped down from the shelf and staggered across to the door, pushing past bodies to reach it. Gigs and several others were already outside. Fin put a hand up to shade his eyes from a sun still low in the eastern sky and saw, out on the edge of the cliff beyond the lighthouse, two men silhouetted against the dawn. The sky was almost yellow, streaked with pink cloud, and ten thousand gannets filled it with their huge beating wings, screaming their contempt for the men below.

Artair and Fionnlagh were a good two hundred yards away, but Fin could see the rope tied around Fionnlagh's neck, looping into his father's hands. The boy's own hands were bound behind his back and he was teetering perilously close to the edge of the cliff, kept from tipping over the edge and dropping the three hundred feet to the rocks below only by the tension that Artair maintained on the rope.

Fin stumbled and slid across the boulder-strewn soup of mud and seaweed that lay between him and the two figures on the clifftop. Artair watched him with a strange smile fixed on his face. 'I knew it was you. When we saw the trawler come in last night. We watched you trying to land the dinghy. Fucking mad! But we were rooting for you, boy.' He looked at Fionnlagh. 'Weren't we, young Fin? It's better than I could ever have hoped for. A father's first-hand fucking view of his boy going over the edge.' He turned back towards Fin. 'Come on, Macleod. Closer. You'll get a grand-stand view. I suppose the DNA results are through.'

Fin was no more than fifty feet away now. He could almost smell the boy's fear in the wind. He stopped, gasping for breath, and looked at his old schoolfriend with a mixture of hatred and disbelief. 'No,' he shouted back. 'You threw up one of your pills, Artair. Prednisone. For asthmatics. It could only have been you.'

Artair laughed. 'Christ, I wish I'd thought of that. I'd have done it on purpose.'

Fin began moving more cautiously towards them now, anxious to keep Artair talking for as long as he could. 'You killed Angel Macritchie just to get me here.'

'I knew it wouldn't take you long to work that one out, Fin. You always were too fucking smart for your own good.'

'Why Macritchie?'

Artair laughed. 'Why the fuck not? He was a piece of shit, Fin. You know that. Who'd fucking miss him?'

And Fin thought about the tears in the eyes of the boy that Angel had crippled all those years before.

'And anyway . . .' Artair's smile curdled on his lips, 'he had it coming. He was here, remember, eighteen years ago. He knew what really happened that year. And there wasn't a day went by that he didn't remind me of it, that he didn't hold out the prospect of public humiliation.' His face was twisted by anger and hate. 'Do you remember now, Fin? Did Gigs tell you?'

Fin nodded.

'Good. I'm glad you know. All that loss of memory shit. I thought for a long time you were putting it on. And then it came to me. Naw, it was real. And you'd fucking escaped. The memory, the island, everything. And here was me, stuck looking after a mother who needed fed through a straw, married to the only woman I ever loved – a Fin Macleod cast-off, pregnant with *his* son instead of mine. Stuck with the memory of everything my father did to us. Stuck with the humiliation of knowing that a whole lot of others knew it, too. Because of you. And you got off scot-fucking-free. Jesus!' He tipped his head back and glared at the heavens. 'Well, not any more, Fin. You're going to get to watch your boy die, just as I watched my father die on these same cliffs. Because of you.'

'I suppose you knew about my kid being killed in the hit-and-run.'

Artair grinned. 'Saw it in the paper, boy. Punched the fucking air when I read it. At last some shit was sticking to the teflon kid. It's what crystallized the idea for me. The chance to ruin your life the way you ruined mine.'

Fin was no more than ten feet away now. He saw the madness in Artair's eyes. And the terror in Fionnlagh's.

'That's close enough,' Artair said sharply.

Fin said, 'If you'd wanted the pleasure of seeing me watch my own son die, you should have been at Edinburgh Royal Infirmary last month. He was just eight, that wee boy. I was there in intensive care when he flatlined.'

And he saw the merest hint of humanity flicker for the briefest moment in Artair's eyes. 'You could have seen my misery close-up, Artair. You could have known for yourself how my life was blighted for ever by the loss of my child. But you won't see that today.'

Artair frowned. 'What do you mean?'

'It would make me sick to my stomach to see young Fionnlagh die here like this. But I wouldn't be witnessing the death of my son.'

Artair's consternation was turning to anger. 'What the fuck are you talking about, Macleod?'

'I'm talking about the fact that Fionnlagh's not my son, Artair. Marsaili only told you that in a fit of anger. Some stupid revenge for having to settle for what she saw as second-best. For having to settle for you. Just so you wouldn't think it had all come too easy.' He took several more tentative steps towards them. 'Fionnlagh is your boy, Artair. Always has been, always will be.' He saw the look of shock on the boy's face. But he pressed on relentlessly. 'All those years of beating that poor kid. Taking out your revenge on the boy instead of the father. And all the time it was your own son you were abusing. Just like your father before you.'

Fin could see from Artair's face that every conviction he had ever held, every certainty he had ever known, had just been stripped away. Leaving him to face a truth that he could never live with.

'That's crap! You're lying!'

'Am I? Think about it, Artair. Remember how it was. Remember how many times she tried to take it back. How many times she told you she'd only said it to hurt you.' Fin took two more steps.

'No!' Artair turned his head slowly to look at the boy he had punched and kicked and punished for seventeen hellish years, and his face contorted with pain and misery. 'She told me the truth. Then realized it was a mistake.' He turned wild eyes on Fin. 'And you can never take back the truth, you know that, Fin.'

'She lied to hurt you, Artair. You were the one who wanted it to be true. You were the one who wanted the boy to blame in my absence. To have a scapegoat. To have a punchbag for all the hate you had for me.'

'No!' Artair almost screamed it now. And he released a feral howl that raised all the hairs on Fin's arms and legs and back. He dropped the rope and Fin stepped quickly forward to pull the boy away from the edge of the cliff. He immediately felt the shivering that racked the teenager's fragile frame. Whether from fear or from cold, he couldn't tell. Artair stood staring at them bleakly, his eyes burning with tearful fury.

Fin reached out a hand towards him. 'Come on, Artair. It doesn't have to end like this.'

But Artair was staring right through him now. 'Too late. Can't take it back.' He looked at the boy hanging grimly on to Fin for support. And all the tragedy of his life was captured in his eyes, every nuance of every moment of pain, every twist of a knife he had ultimately turned on himself. 'I'm sorry.' His voice was barely a whisper carried on the wind, a distant echo of his own father's apology to Fin eighteen years earlier. 'I'm so sorry.' He met Fin's eye for the briefest of moments, before turning without another word and dropping into the void, gannets rising up around him like the fiery angels that would carry him to Hell.

Fin untied Fionnlagh and led him back across the rock towards the blackhouse. Several men came to meet them and put blankets around the boy's shoulders. He had not spoken, but his pain was clear for all to see. His face was a bloodless grey-white. Two hundred feet below, in the creek between the promontories, the crew of the *Purple Isle* stood watching on the deck, and from somewhere out of the wind in the south-west, they heard the sound of blades beating turbulent air.

Fin turned as the Sikorsky dropped from the sky, scattering clouds of seabirds before it, a great red and white bird whose motors thrummed and filled the air with their roar. He saw the words *H.M. Coastguard* emblazoned black on white along one side beneath the rotors as it dipped and bucked in the air rising from beneath the cliffs, before settling finally with a gentle grace on the helipad beside the lighthouse. A door slid open, and uniformed and plain-clothes police officers streamed out on to the concrete.

Fin and Fionnlagh and the guga hunters stood and watched as the policemen picked their way across the glaur towards them, slithering and stumbling among the rocks. DCI Smith led the party, his raincoat blowing out behind him, hair whipping around his head in spite of his Brylcreem. He slid to an unsteady halt in front of Fin and glared at him. 'Where's Macinnes?'

'You're too late. He's dead.'

Smith cocked a head full of suspicion. 'How?'

'He jumped off the cliff, Detective Chief Inspector.' And when he saw Smith purse his lips, Fin added, 'Every man here saw him do it.' He glanced at Gigs, who gave an almost imperceptible nod of his head. Whatever ended up on the police report would only ever be half the story. The whole truth would never leave the rock. It would stay here among the chaos of boulders and birds, whispered only in the wind. And it would die in the hearts and minds of the men who were there that day, when *they* died. And then only God would know.

II

He looked down on the steel-cold waters of Loch a Tuath, the downdraught from the rotors sending concentric circles of broken light across the bay, and then they tipped and veered east, swinging sharply to drop down to the apron behind the terminal building. A clutch of police vehicles and an ambulance were gathered there, blue

471

lights flashing in the sunlight that fell in handfuls through flitting gaps in the cloud, sprinkling like fairy dust across the moor before vanishing again in an instant.

Fin glanced once more at the boy, wrapped in blankets by the door. He had remained impassive for the duration of the flight. Whatever turmoil there might have been in his head was not reflected outside it. Fin himself felt hollowed out. A husk. Emptied of everything that might once have defined him. He looked away again in despair and saw Marsaili waiting for them by the ambulance, George Gunn standing awkwardly at her side. She was wrapped in a long black coat over jeans and boots, and her hair blew back in a stream from a face as pale as an August moon. She looked tiny beside Gunn. And Fin saw in her again the little girl with the pigtails who had sat beside him that first day at school, full of stubborn determination, but vulnerable now in a way she had never been as a child. Artair's death had been radioed ahead. She averted her face from the blast of air and dust thrown out by the blades as the coastguard helicopter touched down on the tarmac.

Fin turned and saw Gigs and Pluto sitting in grim silence at the back of the cabin, their presence demanded by Smith, who wanted to take formal statements back in Stornoway. The others had stayed behind to pack up and make the return trip on the *Purple Isle*. Without a single bird culled. For the first time in centuries there would be no guga eaten on the Isle of Lewis that year.

As the engines wound down, and the door slid open, Marsaili searched anxiously among the faces of the men disembarking. Fin saw her catch her breath as her eyes fell on Fionnlagh, and she ran across the taxiway to throw her arms around him and hold him as if she meant never to let him go. Fin climbed down from the hatch and stood there, helpless, impotent, watching them uncertainly. Gunn approached and slipped Fin a piece of paper torn from a notebook and put a hand gently on Marsaili's shoulder. 'We need to get the boy checked out at the hospital, Mrs Macinnes.' Reluctantly she released her son, before taking his face in both her hands and looking into his eyes, searching perhaps for some sign that he didn't hate her too much. 'Talk to me, Fionnlagh. Say something.' But it was towards Fin that he turned his head.

'Was it true? What you told my father out there on the rock?'

Marsaili looked at Fin with wide, frightened eyes. 'What *did* you tell him?'

Fin clutched the piece of paper Gunn had given him, afraid to look at it. 'That Fionnlagh was his son.'

'And am I?' Fionnlagh looked from one to the other, anger rising visibly in his chest, as if he believed he was being excluded from some secret that only they shared.

Marsaili said, 'You were only weeks old, Fionnlagh. You were crying every night. I had post-natal depression, and every other kind of depression you can think of.' Her blue eyes briefly found Fin's, then slipped away into some distant place from which she had a view back in time. 'We had a terrible argument, Artair and I. I can't even remember what it was about now. But I wanted to hurt him.' She looked at her son, guilt etching the frown gathering in furrows across her forehead. 'And so I used you. I told him you were Fin's son, not his. It just came out. How could I ever have imagined what it would lead to, that it would end like this?' She raised her eyes to a sky rushing past overhead. 'I wished right there and then that I could have bitten my tongue off. I told him a thousand times that I'd only said it to hurt him, but he would never believe me.' She lowered her head and ran the tips of her fingers lovingly down the side of her son's face. 'And you've had to live with the consequences ever since.'

'So he *was* my father.' All the bitterness and disappointment collected in the tears that hovered in Fionnlagh's eyes.

Marsaili hesitated. 'The truth, Fionnlagh?' She shook her head. 'The truth is that I don't know. I really don't. After Fin and I split up in Glasgow I came back to Lewis, miserable and unhappy. And straight into the arms of Artair. He was only too pleased to give me the comfort I was looking for.' She sighed. 'And I never knew whether it was Artair or Fin who had made me pregnant.'

Fionnlagh went limp, his gaze falling listlessly on the flashing lights of the police cars. He blinked away his tears, determined to harden himself to a world of uncertainty. 'We'll never know, then.'

Marsaili said, 'We can find out.'

'No!' Fionnlagh nearly shouted it. 'I don't want to know! If I don't, then he doesn't ever have to have been my father.'

Fin smoothed open the piece of paper in his hand and dipped his eyes to look at it. He felt his throat constricting. 'It's too late for that now, Fionnlagh.' The boy looked at him, a sudden dread in his eyes.

'What do you mean?'

The sound of voices crackled across police wavebands in the nearby cars.

'Last night, I asked DS Gunn to call the lab handling the DNA samples taken on Wednesday. They cross-checked yours and Artair's.' Both Fionnlagh and Marsaili fixed him with looks that carried the hopes and fears of two lifetimes. Fin folded the slip of paper into his pocket. 'Do you like football, Fionnlagh?' The boy frowned. 'Because if you do, I can get us tickets to the next Scotland game in Glasgow. That's what fathers and sons do, isn't it? Go to the football together?'

ACKNOWLEDGEMENTS

I would like to offer my grateful thanks to those who gave so generously of their time and expertise during my researches for *The Blackhouse*. In particular, I'd like to express my gratitude to pathologist Steven C. Campman, MD, medical examiner, San Diego, California; Derek (Pluto) Murray, Gaelic actor and broadcaster; Detective Sergeant George Murray, Northern Constabulary, Stornoway, Isle of Lewis; John 'Dods' Macfarlane, Angus 'Bobby' Morrison and Angus 'Angie' Gunn, guga hunters from Ness, Isle of Lewis; Calum 'Pugwash' Murray and Murdo 'Beag' Murray, skipper and first mate of the *Heather Isle*, Stornoway, Isle of Lewis; Donald Macritchie, teacher of maths and geography at Lionel School, Ness, Isle of Lewis; Evelyn Coull, Gaelic actress and broadcaster; Dr Brian Michie, general practitioner, police surgeon and locum pathologist, Stornoway, Isle of Lewis; An Comunn Eachdraidh, the Ness Historical Society, Ness, Isle of Lewis. I must also offer thanks and congratulations to John Beatty for his book *Sula, The Seabird-Hunters of Lewis*, which provided me with a wonderful photographic and written record of the annual pilgrimage made by the men of Ness to cull 2,000 guga on the island of Sula Sgeir. And I would like to give a special thanks to the people of the Isle of Lewis for their generosity and warmth during my five years filming on the island, and during my researches for this book.

Read on for an extract from the
sequel to *The Blackhouse*:

THE LEWIS MAN

Peter May

AVAILABLE IN PAPERBACK AND EBOOK

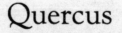

Quercus

www.quercusbooks.co.uk

ONE

Gunn saw the vehicles parked at the roadside from some distance away. The sky was black and blue, brooding, contused, rolling in off the ocean low and unbroken. The first spits of rain were smeared across his windscreen by the intermittent passage of its wipers. The pewter of the ocean itself was punctuated by the whites of breaking waves ten or fifteen feet high, and the solitary blue flashing light of the police car next to the ambulance was swallowed into insignificance by the vastness of the landscape.

Beyond the vehicles, the harled houses of Siader huddled against the prevailing weather, expectant and weary, but accustomed to its relentless assault. Not a single tree broke the horizon. Just lines of rotting fenceposts along the roadside, and the rusting remains of tractors and cars in deserted yards. Blasted shrubs showing brave green tips clung on with stubborn roots to thin soil in anticipation of better days to come, and a sea of bog cotton shifted in ripples and currents like water in the wind.

Gunn parked beside the police car and stepped out into the blast. Thick dark hair growing back in a widow's peak from a furrowed forehead was whipped into the air, and he gathered his black quilted anorak around him. He cursed the fact that he had not thought to bring a pair of boots, and stepped at first gingerly through the soft ground, before feeling the chill of the bog water seeping into his shoes and soaking through his socks.

He reached the first of the peat banks, and followed a path along the top of it, skirting the clusters of drying turfs. The uniforms had hammered metal stakes into soft ground to mark off the site with blue-and-white crime-scene tape that hummed and twisted, fibrillating in the wind. The smell of peat smoke reached him from the nearest crofthouses some half a mile away out towards the edge of the cliffs.

A group of men stood around the body almost leaning into the wind, the fluorescent yellow of ambulance men waiting to take it away, policemen in black waterproofs and chequered hats who thought they had seen it all before. Until now.

They parted wordlessly to let Gunn through, and he saw the police surgeon crouched down, leaning over the corpse, delicately brushing aside crumbling peat with la-texed fingers. He looked up as Gunn loomed overhead, and Gunn saw for the first time the brown, withered skin of the dead man. He frowned. 'Is he . . . coloured?'

'Only by the peat. I'd say he was a Caucasian. Quite young. Late teens or early twenties. A classic bog body, almost perfectly preserved.'

'You've seen one before?'

'Never. But I've read about them. It's the salt carried in the wind from the ocean that allows the peat moss to thrive here. And when the roots rot it creates acid. The acid preserves the body, almost pickling it. His organs should be virtually intact inside.'

Gunn gazed with unabashed curiosity at the almost mummified remains. 'How did he die, Murdo?'

'Violently, by the looks of it. There appear to be several stab wounds in the area of the chest, and his throat has been cut. But it'll take the pathologist to give you a definitive cause of death, George.' He stood up and peeled off his gloves. 'Better get him out of here before the rain comes.'

Gunn nodded, but couldn't take his eyes off the face of the young man locked in the peat. Although there was a shrivelled aspect to his features, they would be recognizable to anyone who knew him. Only the soft, exposed tissue of the eyes had decomposed. 'How long's he been here?'

Murdo's laugh was lost in the wind. 'Who knows? Hundreds, of years, maybe even thousands. You'll need an expert to tell you that.'

TWO

I don't need to look at the clock to know the time.

It's odd how the brown stain on the ceiling seems lighter in the mornings. The crystalline traces of mould that follow the crack through it seem somehow whiter. And strange how I always wake at the same hour. It's not the light that creeps in around the edges of the curtains that does it, because there are so few hours of darkness at this time of year. It must be some internal clock. All those years rising with the dawn for the milking, and everything else that would fill the waking daylight hours. All gone now.

I quite enjoy looking at this stain on the ceiling. I don't know why, but in the mornings it resembles a fine horse, saddled, and waiting to take me off to some brighter future. While at night, when it gets gloomy, it has a different mien. Like some rampant and horned creature ready to carry me off into darkness.

I hear the door open and turn to see a woman standing there. She seems familiar, but I can't quite place her. Until she speaks.

'Oh, Tormod . . .'

Of course. It's Mary. I'd know her voice anywhere. I wonder why she looks so sad. And something else. Something that turns down the corners of her mouth. Something like disgust. I know she used to love me, although I'm not sure that I ever loved her.

'What is it, Mary?'

'You've soiled the bed again.'

And then I smell it, too. Suddenly. Almost overpoweringly. Why didn't I notice it before?

'Couldn't you have got up? Couldn't you?'

I don't know why she's blaming me. I didn't do it on purpose. I never do it on purpose. The smell is worse as she pulls back the covers, and she puts a hand over her mouth.

'Get up,' she says. 'I'll have to strip the bed. Go and put your pyjamas in the bath and take a shower.'

I swing my legs over the side of the bed and wait for her to help me to my feet. It never used to be like this. I was always the strong one. I remember the time she twisted her ankle up by the old sheep fank when we were gathering the beasts for the shearing. She couldn't walk, and I had to carry her home. Almost two miles, with arms aching, and never one word of complaint. Why does she never remember that?

Can't she see how humiliating this is? I turn my head away so that she won't see the tears gathering in my eyes, and I can feel myself blinking them furiously away. I draw a deep breath. 'Donald Duck.'

'Donald Duck?'

I glance at her and almost shrink from the anger I see in her eyes. Is that what I said? Donald Duck? That can't have been what I meant. But I can't think now what I did mean to say. So I say again, firmly, 'Aye, Donald Duck.'

She pulls me to my feet, almost roughly, and pushes me towards the door. 'Get out of my sight!'

Why is she so angry?

I waddle through to the bathroom and slip out of my pyjamas. Where did she say I was to put them? I drop them on the floor and look in the mirror. An old man with a scribble of thin white hair and the palest of blue eyes stares back at me. I wonder for a moment who he is, then turn and look from the window out across the machair towards the shore. I can see the wind ruffling the heavy winter coats of the sheep grazing on the sweet, salty grass, but I can't hear it. Neither can I hear the ocean where it breaks upon the shore. Lovely white foaming seawater full of sand and fury.

It must be the double glazing. We never had that at the farm. You knew you were alive there, with the wind whistling through the window frames and blowing peat smoke down the chimney. There was room to breathe there, room to live. Here the rooms are so small, sealed off from the world. Like living in a bubble.

That old man is looking at me from the mirror again. I smile and he smiles back. Of course, I knew it was me all along. And I wonder how Peter is doing these days.

THREE

It was dark when finally Fin turned out the light. But the words were still there, burned on to his retinas. There was no escape in darkness.

Apart from Mona's, there were two other witness statements. Neither of them had possessed the presence of mind to note the registration number of the car. That Mona hadn't seen it was hardly surprising. The car had thrown her in the air, to come down on the bonnet and windscreen with sickening force before being flung aside and rolling several times over the unyielding metalled surface of the road. That she hadn't been more seriously injured was miraculous.

Robbie, with his lower centre of gravity, had gone down and under the wheels.

Each time he read the words he imagined himself to have been there, to have seen it, and each time he felt the nausea rising from his stomach. It was as vivid in his mind as if it were a real memory. As was Mona's description of the face she had seen behind the wheel, imprinted so clearly in her recollection, although it could only have been the merest of glimpses. A middle-aged man with longish, mousy-brown hair. Two or three days' growth on his face. How could she have seen that? And yet there was no doubt in her mind. He'd even had a police artist do a sketch from her description. A face that remained in the file, a face that haunted his dreams, even after nine months.

He turned over and closed his eyes in a vain search for sleep. The windows of his hotel room lay ajar behind the curtain, opened for air but also letting in the roar of traffic along Princes Street. He drew his knees up to his chest, tucking his elbows in at his sides, hands clasped together at his breastbone, like a praying foetus.

Tomorrow would be the end of everything he had known for most of his adult life. Everything he had been and become, and was likely to be. Like the day so many years before that his aunt had told him his parents were dead, and he had felt, for the first time in his short life, utterly and completely alone.

Daylight brought no relief, just a quiet determination to see this day through. A warm breeze blew across The Bridges, sunlight falling in shifting patterns across the gardens below the castle. Fin pushed his way determinedly through chattering crowds sporting light spring fashions. A generation who had forgotten the warnings of their elders to *ne'er cast a clout till May is oot*. It never seemed quite fair that other people's lives should go on as before. And yet who would have guessed at the pain behind his mask of normality? So who knew what turmoil was hidden behind the facades of others?

He stopped at the photocopy shop in Nicolson Street, slipping copied pages into his leather bag before heading east to St Leonard's Street and the 'A' Division police headquarters where he had spent most of the last ten years. His farewell party had been drinks with a handful of colleagues at a pub in Lothian Road two nights earlier. A sombre affair, marked mainly by recollection and regret, but also by some genuine affection.

Some people nodded to him in the corridor. Others shook his hand. At his desk, it took him only a few minutes to clear his personal belongings into a cardboard box. The sad, accumulated detritus of a restless working life.

'I'll take your warrant card off you, Fin.'

Fin turned around. DCI Black had something of the vulture about him. Hungry and watchful. Fin nodded and handed him his card.

'I'm sorry to see you go,' Black said. But he didn't look sorry. He had never doubted Fin's ability, just his commitment. And only now, after all these years, was Fin finally ready to acknowledge that Black was right. They both knew he was a good cop, it had just taken Fin longer to realise that it wasn't his métier. It had taken Robbie's death to do that.

'Records tell me you pulled the file on your son's hit-and-run three weeks ago.' Black paused, waiting perhaps for an acknowledgement. When it didn't come he added, 'They'd like it back.'

'Of course.' Fin slid the file out of his bag and dropped it on to the desk. 'Not that anyone's ever likely to open it.'

Black nodded. 'Probably not.' He hesitated. 'Time you closed it, too, Fin. It'll just eat you up inside, and fuck with the rest of your life. Let it go, son.'

Fin couldn't meet his eye. He lifted his box of belongings. 'I can't.'

Outside, he went around the back of the building and opened the lid of a large green recycling bin to empty the contents of his cardboard box, and then chuck it in after them. He had no use for any of it.

He stood for a moment, looking up at the window from which he had so often watched the sun and the rain and the snow sweep across the shadowed slopes of Salisbury Craggs. All the seasons of all the wasted years. And he slipped out into St Leonard's to flag down a taxi.

His cab dropped him on the steep cobbled slope of the Royal Mile, just below St Giles' Cathedral, and he found Mona waiting for him in Parliament Square. She was still in her drab winter greys, almost lost among the classical architecture of this Athens of the north, sandstone buildings blackened by time and smoke. He supposed it reflected her mood. But she was more than depressed. Her agitation was clear.

'You're late.'

'Sorry.' He took her arm and they hurried across the deserted square, through arches beneath towering columns. And he wondered if his lateness had been subliminally contrived. Not so much an unwillingness to let go of the past, as a fear of the unknown, of leaving the safety of a comfortable relationship to face a future alone.

He glanced at Mona as they entered the portals of what had once been the home of the Scottish Parliament, before the landowners and merchants who sat here had succumbed three hundred years ago to the bribes of the English and sold out the people they were supposed to represent to a union they didn't want. Fin and Mona's, too, had been a union of convenience, a loveless friendship. It had been driven by occasional sex, and held together only by the shared love of their son. And now, without Robbie, it was ending here, in the Court of Session. A decree nisi absolute. A piece of paper bringing to a close a chapter of their lives which had taken sixteen years to write.

He saw the pain of it in her face, and all the regrets of a lifetime came back to haunt him.

In the end it took only a few minutes to consign all those years to the dustbin of history. The good times and bad. The struggles, the laughs, the fights. And they emerged into brilliant sunlight spilling down across the cobbles, the rumble of traffic out on the Royal Mile. Other people's lives flowing past, while theirs had been shifted from pause to stop. They stood like still figures at the centre of a time-lapse film, the rest of the world eddying around them at high speed.

Sixteen years on and they were strangers again, unsure of what to say, except goodbye, and almost afraid to say that out loud, in spite of the pieces of paper they held in their hands. Because beyond goodbye, what else was there? Fin opened his leather bag to slip the paperwork inside, and his photocopied sheets in their beige folder slid out and scattered around his feet. He stooped quickly to gather them up, and Mona crouched down to help him.

He was aware of her head turning towards him as she took several of them in her hand. It must have been clear to her at a glance what they were. Her own statement was among them. A few hundred words that described a life taken and a relationship lost. The sketch of a face drawn from her own description. Fin's obsession. But she said nothing. She stood up, handing them to him, and watched as he stuffed them back in his bag.

When they reached the street, and the moment of parting could no longer be avoided, she said, 'Will we stay in touch?'

'Is there any point?'

'I suppose not.'

And in those few words, all the investment they had made in each other over all these years, the shared experiences, the pleasure and the pain, were lost for ever like snowflakes on a river.

He glanced at her. 'What will you do when the house is sold?'

'I'll go back to Glasgow. Stay with my dad for a while.' She met his eye. 'What about you?'

He shrugged. 'I don't know.'

'Yes, you do.' It was almost an accusation. 'You'll go back to the island.'

'Mona, I've spent most of my adult life avoiding that.'

She shook her head. 'But you will. You know it. You can never escape the island. It was there between us all those years, like an invisible shadow. It kept us apart. Something we could never share.'

Fin took a deep breath and felt the warmth of the sun on his face as he raised it for a moment to the sky. Then he looked at her. 'There was a shadow, yes. But it wasn't the island.'

Of course, she was right. There was nowhere else to go, except back to the womb. Back to the place that had nurtured him, alienated him, and in the end driven him away. It was the only place, he knew, that there was any chance of finding himself again. Among his own people, speaking his own tongue.

He stood on the foredeck of the *Isle of Lewis* and watched the gentle rise and fall of her bow as she ploughed through the unusually still waters of the Minch. The mountains of the mainland had vanished long ago, and the ship's horn sounded forlornly now as they slipped into the dense spring haar that blanketed the eastern coast of the island.

Fin peered intently into swirling grey, feeling the wetness of it on his face, until finally the faintest shadow emerged from its gloom. The merest smudge on a lost horizon, eerie and eternal, like the ghost of his past come back to haunt him.

As the island took gradual shape in the mist he felt all the hairs stand up on the back of his neck, and was almost overwhelmed by a sense of homecoming.

FOUR

Gunn sat at his desk squinting at the computer screen. Subliminally he registered the sound of a foghorn not far out in the Minch, and knew that the ferry would be docking shortly.

He shared his first-floor office with two other detectives, and had a fine view from his window of the Blythswood Care charity shop on the other side of Church Street. *Christian care for body and soul.* If he cared to crane his neck he could see as far up the road as the Bangla Spice Indian restaurant with its luridly coloured sauces and irresistible garlic fried rice. But right now the subject matter on his screen had banished all thoughts of food.

Bog bodies, also known as bog people, were preserved human bodies found in sphagnum bogs in northern Europe, Great Britain and Ireland, he read on the Wikipedia page on the subject. Acidic water, low temperatures and lack of oxygen combined to preserve the skin and organs, so much so that it was even possible in some cases to recover fingerprints.

He wondered about the body laid out in the cold cabinet in the autopsy room at the hospital. Now that it was out of the bog, how quickly might it start to deteriorate? He scrolled down the page and looked at the photograph of a head taken from a body recovered sixty years ago from a peat bog in Denmark. A chocolate-brown face remarkably well defined, one cheek squashed up against the nose where it had lain in repose, an orange stubble still clearly visible on the upper lip and jaw.

'Ah, yes, Tollund Man.'

Gunn looked up to see a tall, willowy, lean-faced figure with a halo of dark, thinning hair leaning down to get a closer look at his screen.

'Carbon dating of his hair placed him from around 400 BC. The idiots who performed the autopsy cut off his head and threw the rest of him away. Except for his feet and one finger, which are still preserved in formalin.' He grinned and held out a hand. 'Professor Colin Mulgrew.'

Gunn was surprised by the strength of his handshake. He seemed so slight built.

Almost as if he had read his mind, or detected his wince as they shook, Professor Mulgrew smiled and said, 'Pathologists need good hands, Detective Sergeant. For cutting through bone and prising apart skeletal structures. You'd be surprised how much strength is required.' There was just the hint of cultured Irish in his accent. He turned back to Tollund Man. 'Amazing, isn't it? After two thousand four hundred years, it was still possible to tell that he'd been hanged, and that his last meal had been a porridge of grain and seeds.'

'Were you involved in that post-mortem, too?'

'Bloody hell, no. Way before my time. Mine was Old Croghan Man, pulled out of an Irish bog in 2003. He was nearly as old though. Certainly more than two thousand years. Helluva big man for his day. Six foot six. Imagine. A bloody giant.' He scratched his head and grinned. "So what'll we call your man, then, eh? Lewis man?"

Gunn swivelled in his seat and waved the professor towards a free chair. But the pathologist shook his head.

'Been sitting for bloody hours. And the flights up here don't give you much leg room.'

Gunn nodded. Slightly smaller than average height himself, he had never found that a problem. 'So how did your Old Croghan Man die?'

'Murdered. Tortured first. There were deep cuts under each of his nipples. Then he was stabbed in the chest, decapitated, and his body cut in half.' The professor wandered across to the window and peered up and down the street as he spoke. 'Bit of a mystery really, because he had beautifully manicured fingernails. So not a working man. There is no doubt he was a meat eater, but his last meal was a mix of wheat and buttermilk. My old pal Ned Kelly, at the National Museum of Ireland, thinks he was sacrificed to ensure good yields of corn and milk in the royal lands nearby.' He turned back to Gunn. 'The Indian restaurant up the road any good?'

Gunn shrugged. 'Not bad.'

'Good. Haven't had a decent bloody Indian for ages. So where's our man now?'

'In a refrigerated drawer at the hospital morgue.'

Professor Mulgrew rubbed his hands together. 'We'd better go and take a look at him then before he starts decomposing on us. Then a bite of lunch? I'm bloody starving.'

The body, laid out now on the autopsy table, had an oddly shrunken look about it, well built, but diminished somehow. It was the colour of tea and looked as if it might have been sculpted in resin.

Professor Mulgrew wore a dark-blue jumpsuit beneath a surgical gown, and a bright-yellow face mask covering mouth and nose. Above it perched a ridiculously large pair of protective tortoiseshell glasses that seemed to shrink the size of his head, and turn him, incongruously, into a bizarre caricature of himself. Without any apparent awareness of how absurd he looked, he moved nimbly around the table taking measurements, his white tennis shoes protected by green plastic covers.

He crossed to the whiteboard to scrawl up the initial statistics, talking all the time above the squeak of his felt pen. 'The poor bugger weighs a mere forty-one kilograms. Not much for a man of 173 centimetres in height.' He peered over his glasses at Gunn. 'That's just over five feet eight to you.'

'Was he ill, do you think?'

'No, not necessarily. Although he's well preserved, he will have lost of lot of fluid weight over the years. He looks a pretty healthy specimen to me.'

'What age?'

'Late teens, early twenties, I'd say.'

'No, I mean, how long had he been in the peat?'

Professor Mulgrew raised one eyebrow and tipped his head scathingly in Gunn's direction. 'Patience, please. I'm not a bloody carbon-dating machine, Detective Sergeant.'

He returned to the body and turned it over on to its front, leaning in close as he brushed away fragments of brown and yellow-green moss.

'Were there any clothes found with the body?'

'No, nothing.' Gunn moved nearer to see if he could discern what it was that had attracted Mulgrew's attention. 'We dug over the whole area. No clothes, no artefacts of any kind.'

'Hmmm. In that case I would say he'd probably been wrapped in a blanket of some sort before being buried. And he must have lain in it for quite a few hours.'

Gunn's eyebrows shot up in astonishment. 'How can you tell that?'

'In the hours after death, Mr Gunn, the blood settles in the lower portion of the body causing a purplish red discoloration of the skin. We call it post-mortem lividity. If you look carefully at his back, buttocks and thighs you will see that the skin is darker, but there is a paler, blanched pattern in the lividity.'

'Meaning?'

'Meaning that he lay for at least eight to ten hours on his back after death, wrapped in some kind of rough blanket whose weave left its pattern in the darker coloration. We can clean him off and photograph it and, if you like, have an artist make a sketch to reproduce the pattern.'

Using a pair of tweezers, he recovered several fibres still clinging to the skin.

'Could be wool,' he said. 'Shouldn't be hard to confirm that.'

Gunn nodded but decided not to ask what point there would be in identifying the pattern and fabric of a blanket woven hundreds or even thousands of years before. The pathologist returned to an examination of the head.

'The eyes are too far gone to determine the colour of the irides, and this dark red-brown hair is no indication at all of what colour it might have been originally. It's been dyed by the peat, the same as the skin.' He poked about in the nostrils. 'But this is interesting.' He examined his latexed fingertips. 'A fair amount of fine-grained silver sand in his nose. Which would appear to be the same as the sand apparent in the abrasions on his knees and the tops of his feet.' He moved up to the forehead, then, and gently cleaned away some dirt from the left temple and the hair above it. 'Bloody hell!'

'What?'

'He's got a curved scar on the left front-temporal scalp. About ten centimetres in length.'

'A wound?'

The professor shook his head thoughtfully. 'No, it looks like a surgical scar. At a guess I would say that this young man has had an operation performed at some time on a head injury.'

Gunn was stunned. 'Well, that means this is a much more recent corpse than we thought, doesn't it?'

Mulgrew's smile conveyed both superiority and amusement. 'Depends what you mean by recent, Detective Sergeant. Brain surgery is probably one of the oldest practised medical arts. There is ample archaeological evidence of it dating back to Neolithic times.' He paused, then added as an afterthought for Gunn's benefit, 'The Stone Age.'

He turned his attention now to the neck, and the broad, deep wound that incised it. He measured it at 18.4 centimetres.

'Is that what killed him?' Gunn asked.

Mulgrew sighed now. 'I am guessing, Detective Sergeant, that you have not attended many post-mortems.'

Gunn blushed. 'Not many, sir, no.' He did not want to confess that there had only been one before.

'It is bloody well impossible for me to determine cause of death until I have opened him up. And even then, I can't guarantee it. His throat has been cut, yes. But he has multiple stab wounds in his chest, and another in the right scapular back. There are abrasions on his neck that would suggest the presence of a rope around it, and similar abrasions on his wrists and ankles.'

'Like his hands and feet had been tied?'

'Exactly. He may have been hanged, hence the abrasions on his neck, or else he may have been dragged along a beach using that same rope, which would explain the sand in the broken skin on his knees and feet. In any event, it is far too early to be submitting theories on the cause of death. There are multiple possibilities.'

A darker patch of skin on the right forearm was attracting his attention now. He wiped at it with his swab, then turned to lift a scrubbing sponge from the stainless-steel sink behind him, and began roughly rubbing away the top layer of skin. 'Sweet fucking Jesus,' he said.

Gunn canted his head to try to get a better look at it. 'What is it?'

Professor Mulgrew was silent for a long time before looking up to meet Gunn's eye. 'Why were you so keen to know how long the body might have been in the bog?'

'So I can clear it off my slate, Professor, and hand it over to the archaeologists.'

'I'm afraid you might not be able to do that, Detective Sergeant.'

'Why?'

'Because this body has been in the peat for no more than fifty-six years – at the very most.'

Gunn felt his face colour with indignation. 'You told

me not ten minutes ago that you were not a bloody carbon-dating machine.' He enjoyed putting the emphasis on the *bloody*. 'How can you possibly know that?'

Mulgrew smiled. 'Take a closer look at the right forearm, Detective Sergeant. I think you'll see that what we have here is a crude tattooed portrait of Elvis Presley above the legend *Heartbreak Hotel*. Now, I'm pretty certain that Elvis wasn't around in the time before Christ. And as a confirmed fan I can tell you, without fear of contradiction, that *Heartbreak Hotel* was a number one hit in the year 1956.'

COMING SOON

COFFIN ROAD

Peter May

If you had killed someone
you would remember.
Wouldn't you?

The million-selling author of the Lewis trilogy
brings murder back to the Outer Hebrides.

Published in hardback and ebook 14 January 2016.

Quercus
www.quercusbooks.co.uk